A quivering  as jammed betwee re was no telling w or an octopus. He e rudder and playe on of the sucker-stu, kelp-swathed apparition.

Clouds of sand and seaweed swirled up out of the dark, almost blinding Tony's goggle vision. Upon dispersion his light beheld two red-tinged eyes—as large as dinner plates, with luminous yellow and black slit-like pupils. Unblinking, the wide-set orbs hypnotized him momentarily—and a realization set in: from the spacing of the eyes, the creature's head was as wide as a Volkswagon. The eyes rose under an enormous balloon-shaped sinuous pale head, and stopped at Tony's level. The pate of this head was as high as *Zebulon Pike's* 12-foot dorsal rudder! It moved closer and Karas, from experience with small octopuses knew that the bristling skin of the creature was a sign of anger. First reporting his confrontation to the control room by intercom, he motioned Stonefish to come down on the plane and use his chain saw. Tony slashed and sawed with his knife, then relinquished the task to Mason's bubbling saw. The monster, which Tony now recognized as a giant octopus, recoiled at the slashing of its arm, wedging it yet tighter as bluish green blood seeped from the wound and spread in the light beam. The octopus, enraged, unstuck one of its anchor tentacles from its rock lair and curled it slowly upward.

Stonefish's pneumatic saw shredded through the nine-inch thick mass, flinging flesh and gaping suckers in all directions. Severing the tough, mangled arm at the trailing edge of the aileron, he inserted the bubbling teeth between the hull and inboard edge, chewing out the wedged remains. The muscular diver turned triumphantly only to be shocked at what he saw.

PERISCOPE!
by Halsey Clark

SUPERSUB

Halsey Clark

A JAMES A. BRYANS BOOK
FROM DELL/EMERALD

Published by
Dell Publishing Co., Inc.
1 Dag Hammarskjold Plaza
New York, New York, 10017

Dell TM 681510, Dell Publishing Co., Inc.

ISBN: 0-440-08403-2

Printed in the United States of America

First printing—October 1983

"ALL THIS AUTOMATION IS TAKING THE HUMANITY OUT OF WARFARE."

—anonymous American admiral

SUPERSUB

PROLOGUE

COUNTDOWN. . . . One hundred feet below the surface of the Pacific, east of Wake Island, the Trident Class submarine *Michigan* lies motionless, its diving planes and rudders shifting minutely in response to continuous data transmission from the Navdac computer in the 19,000-ton black behemoth's heart. Wisps and chains of bubbles stream from the trim tanks, keeping the 560-foot SSBN precisely level.

Dawn's red sun catches a floating radio antenna buoy. Hardly more than a reed of grass it bends to the current's tug, while 22,300 miles up, traveling at 6,900 mph, a naval satellite beams coded signals . . . unusual signals.

Summoned from breakfast in the wardroom, a communications officer stands tensely by as an EAM (Emergency Action Message) comes in on the radio room scrambler. If it proved out as a missile launch order, it would have come directly from the President, further contingencies to apply if Washington were destroyed. The Lieutenant hands the unscrambled message to the executive officer, a Lieutenant-

Commander, who, in turn compares the format to a daily-changing code kept in the boat's safe.

"Man battle stations; missile," the exec drawls out the dreaded command and, as count-down preparations begin, the message is brought to the Captain for final authentification. Applying his ultimate code to a symbol he, alone is aware of, he closes his eyes momentarily as if for a short prayer, then glares at his exec.

"SET CONDITION *ISQ*."

The Kansan nods and walks briskly to the command center where he passes the word. His dual digit watch reads 0626—Wake Island Pacific time, and 2126—Moscow time. The EAM indicated an unusual MIRV deployment. 1:16—and only one launch. Unless stopped by a counter-mand within thirteen minutes, one 30-ton Trident II thermonuclear missile would be on its way to Leningrad. 5000 miles in twenty-one minutes.

In the Barents Sea, north of Murmansk, there was a mirror-image condition, only the language differing. Low and gutteral instead of twangy plains and down-east on *Michigan*.

Russian.

The Societ exec glances at the digital chronometer in the navigation center. 2126. A nine hour difference from New York City where it was 26 minutes past noon. The Soviet officer checks a computer readout which assures that the final missile trajectory includes the earlier star fix. He too, had noted something very odd about the orders that had precipitated this alert. Only one of the 45-foot SSN-9 missiles was scheduled for launch, and all but one of the re-entry warheads were programmed to abort without detonation. Moreover, what on earth was in Queens County?

He is startled as compressed air whooshes into a missile tube, equalizing the inside to the pressure of sea water on the deck hatch. The boat vibrates as steam builds up in the blast-off tanks below the selected tube. Electronic Technicians are manning the launch consoles as the computer system steadies the Typhoon-Class boat to a graveyard stillness.

The Captain, a full Commander and Annapolis man, takes a small, black cylinder from his wall safe. About the size of a disposable cigarette lighter, he rotates half the cylinder in a memorized sequence: three turns counterclockwise . . . one turn clockwise, and then one-half back again. It emits a shrill buzz as a blue diode lights up on one end.

The doomsday key is now armed!

It is also coded to the waiting female splined jack on the bulkhead behind the Captain's calendar. He makes sure his door is locked, then takes down the calendar. September, 1984. The Captain waits, then, in response to a buzz, picks up his phone.

"*ISQ*, green, Sir." It was the communications officer.

Another voice cuts in: "*ISQ*, green confirm, Sir."

"Thank you Tom." The Captain moves closer to the wall jack, gingerly holding the buzzing key with both hands.

Irretrievable . . . irreversible . . . beyond recall . . .

Fifteen seconds after the mating of plastic and magnetic fields, the pride of American destructive genious erupts into the placid daylight amidst a symmetrical vase-shaped cloud of aerated, rainbow-hued salt water. The solid-fueled projectile, once free of the ocean, ignites and rises . . . first slowly, straining its bonds of gravity—then accelerating vertically into the brightening morning sky.

Simultaneously, the Soviet counterpart to Trident flashes blindingly over the chill sub-arctic Bering Sea. A family of walruses scurry from a vagrant ice floe into the dark safety of the sea. The Soviet rocket, reaching ''burn-out'' at 12 minutes after ignition over Spitzbergen is internally commanded to proceed on recognition radar.

The radar sensor focuses down upon the Norwegian islands and superimposes its current image over a pre-recorded chart compiled by satellites on the same headings and altitudes. Shapes overlapped, the slight discrepencies are fed into the guidance computer, causing retrorockets and vanes to correct course according to program. At fourteen minutes and altitude one hundred, thirty miles, the radar sensor picks up the unique shape of King Oscar's Fjord on the east coast of Greenland. Time: 2140 Leningrad . . . 40 minutes past noon in the Big Apple.

At 16,000 miles per hour, Trident's radar recognizes the Aleutian Islands and Alaska's nose—the Seward Peninsula facing continental Siberia. Continuing, it powers almost directly over the North Pole, sighting the Lomonov Ridge and correcting for a perfect approach over the Franz Josef Islands. Onboard computers, locking into the islands by shape comparision, feed the control surfaces final descent data as the huge rocket completes its polar great-circle voyage toward the proud city of Leningrad.

At minus five minutes, Trident's sixteen contrary warheads are jettisoned, along with the spent carrier into the Arctic Ocean. One fifty-kiloton live warhead—fifty times as powerful as the Hiroshima weapon—screams inexorably toward its target.

On the other side of the planet, SSN-9 ejects all but one warhead into the desolate Sea of Labrador. The surviving red messenger of death streaks over the Gulf of St, Lawrence and pierces the United States' airspace over Maine.

At minus one minute to detonation, it is over New Hampshire—blazing, though lost in the noon sun of an Indian Summer sky.

The lone Trident hydrogen warhead plummets down—a shooting star reflected on Lake Lagoda . . . prompting a lover's wish on the night beach of Gabenova. "Look", whispers the girl to her boy, as the fiery celestial orb is drawn into the glow of Leningrad.

The *Moscow Dynamos,* under the lights at Kirov Stadium, are threatening to break the tie score with only minutes to go. Their star player kicks a wicked side shot at the *Leningrad Sputniks'* unattended goal. Out of nowhere, the *Sputniks'* goalee leaps and deflects the ball. Almost fifty thousand soccer fans roar their approval. The stadium overlooking the Neva River at the tip of Krestovski Island throbs with cheers.

Then everything stops.

And the romantic glow over Lake Lagoda is a fireball.

The *Jets'* quarterback, on a quick call, electrifies the opening day crowd at Shea Stadium with a long pass down the sidelines. Last year's Superbowl Champions, the visiting team is taken by surprise as the Jets' fleet tight end breaks into the clear under the perfectly timed football.

The crowd jumps to its feet.

Following its computerized memory trajectory that included a horse-shoe shaped building surrounded by a network of curving highways and a Worlds' Fair globe, a high-velocity speck zeros in on the 50-yard line as the crowd roars.

And the complex disappears.

Vaporized along with a 747 in mid-air.

All is black.

Until the lights are snapped on.

*　　*　　*

The twin blank screens hung mute before the gathering of scientists in a projection room of the La Jolla building. A young man dressed in shades of brown walked to the lectern while cleaning his eyeglasses. Gripping the stand top with both hands, he waited for questions from the audience. He acknowledged a hand.

"Doctor Mount," a gray-bearded professor boomed, "while I do agree the idea has merit—and the simulation was as good as *Star Wars*—I see a problem. How can we be certain that the, er, enemy will abide by the rules of the contest. They might insert a more advanced guidance package in their system. Mind you, I'm all for having, theoretically, *one* fifty megaton joust than a thousand of them in as many cities."

"We propose open inspection. Next . . ."

"Assuming the Congress buys it, and the warhead is scaled down to smoke bomb or fireworks as you propose, how often will this "demonstration" take place?"

"That will be up to Congress and the Soviet."

"Gentlemen," the CDA moderator called for attention. "We're running out of time. I think we all agree that Doctor Mount's daring idea could prove a valuable deterrent to nuclear war, and I suggest we consider it again at our next meeting. One of the subjects we should prepare to discuss in May is the prospect of building smaller, rather than larger Trident submarines." The moderator smiled at David Mount and a round of chuckles peppered the room. The moderator waved genially to all as he walked up the aisle toward the exit.

In the building's lobby, an attendent had plucked out most of the little white plastic letters from a black sign. All that remained as the last limousine left was:

CENTER FOR DEFENSE ANALYSES

I

NEW LONDON. . . .White-haired Admiral Ben Mount, bareheaded, and as usual, in civilian clothes, knuckled his Burberry raincoat collar against the frigid January wind that rippled whitecaps in New London's long harbor all the way to the old brick lighthouse at Southwest Ledge—exit to Long Island Sound and the oceans. Walking a step ahead of his son and daughter, he seemed oblivious to their presence.

The first of two revolutionary steel whales was nearing completion. Spawned in the sprawling yards of Electric Boat, SSBN 726, *Ohio* was two years behind schedule. Ben Mount felt as if he'd both fathered and carried it—all 18,700 tons and 560 feet. The black hull lay brooding in the dark, ice-flecked water alongside the main floating dock. Tethered with white cables and lined with catwalks, the *Trident* Class submarine, first of a proposed litter of 14 replacements for the *Polaris* fleet had drawn the ire of Congress and the press. With a cost over-run of 70%, it had been labeled a "lemon" and a US Naval "blunder".

Some holiday season! But is was nothing new. Ben had canceled his subscription to *U.S. News and World Report* 3 years earlier when they called his baby "one more massive miscalculation." He kept his fingers crossed that *Ohio's* twin sister, *Michigan,* launched the previous summer amidst the protests of a thousand anti-nuclear demonstrators, and lying at an adjacent slip would have less teething problems.

Even the outgoing administration had fired salvos . . . The Secretary of the Navy publicly accused him of "hampering the construction of the Tridents by creating ill will between the Navy and the contractors."

"Damn," he gritted his teeth—"what do they want? Another *Thresher?* When things are installed less than perfectly, I'll make those moneygrubbing contractors rip 'em out again and live up to their contracts . . . So, a 70% over-run . . . and what hasn't gone up at least 50% since 1969 when we started the project? And what about the inclusion of new state-of-the-art technology, as it happens? The Soviets won't quibble over a few rubles in putting their Typhoon Class together. Forty feet longer than ours yet! So the brass is gonna have to keep the Polaris and Poseidon systems afloat a little longer—"

"Dad," the whining voice startled the aging admiral. "It's too cold for you to stay out just in a raincoat—I mean—" Deborah had to laugh as her father imitated a raincoat flasher. Mount stayed her with a mime's gesture, then reached into his pocket and drew out a pair of earmuffs.

"Bought these in Idaho the year you were born." He sprung the black puffs apart and snapped them on, looking more like a bufflehead duck than the creator of America's nuclear navy.

"Don't remind me," Deborah glowered, sensitive about her age.

"It ain't so bad; you've got another year till the big three-oh." David Mount's nasal delivery was as computerized as his job of troubleshooter for the Center for Defense

Analyses. Like his sister he wore a bulky down jacket, but brown to her blue. Everything David owned was brown—from his diesel Rabbit to his ball point pens, his boxer shorts and bedsheets. Someone had once told his curly brown head that his green eyes were more piercing when in company of brown. First, he was tempted to go to Brown University, but ended up on the Harvard Crimson, graduating at seventeen and managed a doctorate in electronic engineering as his age group grappled with drugs, demonstrations and the draft. David's brown horn rims were thick enough to spare him Viet even without his value in weapons related research. After a stint with the Space Center at Houston during the first moon shots, he was wooed to RAND, the Air Force think-tank, then found his niche with CDA, the Center for Defense Analyses in Washington, DC, preferring the capital to Texas. He'd just come from a special winter meeting at La Jolla, attended by another 39 of the top physical scientists in the country. They'd been invited to update the summer session in view of the new administration. High on the season's priority list, the scrambler telephones and data processors in the charming old Spanish-style buildings overlooking the Pacific buzzed and clicked with topics such as "particle-beam death rays," and "submarine MARVE systems."

"Thanks a lot for rubbing it in."

"We won't count those two years with the *schwartzes* in California—"

"David!" She fumed. "I won't take that."

"Children, children—," Ben stammered. "Do we *always* have to fight? I swear, ever since you both were little—always at each other's throats. As far back as I can remember. It's no wonder your mother is . . ."

"Drying out in Arizona?"

"I'm sorry Debbie, it's mostly my fault. No time for my own family. God damn deadlines . . . greedy contractors. Your mother is a fine woman. I promise . . . after this thing's commissioned . . ."

"It's okay, Dad—we'll all three do it together . . . treat her right when she gets back."

"She deserves it. Betsy is one fine lady . . ." Ben waited till the roar of a trio of Navy Tomcat jets subsided overhead. "Did I ever tell you about . . . how your mother and I got married?"

"You had to?" David smirked.

"In a way, yes." Mount's eyes twinkled. "There was this—"

"Dad, can't we go somewhere warm before you get started on your stories?"

"You're absolutely right Debbie; I know a place. . . ."

The brown diesel *Rabbit* snarled north, past the rickety cliff hanging shacks of old Groton and around the World War II submarine monument near Fort Griswold. The center section of SS249 had been severed and embalmed, then mounted on a concrete pedestal in the middle of a traffic circle. The once-proud conning tower was emblazoned with a bronze plaque acclaiming *Flasher* with 100,321 tons of Japanese shipping sunk—more than any submarine in American history. As a monument to 3505 lost shipmates the gray curiosity vied for attention with its neighbors which included a Pizza Hut and a Radio Shack. Ben Mount crossed his mind's heart as the VW careened onto the clover-leaf feed and onto the spindly Victorian bridge across the Thames. A variation of claustrophobia born of narrow roads over water forced Mount's eyes shut. Off the bascule bridge, they turned south and took 213 through New London toward Goshen Point. Ben, in the "death seat," opened his eyes as they screeched into a parking lot just past Pleasure Beach. A crackling birch fire and a corner booth in "The Neptune" brought color back to his cheeks.

"I might have known," Deborah ogled the mantlepiece above the fieldstone fireplace. Instead of a square rigged clipper ship, a three-foot long scale model of a nuclear submarine reposed in a varnished mahoghany rack, strangely incongruous with the rustic restaurant interior. A polished brass plaque on the base announced in engraved script:

USS NEPTUNE
August 3, 1958, North Pole.

Deborah shook her head pessimistically and looked at the menu. "I hope they have *Groelsch*."

"Is that a fish?"

"No, Dad," David sneered. "It's an exotic fad beer—a sort of cult habit of the extinct flower children species." David ducked as his sister brandished a fork at him.

Ben, mesmerized by the memories of his first nuclear offspring sighed deeply. "Tom Scully was my first cook aboard *Neptune*. He opened up this place a few years ago after he retired. There are photographs of the North Pole trip behind the bar, in case you want to take a look." Ben returned a hand wave to Scully.

"The same shots we have—had at home in the album?"

"Er, I suppose so, Dave. . . . Will you both excuse me for a minute; I should say hello to Tom. Be right back."

"Dave, aren't you gonna tell him what happened at La Jolla?"

"Sis, he's had enough—besides, it was all conjecture. We get paid to think up crazy things."

"Yea, like the neutron bomb." She studied the menu.

"Look, do you want to see Dad sick. Just keep it up."

Debbie shook *no* without looking up. "I wasn't at the demonstration last April when the *Baltimore* was launched. . . ."

"That would have screwed up your so-called "pardon."

"How do you know that I haven't changed?"

"Okay, sis. I'll give you the benefit of that doubt if you get off my back about La Jolla."

"It's a deal," Deborah took a rumpled cigarette out of her drawstring purse and lit it with the restaurant's dolphin-decorated book matches. She inhaled deeply and handed the joint to her brother.

"No thanks—here he comes. Look, let's let him talk about something else for a change; let's ask him something upbeat, like how he married mother."

II

HAMBURG. . . . Snow hung white and heavy, weighing
down the pine branches until they almost touched the
closed mahoghany casket. Over 2500 people, many with
World War II Knight's Crosses tied with red and black
ribbon around the collars of cashmere overcoats, had come
to pay last respects to a sea warrior in the town of Aumühle,
a suburb of Hamburg, West Germany. The mourners were
elderly, and there was a curious absence of women.

"I shouldn't be seen here," Kurt Lutze-Nielson pulled
his gray muffler up over his chin.

"There's little chance that your stepfather's automatons
would be so far from Wolfsburg on a Tuesday afternoon.
That's one reason for meeting here." Peter Nielson turned
away from his son and stifled a rasping cough into his
sleeve. "That's what I get for not wearing a hat in winter."

"Is there *another* reason that you came here?"

"Perhaps nostalgia . . . perhaps guilt. No matter, it was
also a convenient Lufthansa stop—"

"From where? The last time we spoke, you were in Kiev."

"We'll talk later." Nielson's eyes danced furtively as a eulogist droned on. Then a group of men carrying large wreaths pushed their way through the crowd. The wreaths were emblazoned with the red, black and white colors of the Imperial German Navy. Gilt German text lettering, reminiscent of the thirties glinted their messages: "TO OUR REICH'S PRESIDENT" . . . "ALLES FÜR DEUTSCHLAND" . . . "GROSSADMIRAL DÖNITZ— HONOR AND FIDELITY." One of the green wreaths read: "FROM THE SURVIVORS OF U-309." The solemn mourners laid their offerings in the snow around the coffin.

Knight's Crosses with swords and oak leaves, with diamonds, glittered against the snow as ten pallbearers, all former U-boat commanders, took positions around the coffin. One of them, stoically took the old admiral's ceremonial dagger from an attendant's tray of Donitz' war decorations and placed it on the coffin, over the red, black and yellow flag of West Germany.

Former Kriegsmarine Kapitänleutnant Nielson, illegitimate son of Alfred Krupp, snapped to attention as the coffin was lowered into the cold earth cubicle. The speaker's words echoed in his tired head: ". . . the Bonn Government acted shamefully in trying to disassociate itself from the admiral." . . . ". . . his sentence was a political rather than a judicial decision at Nuremberg." "Ja, ja, so it was," the mourners cheered.

The crowd, fired up, mumbled and exploded. "He did his duty," shouted a paunchy man wearing a naval veteran's cap, ". . . what any decent soldier would do!"

"Ya," screamed his friend, ". . . the allies broke every international standard to send him to jail! He was a hero of the German people!" Pastor Joachim Arp, surprised at the outburst tried to calm the veterans. A flashbulb popped and he threw up his hands in despair, disappearing into his red brick rectory as the graying men gathered around the grave, patting each other on the back and singing bits of the old national hymn, *Deutschland Uber Alles*.

Suddenly a young man wearing the uniform of a West German Army lieutenant, slipped through the crowd of elders and snapped to attention before the grave. Eyebrows were raised as he saluted briskly and left as quickly as he'd appeared.

"The Ministry of Defense will make short work of *him*," Kurt nudged his father, urging him toward the parking area as the crowd started to thin out.

"*If* they find him." Peter Nielson was amused. "It may even have been a prank, designed to indicate the real feelings of German veterans. . . . If it weren't for you, Kurt, I might have applauded him."

"Thank God you didn't—," Kurt hesitated, "*father*."

"Then you haven't told your wife about coming here?"

"Just as you requested." Kurt opened his menu.

"And what will my son have to drink?"

"Perrier, please."

"By itself?"

"You go ahead, father."

"I hope you don't mind—."

"Smoke too, if you want; I'm used to board meetings."

"Of course, Kurt, it's better that you don't. Your grandmother smoked too much—" A waiter hovered impatiently over the high-backed inglenook booth.

"I'm sorry I never knew her."

"She was a wonderful woman. Died so young—" Nielson coughed and tapped his chest. "Perrier for the young man, and steinhager for the old one, please. We'll order later," Nielson shook a cigarette out of its pack and waved off the waiter. "I don't inhale—very much, but these last five years. . . ."

"When you stopped writing, I suspected—," Kurt toyed

absentmindedly with his thick ashen hair, then regained his stiff corporate facade.

"Five years detention, few priviledges. I might as well have been in Siberia during the purges," Nielson lowered his voice. "They wouldn't let me write because they were afraid that I had some secret ink or code."

"What were you charged with?" Kurt was startled as the waiter set the drinks before him. Peter lit his *Murati* and blew smoke toward the stained glass window; curls of white catching the oblique rays of late afternoon sun streaming through a decorative lee-boarded squat sailboat of leaded ambers, vermillions and wood-browns on a tossing aqua sea.

"First, how is Lisa?" Nielson parried his son's question. "You know, once I get started, I'm unstoppable."

"She still gets a lot of headaches, if you know what I mean." Kurt fidgeted with a large gold ring.

"Being the wife of a division chairman must be hectic. Continual entertaining. . . . Travel."

"They've been cutting back lately on expense accounts." A shaft of sunlight glinted on Kurt's ring, highlighting the most recognised symbol in the low-priced automobile world—a wolf and a castle.

"New ring?" Peter noticed it was on the third finger.

"Ten years at the plant."

"And how are my grandchildren? I'll bet they've grown."

"I'll see them this weekend. As you may gather," Kurt twisted his ring, "things have changed with Lisa and me."

"I'm truly sorry." Nielson looked down dejectedly.

"It's been almost a year, now. I'm getting used to it. Can you come to Hannover with me this weekend?"

"Nielson looked at his watch; held it away and focused on the little magnifying date-window. "Can't stay that long." He picked up the slender-stemmed glass. "Prosit." It was drained in one long swig. "Waiter, I think I need another one," he held the empty glass high. "Tell me, Kurt; how are things going at the plant?"

"I'd like to make a change—perhaps a transfer to the States, or Canada." Kurt sipped his spring water.

"It must be difficult—a chairman's stepson."

"And the separation hasn't helped. You know how large corporations can be."

"I've only worked for people with uniforms. I don't think the navy is as cut-throat as industry—at least not to their own."

"Since you took me to this remote bistro, I think I might just join you." Kurt ogled his father's liquor glass.

"Waiter," the graying man beamed, "make it two of these!" He leaned over the four-hundred-year-old table, pocked with unintelligible initials, dates, and from more recent times, submarine flotilla numbers and scratched-out swastikas. "Kurt, I'm wanted by the KGB. They don't know I'm back on the continent."

"You escaped . . . you're on the run?"

"I had help, but the deal is over."

"Why were you held in the first place?"

"I'm suspected of being a double agent."

"And are you?" Kurt's face paled.

"It's a long story—but something you should know. Somebody should know. At least I can leave you *that*."

Kurt was puzzled by the remark. "I don't have to be back in Wolfsburg till tomorrow afternoon."

"Good, you'll stay with me at an old shipmate's house, then I'll buy you breakfast before you leave."

"Where will you go afterwards?"

"Who knows? Perhaps to the fiords in the Norland where I was born . . . there's a certain stream I used to fish. I don't think the KGB will find it."

"I'll practice my fly-tying, in case you want some company."

Nielson grinned as the drinks arrived. "There once was a man named Peter Nielson," he began jokingly, then his eyes bulged and he seemed to lose his balance.

"Father—"

"It comes and goes." The high-domed man sipped his clear liquor and set the glass down carefully. Next, he drew a small, silver box out of his vest pocket. "Nothing to worry about," Peter popped a tiny white pill into his mouth. "Now where was I?"

"There once was a man. . . ." Kurt closed his eyes.

tapping his knee expectantly. Anticipation gave way to a broad smile as the toy surfaced beyond the two battleships.

"Kostya," a high pitched voice preceded the robed woman into her husband's sanctuary. Kulov dried his stout hands on his grey cardigan. He groaned and got up. "Tanya!"

"I'm sorry, I forgot; you're home so seldom lately." She picked up her Blue Persian and stroked its long fur. "Papa likes you but not in his study." The tall, black haired woman carried the cat to the door and set it down outside the room. She closed the door, sauntered in and sat on the edge of Kostya's menacing black leather chair.

"My poor dear, you're working so hard. Were you up all night again?"

"The titanium test strength still varies—I've got to find out why. Just a day or two more." Kulov carefully set the model of *Mikasa* into a wall cabinet next to *Fuji, Asahi* and *Nisshin,* on one shelf. Four shelves in all, the prominent units of the navies of Japan and Russia in 1905 were displayed. The 22 Russian ships that were sunk in the battle of Shushima bore small, black Maltese crosses on their bows, while the two light cruisers lost by Togo's fleet were decaled with tiny chrysanthemum motifs.

"Then we can spend a few evenings of your leave together; go to the Kirov. They're doing Romeo and Juliet."

"And I'd promised that we'd go to Cairo and enjoy the sun for a change," Kostya walked over to the fireplace and prodded a smoldering log. He looked up at the framed portrait above the mantel. "What would my great-uncle do?" The striking naval officer commanded Kostya's study: piercing eyes under a high-domed bald forehead and a long, fair forked beard, he was known, even in the era of long Russian beards as 'Beardy' before he went down with *Petropavlovsk,* his portrait artist, Verestchagin, and over 600 men after hitting a Japanese mine at Port Arthur in 1904. "Stefan Osopovitch, what would you do if your opponent was Admiral Benjamin Mount?"

Kulov hummed his favorite tune in mock anticipation of the portraits' answer. "It's coming to me, Tanya . . ." he looked out the frosted window at the frozen Neva, at the gold-glinting spire of the Admiralty Building . . . at the revolving globe of the 'House of Books' building, originally built by the Singer Sewing Machine Company in 1902 . . . at the swarm of strollers and holiday shoppers on the Nevsky Prospekt, Leningrad's Fifth Avenue. Changing to whistling of Prokofiev's *Alexander Nevsky* film aria, he turned dramatically toward his wife. *"Beardy* says that Admiral Mount's parents were born in Russia, and we should never trust another Russian, especially a Jew. *Beardy* also cautioned me that the Americans are really farther advanced on the *Ohio* and *Michigan* than what we are given to believe in their press. It's all part of a double-think ploy . . . a gambit by the CIA."

"Some day, dear, you'll get the credit you deserve. You've done as much as the Jew—but with no accolades. He's such a publicity hound. Nobody even knows my husband's name, except as a competent line officer like all the others."

"It's the best way—we don't engender as much jealousy in ranks as do the Americans. The Typhoon program should leapfrog us over America's Tridents. That's why the titanium hull is so important. We'll be able to go down deeper than *Ohio.*"

Tanya reached up for her husband's hands and pulled him down next to her. "Why don't the Americans use titanium?"

"That's a good question, perhaps it's too expensive— the *Ohio* already has cost over-run of 63 percent, my darling."

"That, may be the titanium—disguised," she laughed.

"Clever girl," Kostya put his hand inside Tanya's robe.

*   *   *

Kulov stacked his notes neatly as the bells of St. Isaac's rang a muffled two A.M. He slouched back into his leather chair. Tanya's robe hung from an armrest; she had long since retired to the bedroom of the small flat in a seven storied neo-classic apartment building on Suvorovsky. He closed his eyes and imagined the slapping of summer waves against the hull of his last command, a *Delta 1* Class SSBN, in American terminology, the initials standing for Nuclear-Propelled Ballistic Missile Submarine. That was back in 1971; since then he'd been 'promoted' to a desk job—that of putting together the Soviet answer to the American 'Trident' system.

The sound of gently lapping waves gave way to a strange purr and the admiral jumped out of his reverie to find Beluga, his wife's blue-black Persian cat drinking out of his free-form indoor lake, a sort of large bird bath, one foot deep that took the space of the average double-0 model railroad complex. Built of caulked marine plywood, the 'shore' was landscaped with modelmaker's grass and trees. There was even a bluff on which was mounted a miniature radar station.

He was too tired to chastise the cat; better Tanya should sleep. He got up and Beluga, whiskers dripping, hissed and scrambled out of the study. "I'm really not that bad," he called after the cat. "I don't dislike you, it's just that I can't stand cats, period." Kulov went to the window. It had stopped snowing. A full moon hung low in the north. One of those magic nights.

He put on his fur coat and hat, fur-lined boots and tucked his mittens into a pocket. The automatic elevator ground to a jolting stop and soon he was crunching his way up Nevsky Avenue. Turning right at the Fontanka River, he crossed the foot bridge to the opposite bank and walked past Pushkin's statue and the floodlit though deserted State Museum to the Summer Garden. After brushing the snow from a bench facing the Neva, he sat down and extracted a Havana cigar from a protected inside pocket.

Across the river to his left loomed the fortress cathedral of Peter and Paul, repository for the marble crypts of the early Tzars. He lit his cigar and blew a cloud of smoke toward an ironclad warship moored at the intersection of the Bolshaya River near the Lenin Memorial. The battle-cruiser *Aurora*, symbol of the revolution, lay icebound and dimly lit. Kulov blew another cloud and envisioned it as coming from the ship's stacks. Alternately removing his mitten and putting it back on, he smoked the Havana to a stub, until his ears tingled under the flaps. Figures from the past mingled with his breath frost and danced on the frozen river, on *Aurora's* decks and in the lamp lit snow before him.

The years melted away and he was at sea again . . . young Lieutenant Konstantin Osipovitch Kulov, heir of two passions——the Navy and the neutron.

Chapter 1

"Peter, I'm leaving you—and that's final!"

"I can't hear you, Eka. Bad connection. A temporary field military phone . . ." Nielson couldn't describe the devastation about him. Orders! As if the allied bombers hadn't done enough; the Russians were closing in and the evacuation of the rocket facility at Peenemunde was beginning.

"I said I'm leaving you."

"Eka, where are you calling from?"

"Zurich. I'm in Switzerland."

"How did you get out of Berlin?"

"You've heard of Toni Lutze. . . ."

"Eka, you couldn't; not with that fat pig."

"I'm divorcing you, Peter, I can't live this way."

"You can't be serious, my love. Look, the war will be over soon. I'll come home. I know you've been through a lot. . . ."

"Peter, you lied to me about Krupp."

"He's ill, but he promised that I'd get my share. You've got to be patient, Eka. These things take time."

34

"Hah," she shrieked, "the old goat's senile, and his lawyers will cut you to little pieces, Mister Peter Krupp von Bohlen und Halsbach. All one big lie, and I fell for it."

"Eka, let's be reasonable. Let's think of the baby. You just can't—" Nielson suddenly realized he was shouting, to the amusement of the phone queue, an assortment of military and civilian personnel at Trassenheide Barracks on Usedom Island.

"Come on, sailor. Settle your family squabbles on your own time. Your three minutes are up." The Wehrmacht Major shrugged impatiently, his address book open, as the last-ditch Peenemunde detachment waited their turns.

"Yes, of course, Major." Nielson lowered his voice. "Eka, it will not be good for the baby."

"I'm having the baby in Zurich; it's all arranged—the best doctors and surroundings."

"You're right, look, give me your address. I'll get in touch; hurry, please."

"Sorry, Peter. It's better this way. Toni's got lots of money and friends. We'll be all right. Don't you worry. Goodbye!"

"EKA. . . . EKA!" Nielson screamed and dropped the receiver, then pushed dazedly through the crowded operations room and ran out to his bicycle.

"Let's go, Godamnit," a tweedy scientist shouted to the Major as he groped for the swinging phone, "the Russians are coming!"

Peter cycled south, toward the village of Bansin where he was quartered. Taking the river road, he looked back at Peenemunde Village where six submarines were lying, being fueled and provisioned. He'd been assigned to one of them, U-3505, as first watch officer under Korvettenkapitän Freiherr Lothar von Maltzan, an engineer and weapons systems genius. Now he would be merely a submarine bus driver, delivering a boatload of V-2 scientists and technicians to the enemy, the *good* enemy, rather than allow them to be captured by the bad enemy. Word had only a few days earlier, been received that the Americans were stopping at the Elbe River—giving the Baltic seacoast and Berlin to Stalin.

Major Vavolov's 2nd White Russian Army battalion was already in Neubrandenburg, some fifty miles away and scattered small units had penetrated and looted even closer.

Clouds of dust and a motorcycle appeared on the approach to the Wolgast Ferry. The BMW sped past Peter, then spun and screeched to a stop. "Peter," the helmeted speedster called and cut his motor.

Nielson swung his bike around, confused all the more at the mention of his name from this apparition on wheels. The rider kicked his stand and whipped off his goggles, exhibiting a buck-toothed smile as he extended a gloved hand.

"Helmut, what on earth are you doing here. I thought you were in Bleicherode."

"I was, but the Americans came in and before we knew what happened we were processed and given temporary leaves. It's called 'Operation Paperclip.' I told them that I'd left my doctoral thesis at Peenemunde and it was important regarding missile tracking and they gave me this machine saying 'go get it before the Russians do.' I left it in a safe at the Development Section building."

"Can I get through to Bansin? What's wrong, you look pale." Nielson set his bike down and fumbled for a cigarette.

"I wouldn't go, Peter. Remember Rumschöttel?"

"Zanser's adjutant? The one who resigned last week?"

"He was shot by the Russians. Some drunken Siberians—a small "recon" party without an officer. They broke into the room as Rumschöttel was packing. Nobody expected recon for another twenty-four hours since the 2nd was still encamped. They tried to rape his wife and he went for his gun. Both of them cut down with machine pistols. You'd better forget about Bansin. Save your life, not your belongings.''

"I guess you're right, Helmut. So I lose a good camera and a few lenses, and who needs a change of uniform anymore?''

"I've got extra clothes, even American underwear I bought at their PX,'' Helmut patted his saddle bag. "Come, get on behind me. You won't need the bicycle either. I take it everyone is leaving now.''

"You got here just in time. There are six boats loading up and leaving at dusk. I'll get you on mine.''

"Thanks—then you can have your Ami shorts.''

Nielson held on to Helmut Duttman's back as the BMW cycle bounced over the bomb-pocked road. It was a time to think of survival, not losses. The realization of what his wife had done would be put off until later, if only for the child's sake. It was a time to be strong—and clever. The rush of salty Baltic air against his face revived him and made him forget.

U-3503 led the assorted U-boat pack from the Peenemunde Village dock, past the power station and across the darkening bay under the looming iron skeletal dish of the Wurzburg radar nicknamed "Riese" or giant. A demolition squad waved to the boats as they set explosive charges around the concrete base.

Looking back from the streamlined conning tower, Nielson could just make out the oxygen plant ruins and a row of smoldering test stands. The five other boats, all with inexperienced crews, followed in single file—two more large "electro boats", one smaller coastal electro and two standard VIIC's—ducklings in the wake of the powerful.

The emasculated armada, without torpedoes because there weren't any more available, slipped into Greifswalder Bay and made for North Point on the resort island of Rugen where the course would be plotted for Falstebro, Sweden, almost 100 miles away—the land's end and gateway to the Kattegat.

Korvettenkapitän von Maltzan spat a mouthful of coffee to leeward, eyes blinking in the red glow of the conning tower instrument repeaters. "Nielson, you better get us there before this ersatz mud poisons us all. I think it's really some kind of lubricating oil."

"In that case, the oil will be on the top, sir. I know the cook put water in the pot with the powder."

"Hmpf, yes. Hah!" Von Maltzan sniffed at the cup then flung it into the descending darkness. "How long till we're into the Kattegat? I'm a little rusty . . . two years since my last sea command."

"We should make it in eight hours—if the wind stays as is, and we don't have to dive."

"And the minefields—"

"I have the latest charts. At Falstebro the mines are restricted to the Danish half of the sound. We'll stay on the Swedish side. Our new echo navigational system will allow us to go through without periscope if necessary. Depends on the visibility."

"All the same, I prefer to stay on the surface," the paunchy officer buttoned up his oilskin as salt spray came up from the dark waters. "My last command was U-464."

"Sunk in Biscay. You were lucky; the other two 'milch cows' were lost with all hands on that operation."

"Our JU-88's were no match for the Mosquitoes and Beaufighters, not to mention Leigh lights and MAD. We should have expected magnetic detection and developed a nullifier."

"The tankers were too slow in diving. We should have underwater refueling systems." Nielson uncapped the speaking tube. "Helmsman, half ahead, port", then picked up the intercom. "Radio room, send this to the others—short range: 'Proceeding 10 knots, will advise.' It's getting a little sloppy."

"For a line officer, you've got some good technical
ideas, Nielson. Too bad you didn't get more into the
missile program. We could have used an engineer with
some ocean-boat experience. I understand you are a university electrical graduate."

"I got sidetracked into 1-M."

"Ah, poor old Canaris; I'd hate to be in his shoes now.
Prisoners do not leave Flossenbürg—and now, with Ba-
varia almost done for. . . . "Yes, I was very lucky."

"And so was Germany. Without your logistic genius the
V-2 program would have lagged," Peter flattered the Junker.

"True, true; but I'm most proud of my work on the
torpedo loader. We'll have to find some eels to demonstrate to the English scientists when we meet them."

"We? Do you suppose I'll go along with the scientists?"

"I'll put in a word for you, but you know how it is.
They'll want to see documentation, hard evidence of your
accomplishments. I am well prepared with photographs,
plans and letters from important people in industry. It
always helps to have contracts with those who transcend
mere wars and build up again for whatever the new market
will need. Went to school with Alfred Krupp for a time.
My family owned a lodge near their place in the Bayerische
Alpen. You've heard of Mount Hochkönig, and the
Königsee— ach, such incredibly beautiful country, especially in the summer. . . ."

Nielson's blood boiled despite the wind's veering to
northeast and the plunging of the invisible bow. He held in
his feelings. "It must be nice, not to have to worry about
survival—that losing a war will not change your style of
living."

"Let me give you a piece of advice, Lieutenant. Always
go where the money or the power is. Some of us have
better credentials and arrive with little effort and some
have to work hard for it. I'll probably go to America until
things are better in Germany."

Go where the money or power is! The phrase echoed in

Peter's head as the wind screamed into a gale. The gale shouted to him—primeval voices from the land of the bear: *Come to where the power is, come . . . come. . . .* The voice chided him: *Nielson, comrade, your place is not with the West. They will treat you as Krupp has treated you. They are all capitalists, the Germans and the Allies. Without credentials you will be lost among the wolves.*

Suddenly, Peter had a plan. He *did* have a credential: U-3503! "Sir, you say that British Naval Intelligence expects to contact us off Göteborg." Peter feigned indifference, inspecting the bridge instruments. "What is the signal?"

"That is top secret—the war is not over yet."

"Of course, I understand."

"I'm going below, Lieutenant. I'm sure you can get along without me till the next watch."

Peter didn't answer as Von Maltzan struggled down through the hatch. Behind his back, one of the two watch ratings directed an obscene gesture at the Baron. The *Naxos* radar detector revolved and flashed intermittently as it picked up the red instrument glow.

Buffeted by huge waves, the 2100-ton welded steel craft, double the displacement of each of the two standard VIIC's and nine times that of the tiny XXIII electro coastal boat, pitched and yawed, making the nauseous land-scientists curse these products of their technical wizardry.

"For God's sake, let's submerge and get this over with," Dr. Fritz Kohn, a propellant specialist staggered toward the 'sick barrel' in the control room.

"Fritzchen," he was chided by an associate, "this is the best way to make speed—on the surface. The weather will keep air reconnaissance to a minimum. You should be glad you're on an XXI." Poor Schraeder, on the tiny boat would gladly change places.

"That's true," Kohn sidestepped forward, accepting the proferred hands for balance, and squeezed past the sound room and officers' quarters, then took his assigned place in the torpedo room under the gray mantis-like reloading arms.

"Captain to the sound room." Von Maltzan fell out of his bunk, the only private one, at the loudspeaker's blast. He wished he had a white-crowned cap to distinguish himself as nominal captain.

Forty-eight extremely sensitive hydrophone heads, arranged in circular rows within a plastic bulge under the boat's bow were receiving continuous impulses from all quarters and depths. The aft-directed units received the sound of the boat's own screws, port and starboard, the swish of water, and forward, the pounding of waves. All these impulses were accounted for. But the hydrophones of the upper ring at about two o'clock were receiving more than the usual ambient sound.

Petty Officer Ernst Knittel cocked his head and counted under his breath, then looked at his sweep-second wrist watch. Both hands were fingertipped on the stainless steel directional wheel. He took one hand off, then pressed the headset tight on one ear while the other remained uncovered for normal listening. Above the wheel a dial pointer oscillated around the 60 degree marker.

"Well," von Maltzan boomed, leaning into the soundroom.

"High speed screws, sir—range about 6500 meters and bearing on an intercept course."

The officer grabbed the intercom. "Bridge." Knittel switched it on. "Bridge . . . Nielson, are you there?"

"Right behind you, sir."

The Junker was startled. "But you're on watch—"

"Relieved at 20 hundred hours, sir. Lindemann's on."

"Hmpf . . . well, what do you make of it?"

"Coming from the east," Nielson rubbed his chin stubble. "How many screws, Knittel?"

"More than two, sir."

"Cruiser, at least," Nielson deliberated. "We've got no big warships out here. Seems to be coming from Bornholm—or Kronstadt."

"Dönitz is bringing back troops from Danzig."

"We don't have any transports with four screws, sir, at least not in service. We can't take a chance, especially with no torpedoes. There's no choice but to take her down. Knittel, signal the others."

"Do we have to?" murmured von Maltzan as he left.

Peter watched the Baron disappear into his green sanctum and wondered whether he'd lost his own ruthlessness.

U-3505 plunged under the roiling surface, the last hope of the thousand-year Reich. Ninety-one XXI's were at sea, working up and training crews; twelve were about to be commissioned and join the two in service. One, commanded by Adalbert Schnee was in the Atlantic. The sleek boat, its retractable hydroplanes cutting sharply, had submerged in nineteen seconds. The standard U-boat could do no better than thirty. Nielson felt a tinge of futility. The most revolutionary submarine of the century was all but perfected, and now might never be used. Capable of 17.5 knots underwater, it could outrun many surface craft, if only for several hours—but that was enough! In addition, Allied Asdic and Sonar could not track at speeds over twelve knots and the electro-boat, with its trebled battery power could run submerged at that speed for eight hours. The standard boat, such as had been in action for five years could only do six knots for that duration, vulnerable to detection.

Nielson's fingers itched for a chance to switch on the automatic acoustic torpedo aiming system—and sink whatever was bearing toward them on surface. But he'd forgotten; no eels!

He felt safe and snug in this boat, almost as if it were part animal, with its non-metallic coat called "Alberich", a combination of rubberized plastic that absorbed, rather than reflected enemy radar when running on the surface. Even the obstreperous schnorchel wore a coating.

Should the boat be detected underwater, it was equipped with "Pillenwerfer", literally *pill-thrower*, a system whereby clouds of effervescent bubbles could be ejected, confusing the Asdic! What a comic scene would ensue with the English.

The destructive potential, prime reason for all submarines was enormously increased over its predecessor. The hydraulic torpedo loader could reload all six bow tubes in twelve minutes, while a VIIC needed fifteen minutes for *each* tube, and the larger boat carried 24 torpedoes instead of 14! Four times the destructive power plus automatic aiming from below the surface, without seeing or being seen. Yet more incredible designs were on the drawing board. A proposed model called for an extra twelve tubes, located on the sub's sides. Imagine, a salvo of eighteen let loose to home in on a convoy or fleet and no fear of detection and "wasserbomb" retaliation.

"Screws closing fast," Knittel rolled his eyes toward the glossy white ceiling as the U-boat glided silently on its 225 horsepower silent-running motor. A fast speed, though preferable, was impossible because of the slower VIIC boats. In the control room, or "zentrale" the manometer indicated 250 meters—two and one-half times deeper than the newest English "V" class boats could dive!

"Range, 1000 meters, angle, zero-seven . . . seven-five-zero . . ."

"All stop." Nielson was sweating despite the luxury of air conditioning, something the Americans had enjoyed for years on their fleet boats. All that could be heard aboard was the heavy breathing of over a hundred men, twice that designed for the air purifiers.

"Screws diminishing . . . bearing one-eight-seven," Knittel sighed and slipped off his headset.

"If he's Russian, he's probably headed for Fehmarn

Belt. He'd like to have a look at some of our equipment in Kiel before the English get there. They were in Lubeck already when we left Peenemunde.'' Nielson ducked across the corridor as the Baron emerged from his lair.

"This is one boat a Bolshevik will never board as long as I'm on it. Let's get back on course, kapitänleutnant,'' barked von Maltzan. "I'm getting tired of our ingenious German food.''

The gaunt admiral leaned over his cluttered desk and looked out his window. The lake was smooth and the blush of spring belied the hopelessness of the rubbled cities. Safe in the resort town of Plön, noted for its miniature reproduction of Versailles, BdU Grandadmiral Karl Dönitz presided over his once-proud fleet.

A rumble from the south interupted his reverie as he packed the photographs of his two sons. Almost thirty thousand German submariners had been lost, and he had given more than his share. The Kriegsmarine was done for; supplies, fuel and ammunition were almost non-existent, morale at its lowest. But he had to keep going, moving ahead of the enemy's advance, buying time to direct the immense effort of bringing home hundreds of thousands of retreating troops from the eastern provinces. Now it was time to move his headquarters further north, away from the British under Montgomery. He had chosen Mürwik, a small town near the Danish border for his last stand.

Sorting out his papers, he put aside the important ones and stacked others to be destroyed. One letter caught his eye. It was a transcript of a radio decipherment from the Chancellery in Berlin:

30 April 1945
. . . Fresh treachery afoot. According to enemy broadcast Himmler has made offer to surrender via Sweden. Führer expects you to take instant and ruthless action against traitors.—Bormann.

Dönitz picked up another transcript, handed to him the same day in the presence of Admiral Kummetz, Naval Commander-in-Chief, Baltic and Albert Speer, Minister of Munitions.

Grand Admiral Dönitz:
The Führer has appointed you, Herr Admiral, as his successor in place of Reichsmarshall Goering. Confirmation in writing follows. You are hereby authorized to take any measures which the situation demands.
—Bormann.

The admiral shook his balding head in disbelief as he read a third letter:

Grand Admiral Dönitz (Secret and Personal).
1 May 1945
Will now in force. Coming to see you as quickly as possible. Pending my arrival you should in my opinion refrain from public statement.—Bormann.

"Führer's will now in force." All Dönitz could deduce was that Hitler was no longer alive. What a strange way to communicate the news. The admiral assumed that the Führer had died in battle, the way he'd indicated he would.

The admiral had issued the appropriate proclamations and arranged the surrender. He would wait till the air raids halted, then meet his adjutant, Admiral von Friedeburg at the Levesau Bridge over the Kaiser Wilhelm canal near Kiel and drive to Muerwik. Dönitz bound his papers in a leather case then reached into his desk drawer. He placed the Mauser pistol carefully in a small handbag, first checking the safety catch. The catch had been off only once—on the evening of 30 April, when Himmler came to Plön with six armed SS troops to argue that *he* should have been named as Head of State. The pistol was under some papers on the desk as Himmler was shown the Chancellory transcripts. Dönitz was relieved when the dreaded SS chief, decorated with death's head insignia accepted the decision, but asked to be "second man." A contingent of boatless U-boat sailors armed with machine guns were hidden on the grounds in the event of trouble. The admiral looked at his watch, then walked over and opened up the half door. An armed seaman snapped to attention. It was good to have The Dönitz Guard Battalion to count on. What was keeping Field Marshall von Greim? There were last-minute details to work out before leaving Plön . . . and what was Himmler up to? What was his reaction upon being denied a position in the post-Hitler government, and where had he gone?

There was a sharp rap on the door that led into the headquarters room. "General von Greim and Fraulein Reitsch to see you, sir."

"Just a moment," Dönitz rang for his orderly. "Donnerwetter, a woman. Hurry, we've got to clean up this mess. There, Bernhard—my socks under the bed . . . and a tablecloth . . . and do something with the bathroom. That's all I need—the Reich has troubles enough, and they send me a woman. I don't care what she does, a woman does not belong on the front." The admiral threw some dirty linen into a closet and locked the door. "Bernhard—the Führer—where is he?"

The orderly, a tow-headed underage recruit, was aghast. "In Berlin, I think, sir."

"No, I mean the Führer's picture."

"Packed, sir. Shall I . . ."

"Yes, and hurry." Dönitz bumped into Bernhard as he ran into the bathroom, rubbing his white two-day beard.

". . . and we were coming in over the Berlin Zoo when we were hit by Russian flak," the World War I flying ace and replacement for Göring, demonstrated with his hand. I lost control, but good old Hannah leaned over me and grabbed the controls. Narrowly missed some linden trees, we were that low, trying to evade flak.''

''I didn't think the Arado would hold together, it was rattling so.'' The slight aviatrix with a flashing, toothy smile stirred her coffee. ''We would have gotten here sooner, but we had a problem finding fuel.''

''And we did rest for a day after leaving the ''Hundes-bunker.'' The distinguished Luftwaffe General winked at Hannah.

''I toast the new Reichsführer of the Luftwaffe,'' Hanna raised her cup. ''He well deserves the promotion.''

''*Marshal* will do,'' Greim laughed. I could never fill Göring's shoes . . . or pants.''

''How was it—in the Hundesbunker,'' asked Dönitz grimly. He was changing his mind about women—this woman. She had spunk, something he'd not seen for some time regardless of sex. She was a pixie, a tom-boy with frazzled wind-blown hair, a scrunched-up nose and her ears were a bit large. He caught himself staring at her in an unprofessional manner. Perhaps Greim was right. The general was only a year younger than he, but look at the fun he was having.

''It was getting to be a *hexensabbath*,'' Hannah replied, closing her eyes. ''Liquor . . . Generals—not you darling—chasing half-naked signalwomen through the corridors . . . Doctor Kunz's dental chair . . . I'm glad he ordered us to leave when he did. And the girls, Gerda, Else and Trudl—the Russians are untamed beasts.

''Maybe they got away without—'' Greim stopped.

''We offered to stay with him and sacrifice our lives for the Luftwaffe's honor. But he wasn't the great man I'd known; his personality had disintegrated completely. When we left, he was waving messages and moving pins on his war map like a little boy playing war games. 'Move this unit here . . . Ritter, you get your planes to such and such."

"That we came all the way from Munich was absurd, looking back at it. He could have promoted me by phone. It would have been much easier to fly directly here."

"To say nothing of losing ten of our fighter cover 190's on the flight to Gatow. Sheer waste of good planes and pilots." The 33-year-old *Flugkapitän*, as she was known in Hitler's circle put her small hand over von Greim's. "I think I ought to leave you to talk about your business."

"Tell the admiral about your plan to reverse the war by piloting V-1 missiles at the Allied Fleet. Perhaps the Admiral will follow up since our Führer gave you a go-ahead."

"He did!" Dönitz stiffened and opened a note-pad.

"He gave permission to commence experimenting on the project providing I didn't bother him during the development stage."

"I see," Dönitz was drawing a V-1 on his note-pad. "He didn't tell me about that one. When did he agree?"

"It was at the Berghof last year—in March, I think."

"It might have made a difference at Omaha Beach, but I didn't think the weapon was operational then."

"Except for an accurate guidance system, it was ready." Hannah got up from the table. "Excuse me, I'm going to freshen up." The two leaders watched her spirited exit.

"Baron," Dönitz reached for a bottle of *Asbach Uralt*. "You know it's hopeless and idiotic to continue." He poured cognac into the coffee. Ritter nodded. "The Führer did you a great favor by ordering you out of the bunker; the both of you."

"I think he was fond of Hannah; he promoted me so I would bring Hannah to say goodbye. There is no Luftwaffe left."

"You knew him during the last war?"

"Just after. I took him for his first airplane ride in 1920. He was still a corporal when we took off from Munich. He

wore a goatee and Eckart posed as a newspaper dealer.
That's how we got them through a Bolshevik trap. The
flight was bumpy and he got very sick.''

"Maybe he wanted to see you also.''

Greim shrugged. "The main reason for coming here is
that he ordered us to find Himmler and denounce him for
treason.''

"Any reason to live is a good reason.'' The admiral
swirled his coffee cup as if it was a brandy snifter. "Himmler
was here yesterday; we have no idea where he is now.''

"Weren't you supposed to—''

"Have him *liquidated?* Then it wasn't only Bormann's
idea.''

"I'm afraid not,'' the general stood as Hannah came in.

"Am I interrupting?'' Lipstick had changed her. Hannah picked up the Baron's crutches. "Here,'' she scowled
jokingly.

"We have just decided on a plan that can't lose,''
Dönitz escorted the couple to their quarters. "But don't
ask us, it's top secret.'' As they walked slowly around the
lake, listening to sounds of spring and rebirth, the admiral
felt a shiver as the death's head insignia of Himmler
reappeared among the lights and shadows of late afternoon—
and came to rest, a glowing apparition, on General Ritter
von Greim.

The Naval College at Mürwik in Flensburg was about as
far as a German could retreat without leaving the country.
Overlooking Flensburg Fiord, it faced Denmark. Dominated by the high spire of medieval Nikolaikirche, the
seaport was known as 'the gateway to Scandinavia.' It was
from here that the admiral negotiated the surrender. The
British Army was already in Lubeck on the Baltic; the
peninsula of Schleswig-Holstein was all that was left of
Germany. There was a day of tenseness as he waited for

word from his courier, Admiral von Friedeburg, who had been sent to confer with the British commander, famed hero of the desert wars, General Montgomery. One of the conditions put forth by Dönitz was the allowing of German boats to continue bringing troops back from the Baltic ports.

Word came that 'Monty' had agreed, and would honor the point *providing* that the admiral issue a directive that forbade the scuttling of boats and destruction of weapons and facilities. This he did, despite the grumbling of his subordinates. They reminded him of his vow that rather than be captured, the German Navy would be flashed the codeword 'Rainbow' as a signal for mass scuttling. The cancellation message was received by British monitors and adjudged authentic and final. He gave as his reason: we need the ships for evacuation of our troops to the west.

The decision was accepted by the surface fleet commanders but, in most cases, rejected by the submariners. Some unknown junior officer sent the signal by wireless. RAINBOW. Soon it was on everyone's lips. Crews fell out of their barracks and rushed to their moored boats. Excited captains shouted the codeword over intercoms in the Baltic, the North Sea and the Norwegian fiords.

Like sea-going lemmings the U-boats left their docks—crews' belongings safely ashore. In swarms they chugged down the rivers and harbors of Hamburg, and Emden, at Kiel and Eckenförde, into the coastal waters where so many of their comrades were interred. To the islands of Wangerooge and Spiekeroog; to Helgoland and Scharhörn; to Hiddensee and Poel. from Travemunde, from Neustadt and Wilhelmshaven—and while Dönitz slept, past the Naval College in Flensburg.

At dawn on May 5th, as the swastika was lowered over Mürwik, 215 submarines of all standard and experimental types were on the bottom. But there were still a few mavericks. One, U-977, lying off the enemy harbor of

Southhampton, voted by lot, to make for Argentina. Most of the boats in Norway's harbors surrendered. A special boat, on its way to attack the Panama Canal, had also received word of *Rainbow*.

Chapter 2

Blond, sharp-nosed Korvettenkapitän Adalbert Schnee tore the deciphered radio transcript into little strips. His first officer, an engineer of the same rank, chuckled and patted him on the back.

"Adalchen, wouldn't you know that something like this was in the cards!" For more than a year, the two high-ranking officers, picked for their success and experience in the sea war had lived with U-2511. They'd studied the plans, made suggestions and watched the keel laid at Blohm and Voss in Hamburg. Schnee was a picture book U-boat hero, one of the few hundred-thousand ton aces to survive the war. A favorite of 'Uncle Karl', he'd been given the plush command of the first operational electro-boat after dividing his time between functioning as an adjutant to Dönitz and the development of the first 'super-sub.' Suhren, an engineering wizard, had compiled an enviable record as exec and commander from the Mediterranean to the waters off Miami Beach. Together they had been assigned to work the bugs out of U-2511 while mounting a surprise attack on the Panama Canal area. It was a matter of conjecture and betting among the crew whether the prime targets were American naval vessels or the Canal itself.

Schnee retired to his cabin as his boat, having easily run under the British harbor gauntlet around Norway's Bergen harbor broke through the cold waters with its *snorchel* and set a course around the Faroes, an archipelago 400 miles west of Bergen. He was taking no chances with the overwhelmingly superior Allied forces in the North Sea regardless of the XXI's vaunted invincibility. There was something wrong. The message from BdU, Mürwik called for returning to the nearest port and surrendering. The radio, between military concerts and Lala Anderson shouted 'Rainbow.''

Schnee lay back on his green bunk under a framed cartoon of a snowman, the insignia painted on the conning tower of U-201, the command which had won him the Knight's Cross. The ''schneemann's'' coal black eyes penetrated him, and the crooked carrot nose mocked:

''Herr Adalbert, you didn't acknowledge the message?''

''That's correct, Herr Snowman.''

''Then why don't we see what we will see. Let's give it a day or two. You know the Soviets and the Allies will have all the fun—and you deserve the first satisfaction.'' Snowman stomped his broomhandle on the deck and knocked his high hat off. He had to leave the frame to retrieve it.

''But what will I tell BdU? I can't suddenly change my mind tomorrow—or the day after, and return to port. We're on our way to Panama.''

''Well, then let's go to Panama. I've been to the tropics before—and survived the heat. I hear there are pictures of snowmen carrying Coca-Cola bottles and I for one . . .'' The screeching of Klaxon horn rescued Schnee from his absurd reverie. He jumped up and pushed through the heavy curtains.

"Asdic, sir!"

Schnee held the spare headset to an ear. Remote, weak 'pings' were being picked up by the hydrophone array. The indicator needle wavered erratically. "Three or four boats," mumbled the commander.

"Hunter-killer group, sir? Headed directly for us." Radioman Pepi Fuss fine-tuned his gain knob as Schnee motioned the control room mate to raise the attack periscope. He went up the ladder and reached his 'saddle' just as the scope locked into place, its needle eye a meter forward of the rubber-coated schnorkel head. Schnee flipped the magnification to high as the automatic condensation control cleared the calibrated image plane. He focused on a faint, white halation, seemingly above the horizon. It disappeared. He turned the instrument a degree to starboard; found another bright speck . . . and another, as the distant flotilla, by units in turn reflected the bright sun from their bow waves.

"Go over to motors," Schnee's blue eye was still pressed into the rubber ocular as Suhren called out the orders:

"Electro-room, start your motors . . . control room, stand by to retract schnorkel . . . engine room. . . ." The orders were relayed aft by intercom.

"Single screws closing at sixteen knots," Fuss called from his sound room, as the various diving details scurried past.

"Flower Class corvettes," Suhren took the protective plastic cover off the 'S' system torpedo computor.

"That's their top speed," Schnee grinned white under the black rubber. "I can make out one of them; she's modified."

"Stand by?" Suhren meant torpedo room.

"No, take her down, and 30 degrees to port. Let's see how fast this thing can go."

*   *   *

"I say, Nevins—what 'appened? We 'ad it dead on."

"Sorry, sir—maybe the equipment, its been actin' up lately." The asdic operator shook his headset and jiggled the control knobs on the console.

"Carey," Lieutenant-commander Jack Wilkins-Smythe bellowed above the din of *Willowherb's* pounding 30-inch stroke cylinders, can you see anything?"

"No sir; I'm on the last fix." The lieutenant replied from his position behind the giant ranging binoculars mounted on the open bridge over the 4-inch gun.

"Dammit, Nevins, the war's over in half an hour and I've not gotten one of the bastards yet. There goes my promotion. A sure kill and the bloody Asdic gives up the ghost." The short commander rocked on his heels and fumed. "Nevins—if that unit of *yours* has not had the proper maintenance, there's going to be hell to pay . . . for someone!" Wilkins-Smythe slammed his binoculars down on the instrument console, shattering one of the objective lenses. "Now, see what you've made me do!" The officer threw up his hands in despair and clomped aft toward his day cabin, emitting a mournful wail.

"I say, Nevins," Lieutenant Carey mimicked his superior, "can't you do anything right?"

*   *   *

The six boats, scattered in the dark, surfaced one by one. Guided by semaphored light signals and the Klaxon horn, they regrouped behind U-3505 in a column and set on the last leg. Diesels were strained to the maximum to gain back an hour lost and reach the dangerous channel of Öresund at slack tide for better maneuverability through the mine fields. The gale had veered north and was tamed by the high bulk of Sweden's immense peninsula. The eastern sky changed from dull rose to crimson as a soft rain pitted the southern Baltic. Junior lieutenant Konrad Lindeman unbuttoned his oilskin collar and pecked at his steaming coffee.

"It's decent of you to stay past your watch, sir."

"Mornings are not considered work to me. Best part of the day—besides, it's getting gamey down there." Nielson inhaled by mistake on his cigarette, then thought of his mother and flipped the butt overboard. He breathed in the salt air deeply. "One thing to be said for war, Konrad, is that it gets one up early to watch sunrises. Sunrises are much more positive than sunsets—which are over-rated. There's promise and birth in a sunrise—and the opposite in the sun leaving us . . . the cold and unknown creeping in. Take our captain; take any silver-striped shore officer, sitting in stuffed chairs, and filling up waste baskets. They lose their touch with reality. If I were von Maltzan, I'd be up here, just for the change of scenery . . . the fresh air. This trip could have been a tonic for him. Just one sunrise like this . . ."

"The men said he forgot his deck-chair."

"Now, now, Konrad—"

"Do you believe in evil omens, sir?"

"Some have basis in fact and science."

"Is there basis in the one about silver stripes aboard?"

"We have too many; the boat won't sink because the curse will be short-circuited."

"And red sky in the morning?"

"What other color did you expect from Russia?"

"It's nice that you can joke at this time," Lindeman snapped off the instrument repeater illumination.

"One learns to take war humorously—especially defeat. It's a safeguard against going mad."

"It is funny!"

"What is?"

"My first—and probably only mission is to surrender."

"That's an essential part of war too. Some people don't know when to give up."

"That is unusual—hearing it from you, sir. What was your position about the attempt last July? I'm sorry, sir. I had no right to ask that."

"I have no qualms about that, lieutenant. My position was one of deep shock, and loyalty to our war effort—*then*."

"And now, sir?"

"We must think of ourselves, Konrad."

"You're right, Commander—look, gulls . . . ahead." A chattering and screeching toward the skywatch seamen from their sectors on the conning tower.

"We should be sighting Falstebro shortly, Lindeman. The gulls are from Sweden. I heard one say 'vilkommen.' "

"You're kidding me, sir?" The nineteen-year-old was caught off guard.

"Well," the thirty-year-old veteran joshed, "it sounded more Swedish than Russian. 'Welcome' in Russian is *NEH-zuh-shtuh.*"

Land was sighted at 0630 and the procession slipped quietly under the smooth waters below the southernmost land's end of Sweden. At snorchel depth they took advantage of the fog bank and cruised at eight knots on diesels around Falstebro Point and took the final land bearings to starboard of the fog, which clung over Copenhagen. The city, though occupied by Nazis, had more than its share of British sympathizers and agents. Triangulation on the ancient fortress ramparts of Malmohüs and the island of Saltholm were sufficient fixes to set the gyrocompasses to hold a course starboard of the mine fields at a depth of 200 meters—well below the range of airborne magnetic sensors— around Ven Island, and through Helsingborg narrows into the sprawling Kattegat.

Millisecond 'spurt' transmissions instructed the other boats before the radio antennas were retracted upon diving: PROCEED MAXIMUM DEPTH ÖRESUND CHANNEL 332M 4KNOTS FOLLOW AND SURFACE APPROX 60KM AFTER HELSINGBORG 312M PLAN B CYPHER 2200HRS.

"Acknowledged and understood," Radioman Fuss

checked off the boats as they replied: "U-1008 . . . U-3523 . . . 2365 . . . 534 . . . 2521 . . ." Fuss turned up the volume on another frequency he was monitoring and transcribed a message which he carried across the corridor and handed to von Maltzan. "Picked up from Naval Radio in Copenhagen, sir."

The Baron, already red-faced from reading the spurt message, crumpled up the second one which confirmed that the German forces were still holding all of Denmark. There was no chance of turning in to port and surrendering safely. Now he'd have to take his chances at being blown out of the water by new allied weapons before reaching the rendezvous, northwest of Goteborg, almost 200 miles distant. He called Nielson into his cabin.

"Donnerwetter, lieutenant; what is this *four* knots submerged when we can do at least ten knots for ten hours! Why should we be slowed down because of the small boats? The three electro-boats should not take unnecessary risks, and we carry most of the important scientists and equipment. I say the boats should be on their own."

"But the smaller boats—the VIICs cannot navigate the channel submerged. Their echo-ranging systems are primitive. We can't just *leave* them here. Let's discuss this with some of the others."

"Who?" von Maltzan was impatient.

"Doctor Werfft. He's the senior civilian."

"Very well, lieutenant. Call him in."

"Baron," the white-maned physicist peeked quixotically over his nose-perched glasses, "I agree with you in principle—but as a mathematician. Unfortunately I am also a humanitarian—especially when my colleagues are involved. May I suggest a compromise. Let's go half the way as a group. At 2200 hours tomorrow—we surface as planned, if we make it—and disperse, so as not to present a massed target. The small boats will have to run on the surface to charge their batteries anyway . . ."

"We can give them an alternate rendezvous further south, and get the British to agree," Nielson unfolded a chart.

"Or simply have them wait," Doctor Werfft added. "Interesting," the pysicist deliberated, "six boats . . . six is a very unusual number. It is the one mathematically perfect number under 28. Its divisors 3, 2 and 1 add up to its own value. After 28, we have 496 . . . 8128 and 33,550,336. There are eight more perfect numbers known, all progressively larger, in the billions and quadrillions and so on. Three large boats, two small, and one very small; each group an entity."

"All the more reason. I don't much like *six* myself . . ." the stocky Korvettenkapitän waxed authoritative. ". . . the six-pointed star of David, for instance."

"RAINBOW . . . RAINBOW—Shouts rang from the radio room and reverberated as U-3505's radio antenna skimmed inches above the Kattegat a few minutes before 10 PM. Fore and aft the crew gathered in groups, tensely awaiting word from the commander.

"Herr Lieutenant Lindeman," crew spokesman Horst Stolle and his diesel stokers backed the young man into a bulkhead. "Are you going to lead us—or do we have to . . ." The grimy Obermechanik held a heavy wrench in his hand.

"Stolle," Lindeman pleaded. "I'm only a conscript—he won't listen to me."

"You're an officer and you better act like one—or do you want to give up like a swine too?"

"Of course not." Lindeman shrugged defiantly.

"Then tell him to scuttle. According to the wireless, only the cowards in Norway are not doing what they have pledged. If you don't—"

"If I don't?" Lindeman squirmed uneasily.

"We don't have any eels, but you should fit in the tube nicely. Fresh young sharkfood."

"I'll see what I can do."

"Tell von Maltzan that you overheard the crew talking about blowing up the boat with all hands if it couldn't be scuttled honorably like all the others. We don't want the Bolsheviks or the English and we'll take our chances on the rafts—got it?"

"I'll see what I can do."

"No tricks, now, little boy, or you won't live to regret it."

"$17,543 apiece!" Helmut Duttman handed Nielson several pair of US Army issue cotton shorts. "Not the shorts," he laughed. "If we could sell this boat—"

"That is if the entire crew voted to go." Nielson hid the folded chart between a cabinet and the refrigerator. It was a good place to talk privately on the crowded boat as the freezer motor whined and cut out. "We've got just enough fuel to make it—with no detours."

"How far is it?" Helmut had looked at the coastline of Argentina before Nielson folded the chart.

"Almost 9000 miles, unless you like Biscay."

"No, thank you," the studious young scientist frowned.

For a moment, Nielson considered running to the Argentine. If it only weren't for the cargo of brains. Duttman would go, he was sure of that, but von Maltzan, and the rest. No, they wanted no complications. No raft to shore—no hard times, for they were the international set, and their loyalty was to the mark, the dollar, or the British pound, whichever was easier and safer. But there would be no such exchange for Peter Nielson—unless . . .

*   *   *

U-2511, white snowman painted on the streamlined conning tower, swung around and set a course back to Bergen. Commander Schnee was a professional; flesh and soul welded to his boat and steered by his almighty orders, like many a German before him. From a prominent family, he did not have to escape or prove anything. He had his glory in his pocket.

Eighty miles southwest of Utsira Light, entrance marker for Norway's lower fiord network, multiple screws were picked up by the hydrophone array. Once more in the tower saddle, he swung the attack scope to the bearing on the azimuth ring reported by the sound room. Schnee's knuckles turned white and his body tingled with a combination of fear and delight. A heavy cruiser, escorted by four destroyers were steaming along the horizon ahead of him— oblivious of his presence! A training manual exercise; the proverbial 'sitting ducks'. His hunter's blood bubbled. They just had to be English or American; Germany had no surface warships at sea. They were all bottled up in ports.

"A cruiser and four escorts," he whispered to Suhren, who thumbed through the Weyer ship identification book. "Steuersmann, go to eight-five."

"Eight-five" repeated the excited helmsman.

"Motor room to half ahead and stand by". Half the 4200 horsepower in the many-tiered lower hull batteries were shunted off and the boat slowed down to 6 knots.

"Switch to silent running."

The two main motors cut out as a special small motor purred, moving a belt system that turned one shaft.

"Bearing port 32 . . . speed 16 . . . range 4000—Mark," repeated Suhren as he fed the data into his clicking torpedo computer forward of the commander's position.

"Down scope, sound room follow . . ."

"Sound room following," came the confirmation from below.

"Locked in," the exec watched a pulsating green light.

"Take her down to fifty . . ."

"To fifty meters," the diving officer hovered over the

planesmen in the control room as the sleek black shark-like craft put its bow down, then leveled off.

"*Phantastich,*" Schnee watched the green computer light that indicated the bow hydrophones were transmitting relative course and speed of the cruiser to the computer, which in turn, mixed the data with the course, speed and depth of U-2511, feeding a continuously corrected setting into the six bow torpedoes. And yet, the sharp bow was pointed parallel to the cruiser's heading—ready for a maximum speed getaway in the opposite direction. The six 'eels' were programmed to fire forward for a hundred meters, then turn toward the target, maintaining the proper lead, and at the same time rising from a fifty meter depth to seven meters below the surface, the running depth for magnetic-fired torpedoes under a cruiser of the type observed. Schnee had pointed to the silhouette of a 'Town' type British cruiser in the recognition manual. Suhren noted that four of the nine cruisers in that class had already been sunk.

"Probably the *Norfolk,* type three. She has extra 40s"

"Right, sir," Suhren looked at the specifications. "Five point eight draught." The engineer set a dial to program the torpedoes to run one meter under the cruiser's keel.

"Spread, one-point-five . . . range 2000."

"Set," replied Suhren. The computer clicked and the six shot salvo was programmed to fan out into a lineal spread that, at 2000 meters would be about double the cruiser's length of 176 meters, insuring a hit or two despite the most evasive last minute action conceivable! Little did the commander comprehend at the time that the incredible technological advances of his boat would form the basis of the true Supersub in less than two years.

Schnee's palm sweated over the firing button. How strange—to pursue an unseen enemy, by watching little lights, calibrations and digits . . . listening to the whirr and click of a machine . . .

"Two-five-zero-zero," Suhren repeated the message from

the sound room and counted under his breath as the range
indicator moved toward the firing setting. The first officer
watched the commander's face for a sign. A red light
flickered; bow tubes were flooded and ready. Was he
going through with it? Only he and Schnee knew what the
message contained. Even Pepi had no access to *Captain's
Cypher*.

CEASE FIRE IMMEDIATELY . . . STOP ALL HOS-
TILE ACTION . . . No question that it was authentic,
using the cypher that was specified for exclusive use on 4
May. The Captain had not yet acknowledged receipt, so as
far as BdU knew, 2511 was still at war. Suhren was in
agreement. Yes, they should go through with it. Years of
development, countless blind alleys overcome, materials
synthesized . . . priorities gotten at great expense to the
other boats—the ones that were sunk for want of a snorkel
or a repair.

The commander tensed his hand, balancing the palm on
all five fingers over the button like a crab stopped on its
ascent up a piling. Schnee closed his eyes for a moment.
No longer would the hunter delight in seeing the flash of
victory and destruction that told him he'd done his job. He
could only replay the film of his memory, and synchronize
the image with the concussion—but how, since the concussion will happen *after* the flash.

A blue light intensified, signalling the ten-second count-
down had begun. 'The log!' Suhren suddenly remembered.
Fuss had recorded receipt of the message: the code key
. . . the time of day. "Adalbert . . . no . . ."

But Schnee's hand had already slammed against the
control panel. Suhren winced. Too late, but then his jaw
dropped. There'd been no jolt, as was expected when ten
tons of deadly eels were spot out of the bow. A malfunction
of the 'S' system? Thank God. Saved! Certainly averted a
court-martial. "Adalbert—we're fortunate something went
wrong . . . the radio log . . . the message . . . He stopped

short as he saw it. The computer lights were out; it was quiet . . . but who?

Schnee was grinning at him. "I hit the abort switch just before zero . . ." The two whispered out of the helmsman's earshot.

"But, I don't—" Words didn't come to Suhren.

"I couldn't let you in on the whole plan, Reinhard. Orders. It was imperative that no one knew, so all systems down to the last second would check out—including my first officer. One of the things we couldn't test out on trials was the variable of ourselves under stress . . . under an actual attack.

"Then it was a success."

"Absolutely; on paper, HMS Norfolk is on the bottom."

"And we haven't been detected.

"Let's get out of here before we are," the capless commander climbed down into the control room. "Take over, please, Reinhard. I've got to write a letter to Uncle Karl."

Chapter 3

Second Lieutenant Stefan Zajonczek touched his forehead against the cold plexiglas of his cramped station below the turret gunner's fleece-lined boots as he stared into the blackness at the fleeting bright ellipse. He grunted painfully as the bombsight pedestal controls ground into his left hip—but hands and knees into the nose was the only way to see in this particular version of the American Liberator bomber.

Stefan pressed his throat microphone and asked Pilsudski to give it one more try. Snapping off the five-million candle-power Leigh light under the starboard wing, he swung himself into a more comfortable position for the next pass.

The twin-tailed PB4Y-1 droned and banked to come in on the same bearing again. This time, Pilsudski brought it in lower and the wave-skipping patch of light was larger. Zajonczek cupped his eyes with his hands, one of which held the bomb release remote switch. A quick check ascertained the bays were open.

So he'd bet the navigator that the blip he saw ten

minutes earlier was a boat. They laughed at him until he
took out his money. 'Zag,' they said, 'you're always
seeing things that are not there.' Now they were laughing
again. 'The radar,' they said, 'was very sophisticated according to the English, and could only be understood by
sophisticated observers—not farm boys from Jaroslaw.'
Stefan felt inside his flight jacket, then pulled out a chain
with the medal of St. Stanislas, martyr of Crakow, friend
of the soil and patron of all Poland. He kissed the warm
metal and quickly zipped it back inside. No sooner had he
concentrated on the ellipse again than he saw, on its
periphery, a bright reflection . . . and a second one—ahead
of the first. Stefan screamed into his microphone and
Pilsudski banked and the bomber went into a dive at the
bright spot. A 'stick' of eight 250-pound depth charges,
six-foot long cylinders with breakaway tails tumbled from
the bomb bay, straddling U-2521. Pilsudski raised the rest
of Squadron 311 on the wireless and the skies were filled
with Polish war cries.

Nielson, last through the hatch, cursed and slammed the
klaxon button for an emergency dive. The Leigh lights, like
screaming meteors, blinded him temporarily and he dogged
the hatch from feel alone as the boat's electro motors
whined to gain diving headway. Five seconds . . . ten . . .
Nielson counted as he felt the boat nose over. Not fast
enough . . . he shook off the pain of bruises from his blind
descent and dragged himself down into the control room.
Fifteen . . . twenty . . . twenty-five. His vision came back
in wavering spurts and he heard someone shouting. It was
von Maltzan in the sound room screaming into a microphone:
"CLAVICHORD, do you hear me? CLAVICHORD, come
in bitte . . . schnell!"
"Ten meters," reported the control room mate. "Fifteen . . ."
The boat was under. "Hard to starboard, full rudder,"

Nielson took over and a rumble shook paint from the white ceiling. The lights blinked. "Wasserbomb!" shouted Lindeman. "Rig for depth charges!" The boat shuddered as several charges went off at once; a giant iron hammer had struck the hull. Glass tinkled and light bulbs burst. The boat groaned and lurched, throwing crew and terrified passengers in heaps against the mazes of conduits and valves—but it held together, and that was what counted. Another charge went off just amidships forward of the tower. The impact was so jarring that the boat rolled over and a section of the snorkel head was ruptured. But 3503 went down, under full power and control—down to the safe caress of its maximum operating depth, 250 meters, far below the settings of the enemy's missiles.

The 'S' system picked up a shoal to starboard which coincided with a sounding of 10 meters on the chart and Nielson called for full speed, which, in two hours would allow them to surface in the shadow of Anholt Island to assess hull damage with minimum chance of radar detection.

Approaching the island, the snorkel jammed before it could be raised and they went in almost to the beach before surfacing. The damage was not reparable so the scientists voted to go ashore on the sparsely populated five-mile long island.

As the others were wading, hip-deep on the low tide sandbanks, pulling rubber rafts crammed with books, technical data and personal belongings, the Baron commandeered the radio room and had Fuss send repeated messages on a spectrum of wavelengths. When cautioned by Nielson, von Maltzan threatened to have him courtmartialed for hindering the mission. He was sending the codeword for Royal Navy rendezvous: CLAVICHORD.

Nielson and a few key crewmembers were ordered by the blustery Junker to scuttle the boat in deep waters. It was still two hours before dawn when the bow anchor was hauled off the sandbank and the powerful electric motors put in reverse. Damage to the intake system was such that the diesels were inoperative. Running on the surface, several miles north of Anholt, Nielson called for full stop and ordered the helmsman and motor crew to break out an inflatable raft and go over the side . . .

"I can handle this alone," Nielson reassured the four seamen as they scrambled into the raft, perplexed by the sudden change of events. Even Nielson himself was surprised—the nebulous plan that had occurred to him on the bridge during the height of yesterday's gale became strikingly clear. 'Go to where the power is' von Maltzan had said, meaning America. But Peter Nielson could not go to America—nor England. He would be hunted down as a war criminal. Benjamin Mount and William 'Moxie' Mulford would see to that. Peter Nielson would not be fought over by the Western industrial-military complex for his knowledge of Germany's submarine-fired missile experiments. He was with Steinhoff in a frigid lake, secluded high in the Austrian Alps, when the first rockets were fired from a submersible, manned platform. He was with Doctor Ebeling at Poel when the submersible V-2 container was tested—he! Nielson, the liaison officer between scientist and sailor. There would be a job for him—especially if he brought his own demonstration equipment, a complete XXI. And who would 'buy'. The other place that possessed the 'power'. Russia would give him a job.

Nielson studied the chart and decided to make for the tiny island of Hornfiskrön. Off the southern coast of the large island called Laesö, it had the advantage of a reef to hide behind, and it was totally uninhabited. He could be there by dawn. Throwing the motor levers into half-ahead, he ran through the control room and scurried up to the bridge for a compass bearing before taking the helm and putting the boat on a course to Hornfiskrön. He was about to go down to the motor room to rev up to maximum, when, suddenly the boat accelerated on its own accord. Perhaps something was wrong. He slid down the ladder.

"Hello, Peter!"

Startled, Nielson whirled and leaped from the ladder, pistol in hand.

"Peter, you know I can't stand firearms."

"Helmut, I saw you get off at Anholt," Nielson stuck his Walther P-38 into his belt.

"So you didn't see me get back on."

"You've got to get off."

"But Peter, you can't handle this monster alone—besides, I brought your underwear. Somebody has to think of you. The smooth-skinned young man rummaged through his shoulder bag.

"You don't understand, Helmut. I want to do this alone."

"You *vant* to be alone like Garbo." Helmut posed coyly.

"I'm serious—" Nielson whipped out the pistol. The lustrous oiled barrel gleamed in the red conning tower light. "Get on up the ladder."

"Don't point that thing at me, I'm going."

With the boat on automatic pilot, Nielson inflated another rubber raft and told Helmut to wait while he went below and cut the motors. "I've always wanted to go to Denmark—they're so progressive according to some of my friends . . ." Helmut held tightly onto a deck stanchion as the black water rushed by.

When Nielson returned to the bridge, Helmut was gone. Nielson played the flashlight fore and aft. Suddenly he felt sick; the raft was still secured but dragging over the side on the starboard saddle tank. He had killed a friend, just as sure as if he'd put a bullet through him. Helmut was weak and would never be able to swim to shore, especially without a lifejacket. He cursed himself for leaving the boy alone, and shouted into the blackness, but all that answered was the wind.

Nielson climbed down to the deck and hauled the raft up, then tied it down. It was the last raft, and it still might be needed. He noticed something in the raft. Helmut's shoulder bag. Opening it, he shone his light on several binders neatly stacked with papers and marked with index tabs. Helmut's doctoral thesis! Nielson's first inclination was to fling the bag into the sea. Instead, he tenderly closed it and carried it up to the bridge—almost as if it was alive, or a body.

The black bow nosed gently into the sandy beach of Hornfiskrön's tiny, nameless neighbor, a mustard seed on the chart. The islet, part reef and part dunes with a scrub-covered rise on one end was a quarter mile east of its parent, a haven for sea birds.

The flapping of cormorants and screeching of gulls greeted sunrise as well as U-3503. Peter had chosen a tidal flat indentation and allowed the sea itself to power the boat slowly through the secluded inlet. It was low tide—a very important factor in entering any unfamiliar or uncharted harbor. On the southeast side of the islet, the boat was well out of visual range of Denmark's mainland, fifteen miles east, and invisible to the Danes on Laesö, a mile north, as well as to the herring fishermen who plied to Hornfiskrön.

A hydraulic motor purred and a forward bollard rose and locked into position. Nielson then went up to the bow and looped a one-inch mooring line over it and climbed down into the hip-high water, hauling the free end of the line with him. After securing it to a rock on the beach, he pulled himself up on deck and went below through a forward hatch to the radio room. After setting a timer to buzz every ten minutes in order that he be reminded to go to the bridge for a quick scan of the beach, he switched the receiver on and monitored the Soviet Naval frequency. Finding some traffic, he composed a short message with help from a Russian-German dictionary. While having

some conversational knowledge, he was vague on technical terms and chastised himself for his lack.

What he didn't tell von Maltzan was that among the last
messages received from BdU before leaving Peenemünde
included the information that a Soviet battle cruiser had
threaded the 'Sea Urchin' minefield, a system that he had
taken part in laying by U-boat years earlier, bottling up the
Soviet fleet at Kronstadt. He was certain the multiple
screws picked up on the hydrophones a day earlier was
that cruiser. It was probably *Sevastopol* since *Petropavlovsk*
had been badly damaged by a Luftwaffe attack.

At 0625, Nielson tapped out several repeats on the
wireless in Russian on the Soviet frequency:

HURRY HORN WEST . . . HURRY HORN WEST . . .

At 0719, a seaplane circled over the islet, noted the
white sheet rippling from the attack periscope standard and
left. Nielson was right; of the four *Gangut* Class cruisers,
only *Sevastopol* was equipped with a seaplane catapult.
Simple arithmetic told him that the seaplane, with a maximum speed of 180 miles per hour, had come 120 miles in
the 40 minutes since he first sent the message. *Sevastopol*'s
top speed of 23 knots would get her to Hornfiskrön in
something over five hours.

Nielson visited the galley and brought up an armload of
wursts, black bread and apple juice. Then he set himself
up behind the twin 37 millimeter AAs in the forward
bridge gun turret and waited.

The old grey battle cruiser, bristling with obsolete hull
parapets housing 6-inch guns, and four deck turrets with
three 10-inchers each lay curiously at odds with the tranquil sea. The two center turrets were pointing directly at
each other, separated by the aft funnel. The forward funnel,
sprouting from the superstructure base behind the cluttered
mast, had been redesigned to rake back at an absurd angle
in order to correct certain mistakes by the British shipbuild-

ing firm of John Brown Ltd. which upon the first sea trials
in 1911 enshrouded the proud, medal-festooned commander
and his admirers on the banner bedecked observation bridge
in greasy black smoke. O the summer-white uniforms and
gold braid!

Nielson stood, hands on hips, on deck as a sparkling
power launch putted toward the beach and disgorged its
platoon of armed marines, a flanking operation. Another
launch came directly at the beached submarine and leveled
an ugly bow gun directly, as it seemed to Nielson, between his eyes.

While the marines skittered from dune to dune, moving
in on the black bow, an officer aboard the seaward launch
raised his electrified speech amplifier. In compliance with
the demands, the German Lieutenant, *sans* uniform jacket
and cap, put his hands behind his neck as the marines,
wary of a trap, climbed aboard under the covering machine
gun positions of their mates on shore.

Captain, 2nd Rank Konstantin Ossipovitch Kulov waved
his marines on into the German mystery craft. He'd heard
about such boats; the retractible diving planes were one
indication, and another was the AA armament. Remote
control turrets fore and aft of the slimmed-down bridge. If
indeed, it was the electro-boat, he would have a plum, an
entire orchard. For it was he, Konstantin, a great-nephew
of Stefan Ossipovitch Makarov, Admiral of the Imperial
Eastern Fleet and torpedo boat genius in the victory over
the Turkish Fleet at Batum. He was the first Makarov to
serve in the navy since the ill-fated *Petropavlovsk* of 1904
went down in less than two minutes, victim of a Japanese
mine. The incident served to keep the Makarov name
below other admirals of less accomplishment and bravery.
Kirov, Nakhimov, Ushakov . . . fine warriors but none a
Makarov.

Kostya studied the formidable craft though his captured
German binoculars. He hated Germans, yet admired them.
Was it jealousy that drove the entire Soviet machine to

victory. Jealousy of the west? Or was it animal spirit . . . basic hunger, that brought the Soviet forces together? A promise of a better world. For him it was neither—as far as a young man could know about his own motives. He was a sailor in the mold of his great-uncle, an innovator in weaponry . . . tired of the clumsy old-line ships and eager to put his training and interests to task.

Kostya focused on the blond German. Why had the German given up? Or was it a trap? He detested the pompous Nazis, but admired their technical ability and fanaticism, a trait necessary to war. He detested cowards most of all, no matter for whom they fought or retreated from. The German looked like a model for a Nazi poster— the type that Tanya taunted him about. Dark-haired Tanya Petulnya, and her gypsy dream of Prince Charming.

He watched the marines swarm over the long, black submarine; disappearing into the tower, popping out of deck hatches like puppets with toy guns and swimming around the boat, searching for demolition charges and booby traps. The launch radio crackled.

"Lieutenant Grechko, sir—vessel checked out. All clear and safe. Standing by, sir," the walkie-talkie hummed.

Kulov took the microphone from his Petty Officer. "Very good, Grechko, we'll come alongside." The launch motor revved up and two seamen climbed forward, one with a mooring line, the other with a machine carbine trained on Peter Nielson.

"One of the by-products of schooling abroad is the acquisition of another language, and, as an electrical engineer I found German indispensible. Kulov's short, hairy fingers explored the torpedo reload mechanisms. He motioned·to the accompanying marine guard to leave them alone.

"For me, it was the English language that was most important. My field is the same as yours."

"Quite a co-incidence, Commander, that we are both here—both in the electrical *field*, pardon the pun . . . and aboard what is known as an electro-boat. By the way, it won't be long that Russian will be indispensible as a language of science. We are on the threshold of vast technological advances. The west has had their day; tomorrow will be for the Soviet."

"And the Chinese?"

"That, Herr Nielson, will be the day *after* tomorrow." Kulov ushered Nielson into the control room. "What happened to your crew, Commander? Do I pronounce your name correctly?"

"Under international code, I am not required to tell you more than I have already."

"Come now; when have the Nazis honored such laws?"

"How do you know I'm a Nazi, Captain?"

"You certainly look like one," Kulov grinned."

"Does Goebbels look like a Nazi?"

"Touché, Herr Nielson. On second thought, your name is not *very* German. Cigarette?"

"Have one of mine."

"I will, thank you. Russia is better with vodka. What was your original mission, Commander? A boat of this type would not come this far without a crew, or a good reason—and where are your acoustic torpedoes. I was looking forward to seeing one."

"Would you like to see the accoustic torpedo computer system? It can track and fire from fifty meters down." Nielson pointed up the conning tower ladder.

"By all means, but I'm very happy that you didn't get a chance to use it against my poor old ship. *Sevastopol* is even too slow to maneuver away from a torpedo it can see. But first I should report to my superior and arrange for salvage."

"Use our radio."

"No thank you, Commander. Our procedure will not allow use or tampering with equipment. We don't want any 'accidents.' " A gleam flitted before the Russian's searching eyes. "Who else knows about this?"

"BdU was informed of our plans to scuttle."

"*Our?*"

"My captain and crew took to the rafts. I volunteered to scuttle. There were several men . . . I ordered them off when I decided on this action."

"Unusual story, Herr Nielson, but somehow I believe you. Whether the others will . . . but no matter. For whatever reason, you are making *us* a present of an advanced weapon." Kostya looked furtively around. "Will you show me all you know about this boat? It will take a day to tow it to Riga. I may be able to put in a good word for you."

"What can I lose?" Nielson climbed up to the conning station.

Kostya's brown eyes simmered under his thick brows. There was something of the Tartar about him. Even his brain salivated as he looked at the tower equipment, light-years ahead of any warship he'd ever seen or dreamed of. It could be his; it could be a way to reinstate the House of Makarov, suspect and belittled for so many years.

Chapter 4

"Commander Mulford? I'm Calvert Crowe. I believe we have a friend in common," the American officer took his reading glasses off.

"Eh?" W.E. 'Moxie' Mulford wheeled toward the somewhat tenor voice and eyed the pale, thin man suspiciously. "And what might be 'is name?"

"Commander Benjamin Mount."

"Well, put it there, Yank," Moxie squeezed Crowe's hand so hard, he winced. "Any friend 'o Ben's is a friend 'o mine—Calvert?"

"Cal."

"Did you serve with him?"

"I knew him at college, before he transferred to Annapolis. We keep in touch."

"No little fish," Moxie looked at Cal's insignia.

"I'm not a submariner, in fact I don't go on boats very much—except in drydock. I'm with the Bureau of Ships. Ben wrote me to look you up. He said you you might be going to Hamburg, so I inquired what flight you were on."

"What's 'e doing now, I expected him to call me. He wanted to take a look at the electro subs."

"He's on a special project with ComSubPac. That's how I got to come here in his place."

"He's playing with his little rockets?"

Cal whispered, "How did you find out?"

"It's no secret, the krauts did it two years ago—from below the surface. What boat is he on, lad, I'll drop him a line." Mulford rubbed condensation from the window next to him and looked down on the ruins of Hamburg.

"Chimera. He's with Jack McCrary."

"Those two. On the same boat?"

"Something wrong?" Cal was perplexed.

"No . . . nothing at all," Mulford lied; he was thinking of Betsy Kirkland. "You're not regular Navy, then?"

"How can you tell?"

"Most university people aren't. It's the same over here. What did you prepare for at college?" Moxie reached into his duffel and extracted a packet of Rattray's 3 Noggins, whose contents he shook and tamped into his well-burned pipe bowl with an index finger.

"My major was physics."

"Is that what Ben studied when you first met him?"

"We took the same undergraduate course, but I went on to graduate school in a Naval Reserve program."

"You could have been deferred—or done well in those lucrative laboratories I've heard about." Mulford chewed on his pipestem and sucked in air as the passengers were gathering their gear and snapping safety belts.

"I wanted to see the world before getting glued to a chair and coming out of a lab with a long white beard." Cal stroked his smooth chin.

"Yer a bit younger 'n Ben."

"I was 15 when I started at Columbia."

"Ye don't sound like yer from New York."

"I'm from upstate New York, a little town near Schenectady called Quaker Street.'' Cal gripped his canvas seat as the transport banked into its landing approach.

"Quaker Street,'' Mulford chuckled. "Imagine a street full of people in knickers and black hats.''

Moxie shaded his eyes as he studied the bow section of an electro-boat, shrapnel-pitted from 8th Air Force raids that preceded the British 2nd division into Hamburg. The disjointed steel nose hung limply from a high crane by a double-yoked cable. Six other sections had been already fitted together and one section, pierced with openings for six torpedo tubes lay battered in the mud and rubble. The yawning upper cylinder of the assembly was crammed with vents and conduits, waiting to be mated to the next section. A smaller cylinder, below, was closed—a compartment for some of the boat's trebled storage battery array.

Blohm and Voss' marine railways canted down to the oil-puddled Elbe River under mangled steel over-structures, each one carrying several type 21 boats in various stages of completion.

As they flew over the sprawling shipyards prior to landing, Commander Mulford had remarked that the works resembled a graveyard of whales that had been beheaded on a beach.

"Corporal,'' Lieutenant Crowe called a white-helmeted MP, "let's get a ladder over here.'' He pointed up at the inviting aperture, bristling with steel, copper and brass fittings.

"There must be almost thirty of 'em,'' Mulford tried in all his pockets, and couldn't find a match.

"The same as at Bremen and Danzig—and there were another ninety in the water waiting for crews and working up just before the scuttling.'' Crowe was already up the springy ladder.

"Gawd,'' the mustached officer searched his uniform pockets for matches. "We'd damned near 'ad it. Good thing our lads bombed the hell out of the pre-fab barges on the canals or they'd have been finished months earlier. It's amazing the buggers got as far—hello, now . . . what was that?" Mulford drew his Webley revolver and looked under the propped-up hull.

"Moxie," shouted Crowe, a hollow voice from deep within the boat, "it's incredible . . . hydraulic torpedo loaders . . . and . . ."

But the Scotsman was already poking through the cradle underpinnings, revolver cocked before him. "Aha, now I've got ye. Come on out an' keep yer hands over yer head; quick now."

A figure emerged from the shadows, crawling out and shielding its eyes from the sun. Clothes torn and dirty, it staggered to its knees, then fell forward into mud and rubble. Approaching cautiously, Moxie reached out with one hand and turned the recumbent figure on its side. It was surpringly light and small within its oversize ragged clothing. Moxie quickly holstered his gun and called out to the MP. He wiped the grimy face with his handkerchief. "Nasty wound, Corporal," Moxie carefully picked up the limp figure. "the child can't be more than five or six—call an ambulance and hurry, I'll be at the main gate."

Moxie's pipe lay forgotten under the electro-boat as he carried the shivering child up an incline, between the mute, gray, rusting machines of war.

The sandy-haired little boy blinked as he saw the plasma bottle bubbling overhead; he followed the tube down to where it disappeared into a bandage on his scrawny arm. His eyes grew saucerwide as the tan field uniforms and strange insignia came into focus. Anchors and a funny shield on a shirt collar . . . little golden crowns . . . the man with the mustache—no eagles such as he was accustomed to seeing. Eagles with square wings. Instinctively

the boy flinched. The enemy. He turned his head away—
into his clean pillow.

"Don't be afraid, sonny . . . *keine angst* . . ." Moxie
stumbled with his German. "Look what I have." He held
up an enormous Hershey bar. The boy's face brightened;
he tried to raise his bandaged head but couldn't.

"*Wo ist dein mutti?*" The clipped voice of a British
surgeon surprised the boy. He shook his head and started
to cry.

"I think that's enough for today, gentlemen. He's had a
severe shock and the trauma is wearing off. He's frightened that he's alone, with no familiar faces. Another hour
or two out there and he would have been a goner; I don't
think he's eaten for a week." The doctor adjusted the
plasma bottle and pulled a curtain taut around the bed.

"Thanks, Major—we'll stop by again tomorrow; somebody's got to miss the poor kid. C'mon Moxie," Ben
tugged at his friend's elbow. "Mulford, what's wrong?"

"It's just that the child—regardless of his age—it's just
that he sort of reminds me o' my brother . . . may he rest
in peace in that forsaken Scapa Flow."

A week went by, the peace in Europe was already a
month old and found the conquerors picking through the
ruins. Lieutenant Crowe flew to Blankenburg, where deep
inside the Harz Mountains' bomb-proof catacombs he inspected a full-scale wooden model of the first operational
ocean-going closed circuit Walter design—an XXVI model,
the first true submarine, a craft more at home under the
surface than on it. Mulford, taking to the water with a
Royal Navy corvette found, under camouflage nets at the
island of Neuwerk, of Cuxhaven, an intact small Walter
turbine boat, U-1407. Together they seized and shipped
off several experimental hydrogen-peroxide and ingolin-
fueled experimental power plants from Kiel test stations to
England and the States.

In between forays Mulford stopped in at the hospital to see his little friend, who remembered that his name was Rudi. He also showed five fingers as the number of candles on his last birthday cake and had no idea of his last name.

"Wer ist sie?" Rudi pointed to the blonde.

"Rudi, this is . . . er, sie . . . ist Fräulein Ursula."

"*Rudischen, Ich bin Moxie's freunden . . .*" Ursula continued in German as Mulford nodded approvingly. ". . . and we're going to be good friends too, aren't we?" She leaned over and brushed his hair away from his eyes.

"Does Mister Moxie bring you candy too?"

"Darling," she turned to Mulford, you've been two-timing me." Rudi was busily unwrapping a present.

"I'd like you to take care of him for a few weeks, Uschi. The doctor agrees he should get out of here. As soon as I can get the necessary papers, I'll put him up with my parents. My transfer to Rosyth should come through soon. Here, take this," he handed her a commissary card. Buy anything you need; it'll go on my charge."

"Anything?" She batted her green lashes at him.

"Anything," but don't get carried away."

"I understand, darling."

Chapter 5

Stoyonov swung out the hinged map of North America. It was decorated with pink disks. Alaska had two; one near Point Barrow, and another at Dillingham, just west of the Aleutian connection. The panhandle was under jurisdiction of disks in Canada's Yukon and Columbian Provinces in case of a geographical emergency. The rest of the Provinces had one each, except for Quebec with two.

Mexico was represented at Chihuahua, Guadalajara and on the Yucatan Peninsula, while the Central American Republics had one each. Cuba and the Caribbean entities also sported one apiece.

Of the States, only three had more than one. Tennessee, Washington and New Mexico had added additional locations, all within a short drive to seemingly unimportant cities: Pasco, on the Columbia River, Oak Ridge and Los Alamos.

The Assistant Director of KGB, North American Sector, took a small file card out of a drawer and laid it, face up on his metal desk. He opened another cabinet and fingered through the index tabs. Drawing out a wallet-sized snapshot, he placed it on the file card, face down. Sizing up his guest, a fair-complexioned, somewhat dishevelled young man of military age, he picked two more photographs from his file and snapped them down upon the other. Then the stout, dark-suited Russian sat down under a sepia-toned photographic portrait of Stalin. Stoyonov was proud of his part in the real estate system. Started in the early thirties, he inherited it with his promotion from field service with Tass in Helsinki, a congenital asthmatic condition having kept him from the military. One of his favorite pastimes reclined on a wall shelf; a Russian version of the American table game of 'Monopoly'. His superiors allowed him that joke, though his employees were afraid to accept his challenge to a game. Not so with Reino Hayhanen, who, unlike the stereotype agent, did not hide his thirst for vodka and women. Stoyonov pushed the file card closer to the Finn.

''Unfortunately you'll have to get accustomed to an outside privy, but it does have running water and a heated garage.'' Reino cocked his head at the photograph of a white clapboard 2-story frame house with a mountain behind it.

Stoyonov spun his chair and pointer in hand, tapped at a feature on the left side of his map. ''This is Idaho,'' he traced the state's border. ''It's famous for potatoes. But for us, it's now important because a development facility will be built for the construction and testing of atomic-powered engines. We will arrange for our real-estate agent to terminate the current rental because the owner had decided to return permanently. In two or three years you'll be an Idahoan. Your factory training in Turku will get you a job in the construction of the planned facility near the town of Arco. When the time comes you will receive further orders.''

Reino concealed his excitement; he knew better than to

interrupt an Assistant Director of Lavrenti Beria's domain. Such an assignment promised fistfulls of currency and a freedom from red thumbs and party tape.

"One more thing before you ask questions, Mister *Arni Järvi*. We have come to the decision that you should be married. It will look right to bring a bride home from Finland . . . so we have a few possibilities that we've checked out . . ." Stoyanov turned the snapshots over like a draw-poker dealer. "Pick one of these beauties—their statistics are on the backs. Oh yes, I almost forgot; there will be additional funds for the lady. Given to you, of course." The director smiled behind his hands, fingertips touching and fanned out. "Any questions?"

Reino turned two photographs face down and slid the other one onto the director's desk. It landed on a newspaper, over the front-page picture of a burgeoning mushroom cloud.

After the Finn had left, Stoyonov took off his suit jacket and lit a Havana cigar. Moscow could get very hot in August. He picked up the file card. The property, six acres, was 'acquired' by his predecessor in 1933. A numerical code indicated the following:

Acquired from: Family of 3. Järvi; Ahti, 34; Oulu Finland; Karen, 31; NY USA; Arni, 10; Twin Falls, Idaho, USA. Location: Blaine County, 12 miles west of Martin's Ranch, Route 22. Contact agent Alexei.

Stoyonov put the card back and locked the cabinet. Alexei was the 'real-estate' agent for the northwest states and based in Walla-Walla, Washington. His real name was Al Benedict. He owned a billiards hall and a gas station as well as running a real estate office. One of the benefits of being an agent for KBG was access to inside information. Big Al, an eccentric, was so impressed by the Soviets he met on a 'business trip' in 1932 that he converted most of his assets to gold and buried it all illegally as the country went off the gold standard.

The agent with deep-set eyes under bushy brows, blew a smoke ring toward the ceiling lighting fixture, a bare bulb hung by its wire. Only once in his two years in this room had he managed to 'lasso it upside-down.'

He blew another ring toward the hinged map, and another over the newspaper wirephoto from Hiroshima. Seventy-four pink disks glowed in the afternoon sunlight pouring in over the Kremlin's west wall. Seventy-four families—perhaps three hundred people at the most. Liquidated after coming from North America. Picked for the location of their property and simplicity of their existence. All with relatives in Scandinavia, the Baltic States or the Eastern bloc; all tricked by ruse to return; a parent's death in Estonia . . . an inheritance in Poland . . . a business proposition in Finland. Too bad the children had to die, but the party had to plan for the fifties and sixties. And Stoyanov was only 'involved' for two years. He was responsible for only a few 'liquidations.' The 'Monopoly' board was already saturated when he took over. Three hundred! Nothing compared with one bomb over Hiroshima.

He opened a dossier and flipped through its contents. 'Hayhanan, Reino.' Skimming a few paragraphs, he read a capsule history:

Born suburb of Leningrad, 1921. 2 Brothers, 1 Sister. Father a farmer and fireman, village of Pushkin; Mother a cook. Grad Finnish Dept. Ped. Institute, Leningrad 1940, Magna cum laude. Drafted NKVD for interrogation school, Finnish war. Recruiting agent

1942-44. Known as Arni Järvi, Turku Finland, 1943 to present. Trades or occupation: Welder, photographer. Family deceased; Unmarried.

The director turned the lead out a bit in his mechanical pencil and crossed of the last entry of Hayhanan's history.

Chapter 6

Cal Crowe folded his orders and looked out over the twin port Pratt & Whitneys as the R2Y-1 transport version of the Liberator banked over Land's End and headed across the Atlantic.

The south coast of England with its limestone cliffs picked up the western sun. On the other side of the channel sprawled Brittany, deceptively tranquil, and beyond, Utah and Omaha beaches. To the south, the broad expanse of Biscay Bay—'death sea' to the German submariners—stretched into the summer haze. The naval officer was grateful, or was it luck that had spared him a watery grave like the many others he'd known during his two and a half years in the Navy.

Two weeks' leave in Scotland at Moxie's cottage had charged his batteries and he'd been rarin' to go back to Kiel and pitch in with 'Operation Paper Clip' which was inducing German missile and submarine scientists to work for the States. He was sure the Soviets had gotten a head start on electro-boat weapons systems by capturing the

Vulcanwerft plant in Stettin, builders of the highly secret submarine-launched V-2 prototype containers. There just had to be plans, and engineers to be found. But then the transfer orders arrived and reminded him there was still another war in the Pacific. But why the Canal Zone?

Four motors whined as the converted B-24 gained altitude and changed the pitch of its props. Cal looked around him; forward, a Brigadier General and his aide were kibitzing with the air crew. Next to him, a British Naval Commander jerked spasmodically in response to his dreaming. Aft, a group of hot-shot pilot types were trying to make out with five Navy nurses, giggling occasionally rising above the motors' roar.

He'd gotten some information about the flight. First stop, the Azores, and then Bermuda where he was to lay over a day and catch another plane to Panama. He wondered whether the nurses were also going to the Canal Zone. There was one, a blonde, who intrigued him, their eyes having met when he turned. He hoped she hadn't noticed his concern over her shapely knee; skirts were a novelty. Lapsing into fantasy, looking down into the big, soft summery clouds, he imagined the nurse lying on a bed of satin pillows in a Rita Hayworth negligee, beckoning to him.

Five hours later the drafty Liberator landed at Santa Maria Airport, a massive military base just completed by American engineers. Cal was a little slow getting off. Something beautiful had happened to him; he was in love. During those five hours he had courted her and won her. He couldn't make up his mind whether she resembled June Allyson or Lizbeth Scott more. He decided on the latter because he liked sexy voices and hoped the parallel would continue.

Later, in the mess hall, he was outpointed by the Air Force pilots in his few attempts at staking a claim with the girls. It was nothing new to Cal; always the loser in such affairs. Aggressive he was not, but he vowed to prevail at the next stop.

The verdant fish-hook shaped island cluster elicited oohs and ahs from the girls. Visions of post-war honeymoons and breakfasts in bed danced in their heads. Bermuda. White cruise ships, deck chairs and servants. For Cal, it was an uppity Wasp bastion in spite of the tourist trade, and regardless of how many travel posters extolled and cajoled, the only way he would come was by military orders. The plane banked low over the myriad coral heads and shallow turquoise lagoons as it made its approach to the U.S. Naval Air Station's main runway on St. David's Island. A whole new peninsula of white sand had been added to the fish-hook by American bulldozers, projecting indecently into Castle Harbour.

Cal was elated when the Liberator, after refueling, took off with the swaggering pilots. Expecting more competition from new quarters, he was surprised at the vacant barracks, administration quonsets and transient's facilities until a clerk told him that just about everyone was attending a cricket match with an adjoining gambling casino at Bradley's Bay on the next island. The base's cadre and complement, it being Saturday, was not expected back very early. It was a glorious afternoon, one of the 340 sun-spangled days advertised and all but guaranteed out of the year.

Cal stripped to his shorts and stretched out on a bunk in his 'BOQ' quonset. Batchelor Officer's Quarters—was he destined forever to sleep alone? Twenty-five years old in February, he'd gotten a scholarship to Columbia at the tender age of 15. His father, a thrifty Quaker farmer, refused to finance his graduate work, so Cal joined the Naval Reserve in exchange for finishing his education. Farmer Crowe, a conscientious objector to war, disinherited his son, but went to work in a war plant himself after Pearl Harbor because it paid double for overtime.

Cal had read the exciting papers of Iréne Curie, Joliot, and the Germans, Otto Hahn and Lise Meitner on the irradiation of Thorium, and wanted to enter the exciting new field that revolved around the neutron, a theoretical sub-atomic particle.

Discovered by a team of German physicists who bombarded Beryllium, a light metal, with alpha particles, it was found that the resulting radiation could penetrate 2 centimeters of lead. This added to the confirmation, in 1930, of Britain's Rutherford that the mass of uranium was greater than the sum of its constituent parts, and indicated strong 'locked up' energy within the nucleus.

Both Ben and Cal, fired up with excitement, enrolled in émigré Enrico Fermi's class at Columbia. After a year, Ben received his appointment to the Academy and Cal went on to become one of the most outstanding students of the renowned Italian physicist.

Cal recalled the evening he first met the scientist's wife, at an Italian restaurant on upper Broadway. It was just before Ben left for Annapolis.

Signora Fermi was the reason that her husband had left the employ of Il Duce. Had he not, America would have lagged even further behind Germany and France in nuclear theory before the war. She was the reason that he was not then working in Germany. Enrico and his assistants, including one Calvert Crowe, went out to Chicago in December of 1942—and surpassed Germany, under the dank bleachers of the University football stadium by creating the world's first nuclear chain reaction.

All this because Signora Fermi wasn't wanted in Italy.

Signora Fermi was a Jew!

A chattering of female voices woke him from his reverie. The nurses—they were quartered in the next quonset! Cal listened to the schoolgirl sounds and realized how much he'd missed. All study and no play; it was true, Cal was a dull boy, cramming in high school . . . holidays, summers. Fulfilling the super-Christian ethic of his father and the Quakers. Hypocrites!

The better his grades, the more he withdrew . . . from girls, his childhood friends, from everyone. But especially from girls. He built an invisible wall around himself; never went to the football games—not even to the prom.

But it did get him a full scholarship, at least for tuition. Cal earned his room and board by working nights for the Physics Department. Why not a young scientist to wash the retorts and flasks, to clean the bunsens and care for the microscopes and specimen slides.

He became friends with only one person at Columbia; another 'loner', Benjamin Mount.

Now and then, a word reverberated though the corrugated iron, half-cylindrical pre-fabs . . . words that men never said: 'Keen . . . divine . . . scrumptious . . .' Then the strains of a scratchy record. Andrews Sisters . . . *'drinkin' rum and—Coca-cola, both mother—and daught—er, workin' fo'—the Yonkee dol—laaar . . .'*

Lush fragrances curled through the open windows, perfumes from the Cherokee and Multiflora roses, from Calendula, Nasturtium, honeysuckle and the Passion Flower invaded Cal's sanctuary and intruded on the dog-eared copy of *Life* he was trying to read. He immersed himself once again, trying to concentrate on a feature article entitled: 'Your Post-war Dream House.'

A sexy voice mingled with the caption he was reading.

"Okay, let's go for a swim."

". . . the most divine beach—just across the causeway . . . turn right and take the trail . . . very secluded and lots of caves . . ."

"I'll get some cold cuts and soda . . ."
"Goody," someone squealed.

Cal was glad the other two bunks in his room were
empty. Air Force uniforms were draped haphazardly over
them. It wouldn't be that way with the Navy. He was
thankful for the cricket match; it was good to be alone for
a change.

Swimming! The girls were going to the beach. Now was
his chance to meet Lizbeth Scott. No competition from the
fly-boys. Cal dropped the magazine to the floor. Its cover
showed a smoking kamikaze diving at an American warship.
He got up and rummaged through his B-4 bag. Where had
he stashed his old trunks? Finally, for a time, the war was
far away. No bombs, no reports, no admirals to duck. Cal
inhaled deeply of the Passion Flower as he slipped into his
bathing trunks and envisioned the blond nurse cavorting in
the romantic tropical sea. He didn't realize how ready he
was until buttoning his khakis.

The waves sparkled white as they rolled over the coral
reefs that ringed the shallow, turquoise lagoon, gravepool
of Spanish treasure galleons, private yachts and blockade
runners. Cal's pale body glistened with sun-tan oil as he
set his watch bezel to remind him that 15 minutes would
be enough. Behind large sunglasses he looked like a giant
crew-cut insect. Lying hidden between gnarled old cedars,
he peeked over a stand of flowering Yucca at the pinkish
sand beach below. He had gotten there first.

Cal ducked his crew-cut head, chin into sand as the
column of bicycles passed on the trail above. Unseen, he
watched the five girls, all in suntan trousered uniforms file
down the footpath balancing jugs and picnic baskets, giggling and chirping. His breathing stopped momentarily
when they set their things down in a clearing between a

mangrove and a coral ledge not ten yards from his own lair. Three dark-haired, one redhead and his heart-throbbing Lizbeth! Carefully, they laid out light blue blankets and weighted the corners with stones. Suddenly the redhead stripped off her shirt and wiggled out of her pants. Cal blinked and closed his eyes. When he opened them she was standing nude and smoking a cigarette. One by one, the rest did likewise. Cal's heart stopped as the blonde stepped out of her panties and unhooked her bra. He had never, ever seen one nude woman, let alone five at once without himself being seen. He felt feverish as he watched them, bending over and neatly folding their clothes. After a drought, a downpour. He trembled and dug his fingers into the sand, pulsing hot and cold inside. One of them, the biggest and most endowed, shrieked and bolted toward the beach. She was tanned, and seemingly wore a white two-piece bathing suit—but only from the side and back. The others quickly followed; 'Lizbeth' was last. Cal felt both guilty and elated, daring not to move lest he be discovered and run off the base as a peeping Tom. Nobody would believe that he hadn't planned this. He had—but not this way. Girls always wore bathing suits—in Quaker Street.

The five cavorted in the surf for eternal minutes, then emerged and ran dripping toward him, before picking up towels and vigorously drying themselves. Five! Each one different, in size, color and movement. His thighs trembled so much he thought he'd surely go mad and scream out. The scene was unreal, resembling a burlesque show he'd seen in a movie in Schenectady. They sprawled out to sun on the blankets, the redhead giving him such a feet first view that he wanted to stand up and beat his scrawny chest like Tarzan before leaping on top of her.

The red-head, squinting at the sun was first on her feet. She snapped her brassiere on backwards and did an about face inside of it that baffled the perspiring pop-eyed officer. Next, the blonde, his erstwhile promised, walked swayingly toward his hiding place. She came so close that, from his prone position under the cedar branches, all he could see of her was above her knees and below her waist. He could have reached out and—. The luscious alabaster torso squirmed up toward something on the cedar. A flowering vine shook and the branches above Cal rustled. For a very long minute, her charms were displayed in bright sunlight . . . curled, blond and glistening, with a precise detail never shown in paintings, nor formed on a sculptured nude.

Fireworks went off inside Cal Crowe.

His glazed eyes followed her as she walked away, holding a giant, pink hibiscus to her nose. Cal waited till the girls had cycled off, then buried his trunks in the sand and went in for a quick dip. After putting on his suntans, he saluted the stone over his spent trunks and retrieved his bicycle. Good riddance to those. Despite the saggy crotch support of his suit, he'd resisted buying a new one for years. He felt new freedom; now he'd have to spend the money. For Cal, a downturn always became an upturn.

He cycled fast up the road they had taken. Now he had a bond with all of them, especially with Lizbeth. Hot and cold qualms passed over him. He felt like a rapist, or was it deeper than that; he felt part of her. Such carnal knowledge was only for a husband—or was it? It was ordained. It was Kharma. Muddled with guilt, shame and ecstasy, he almost lost control and narrowly missed driving over a cliff into the rocky waters. He braked to a stop passing a stone building. Five bicycles were propped against a tree near the entrance. Leaving his bike against the building, he noticed that it was an extension of a hill, only the entrance and foyer being of standard pattern. Inside, a small sign proclaimed 'CRYSTAL CAVES.'

Cal made sure all his buttons were buttoned, rubbed his shoes on the backs of his pants and polished his tarnished silver bars and set his overseas cap rakishly before descending the limstone steps down to the caves.

*   *   *

"Imagine that—a bird that couldn't fly."

The Navy nurse was startled by the voice behind her. Stepping aside, she looked quizzically at the intruder. Seeing his rank before seeing his smile, she automatically started to salute. He stopped her with a gentle hand on her wrist. "Not necessary indoors."

"I've heard of birds that don't fly. The dodo . . ." she examined the fossil on the cave wall. And how about the ostrich, although they don't look enough like birds to begin with. This one looks like a duck, or at least his bones do."

Cal leaned over and read a caption while thrilling to the scent of perfume—of his beloved. '*Hesperornis*, a flightless diving bird from the Cretaceous.'

"From the what?"

He recoiled at her accent but recovered. "It's a Latin word that means chalky. These caves are limestone, which is a kind of chalk. The bird got caught in a mudslide millions of years ago, and the mud dried into limestone."

"You don't say—gee, you must be a teacher or somethin'. Say, is somethin' wrong?" She looked at her arms and uniform under the spotlight.

"No, it's probably that you reminded me of someone."

"Not your mother, I hope."

Cal shrugged no. "My name is Cal Crowe."

"Hi, Cal; I'm Cynara Sokol," she held out her hand.

Taking it while he cringed inside from her inflection—quite the opposite of Lizbeth Scott, he motioned her to precede him along the viewing ramp. "Nice meeting you Cyna-ra. Where are you from?"

"Brooklyn, and you can call me Sona."

"How extraordinary, I'm from Brooklyn, too."

"Ya don't sound like it." Sona's sparkling green eyes searched the cavern ceiling. "Jeez," she exclaimed at the

hundreds of stone cones hanging down and reflecting irides-
cent blues, purples and greens.

"They're called *stalactites.*"

"I can't remember names like that—hey, I'd better get
going . . . my friends, they're over by the pool."

Refusing to acknowledge Sona's friends, Cal gazed upward reverently. "All this grandeur reminds me of Radio
City Music Hall."

"Reminds me more of the Paramount."

"I've never been there."

"Do you like Sinatra?"

"Is he a singer?"

"Is he a *singer?*" Sona let it go.

"I like classical music," Cal pantomimed a violinist.
You're not married, are you?"

Cal shook no. "Maybe we can go for dinner somewhere.
The Castle Hotel maybe; they've got dancing . . . under the
stars." Cal hoped she didn't like dancing.

"I'll be right back," Sona sprinted lightly on the wooden
walkway.

They lay on the blanket that Sona had brought. It was
nice to be with a girl, thought Cal, who planned in
advance. It was Sona who, after finding a delightful native
sea-food restaurant on St. George, away from the stiff
hotel scene, insisted on a blanket for a beach walk. There
was always a point when one wanted to relax and enjoy
the tropical night. The full moon seemed to get bigger and
bigger and the night sounds got louder. Invisible frogs and
lizards added their croaks and wails to the night concert of
winged virtuosos, even the labyrinthine mangrove roots
emitting primeval chirking choruses. Sona pressed her Lucky
Strike into the dark, damp sand and put her head on Cal's
shoulder.

"It's been a marvelous evening," Cal pecked her on the
cheek.

"And it's not over, yet."

"Really?" Cal stumbled over the word.

"We're still going to walk out to the point; I just love to walk in the moonlight." Sona fluffed up her short bob and rolled over on her stomach.

Cal couldn't help but notice the moonlit shape near his hand. "Sona."

"What?"

"Do you have a boy friend?"

"Nope."

"What about all those doctors," I'll bet they must chase the nurses around."

"They're mostly all married."

"Oh," he moved closer to her. "Cynara is an unusual name."

"I know, especially with Sokol. My mother's Irish and my father is a jewelry salesman."

"Sona, I'm glad you agreed to have dinner."

"And you were surprised I didn't take you up on the fancy hotel and the dancing?"

"My dancing is pretty rusty. I was relieved you didn't."

"I don't like gold diggers," Sona stretched out on her back and wiggled her body deliciously. "Besides, I like small, intimate restaurants."

"The fish was great. What was it again?"

"Red Snapper; I seen it at the Fulton Fish market once."

"You must meet a lot of men."

"That's the truth."

"It must be—well, a pretty girl's got to watch out with so many guys around. Take me, I might have been Jack the Ripper."

"You didn't qualify, I've met enough of those types."

"Maybe I'm a Jekyll and Hyde type," Cal rolled over and slipped his hand over her thigh.

"Okay, Mister Hyde, that's far enough." Sona slid out from under and got up, smoothing her skirt down.

"You've read the book?"

"It was a movie, with Spencer Tracy."

"Oh," Cal shook out the blanket and folded it.

"Stick it under that crazy tree," Sona pointed at a mangrove. We'll pick it up on the way back.

Cal almost said "yes, dear."

They walked east from the air base toward Nonsuch Island, and then north to St. David's lighthouse and rested on a rock overlooking the narrows where Admiral Somers' boat, wrecked in a storm that Shakespeare immortalized in 'The Tempest' was stranded on the shoals and landed the first colonists in 1609.

As Lieutenant Commander Crowe mused about history, Sona climbed an embankment and reached up for one of the many dazzling star-shaped flowers that crowned a coral ledge. Each blossom, blinding white in the moonlight was the size of a sunflower. They looked like illuminated medieval drawings; long petal-rays and globular centers. Sona slid down the bank and handed her flower to Cal.

"If there's a sunflower for daytime," Cal ventured, "Why not a moonflower for night?"

"Mrs. Moonflower," Sona addressed the parent vine, "I only took one and I'll treasure it forever." She caressed it and the fragrance enhanced the walk back. At the base, they exchanged forwarding addresses. Sona's destination was San Francisco.

The next morning, a Bermudan native girl, originally part Mohican from a slave influx during the seventeenth century, noticed Sona's 'moonflower' in a vase while changing the linen.

"Miss Sona, this flower is very rare; it blooms only one night of every year and brings good fortune to its beholder—"

Sona skipped happily to the window and waved to an airplane that was just taking off. They had agreed to do it that way. The Bermudan girl chanted softly while rubbing a black shark's tooth hidden in her hands. The night-blooming *'Cereus'*, to her recollection had never been plucked, but only observed by the fortunate. Perhaps the shark spirit would intercede and forgive.

Chapter 7

"Captain," Cal clutched the cockpit bulkhead as the A-20 'Havoc' attack bomber hit an updraft. "I'm not much in sky navigation, but shouldn't we be heading more south?"

"Why, sir?" The Air Force captain asked his co-pilot to take over and swung himself around.

"Isn't the Canal Zone that way?" Cal pointed left.

"Who said we're going to Panama?"

"My orders—" Cal fumbled in his jacket pocket.

"When were they cut?"

"July 9th," the Naval officer handed a mimeographed sheet forward. "Pentagon . . . Admiral Downey."

"Never heard of him," Captain Benson exchanged orders. "Mine were cut on the 14th—and check the signature."

"I'll be goddamned, the big man himself."

"Can't top that—if he says we go to Frisco, we go to Frisco," Benson offered Cal a cherry lifesaver.

"I'll wait for a lime, thanks. I don't understand why I didn't get a change of orders."

"Even CINCPAC fucks up now and then."

100

"Ain't that the truth." Lieutenant Wiseman quipped as he pulled back on his wheel. "You know, the last time we ferried a guy to a place he didn't expect—London it was—the invasion took place the next day."

"Made sense," Benson added. "The VIP was a demolitions expert. Maybe your orders are some kind of cover."

Wiseman turned around. "Seein' as you're with BuShips, it could be that we're getting ready to send out a lotta men, sir."

"Something's got to happen; that's for sure." Benson unwrapped the *Lifesavers*, exposing a lime ring for Cal.

"Thanks . . . Say, what's the flight plan?"

"We fuel up at McConnell in Wichita and go over the great divide. This is the hottest A-20 in the air; we'll have a beer at McConnell in less than six hours. There's only one attack bomber that's faster."

"The *Mosquito?*"

"Hey, pretty good for a swabbie. But you can have plywood. I wouldn't want to get shot up in one." Benson took the wheel again.

The sleek, stripped two-motored plane lifted off from the Wichita Air Force base at 0310, and flew low, following the glittering night necklace of prairie towns. Pratt, Dodge City, Lamar. Cal, in twilight sleep, nodded, occasionally waking up and looking down, dreaming of cattle-drives and covered wagons huddled around campfires . . . of the blazing saloons . . . Bat Masterson . . . the Cole brothers.

"Hang on, sir. We're goin' up—and better put on your oxygen mask," Lieutenant Wiseman, face eerie in the green instrument glow, pointed at a yellow bag over Cal's head.

"The Rockies? Already?" Cal yawned.

"We'd have done it faster without a head wind."

Cal checked his radium-dial wrist watch. Less than two

hours since Wichita—a distance that took covered wagons weeks! It was 0528. Ahead loomed the dangerous darkness of the jagged Rockies, faintly discernable only from lack of stars, a distant snowy peak catching the first blush of dawn. To the north lay the sleeping plateau of Colorado and sky glow of Denver; and to port, the dark desert of New Mexico.

"Holy mackerel," Wiseman screamed into the intercom, jolting Benson out of his seat.

Cal saw it too—far to the south. A white flash, turning green, then orange and purple.

"Must have been a meteor." Benson blinked awake.

"But I woulda seen a streak," Wiseman shot back. "You know, like you see on shootin' stars when one hits the atmosphere."

"Could be you just caught the flash, or maybe the streak was hidden by a mountain," Benson replied sleepily.

"Could be, *mein kapitän.* I'll try to raise the six o'clock newscast from Salt Lake City."

"What's doing in town?" The olive-drab plane whined past Mount Diablo and descended to its approach altitude. The broad expanse of Pacific Ocean shimmered beyond the intricate coastline of central California.

"Not much on Alameda, sir, but I'd certainly take time off for the Latin Quarter," Captain Benson, in rank, equivalent to U.S. Naval Lieutenant observed protocol. "Make sure you bring some rubbers with you, though. It's like Tijuana."

"Gotcha," Cal squinted for a glimpse of the fabled city.

"There's a dive called Gomez's Café. The old man kicked the bucket last year, but one of his broads is doin' Okay runnin' it since . . ."

"I'll remember that, Lieutenant," Cal grinned. It was nice to come into a strange city and have a girl like Cynara to look up. A few days kicking around, and he'd look her up at the Naval Hospital to which she'd been assigned.

Cal felt a tinge of pride as the converted bomber circled gracefully over the Golden Gate Bridge. Just like a color travel postcard . . . the orange engineering masterpiece of the west coast, silhouetted against the Pacific. It was his first view of the ocean that bordered the mystical and legendary empires of his schoolbooks. He strained for a sign of Alameda and thought he saw an aircraft carrier tied up at a dock. Benson, waiting for landing clearance, dipped his wings and made another approach from seaward, zooming low over the longest single bridge span ever built.

Below, a white wake boiled seaward from under the bridge. "Looks like a cruiser, at least, and boy, are they in a fuckin' hurry. Go get 'em, swabbies," shouted Wiseman.

Leaving the bridge glowing vermillion behind them, Benson lowered the flaps and bounced onto the Naval base landing strip. It was about 0830, and visions of bacon, eggs and home fries . . . ice-cold orange juice and real coffee had replaced, erased the idea of war.

Sweating in his starched suntans, Cal emerged from COMSUBPAC's headquarters building. Expecting a few day's leave, he'd instead received orders to ship out at 0600 the following morning. He was to be ready at 0530 and respond to a knock on his BOQ quarters door only if he heard the codeword 'centerboard'. During the interim he was restricted to the base and 'advised' to remain inconspicuous as much as he could. All personal phone calls and communication was disallowed, though he might write letters that would be posted 'at a later time'. Cal availed himself of the hours between messes by writing letters to his mother in the town of Quaker Street, near Schenectady, New York, and to Lt. Cynara Sokol, care of the base hospital.

Scouring the Bay area's newspapers that evening, Cal found a small notice in the *Examiner:*

EL PASO, July 16 (AP)—Just before dawn this morning, a brilliant flash was observed north of this city, in the direction of Alamagordo, New Mexico. Approximately seven minutes later a shock wave rattled windows here.

A news release from the Corps of Engineers in Albuquerque at noon stated that "an Army ammunition magazine had exploded in an uninhabited part of the desert of southern New Mexico," and that there had been no casualties.

Reports of sighting this flash have also come from Pecos and Alamagordo.

Cal left word with the base orderly room to call him at 0500, just in case his travel alarm didn't work.

"CENTERBOARD," he gave the password.

Lieutenant Commander Calvert F. Crowe was ready, even to the proverbial fifth 'S' which commenced with 'shower' and ended with 'shampoo.' His crisp, fresh uniform felt good as he got into a command car. Bag stowed in the trunk, he was suddenly aware that he was flanked by armed MPs, 45s held between their knees. Another Naval officer of his rank sat next to the driver. An army truck revved up behind them. The two-vehicle column rumbled through the Naval complex and pulled out onto a dock, then sped around an escort aircraft carrier and stopped in its shadow—hidden from the stream of workers automobiles traversing the Bay Bridge to Oakland's round-the-clock war plants. The vehicles pulled up parallel to a conning tower, hardly more than the periscope shears projecting over the dock's edge.

Cal, a glutton for aircraft and ship recognition, could

not place the class of this submarine. It was definitely a fleet design, yet curiously smaller, as if it was a lesser relative of the *Sargo* or *Tambor* Class. Its diesels were grumbling and a deck crew was securing lift tackle to the aft deck boom.

The 'six-by' army truck set its emergency brake with a creak and four MPs with automatic rifles hopped off, taking positions between the truck and the submarine's gangplank. Two husky sailors jumped up on the truck and lowered a metallic can gently off the tailgate to more waiting, tattooed arms. The sailors inserted a steel rod through the can's handle and carried it to and down the steep gangplank, where it was shackled to a boom and winched down through the aft torpedo hatch. A second piece of cargo, less fragile and in a watertight box about 10 feet long was lowered by the forward tackle and set into the deck torpedo compartment under a section of wood slats. The operation took less than ten minutes.

Cables were loosed and the sub backed out, swinging its bow toward Treasure Island. Rounding the Embarcadero under 'Old Town' Cal, on the bridge could make out the cylindrical arch-pierced stone tower that marked the top of Telegraph Hill. Customarily, the boat's captain and his bridge officers took a look at the Golden Gate before relinquishing the view to the assigned watch. Most of the crew came topside to pay last respects to the states—a kind of superstitious observance. An offering to the Gods of survival before committing themselves to the dangers and awesome enormity of a sea at war. For half the submariners who would never return this was the picture last remembered below the waves.

Coffee steamed and bubbled in the stainless steel snack pantry forward of the wardroom. The delicious aroma wafted through 'officer's country' which consisted of a section between the control room and forward torpedo room.

"This boat is one of three *M-Class* boats, built in 1940 under Captain Tom Hart's program for quick-diving boats—more in the range of Germany's U-boats. Our regular fleet boats are larger and have more creature comforts, but they take a full sixty seconds to dive." Captain Warneke spread out the refit blueprints on the wardroom table before Cal and the other passenger, Lieutenant Commander Jim Paulsen. "The German boats can dive in forty seconds or less, so you can see what the thinking was here. The M-Class packs the same wallop as most of our big boats, but is more maneuverable and less detectable. But we never got into an Atlantic war with them so development was stopped. The big ones have plenty of room in the Pacific and they don't have to contend with the more sophisticated detection systems—which the Japs don't have.

"There were two boats—in sequence, 204 and 205. *Mackerel* and *Marlin*. There was a third boat—this one, that was never listed, and as far as the enemy is concerned just does not exist. We set up *Mackerel* with a phony mission where she fired torpedoes at the ghost of a civil war sub off Hatteras—if it wasn't a U-boat, and then we assigned the boats to a training fleet. This one, the *No-name* was stripped of all but three tubes last year and fitted with extra batteries like the German electro-boats to be used for fast and secret assignments. An enemy agent, spotting us, would assume that we were one of the discontinued M-Class, and therefore unimportant game. Our complement is only thirty-nine, making security easier than on a *Tambor* or *Gato*. The crew is hand-picked and doubly checked out. Since we have to maintain communications with CINCPAC for supplies and orders, we do have a code name system that changes on the last day of every month. You are now aboard SS *Marimba*. I don't know what those gadgets are that we're carrying but anything put on this boat had got to be top priority, and we'll do our damndest to get it where—"

"Whoops," Cal bolted his coffee. "It's time." He threaded his way back to the aft torpedo room bulkhead hatch which was guarded by an armed marine. After showing his ID, Cal ducked into the well-lighted compartment. There, beyond a screening curtain, an officer in suntans sat on a bottom bunk. Next to him lay a Colt 45 automatic and a stack of books. Before him, strapped to deck-welded eye-bolts and padlocked, stood a mysterious metal container; polished, brushed stainless steel, two feet high and eighteen inches in diameter. It looked like a streamlined milk can.

"Lieutenant Commander Crowe, reporting for his next class, sir," Cal joshed with Ken Paulsen, his equal in rank who had accompanied him in the command car. Paulsen handed a book to Cal, who sat on the opposite bunk. "Read the first chapter and then we'll go over it together."

Cal turned the innocuous cover open. There was one word:

CENTERBOARD

The term had nothing to do with sailboats.

It meant ATOMIC BOMB STRIKE!

The directions for arming "Fat Man", the plutonium bomb, had been compiled and typed out at MISPLAY.

Which was the codeword for Los Alamos.

After the lesson, Cal set to memorizing the arming procedure while completing the balance of his four hour watch.

Alone, with a lead-lined pot, containing the first pure Plutonium ever made . . . enough for one atomic bomb.

Already twenty-four hours out to sea, the heavy cruiser, *Indianapolis* was steaming east, southeast at high speed. In a guarded, locked cabin, Captain James Nolan, U.S. Army Manhattan Project specialist, sat his third four-hour watch over another, similar steel container. Inside its lead-shielded lining reposed the result of two billion dollars' worth of preparation and the efforts of thousands of scientists and technicians: ninety pounds of Uranium-235.

The brains of MISPLAY weren't taking any chances.

The first team was traveling on the surface with "Little Boy's" markings.

The second team was on a submarine that didn't exist, with Plutonium for "Fat Man." The Plutonium bomb had been tested only one day earlier in the desert.

"Little Boy" was a sure-shot and didn't need testing.

One of them would make it to Tinian. MISPLAY had seen to that; in fact there was even speculation at MIS-PLAY that they, also had a back-up team.

Marimba was lucky. It had to submerge only twice, detecting one aircraft and one boat between San Francisco and Hawaii. After refueling from a Navy tanker off Pearl Harbor, it continued at eighteen knots at a rhumb line toward the Marianas. On July 29th, *Marimba* went under. A scrambler message from Tinian warned of a Japanese anti-sub patrol out of Hiroshima. They were last reported headed for an intercept with *Marimba*. Someone had talked. Someone had found out about the nonexistent boat!

Indianapolis had delivered its deadly cargo to Tinian four days earlier. From there the cruiser went to Guam, then steamed south toward Leyte where they'd planned to refuel before returning to San Francisco for another "milk can."

Running at periscope depth, *Marimba* picked up blips on its new "ST" radar. It changed course, only to be blocked by yet another surface group skirting up from Rota. There weren't many Jap boats left in the Pacific, but what they could muster seemed to be looking for a lone American submarine.

*   *   *

Lieutenant Commander Mochitsura Hashimoto listened on the spare hydrophone headset. His eyes narrowed and his stocky neck throbbed inside its stiff collar. This had to be the boat that his superiors in the Intelligence branch had briefed him on. Just as he'd been assured. It was right on time and heading for Tinian. Hashimoto brought his boat up, tower awash and radioed his position to a following sub chaser.

"Tubes one to six, stand by for surface fire," the bridge watch scoured the darkening waters ahead. Still no visual contact. Hashimoto knew from the rev count that the adversary was doing about ten knots, a normal surface cruising speed for submarines, and he also knew from which direction it was coming. All I-58 had to do was wait, silently maneuvering on its electric motors. Six of the most advanced torpedoes in the world's arsenals were ready. Powered by oxygen, the wakeless projectiles were capable of 58 miles per hour, almost double the speed of comparable American torpedoes! Over a hundred crew and officers were proud of this Japanese engineering breakthrough, and eager to test it.

Suddenly a lookout spotted the plume of a periscope speeding off the port bow. The metal eye, coming out of summer sundown's mist turned toward I-58, and disappeared.

"Too late," screamed Hashimoto, "too fast. Stand by to dive." His second officer agreed that it would be better to let the chaser depth bomb it, rather than fire blindly at the hydrophone's directional heading.

Hashimoto bit his lip; never had he encountered a submerged boat going at such speed.

"But Commander Hashimoto," the Captain of the *Kuri* Class destroyer called through his megaphone as the boats bobbed alongside in the darkness, ". . . our sound tracking equipment cannot follow anything faster than thirteen knots.

This was a most unusual submarine. The illustrious Hashimoto knows that . . .''

The Commander from Hiroshima signaled that he was going after the phantom, and called for full ahead on diesels. If the sub was going to Tinian, there was a chance he could catch it with full surface speed, and who knew these waters better? He ordered the helmsman to make for the tiny island of Aguijan, south of Tinian, and wait—like a trout behind a stone.

"High-speed screws to port, sir."

"What's our position?"

"Seventy-five miles northwest of Guam, sir."

Hashimoto rubbed his prominent chin; he was surprised he had gone that far in search of another contact with the elusive quarry. He steeled himself and vowed to be better informed and not let his anger get the better of him again. A bird in the hand applied here. The screws were rare at this hour. Hashimoto ordered a change of course and ran west for an hour, then went under to periscope depth. Whatever it was was coming closer; contact was made on the "wet" radar, skimming along behind the periscope head. Now it was fading again.

The second officer indicated a zig-zag with his hand.

"You are right, Higa."

The twenty-eight hundred ton boat stayed on course and the soundman held up his hands in dismay.

Hashimoto ordered a radar sky-sweep, then surfaced enough for the long range unit to scan the moon-swept horizon. Gone! Another near miss. The previous day he had sent two of his six Kaitens off on their suicide mission after sighting a tanker and its escort warship. The young pilots of these kamikaze torpedoes went happily to their fate. Explosions were heard, but 1-58 had its orders and did not stop to look. Now he was dishonored. Three contacts in two days and nothing to show for them.

"Surface," he snarled, and the bridge watch scampered up into the tower. It was a time to leave the commander alone. The thirty-five-year-old father allowed himself one more look. He panned with the night scope. Nothing. Nothing but a gleaming thought in his mind. His ceremonial sword was superimposed on the etched periscope field calibrations. Jeweled handle. Razor edge sparkling over the calm, glittering sea.

"Bearing two-seven-oh," a lookout shouted from the bridge. The watch officer trained his binoculars over the port bulwark and bent to the voice tube.

"Captain to the bridge."

Beads of sweat on his forehead, red battle light streaming from the open hatch, Hashimoto took the glasses. His mouth opened slowly as he focused on the horizon. The moon had been good for him; it shone on the enemy for him to see, a fortunate circumstance, for had I-58 surfaced beyond the ship, it would be the submarine that was visible. His mouth tightened grimly under the rubber-coated glasses. It was a large ship; its superstructure had six levels within its tripod tower. He could see the shape of a seaplane on a launching ramp aft of the forward funnel. Huge radar antennas bristled in the tops. It was an American cruiser, Portland Class. Hashimoto's teeth glistened in the moonlight.

"Crash dive," repeated Lieutenant Higa.

Six torpedoes spurted out of I-58 's shark bow at two second intervals. At 1500 yards, the spread of three degrees would amount to 200 yards upon reaching the target—approximately the length of *Indianapolis*. At almost fifty miles per hour, Hashimoto's sweep-second would not make a full revolution. He gripped the periscope handles tightly as he counted down.

"A hit . . . and another!" He stomped loudly on the deck as high plumes of water exploded into searing orange fireballs. The torpedoes had struck the fore and aft magazines, under A and C turrets. Hashimoto waited till the cruiser's bows dipped, and the whirling propellers tore out of the water before diving.

An hour later, tubes reloaded, I-58's periscope panned a full circle. Nothing but moonlit ocean. The huge boat with its little men came up for well-earned air, and the fishy aroma of Japanese cigarettes curled from the conning tower and open hatches. Long-hidden bottles of Kirin and saki were opened and shared while a long-necked samisen plinked to the happy sing-song wail of a popular Japanese ballad.

In the twelve minutes before the final plunge after the torpedoes hit shortly after midnight, about 800 of the ship's complement of 1200 managed to get clear of the inferno—many of the crew had opted to sleep on deck because of the oppressive heat below. Captain Charles Butler MacVay III, among the survivors, was thankful, though he privately cursed himself for giving the order to stop zig-zagging earlier that evening. But he was confident of being rescued at daybreak. His last order before abandoning ship was to the radio-room . . . to saturate the frequencies with SOS calls. What the Captain didn't know was that the emergency power lines were out and not one message was sent!

For fully three days the survivors clung to debris and overcrowded rafts. One by one, hands let go under the searing sun. One by one, men screamed as schools of sharks swam under them—until the survivors numbered about 300. On the fourth day, they were spotted by an American aircraft.

In all, 883 men were lost—the greatest single disaster in the US Navy's history.

In the Pentagon, a hulking two-starred general riffled through CENTERBOARD files in his safe and plucked out a bar of nutted chocolate. The top-secret files safe had proved to be the best place for keeping chocolate. The mustached general popped a hefty chunk into his mouth and read the message concerning the loss of *Indianapolis*. He would have to hide his relief—and consider other ways of delivering the next bomb. The coincidence gnawed on him. Only five days earlier and the entire Manhattan Project would have crumbled. He made a note to consider the transfer of nuclear material to submarines at Hawaii.

The last four-hour watch was almost over. Three times a day, for sixteen days, he'd sat on the bunk, guarding the milk can . . . checking his pistol . . . wiggling his toes awake. Forty-eight times he had entered this metal crypt, and forty-seven times Paulsen had replaced him. Having read every book on the boat, from lurid paperbacks with eyes in keyholes to the captain's navigation manuals, Cal regretted not bringing a copy of *War and Peace* aboard—something that he would never have time nor patience for ashore. The omnipresent brushed steel container had assumed many roles and images since leaving Frisco. It had appeared, etched on his brain in nightmares, at the mess table as an enormous salt-shaker; and even in the privy. One wave-tossed night he dreamed the can was as high as Fujiyama, and had a long fuse that trailed all the way into the sea. His job to light that fuse. He donned diving equipment and applied an acetylene torch to the end. Powder sputtered and crackled along the seabed scattering bottom fish and scaring mollusks into burying themselves deep in the sand. The flame emerged on a beach south of Tokyo, frightening bathers and rice-paddy workers, singeing forest brush and finally entering the miles-high cylinder.

Instead of an enormous cataclysmic explosion—a silence. Cal woke up in a cold sweat. But Paulsen had described "Trinity" to him. The Alamagordo test had occurred before dawn on July 16. It was not a meteor he'd observed from the speeding bomber before climbing over the Rockies only two weeks earlier. It was the plutonium bomb; the predecessor of the one in front of him! Calvert Crowe had worked with Fermi at Columbia, had been on the squash court in the Chicago stadium that day in December, 1942, when the first nuclear chain reaction had happened. As a scientist, he knew the potential of fission. There were papers available in 1940 that explained the potential power locked up in the heavy isotopes. Less than a hundred pounds of plutonium would yield a destructive force equal to 20,000 tons of TNT—and it would require a fleet of 1000 B-29s to deliver such a conventional bombload.

There were those who asked him why he didn't get a job at Los Alamos or Oak Ridge, and make lots of money since he could have been deferred for his specialty. To this he answered that he was a rare bird—a patriotic type, and he wanted to be part of the world before bolting himself to a laboratory table. This was only partly the truth. In reality, Cal was ashamed of his father, his uncles, and his community in the small town of Quaker Street, near Schenectady, New York. Quaker Street, four corners on Route 7. A filling station, a post office and a general store. Population: about 500. Mostly Quakers with small farms. His father's farm consisted of some ninety acres. There was a ramshackle barn and a chicken coop with excrement four inches thick over everything. One milk cow was kept in the barn, next to a rusted-out Model T on cement blocks with weeds growing through the floorboards. Mortimer Crowe didn't work the farm; he hired "underprivileged" boys from New York to shape the place up from June through September. Thirty dollars a month and board for a twelve-hour day, six days a week. Mortimer had a well-furnished house with piano and fancy library. One of the two cars in the attached and heated garage was a Lincoln Continental. Farmer Crowe had a taste for the extravagant—and could afford it.

"Farmer" Crowe worked at General Electric in Schenectady and made double and triple time for overtime.

So did Warner Crowe, and all the other uncles. So did all the healthy draft-age Quakers in Quaker Street. Up the main road stood a pristine white Meeting House; windows bright and lawn always trimmed by the hired city boys, there was one unusual thing. Meetings never took place in the house. It was a front to bamboozle the draft board of Schoharie County. And it had worked.

So Calvert Crowe, a scholarship student at Columbia, entered a study program with the U.S. Navy's co-operation. As a scientist, he hated pretension—and his people were pretenders. Conscientious objectors, but for monetary gain— and cowardice.

Besides, Cal wanted to be a man—and scientists were notoriously poor lovers. He was afraid his preoccupation with "making out" and losing his virginity was a deterrent to scientific concentration. What better solution than the Navy? But, alas, it had not transpired—yet. After two years in uniform . . . and he too, was ready to explode. How close he had come on the beach at Bermuda—and then *this* happened. He stuck his tongue out at the Plutonium container and tried to think of Cynara, on the beach. But each time he envisioned her, the Brooklyn accent turned him off and he conjured up the redhead.

"Brighter than a thousand suns . . . metal tower vaporized . . . white sand fused into a green ceramic dish as large as the stadium in Chicago . . . observer knocked off his feet at two miles by shock wave . . ." Paulsen's words haunted him. "Great, green super-sun . . ."

Cal was back-up man on the second bomb. Back-up in case Paulsen came down with beri-beri, or sprained his wrist and couldn't assemble the components. Chances were slim that anything else would happen, since it already did—at Wendover Field. Paulsen's original back-up, an Army major, after months of orientation, was found to be too fond of luncheon martinis.

Four cities had not been hit by Le May's bombers: Kyoto, Hiroshima, Koruba and Nagasaki. They were being "saved" for the big one ;it was the only way to measure the force of the atom weapon. The Japs were jittery. In

Hiroshima, an important Naval Base, the officers had joked that the reason they'd been spared firebombing was that Truman's wife had relatives in the city.

"Olympic" and "Coronet" were already under way. The first operation, code name for the initial assault on Kyushu, with over 800,000 American troops, was scheduled for November 1st. The second was to commit well over a million fighting men to the beaches around Tokyo in the spring of 1946. Submarines were coming off the ways fast. The powerful, new *Tench* Class was ready, a state-of-the-art boat that combined all the developments needed for the Pacific war. But there were no more enemy boats to sink. Few boats worthy of a torpedo. COMSUBPAC took to their deck guns and lobbed shells at barges, wooden junks and anything else that did not fly the stars and stripes. If they weren't on intelligence sorties or mine-data runs for "Olympic", they stole into harbors and shelled shore installations or blew up freight trains.

Cal trembled when he thought of the invasion of mainland Japan. Two million American troops faced with an enemy who wanted to die—expected to. Strapped to mines and inside suicide torpedos, carrying live explosives—waiting behind rocks and trees all along the island coastline. It was possible that the bomb, made from the contents of the can before him, guarded by him, could end the war; could save a million American lives. On the other hand—and he had discussed the topic with Paulsen—it might have been proper, inviting Emperor Hirohito to Alamagordo to see with his own eyes. But then the Japs didn't warn us about Pearl Harbor . . . and with only two bombs completed, they would certainly go after a lone B-29 with kamikaze. No. One does not pet a rabid dog.

The somber cannister glinted, reflecting caged light bulbs and empty pulled-up bunks . . . the vertically elongated man in uniform sitting and waiting. How many knew what was in this can . . . what was the 4 x 6 foot crate that was stowed below the forward deck gratings? The crew guessed:

a secret rocket? Gold bullion to bribe the Japs to surrender? A shipment of mail order goodies from Abercrombie & Fitch for the Admirals of COMSUBPAC?

Rocket weapon! Cal studied the vertical container and imagined it to be inside a V-2 missile. In his mind he drew a tube that was perpendicular to the deck, that extended through the pressure hull and up as high as the bridge. Why not fire an atomic bomb *from* the submarine itself, instead of transferring it to a bomber? The V-2's range was almost 200 miles . . . *Marimba* could sneak, unseen, within range of any city in Japan, then surface so the ejection tube was clear of the water. . . .

*   *   *

On the 6th of August, Hiroshima was destroyed. The scientists had won the war and started another.

Chapter 8

Led by Halsey's flagship, USS *South Dakota* and a section of Task Force 30, a fleet of submarines left Pearl Harbor for the victory run to San Francisco—*Puffer, Baya, Kraken, Loggerhead, Pilotfish, Stickleback* and *Chimera*.

On October 15th, the procession passed under the Golden Gate Bridge. Bringing up the rear behind the subs were three destroyers, a light cruiser and three more battleships.

The colorful Bay City went mad that evening, and far into the morning. There were toasts lifted on Fisherman's Wharf, in Chinatown and The Latin Quarter. The submariners drank to five million tons of Jap shipping on the bottom and over 200 Imperial Naval vessels sunk. In quiet corners, somber thoughts were held by contrast, for 3500 shipmates who did not come home.

Ben Mount proudly demonstrated his facility with chopsticks to Cal Crowe and the two Navy nurses. Sona was attracted to Ben—there was something familiar about him.

"I confess that my first experience with these was in Chinatown back in New York. The guys used to walk over the Brooklyn Bridge and go have egg foo yong on Mott Street. It was either that or a subway to Times Square."

"I'm from Flatbush myself, near the Williamsburg Savings Bank," Sona Sokol's eyes brightened and Cal suspected that a chemical reaction was taking place between her and his old friend. He didn't mind much, as the redhead, Dottie, had a voice like Lizbeth Scott. Cal imagined Dottie doing an about face inside her bra.

"I suppose you're going back to Columbia," Ben changed subjects as he thought Sona was Cal's choice.

"Back east, yes—but not to New York. There's a spot open in the Naval Research Lab in Philly. You've heard of Gunn and Abelson?"

"Weren't they involved in the bomb?"

"Indirectly. Their method for isolating U-235 was designed for fueling an atomic reactor. Manhattan Project came in with a higher priority but used their extraction formula."

"Now they're back on propulsion?"

"Ben, what would you say to a submersible that could stay under for sixty . . . eighty days. Without surfacing or snorkeling?"

"I'd say the crew would go crazy."

"But the boats will be larger, more comfortable. Individual private bunks, television, exercise machines, frozen foods."

"You think it can be done?"

"It has to be done." Cal poured more saki into the tiny china cups. Ben burned his lips and quickly emptied a glass of icewater, to the girls' amusement. "You can bet the Russians are not standing pat on submarine propulsion. Right now they're probably taking the German Walter boats apart."

"Walter who?"

"The closed-circuit peroxide motor. You know how

they copy things. In five years they'll have the most powerful sub force ever gotten together. The Soviet Navy doesn't have to worry about funding. Nobody's going to tell Joe Stalin to put the expenditures into worker's benefits or public housing. It's going to take a big selling job to get anywhere here . . .''

"Gentlemen, the war's hardly over and already you're starting another one.''

"Dottie's right, Cal. Let's continue this some other time; I want to know more about those German boats you looked at with Moxie Mulford.''

"And you checked out the Jap I-400.''

"Big and primitive,'' Ben took out his wallet. "One thing about pig boats—you can't spend your money as easy as on the big ones. Let's go see what makes this town so big with the sailors—and sailor-ettes.'' Waiting until the girls had gone to powder their noses, Ben confided to Cal: "Nice, very nice. But I'll have to beg out of tomorrow.''

"Betsy Kirkland?''

"Yeah.''

Cal understood. One doesn't argue with an Admiral's daughter.

Chapter 9

"Ben."

"What?"

"Do you love me?"

"What a silly question," Ben buttoned up his shorts and went over to the window.

"Do you suppose she is still mad?"

"Who?"

"Betsy."

"She'll make out." Ben looked down on West 8th Street and watched an artist struggling with a large canvas against the December wind. A stream of young men on the street, carrying books and brief cases. Hardly a woman among them. They wore Air Force flight jackets, emblazoned with unit insignias, bombing mission symbols; wore combat boots and Navy peajackets. Even from the third floor of the Marboro Hotel Ben could feel the excitement of the students. These were the first wave, come back from the European Theater, from Iceland and Africa in time for the Fall semester. Soon, in a few weeks, they would be coming from Okinawa, India and the Aleutians, marching with fire-belching dragons embroidered on their service coats, eager to make up for the lost years—and dreams.

"Ben."

"Yea."

"Was it this article?" Sona Sokol rolled over on her stomach and picked the New York Times up from the end-table. She read:

'SUBMARINE NAVY WITH ATOM FUEL AND HIGH SPEED HELD SAFEST AGAINST ATOM WAR'

'Doctor Sidney Weinstein Tells Senate Group Warships of Future May Operate 1000 Feet Below Surface.'

'Washington, Dec 12—Dr. Weinstein, a 30-year-old physicist told the Senate Committee on Atomic Energy today . . .'

Ben sat down on the bed and took Sona's hand in his. "I'm thirty years old, Sona, and what am I doing?"

"You're a damn good officer with a great future and a loving fiancée who is lucky she does not have a class this cold morning." She pulled Ben down and purred, nude under the sheet. "And, in four years you'll even have your own personal physician to sleep with. We'll have an apartment in the Village and a summer place on Fire Island."

"Sona."

"What?"

"I've got to get in on the ground floor. Sure, I know what I'm doing as a line officer, but I'm not really one of *them*. I don't play their kind of ball game. I can't brown-nose to some shithead I don't respect. That's what you've got to do to make rank. It's the same in business, in politics.''

"You should take lessons from Jack McCrary.''

"That's part of it. He's doing something. You're doing something, and I'm doing what the Germans did two years ago, only worse. So I make sure we cut up our old boats and stick extra batteries in 'em. What do I do after that?

"Moxie's working on advanced propulsion systems, Cal's developing a reactor engine, and you're studying medicine. And Ben Mount. I'll be shuttled around from desk job to desk job; old Ben Mount, Officer-in-charge of spare parts for obsolete submarines . . .''

"Ben,'' she kissed his shoulder, "I understand. You've got to do what your heart tells you to do.''

"Look, there's a nuclear physics course at MIT. My year at Columbia qualifies me, and the Navy will pick up the tab . . .''

"Do it, Ben.''

"You won't mind—it's a three-year grind?''

"We can meet half-way on weekends—if you don't get too much homework.''

"Secluded motels on the Wilbur Cross Parkway . . .''

"And after we're married—romantic country inns.''

"Thanks, Sona, for making it easy for me.'' Ben got up, pulled down the shade and slipped under the sheets. The bed was squeaky, so he reached over to his portable Zenith. All newscasts.

"Try QXR, it's way over on the right.''

They waited till *O, Come All Ye Faithful* had ended and tried a *Jingle Bells* medley.

May 17

My dearest:
I tried to call yesterday but your dorm phone was busy and you weren't in this morning. I'm catching a

plane to Washington, and it'll be a day or two before I find out whether I'm accepted on a new team that's going to Tennessee. My old friend, Admiral Sawyer put in a word for me and the next thing I knew I was packing. Apparently something big is brewing and this may be our chance to get in on the ground floor. If this works, I'll continue on an MIT extension course until the operation is finished. I can't say much more because this is one of those security things.

It looks like we'll have to reschedule things if I get stuck in Tennessee. I know how much you wanted a June wedding—and so do I but . . .

Sona dropped the letter and flung herself on her bed. The dorm was empty; all the girls were in class. Mostly Liberal Arts and Education majors. Very few Pre-meds. Now there would be one less. She sobbed because she felt so alone, now more so.

The Dean was encouraging; he advised her to try something less competitive, perhaps lab work. It wasn't just one class—the grades were consistently low. Had she been fooling herself all these months? Hoping for some miracle where all the complex formulas and procedures would suddenly become lucid.

Cramming and extra help had not overcome a basic deficiency in math and the sciences. Now she knew it was the high school itself. Though she received high grades in biology and chemistry, the level of the school was low. An "A" at Girl's Commercial was equivalent to a "C" at Bronx High School of Science or Abraham Lincoln. That's what came from living in a section of Brooklyn where most people worked with their hands for a living.

She sobbed and wondered why she had not stayed in the Navy and let well enough alone. But no, she wanted to please Ben; make him proud of her, even with her Brooklyn accent which she'd worked diligently upon in order to improve her image to Ben's friends—especially the well-turned-out Miss Kirkland. It would have been wrong to be a "service couple," both getting paid on the same day, once a month and both griping about their commanding officers. There was no returning either; the Navy had cut back on nurses; there would be no reinstatement, no commission.

It was peacetime.

Sona felt some elation at not having to face Ben, not having to tell him she wasn't good enough. But she had counted on the marriage . . . a last straw to cling onto. And she couldn't tell him now. There was still the summer to work things out. She'd get a job somewhere. Perhaps something would happen and solve it all.

Ben called, and it was as she'd expected. He'd gotten the assignment and was embroiled in it. He came to New York in late June and met Sona's family; discussed the possibility of a wedding in September, when "things were more straightened out."

Sona's father, Saul, worked in a diamond mart on 47th Street. But he was a minor salesman in a stall that specialized in decorative jewelry. He was proud of his bright green sport jacket and wore it to Chinatown when Ben picked up the tab. Saul volunteered to use his connections in buying a "colossal rock", at least two carats for his daughter Cynara.

Her mother, a daughter of Erin, blamed her father, bless him for her habit of "perfect Manhattans." One of the things that had impressed her about Sol was his abhorrence of alcohol. Unfortunately it hadn't rubbed off on her. She got worse because he was such a bore. Ben and Sona agreed that it might be a good thing to plan a life elsewhere—at least two states away. Ben gave his old Plymouth roadster to Sona for safekeeping. There was to be a staff car available at Oak Ridge.

*   *   *

The Bureau of Ships in Washington, opened its files for Ben Mount. With the job came a promotion. The Navy wanted a man with practical sea experience to ride herd over the brilliant, younger selectee officers in the nuclear group. A condition was that Ben take special courses to augment his Electrical Engineering degree, since two of his group had their Masters' diplomas.

As a Captain, Ben cut swaths in Washington. He requested top secret files and got them from their dusty crypts. He had to know all there was about atomic fission.

He found papers of Cal's boss, Dr. Ross Gunn from early 1939 that proposed an atom-powered ship. He read of research fund appropriations that had been shelved. He was amazed to find that the original military advisory people in 1940 were more interested in propulsion than a super-bomb.

A group within Manhattan Project wrote nine months before Hiroshima:

'The government should initiate and push, as an urgent project, research and development studies to provide power from nuclear sources for the propulsion of naval vessels. It might be advisable to authorize the initiation of these studies at once, without waiting for the postwar period, in order to utilize scientific personnel already familiar with the pile theory and operation . . .'

On a hot summer evening, Ben's perspiring fingers held up a schematic drawing found among some of Dr. Phil Abelson's papers. It was accompanied with proposals and ideas that would change the life of Ben Mount, and others, as well as revolutionize the military and political posture of the entire world.

The drawing lay, partly curled from inadequate temperature and humidity control, on the cluttered desk of Admiral Clay Randall, Assistant Chief of the Bureau of Ships. It showed elevation, plan and section of the last two compartments of a German experimental submarine, the hydrogen-peroxide powered type 26.

Abelson had made one major change. The propulsion components were labeled with unusual names: Pile Core, Potassium Sodium Heat Exchanger, Feed Water Pump. The scientist had replaced the Walter power plant with a nuclear reactor system. Ben felt like a child who had been given plans for an "Erector Set" without the miniature beams and trusses, except he had the money and was itching to go to the store.

The accompanying report was a bombshell that rattled the rambling building to its cinder-block foundation. Admiral Randall read it aloud and was astonished. It stated that, with a proper program, it was possible to build an atomic-powered sub in two years, capable of operating submerged at twenty-six to thirty knots for many years without refueling, and added that speeds could be doubled in time.

The report concluded with ". . . this fast, submerged boat will serve as an ideal carrier and launcher of rocketed atomic weapons . . ."

Ben had heard similar words before—in San Francisco, from Cal Crowe. They had excited him once, but now it was becoming an obsession. Ben Mount, son of an immigrant tailor—from Russia, yet—had a chance to do what had never been done by anyone!

"Of course, we knew these papers were here someplace," the overweight Admiral started to stack them and pulled a file drawer open when Ben snatched them from his hands.

"I'll give them back to you, sir, after I've made copies."

"Of course, Captain."

"By the way, sir—er—Clay," Ben occasionally had trouble remembering that his new rank, Captain, allowed him a little less formality with the next higher rank, ". . . where are those two physicists now?"

"Still at the Naval Research Labs, but both have put in

for transfers. Gunn got a $25 raise, which brought him up to ten grand—the highest allowed to civilians in the Navy Department. I can't blame him for leaving. Abelson is going back to Carnegie Institute.''

''All the good brains are leaving because the Navy chiefs not putting any money where their mouths are,'' Ben slapped a bronze and brass 37mm shell cigarette lighter on the desk, startling the officer.

''Look here, Ben; it's been a long war and it's time to relax, play a little golf, spend time with the family. Give it time; we all have to reform our flotillas and chart new courses. Go on out to Oak Ridge and write your reports. Ol' Clay will put 'em into the right slots.''

That summer, while the Navy was concerned with the Bikini atom bomb tests—which were to prove little and turn public opinion against nuclear endeavor because of fall-out—Ben, by dint of new-found energy and perseverence beyond hours, became the spokesman and den-father for the younger officers assigned with him to Oak Ridge. He coordinated, condensed, evaluated and forwarded precise information and recommendations to his superiors.

In August, General Electric stimulated the propulsion program by presenting a plan for the production of a reactor to power a destroyer-sized vessel. Now that industry was interested, so were a few admirals and congressmen. After the presentation, Ben was driven to the Pentagon and introduced to the Director of Manhattan Project, Lieutenant General Jason Wood, the chocolate eating production mentor of the bomb that saved a quarter million young American lives. The short meeting had good results; Wood picked up his phone and Ben's snagged top-secret security clearance was implemented with one sentence.

Ben called Sona and the wedding date was put off again.

*   *   *

General Wood's deputy, a brilliant engineer, invited Ben to fly with him to Oak Ridge. The two-hour flight over the verdant Alleghenys was charged with excitement that ignored the updrafts and scenery. Ben bombarded Colonel Starret with questions and proposals that taxed even *his* experience. He was so taken by Ben's insights into modern warfare that, after arriving at the nuclear complex, he had him assigned as deputy to the commandant, Colonel Richards.

At the time, in one of the many Oak Ridge buildings, Monsanto Chemical Corporation was preparing a "pile", as a reactor was called. Westinghouse, Allis-Chalmers and other large companies were also setting up energy labs to develop power for peace.

Captain Ben Mount gave himself yet another duty: he used his priority influence to make sure that the scientists were given comfortable quarters in private dwellings rather than the barracks that had been hastily cleared of two-year-old newspapers and pin-ups. These were the men the Navy and the nation would depend on to keep America strong— and make a poor boy's dream a reality. The five officers in Ben's group were assigned specific companies to "infiltrate" with an eye to powering a submarine.

Eventually, a few senior officers at the Bureau of Ships were advised of Ben Mount's budding threat to divert Naval funds into submarine propulsion at the expense of the larger vessels. Should Ben succeed, it would mean a shuffling of contractors, certain regions losing work and many long-time "understandings" between high brass and industry shattered. BuShips got in touch with the Naval Project officers at Oak Ridge and advised them that they need not report to Captain Mount anymore.

Initially furious, Ben called a meeting.

"Gentlemen," he addressed his five juniors, "do what you want—bypass me if you are afraid of those fat-assed

Admirals with their Naval coloring books—but remember one thing,'' there rose a glow in his eyes, ''I'm in charge of your fitness reports. As senior officer, it is my job to fill out semi-annual report cards on each one of you. The information I enter on your card will be read, not by BuShips, but by an impartial promotion board. Any questions?''

Noticing the Captain's melodramatic delivery, the five officers conferred momentarily, then elected the most eloquent to reply. Lieutenant Gillespie stood up and cleared his throat. ''Sir, we have duly deliberated your ultimatum, and our vote is unanimous in compliance with your wishes.''

''Excellent, Gillespie. Now Lieutenant Livoti . . .''

''Sir . . .''

''You know the two Waves who have been assigned to us.''

''Yes sir,'' Livoti jumped to his feet.

''Which is the sexy one?''

''Alicia Blair,'' the Lieutenant sighed.

''Get her transferred out of here; she can't spell, besides I want to streamline our operation a bit. Then get the other one and give her instructions not to open any more official US Navy mail. Have her stack it all in a corner somewhere. When I'm ready, I'll go through it myself.'' The young officers decided that it would be a good night to go to Knoxville and tip a few.

A month went by in which Ben's group accomplished more than had been done since the war ended. The pile of unopened letters was overflowing the closet and a coat rack had to be requisitioned while the mail was locked in.

Ultimately a telegram arrived from Naval District Headquarters, It requested the forwarding address of the former Oak Ridge Naval Group. By then, the group's reports were ready, organized into coherent, decisive missives. By some quirk, they reached the proper channels, and were so well received by the Naval and Atomic Energy Commission Libraries that the subsequent reports became known and looked for as "Mount's Memos."

On October 30th, as street urchins slammed flour-filled nylons at parked cars and each other, Sona Sokol went down to the vestibule, as she did hopefully every day and put her little key into the family mail box, one of ten in the tan brick building on the corner of Flatbush and Seventh Avenue.

One of the letters was for her; it was postmarked Washington DC. Excitedly she opened it, but it was not from Ben. It was from Dottie Frazer, the redheaded Navy nurse. Dottie was still seeing Cal who was at a research lab in Philadelphia, but the affair was difficult because of Cal's traveling out west so often. It was hard to work out a mutual schedule, but she still had hopes of snagging him when all the meetings were over, like he said.

In her last paragraph, she reported that Admiral Kirkland had been transferred from Frisco to the Pentagon, and Betsy had landed a job with *The Washington Post* and was doing a supplement interview series about prominent area personalities.

One of the "personalities" she'd been seen dining with was Captain Benjamin Mount.

Gaudy red and green neon reflected from the rain-pattered asphalt below the elevated tracks over the intersection of Flatbush and Myrtle Avenue. It was almost three in the morning; a blustery, chill November storm had clogged the sewers to overflowing. Relieved at managing to cross the Manhattan Bridge, her white Plymouth roadster buffeted by the nor'easter over the dark river, Sona relaxed as she passed by the rainbow-lighted square, Squibb Building. Over Brooklyn at last. She rubbed her eyes and tried to shake off her dizziness, which came in short spells. She'd been to a party thrown by her former classmates down in Greenwich Village. They'd tracked her down and insisted she come and talk to a professor, one of her first-year instructors, who offered to give her a job on campus.

As it turned out, the doctor, a smooth operator, got her to drink "just a little" bourbon in her ginger ale. Giddily, she accompanied him to his office across the street where he was to explain the position he had in mind.

The position was dependent on sexual favors and she managed to clear her head enough to slap him, race out of his office and run frantically to her parked car in the downpour.

Sona drove off the ramp and accelerated past the all-night bars. The broad, wet avenue was empty and glistening like a circus. The lights seemed to be all with her; she crossed Tillary Street . . . Johnson Street. Another few blocks and she'd be home. But the dizziness set in again, accompanied by a strange exhilaration. She imagined herself on a high-wire in the circus—a clown balancing . . . red, green, blue flashing lights. Suddenly, a pair of white lights blinded her and she swerved, fell off the high wire and all the cheering stopped.

The 17th Precinct book noted that "the vehicle had skidded a hundred yards before *impacting* with elevator pillar number M-291S," and that the MV operator had died instantly.

The obligatory post-mortem stated that "a small amount of alcohol had been found in the victim's blood."

At the funeral home, on Flatbush near Church Avenue, Sol Sokol stared blankly at Ben, small eyes cabalistically piercing Ben's jumbled brain and tearing at his nervous system, until the officer, in dark civilian suit, had to lower his head.

In Cypress Hills Cemetery, Sol said nothing and continued his dybbuk role in skull cap and long coat as his wife looked on, glazed from the previous night's drinking.

On the ride back to Flatbush, Ben sat in the limousine back seat with the Sokols. Sol, wearing a wide-brimmed black hat was in the middle. He reached solemnly into an inside pocket and drew out a small velvet box. With a trembling hand he opened the lid. A solitaire diamond glinted, a counterpoint to the black trappings about it.

Ben Mount would never forget that diamond.

Chapter 10

Two violins and a piano were doing a somewhat exotic version of the hit song from "Annie Get Your Gun."

Alys Southerland drew closer to her dancing partner on the crowded floor of "Le Continent" and sang lightly to him: "Falling in love is wonderful . . ."

Nuzzling into her long, blond hair, Jack McCrary bit her on the left ear. "I can do that, and if it weren't for all these people, I'd go right down your neck . . ."

"Promise?" Alys broke away into a Lindy as the medley switched to "Doin' What Comes Naturally." One of the violinists, a buxom dark-haired woman in her late twenties, wearing a peasant blouse and a red-flowered full skirt strode past the lush, red velvet dining booths and without missing a beat, chatted with the guests. Waving her instrument and bow to the raucous Irving Berlin score, she made her way around the dancers to a corner booth, leaned on the red, tufted backrest and plucked lightly *al pizzicato*.

"I can't help it, Jonny boy, it's the gypsy in me."

In blue velvet evening jacket, flashing an emerald-cut

pinky ring diamond which matched his tie-clip stone, a ruddy-faced, broad-shouldered man with a white handlebar chewed on a fat Havana. He acknowledged the voluptuous violinist and craned his head for a view of his daughter and her fiancé.

"Jonny boy, your little Alys, she not so little anymore."

"She'll have to go a ways to catch up with you, love."

Jonah Southerland guffawed and pointed out his choice of dessert to a black-tied waiter. The piano player, meek husband of Roszika concluded the show tune medley with a baroque flourish and changed into a romantic Hungarian theme. Roszika leaned over the table and admired Alys' gold evening handbag. The Maryland Senator took advantage and sniffed at the rose at her cleavage.

"Jonny, the people—" Roszika backed away.

"They're all *my* people, Rosie."

"Forgive; I sometimes forget how important you are."

"One reason I love you."

The gypsy smiled and picked up her bow as Southerland's hand moved over the backrest and waited. Roszika knew that Jonah was palming a twenty. It was a game, a ritual and she played it well. With a flurry of bowing to the heart-rending melody she twirled into the booth, against Jonah's waiting hand. He hid the twenty within her voluminous decorative skirt. As a signal that he'd placed the bill in her skirt pocket, the congressman pinched her and she reeled off.

The game had started with fifty-cent pieces dropped into her bodice in a run-down dive near the waterfront shortly after Pearl Harbor when reserve Commander Southerland and his fellow sea-lawyers had gone slumming. In trouble with the immigration authorities when Hungary declared war on the United States, Jonah fixed up her papers, for which she and her husband were eternally grateful. Albert, her husband was a result of a family match-making in Budapest. Much older, he chose not to know what was going on between Roszika and their benefactor. Where she got her money was inconsequential. There was enough to allow him to work on his pet project, a light opera based on the life of a twelfth-century Hungarian King, Bela III, called *The Golden Bull*.

Commander Southerland withdrew some of his Maryland family inheritance and bought a town house three blocks from the White House. He refurbished the top floor as an apartment and put Roszika in charge of overseeing his lavish, new restaurant and club on the main and second floors while he was stationed in Australia.

A year later, Jonah returned, arm in a sling. For all purposes he was a hero in his home state. While in Port Moresby, New Guinea on a legal assignment for the Seabees, a Mitsubishi 'Betty' got through and dropped a stick of bombs.

Though Jonah should have been in a shelter after the air raid siren, he wasn't . . . and never expected the enemy's aim to be so bad as to hit a whorehouse in the suburbs. He got back to Annapolis just in time for the '44 primaries and ran on a low-profiled hero's ticket.

The hitch in the Far East had not hampered Southerland at all. He came back—armed with contacts made at MacArthur's and Nimitz's staff levels, knowledge of shortages and priorities in ships and supplies, in-fighting among the commands, and a few secrets apt to be garnered by lawyers for personal gain.

"Le Continent's" clientele had changed in the eighteen months since the war ended. But only in appearance; the uniforms were fewer, but the people were the same. Many flag-rank officers were now with large industry in the Washington area. During the war, an admiral would be wined, dined and introduced to whatever his pleasure was, at no cost, with no record, just a table number. And now, the privileges remained. Habits formed during the war, away from their families, were continued by the steel and concrete "admirals", by the "big ship" advocates and chairmen of munitions empires, drawing military retirement pay as well as corporate salaries and the requisite "perks".

"Le Continent" was the watering hole for the shipbuilding interests, both Naval and industrial. The first floor was a very proper facade as a first-class restaurant. Southerland did not have to "buy" his three stars in the local newspapers' dining guides because he'd already bought the best chefs and decorators.

On the second floor, "aft" as it was put to the admirals, was a private dining room called "The Med." It was also accessible by a back stairway which led to a courtyard behind the Rochambeau Apartments, screened from the Army and Navy Club.

The Med featured a four-walled mural depicting iron-clad warships of all nations during the vintage "mahogany" years from 1860 to 1910—the "sway of the grand naval saloon". The theme of "on Mediterranean Station" was one dear to the hearts of traditional naval people—a cherished and fought-for assignment studded with fancy beaches, villas, classic architecture and gastronomy.

Painstakingly illustrated in a slightly primitive style, the American Civil War *Monitor* cruised off Ibiza with a parasol sun tent. Below the Italian boot steamed a resolute HMS *Dreadnought* of 1908, while the French *Vainquer* prodded Tripoli with her red ram bow and twin Dahlgrens, circa 1880. Conspicuously absent from the array of "allied" warships of history were the Russians, who had yet to prove themselves on the sea, much less during the mahogany era. At average eye-level, the mural's turquoise waters were punctured with port-holes, glass openings in aquarium tanks set into the walls and stocked with interesting fish and mollusks representative of the world's oceans and seas . . . Purple squid, needlefish, piranha, anglerfish in a dark tank with green incandescent tentacles, and even a baby hammerhead shark.

Food for talk, and for contracts.

The tables were all mahogany reproductions of those

found on the *Great Eastern*, complete with fiddle-rails, and all enclosed in private cabin-like booths. Six to a table, the Med Room could seat thirty-six, though any two VIP's could reserve a complete cabin for their own pursuits. It was a world of gilded figureheads and brassbound binnacles trimmed in gold braid.

The senator finished his *pêche melba* and lit an enormous Havana. He snapped out sixteen matches from the restaurant matchbook and set them down in groups. One table for Corcoran from the Bethlehem Yards. We'll put him with Hays from BuShips and Labine of DuPont. Jonah pushed the matches around.

"Dad, we've decided on the Riviera for our honeymoon," Alys Southerland whooshed onto the divan as the little gypsy combo took its break and the murmur of dinner conversation once more prevailed. She shook her long blond hair behind her neck.

"Alys mentioned that you had a restaurant, but this—"

"It's not as big as some in town."

"But it's something else," Representative Jack McCrary dug into his dessert as a Bahamian waiter poured coffee from a silver urn.

"Style will always prevail," the senator opened his 45-inch hand-tooled belt a notch. "By God, I wish I could join you kids on the Riviera—at a distance of course, but this reactor business. Perhaps when we've solved it . . ."

"The Oak Ridge crew?"

"That little Jew has got to be stopped," whispered Jonah.

"Oh, Dad," Alys feigned shock.

"If that project is not . . . 'diverted', certain powerful interests will get very angry, and certain aspiring young congressmen will not be re-elected."

Alys frowned and lit an Old Gold.

"What are we going to do about it?"

"That's the spirit, Jack." Southerland picked up the

loose matches and lit them, one at a time with his cigar, then dropped them into an ashtray. Without looking up, he let the last match burn lower as he held it. "What do you think of Captain Duillas?"

"Plodding, not very bright—a red tape man . . ."

The senator wheezed and blew out his last match. "We're going to have a Naval commandant at the Oak Ridge facility."

"But he doesn't outrank—" Jack shot back.

"He will!"

Chapter 11

It was a grueling trip. Eight states and a dozen plants and laboratories, including the plutonium facility at Hanford, Washington, the AEC lab in Chicago, the Knowles lab in Schenectady, and the sprawling center of bomb technology at Los Alamos.

There were very few important scientists who escaped an audience with the Oak Ridge Naval Group. For Ben, there was no such thing as "normal" working hours or holidays. He saw to it that everything of note was recorded and all potential lobbyists and brains for his program were recruited.

At Los Alamos, the senior fission and reactor physicist, Dr. Edward Teller, was so taken with Ben's group and their story of research and development roadblocks that he wrote to an influential friend in the Defense Department, recommending that funds be allotted and engineers procured for atomic propulsion.

In September, the Naval Group presented their proposals to Admiral Randall, who had just been promoted to

Chief of BuShips in Washington. The recommendations included establishing a Task Force that was independent of red tape.

To the Group's surprise, the Bureau shelved the report and ordered their dissolution, effective immediately. The five junior officers were transferred into remote sections of the Bureau, while Ben, almost as a penance, was reassigned to Oak Ridge as a document declassification officer. Luckily, Admiral Gar Kirkland, just back from a tour of duty in the Middle East, interceded and Ben was made the first claimant to a new Pentagon job called "Special Consultant in Naval Nuclear Matters."

A large, wrapped box was delivered to the suburban Annapolis home of Admiral, Ret. John McCrary Sr. In the box, a case of Chivas Regal; on the card in a sealed envelope: "thanks, J." The maid accepted the delivery and had the gardener put it with the other boxes in the garage to await the Admiral's return from Palm Springs, where between rounds of golf, he was attending a meeting of West Coast shipbuilders.

"At least you got a good tan," Betsy handed Ben a fresh cup of steaming tea.

"In New Mexico, you can get a tan through a window in August—if you don't get broiled alive first."

"I still can't figure out why they split up your group; didn't you tell me that Randall was on your side?" Betsy stretched a nyloned leg out under the tiny table and accidentally rubbed Ben's lean shin. He tingled inside. The first touch of a woman since Sona. He felt ashamed for liking it.

"There's nothing to say. Somebody got to him; it happens."

"Ben, you know I'm not 'interviewing' you now. I

want to help. I believe in the *Neptune*, and what's more, Dad is serious about burying the hatchet.''

Ben set his chopsticks carefully across his empty rice bowl, in the figure ''X''. ''Are you trying to tell me that Gar did me a favor because he's changed his mind about what I'm doing?''

''We saw a few more Russian submarines in the Gulf of Aden than we expected . . .''

''You saw?'' Ben blew on his tea.

''Well, you know Dad, and how he carries on.''

''For whatever reason, I'm grateful,'' Ben motioned to the waiter. ''I could have been collecting dust in the Oak Ridge archives.''

''People do change, Ben.''

''Have *I*?''

''You seem more . . . mellow, but then what you've gone through—''

''Cynara.''

''She was a fine woman—''

''It was my fault.''

''Let's drop it, Ben.''

''All right.''

''You wish to order?'' The waiter was central casting.

''*Hai*,'' Ben changed his voice inflection. ''*Gohan ga-zai kari desk-a . . .*''

The waiter bowed and was about to pick up Ben's empty bowl when he retreated.

''Sorry, I forgot,'' Ben took the chopsticks.

''Sorry you forgot what?''

''Sorry I forgot how to say sorry in Japanese,'' he quipped. ''No, actually crossed chopsticks are meant to keep evil spirits away from our table, or our hearths. For the waiter to break the spell, it would be some sort of sacrilege.''

''Ben, you're so full of goodies, I could listen to you all day, even without all the intrigues of your job.'' Betsy watched the rice being set before him. ''How can you eat that without soy sauce? It must be so dry—and that, that cold, raw fish!''

"The Japanese eat it this way—in Japan. Americans are too used to dumping ketchup on anything that doesn't have instant flavor. Good rice has its own subtle flavors.'' Ben picked up the bowl and deftly worked his chopsticks. "Another thing—'' he poised a clump of white in mid-air, "you don't see many overweight Japs. They're very ascetic; we can learn from them.''

"We sure did, one Sunday morning.''

Ben didn't answer, or try, with a cheekful.

"I think you're very ascetic—in a good way,'' Betsy picked at her teriyaki steak tidbits.

"But I'm no saint.''

"Or rabbi.'' Betsy chewed suggestively.

"Sometimes I look more like a rabbi.''

"Don't be so hard on yourself.''

"I like it, I like it,'' Ben rolled his eyes ecstatically.

"Oh, my God,'' Betsy smirked, "and it's only lunch-time.''

"You're right, it is a working day.''

"We could continue after work, Ben, that is if you get off on Friday nights—and please don't answer *that* one.''

Ben's eyebrows raised comically. "A weekend. Already?''

"How about my place, at seven. I make a mean lasagna.'' Betsy's long, dark hair fell over one eye as she stretched, tightening her white sweater so that Ben felt a weakening.

"Can I bring something?''

Betsy just smiled.

Chapter 12

Ben sorted out his office things; one box for keeps, one for throw-outs. He'd packed hastily at Oak Ridge and now realized how small his Pentagon office was. It had been a ladies' powder room until after VJ day, when the typing pool was cut in half. After that it functioned as a store-room for used swivel chairs, most of them worn through by the countless behinds of desk officers. He picked out the best one, tested it for squeaks and shoved the rest, including a discolored green ladies' relaxing couch into an elevator and pressed the ''down'' button before jumping out. For a desk, he made do with a piece of plywood tied down on a wall-hung basin.

From a cardboard box marked with a symbol for radioactivity, he culled out his desk paraphernalia: progress book . . . phone index . . . sharpener . . . appointment calendar, and set them on the plywood. Before he was aware of it, he'd also opened a leather photo easel and set it up. Momentarily taken aback, he closed it and put it into the ''out'' box. He'd forgotten where he'd stashed it al-

most a year earlier after Sona had died. Pondering a
moment, he leaned down and slipped the photograph out.
Then he walked around his new office till he found, on the
floor, a suitably defunct book. Sona, with a backdrop of
the Brooklyn Bridge, was inserted in a thick manual of
steam engineering.

Ben sat on the floor and brooded, then got up and
looked out of the tiny window at the interior courtyard—a
grey concrete pentagon with scrawny trees at precise
intervals. He felt like shouting an obscenity to listen for its
echo.

But instead, he picked up the phone.

The Clinton Lab at Oak Ridge was still almost deserted.
Only one of the several corregated tin shed-like buildings
in the reactor sector had a guard posted. Ben walked
briskly over to it and showed his credentials to the negro
MP.

"Damn, sir—I mean I didn't . . ."

"You did the right thing, Corporal; don't trust anyone
out of uniform. They could be communists." Ben put his
burberry raincoat collar up, and sneered behind it in mock
imitation of a foreign agent. The corporal, with a big,
white grin held the door open and Ben skipped inside.

"Ben Mount, you old son of a—" Cal Crowe, in tan
coveralls, came sprinting to meet his old friend. "Why
didn't you call?"

"I did—to make sure you'd be here." They walked to a
staging area in the vast shed. Boxes, plans and construction wood lay everywhere around. One section of the floor
had been freshly concreted and was roped off in an irregu-
lar shape.

"Tolerances are doubly acute on projects this size, so
we refigured the site," Cal surveyed the floor.

"One of those big heat exchangers?" Ben winced.

"That's what they want at AEC. That's what they get."

"How long will the moolah last?"

"I can keep a small crew on another six months."

"Not enough time for anything tangible."

Cal shook his head disdainfully. "We're kidding ourselves. Lost two of our best engineers already."

Ben rolled his tongue around and draped his raincoat over a barrel. He looked up, sideways and around, mentally measuring. "Cal, is anybody really expecting you to build something?"

"No, it's mostly for the theory. Basics."

"Could you get to the nuts and bolts stage of a small reactor? Compared to this, an itsy-bitsy one?"

"You mean something that might fit into a you-know-what?"

"The Daniels Pile is just sitting in the next room."

"We can give it a good try, but what about Duillo, he's got sensitive toes." Cal Crowe exhaled disgruntlingly.

"I'll talk to Randall; you just order what you need. If anybody asks you why, tell 'em Mount said so . . . and, oh, say hello to Dottie. If it's a boy, I'll appoint him to the Academy."

"It's a deal."

"I just don't like it," Jonah Southerland closed the mahogany door of Cabin 'A' in the Med Room and took his place at the ship's table. He grabbed the handle of the brass telegraph pedestal and rang out 'All Stop.' Repeaters in the kitchen and bar signalled that Cabin 'A' was not to be disturbed until further notice. All six cabins in the private room, upstairs at "Le Continent" were occupied and reveling. The Christmas Season "smoker" was in full swing. 1947 had only a few days left.

Maryland State Representative Jack McCrary glanced at his father, then turned to the Senator. "Nobody, not even Dad, can buck Nimitz."

"What I wanna know," slurred the retired Admiral, "is

how th' hell can a little . . . squirt like Mount get around us? I thought we'd already deep-sixed 'im.''

"It was a mistake to go along with Kirkland," Jack drained his Jameson's Irish whiskey and slammed the glass on the table.

"Maybe he had it in for us because of you and Jonah's daughter," Jack, Senior, opened his black tie and wiped his brow. He picked an ice cube out of his gin and put it on the ashtray. "Who do they think I am, an Eskimo?"

Jonah sucked hard on his Havana, examined it, then put it forlornly into the ashtray. It had turned to mush from the icecube water. He flipped up the binnacle voice tube lid and called to the coat room. "Sally, send up a couple o' my stogies, heah." He ogled his guests solemnly, clasping his fidgety fingers. "I think there's a pack out there knows more'n they let on. How come we didn't find out about Mount's personal Naval Pile till last month? I thought we had friends in the AEC."

"We have, but nobody expected him to go as far as he did," Jack stifled a hiccup.

"And nobody ever 'spects a moccasin to bite less you step on it. I tell you this guy is dangerous. He don't think like we do. Funny name, Mount. Wonder what he changed it from." Southerland grunted his heavy body to the door and peeked through the porthole. He opened the door, allowing a tall brunette with black net stockings and a scanty Santa Claus suit in.

"Melinda heah, is from th' South Pole, ain'tcha honey?" She wiggled her breasts as Jonah took a fistfull of cigars from her tray and patted her on the backside as she left. McCrary, Senior almost toppled out of his captain's chair.

"I've a hunch," Jonah lit up and disgorged smoke that brought tears to Jack's eyes, "that the whole thing is a set-up. That little Hebe could buttonhole a whale if he wanted to. I'll bet he got a few of those dumb gung-ho ComSubPac jockeys to hand-carry his proposals to the brass . . ."

"That's why my contacts at the Pentagon and Atomic Energy Commission didn't call me. I never missed anything in reg'lar channels, damn it. He don't play fair," the Admiral growled.

"One thing we've learned, gentlemen. If Mount doesn't do things by the book, we can't stop him by the book."

"In spite of Nimitz?" Jack grimaced. "I don't see how we can influence him once he's made up his mind."

The white-haired Senator smiled and sipped his Jack Daniels mash. "As I see it, Captain Mount still hasn't cleared the AEC," he hesitated, "an' besides that, ah hear he's takin' a trip out to Scotland soon . . ."

"But what has that—"

"Jackie, boy, all politicians like to see the opposition get out of each other's territory once in a while. Makes for more stompin' room." Jonah made a mental note. There was another way to deal with immovable opposition. Distasteful? Yes.

But there were those who agreed with what happened at Ford's Theater on Good Friday in April, 1865, including Jasper Southerland, though the Confederate Colonel never went on record. Certain letters in the family's collection had been disposed of before going to Georgetown's library. It was only a brief flash to Jonah, but he dwelled on it privately until all the cabins in the Med Room were open and off-key renditions of college songs reverberated throughout the building and into the stage-like streets of the marbled city.

Chapter 13

Hardly had the Fugenzu, Fukurokuju and Kwanzan trees along the Potomac shed their pink blossoms and the Cherry Blossom Festival crowds departed when Westinghouse called the AEC and presented a proposal to compete with General Electric in the reactor race. They would tackle the water-cooled heat exchanger, as GE was designing a unit that used liquid sodium as a coolant.

Ben tried another tack. He organized a public relations campaign that emphasized "atoms for peace" while accepting the aid of Betsy Kirkland, who interviewed personalities and industrialists on the panaceas of nuclear energy. The big-ship advocates sat back again and went out to the ball park and golf courses, content that the word "propulsion" had disappeared from Mount's Memos and the press in general. Admiral Randall was relieved at the respite—not having to ride herd on Ben—and finally managed to spend a quiet "post-war" week with his family in Newport.

But when he came back, the boom was lowered. Ben had plans, and he acted decisively.

"This is it, Clay," Ben spread out a fan of neat reports before the congenial Chief of BuShips. "It's either Duillo or me. I've been doing all of his work, so I want the credit—and more than that, he's getting in the way of our program. The only thing that's changed since the Oak Ridge Naval Group was scuttled is that Captain Duillo's name is on the letterhead. I let it go for a while; there was no choice. Maybe you guys were right, maybe Duillo knew something that I didn't . . . how to handle the armchair admirals. No offense, Clay . . . but as things went along, I realized that it made no difference. I kept the same old treadmill going, but now I've had it . . ." Ben unfolded a letter and set it down before Randall. "Triplicate . . . my request for a transfer. It's up to you, Clay. It's Duillo or Mount; take your choice."

"Crab" Randall, the nickname derived from Barclay (some called him Clay, and others, a backwards version of Barc because of his tendency to move sideways when confronted), rolled his swivel chair to the right. "Ben," he dropped his large hands on his lap, "I've been aware of this for some time, but who wants to make waves?"

Ben moved his chair closer to the desk. "Clay, you know he's a loser; anyone who stays put is a loser, so they don't step on toes . . . they turn in reports that don't bug anyone. Fine! That's better than nothing. But do we want *nothing*? Do you want to go back to Newport in three or four years on half pay and just play golf? Or chase striped bass and tuna?"

"Ben," the aging admiral picked up the transfer papers. "You keep these for now." He rose and smoothed out his uniform, then put his arm, one broad and one narrow gold stripe, on Ben's shoulder. "I've put in a lot of good years in this Navy, and not a one that I'm ashamed of. Do you think I'm about to screw up now?"

*   *   *

With a green light from Bureau of Ships, Ben was on the spot. All the incessant pushing had given him callouses, and callouses were not good for go-aheads. At times, he felt like he was pushing a giant marshmallow—only to fall into it. At others, he was a three-inch long lizard leaning into a one-ton rock—trying to move the dark boulder into life-giving sunlight, the sun, ever moving beyond his one-inch successes. As promised, experts had been added to his staff, and his offices extended beyond the ladies' powder room in the five-sided mausoleum, but he could not relax his efforts.

His soirées with Betsy were usually followed up with Sunday supplement features reporting the grave shortages of fossil fuels and depletion of hydroelectric power.

Not the least of catalysts to help move Ben's boulder were the Soviets. Naval Intelligence had revealed that Russia was building three submarines for every one of ours. Sabers started rattling in the naval closets from Bremerton to Key West. Because of the Soviet blockade of Berlin in June of 1948, President Truman signed a resurrection of the Selective Service Act and alerted two million young men for the emergency.

In Washington, Captain Arleigh, "31-knot" Burke of World War II destroyer fame presented a report to the Navy Department that curled their hair. It stated that Russian naval capability based on their development of the German electro-boats was far greater than that of the US Navy. Admiral Momsen, of aqua-lung note, and Admiral Spruance, victor of Midway, lent their support.

Now Mount was going "full ahead."

He advised Westinghouse and GE of great profits to be had if they accelerated their industrial atomic power projects, and the best way would be to first build small reactors for the Navy. This was the only way to expedite nuclear development since the military was the only agency that had ready access to uranium and plutonium aside from the bomb producers. Once a reactor was in operation it would be a simple matter of conversion to a larger stationary model. With drive reminiscent of a Kaiser or a Ford, Ben lassoed those divisions of corporations that were important to his program and moved their centers closer to his new empire, thus eliminating fiscal and managerial bottlenecks. Ben felt he was indeed "chosen" to succeed—and mere money, taxpayers' or otherwise, would not stand in his way.

By inserting his hydra-headed machine between the military and the contractor, it was he who pressed the buttons that kept the funds flowing commensurate with production. His infiltration of BuShips and AEC was no less brilliant than any civilian conglomerate coup. It allowed him to, for the sake of progress, pit one against the other; in effect, he answered his own letters.

If a problem occurred, it went straight to Ben. If it wasn't sent to him for some goof or oversight, he'd find it anyway because of his insistence on screening all documents and letters even in rough form. Mount graded these letters as a schoolteacher might, then re-routed them back for correction, many with a "D" because of bad spelling or vague thinking.

On one occasion, a project engineer called from Schenectady and bleated that he couldn't meet Mount's deadline.

The finger-tapping Captain listened for a short time, then interrupted: "What time do you get out of bed every morning?"

"Seven," came the scientist's reply.

"Why don't you try getting up at six?"

Two camps were forming; one that produced and got promoted, and another, the plodding regulars and Department of Defense civilians, who deemed their rank and seniority sufficient for recognition, all things equal. After a few bouts with himself, Ben eliminated all pompous office titles and even posted lesser ranked people over higher ranks when there was no question of who demonstrated more talent or initiative.

A man wary of promises and the unknown, he had a rubber stamp made to imprint on all technical data, reports and articles from outside his domain:

N I H. It meant "Not Invented Here."

One of his pet expressions that settled many an argumentative meeting and technical impasse was:

"Talk with me, not *at* me."

By osmosis, intimidation, brilliance, money and necessity, the propulsion plans were ready. Ben's thumbs-down policy on a spread-out system had paid off. The reactor, on paper, was to fit within a thirty-foot diameter cylinder. BuShip's draftsmen came up with hull plans for a mockup to set the reactor in. There existed underwater streamlining technology, but the decision was to go with the standard "Guppy", (greater underwater propulsion) design, since the reactor was problem enough.

Neptune was to be slightly longer, at 324 feet, than the postwar diesel *Tench* Class Guppy conversion, but beamier and deeper, a thousand tons heavier. Not a playtoy, it was to be equipped with standard forward torpedo tubes.

As the nuts and bolts stage was reached, all but the die-hard opposition became quiet. Scale models were built, with cross-sections of accomodations and power plant. The big-ship advocates began to think of atom-powered aircraft carriers while the populace cheered the sentencing of a dozen top Communists to jail for advocating the overthrow of America.

Chapter 14

Buffeted by a chill November wind, the rusty bow of S.S. *Scythia* was snubbed up to its Quebec pier. Children on the dock looked up at the steamer's stern and tried to pronounce "Cuxhaven". A whistle blew, and the brash came rushing down the gangplank, vanguard of some fifteen hundred refugees from Germany and the Baltic.

Knots of people formed on the dock. Foreign shouts peppered the air, and there were embraces among men and women alike.

But one tall, lean man of about fifty, was not in a hurry, nor was there anyone to embrace. Carrying two large suitcases, he threaded the crowd and waited patiently on the customs line outside a small brick building.

Andrew Kayotis was scrutinized by an ancient customs guard who was about to open the suitcases when confronted with the passport. Kayotis, according to the book, was an American citizen, residing in Detroit. The guard muttered something in French and waved Kayotis through. There was nothing unusual about a man from Detroit getting off at Quebec. Most likely to take the Lake steamer the rest of the way. There was nothing unusual about the man himself—sharp, almost hawklike face, rumpled but clean clothes, grey tweed jacket, no tie, scuffed-up black shoes.

The unusual fact about Andrew Kayotis—the real Kayotis—was that he was dead. Like Eugene Järvi from Idaho, Kayotis had visited his home country, Lithuania, the previous year, but had become ill. He wrote friends from his hospital in Memel, that he intended to stay indefinitely in the Baltic country and that his trailer house, on blocks in a worker's camp near Convair's missile assembly plant on the outskirts of Detroit would be rented in the interim. Then the letters trickled and stopped. A small family moved in and sent their rent checks to a real estate agent in Cicero, Illinois.

Kayotis, once immersed in the Bohemian French Quarter of Quebec, left the dead man's passport off at a KGB drop and assumed yet another identity. He got on the Lake Steamer to Detroit, but disembarked at Rochester, complaining of sea-sickness. Peeling twelve hundred dollar bills out of a sheet-film holder he bought a surplus Jeep with an all-weather top and drove to Eastman Kodak where he stocked up on 35mm and 8x10 color film. Then he bought a used Deardorff view camera to supplement his Contax, and a sleeping bag.

On Thanksgiving day, 1948, Emil Goldfus, of Manhattan—artist-photographer, wheeled onto US 33, westbound. Aside from his identification, he carried a letter of introduction from a West Berlin stock photo agency, outlining his assignment to photograph the Rocky Mountains and the Golden West.

On the same day, the Assistant Director of KGB, American Sector, moved a blue-headed pin on a wall map from Rochester to Chicago. Anatol Stoyanov followed the route planned for Colonel Rudolf Ivanovich Abel: Idaho, Washington, Berkeley and Los Alamos.

The Assistant Director put his thick hands on the radiator. Lukewarm!

Stoyanov slipped into his gloves and locked his office door. Should a party functionary try to enter unannounced, it would be simple enough to regain his content composure before opening the door. Gloves would be a complaint.

He opened a book that contained clippings from American newspapers and magazines. One article, from *The Washington Post*, by a woman, featured a photograph of Captain Benjamin Mount, the American version of the Peoples' Submarine Engineer, Captain, First Rank, Konstantin Osopovitch Kulov.

Stoyanov snickered as he read Betsy Kirkland's article:

". . . in order to guarantee electric power for the seventies and eighties—for our children, and our grandchildren, it is imperative that we back industry now, before the atom gets side-tracked by the military . . . and, as Doctor Gunn said, 'the atom must be used to turn wheels . . .' "

Fools, thought the Assistant Director. Those *wheels* are under howitzers; they turn propellers and activate missiles.

There was a lot to learn from America, not the least of which was *repetition*, the core of the American dream—through their huge machine called "Advertising". What is advertising but a capitalist's manifesto. Promises no less empty than the five-year plans, the difference being that the profit in America went to the rich, not the government. Is it better that the rich hold sway? Stoyanov shrugged *no*, and he believed it, regardless of "inconsistencies" within the Party. These would be ironed out, but one could never iron out the animus of self-perpetuating greed unless the books were open. Stoyanov *believed* that the two systems were equally bad—or good, and that made fair game.

Chapter 15

HMS *Comet* skimmed south, down the narrow channel past Snab Sands and Rampside Pier, a breakwater that extended some half mile into the harbor of Barrow-in-Furness, an industrial town of England that looked over the Irish Sea.

The sleek, black craft, its low conning tower and decks awash, snaked around Cas Isle and scraped her keel on Foulney Twist shoal before nosing west past the lighthouse at Haw's Point into the Irish Sea. It was warm for the first of April. Sunning their bleak faces on the station tower were two British Naval officers and a wizened civilian shrouded in a Burberry raincoat.

"Vickers-Armstrong did a top-ho job on this boat—fitting in some creature comforts. Cold bastards, those Huns," the mustached officer tamped down his pipe mixture of Rattray's Three Noggins. "Only one thing wrong, the bloody fuel is so combustible that we canna' smoke while underway. So for ol' Mulford it's either chewing tobacco or m' cold pipe." *Comet* rounded Hilpsford Point and edged into deeper waters to evade several surf-casting fishermans' lead missiles. " 'At's it Oliver, m'boy; we wouldn't want to collect our dues by gettin' skulled by our own people, now. One thing, Ben, about Barrow—it's not like Portsmouth or Rosyth, with all the gawkin' tourists about. It's a wonder we have any secrets at all in this man's Navy. Now, where was I? Ah, yes—my glorious pipe. This tobacco here—it's from Edinburgh—is so good that ye needn't light up." Mulford sucked in deeply.

"It functions more like a baby's teething nipple, I'd say."

"Come now, Ben; you know I'm really practicing for a nice, round woman's tit. Here, now, Oliver," he addressed the boat's commander, "I 'ope yer not offended by m' language, but where else can a man talk free?"

Lieutenant Commander Oliver Casell kept a straightforward military demeanor. "You are most certainly right, sir."

"You're damn right I'm right, Oliver. Some day you'll be able to swear like the rest of us, but without a war, it'll be that proverbial cold day in hell before it happens."

"I'm looking forward to it, sir," Oliver cracked a forced grin, then picked up the sound-powered intercom. "Stand by to dive." Casell waited courteously as his elders descended through the hatch, then followed as the cox'n dogged it behind him.

A flurry of activity pinned Ben against the periscope in the confined control room of His Majesty's experimental boat. It seemed as if the entire boat's complement of nineteen were all in the same compartment at once.

Ben had been briefed earlier about the turbines; they were driven by a superheated mixture of steam and carbon dioxide produced by diesel oil combustion in an atmosphere of decomposing hydrogen peroxide. The "closed" system of a German scientist manufactured its own oxygen, eliminating the need of natural air. The *Comet* motor, an enhanced version of the unit captured at the war's close, had one major inherent flaw——the intense heat required that the engine compartment be evacuated of crew. Temperatures in excess of 160 degrees were generated during operation.

"I forgot to tell ye, Ben," whispered Moxie, "In a boat this small, it pays to be like Casell here. 'E likes men as well as women . . ."

"Rule two, paragraph five, His Majesty's Naval dissertation on picking crews for tight quarters," Oliver joked, ". . . in submersibles of less than 400 tons, it is advisable to discern the sexual proclivities of applicants lest performance be affected by the proximity of bodies . . ." The younger officer looked at his watch and changed from a witty to a grim composure.

Oliver signalled the second officer by hand.

"Stand by," a controlled voice replied.

"Turn out the foreplanes."

"Close all vents."

"Flood."

The crew scrambled to valves and levers and those not on dive duty held on as the bow dipped sharply and the RPMs increased.

"There's another thing about *Comet*," shouted Mulford over the din, "Sometimes the controls don't respond until you give them an order in German."

"Since it was a German boat," quipped Ben, "you should have given it a sauerkraut name, like . . . the *Blitzwurst*. Who knows, it might have meant an extra knot or two."

"Oliver, make that recommendation to Whitehall," Moxie hung on as the motor crew squirmed past, and into the bow. One of them, Danny Towers from Londonderry in Northern Ireland, could not avert a sixth-sense glance from Ben Mount, whose sharp-honed ability to pick up alien vibrations was as good off England as it was in the Washington, DC jungle.

"Periscope depth, sir," the tube whined up.

"Thank you, Simms," Casell pressed into the ocular and swung the scope a full circle. "Looks like all clear."

"Then let's go," Moxie squared off.

"Down scope—seventy feet and trim."

"See this console," Mulford pointed, "it's a remote for the propulsion system. We can control it from here without scalding ourselves. Everything back 'o that heat shield: ventilation, auxiliary helm, and the pumps as well."

The knotmeter indicator was steady at six, a normal maximum underwater speed.

"Rig for high," Oliver waited.

"All rigged, sir."

"Full ahead."

"Aye, sir," the chief engineer eased the throttle forward.

"Jesus," Ben's jaw dropped as the indicator moved . . . seven . . . eight . . . nine . . . He riveted on the guage, daring not to let his claustrophobia take hold. Ten . . . eleven . . . twelve . . .

"As they say, you ain't seen *nuttin* yet," Moxie laughed.

Ben held tight to a conduit as the speed approached twenty knots. "Incredible—to think that these boats were almost ready. We would have been wiped out." The turbine's 2500 horsepower thrummed through the deck and into Ben's very bones—imparting to him an exhilaration that he would never forget.

"Our poor blokes upstairs wouldn't ha' even picked up this infernal machine on the Asdic . . ." lamented Mulford.

"And the Soviets are developing more of these?" Ben was aware of a blast of heat from behind, like the heat from a glowing pot-belly stove.

"They've got double what the Allies got, and that without sinking even one German warship. I'll never understand your Mister Roosevelt for knuckling under to those Siberians."

"Unofficially, I'm with you," Ben loosened his collar and glared at the aft bulkhead.

"The Russkies must be 'avin the same problem," Moxie

wiped his brow with a sleeve. "However, they'll have better use for these contraptions—as ice melters!"

"Have your engineers tried rocket ceramics?"

"We're working on it."

Stoker Towers considered the options. For 5000 sterling, he'd have had a go at Churchill himself. That the IRA had given him the job was enough in itself; any way of weakening the English was worth it, especially alienating the Americans. What was the life of one obscure Naval officer when balanced against the injustices of the crown? 5000 pounds. He might even 'disappear' with a stake like that. Maybe Australia.

The American would be around for three day's tests aboard the *Comet*. If he couldn't be eliminated at sea, he could be stalked ashore. Yes, it would be easier on shore. But how? Danny absentmindedly toyed with his rigging knife awl.

"Give it a bit more," urged Mulford. "Let's try for a nice round twenty-five, like it says in the specs."

Casell checked the instruments; the speed hovered at twenty-three knots and they'd been running for only twenty minutes. There was fuel enough to run for five hours. Over a hundred miles at top speed! The Lieutenant-Commander gave the order.

"Whoa," Ben gulped as the temperature indicator jumped along with the speed. It stopped at the limit pin: 200 degrees! At twenty-five knots the hull began to shudder and a black eye-searing jet of smoke puffed from the bulkhead hatch. Casell grabbed the fuel throttle and pulled back.

It was jammed.

The smoke intensified and backed up through the ventilating system. The control room was darkening and racked with coughing.

"Where's the fuel cut-off?" Ben shouted over the din.

"Get 'er up. Hurry," Mulford took over as Casell seemed to be in a temporary daze. The planesmen held their controls to full rise and the hull groaned as it strove to tear out of its line of horizontal momentum. Slowly, *Comet* nosed up and all grabbed for handholds lest they slide back to the heat shield. The 400-ton steel projectile bolted toward the surface at twenty knots, and amidst a geyser of foam, shot free, leaping half its length out of the Irish Sea like a crazed whale. With a crash that shattered glass dials and bulbs, *Comet* landed harshly on its belly, rolled to port and righted itself.

In the sooty blackness below, Ben had found the fuel cut-off and thrown the lever. *Comet* sped along the surface, planing and dipping erratically until the fuel lines had been exhausted and the hatch opened, belching black smoke like an ancient sea-going locomotive. The crew climbed out, dazed and coughing, their faces covered with oily soot.

Gathering on the forward deck because of the heat aft, the crew stood head count. All present except—

"Captain Mount," Mulford repeated.

Nobody answered.

The veteran Commander flung his pipe overboard and tore off his service jacket and shirt. He drenched the shirt overboard and wrapped it around his head as he climbed up the tower and went down through the hatch.

A long minute later, he emerged, carrying a limp figure. Eager hands reached up and lowered Ben Mount to the deck as Moxie climbed down. " 'Ere, let's have a look at him," Moxie pushed through the inexperienced sailors. "Nasty crack on 'is head—Oliver, get on the wireless and call a boat and a doctor . . ." Mulford pressed down and up on Ben's chest.

"Ow," Ben blinked and felt the side of his forehead.

"Ye must have cracked yer noggin when we hit the water. Good thing we had a muster, or that smoke would ha' done ye in for sure."

Danny Towers sat on the bow, clinging to the fending

wire. Feeling something in his pocket, he reached in and palmed it. He'd forgotten in the confusion! Leaning over, he dipped his hand into the slapping waves and let a heavy spanner drop, unseen.

"It's been a long time since I shouted you a brew, Ben," Moxie said, as they sat at the bar of the Imperial Hotel, overlooking Barrow's harbour, a squarish basin formed by long Walney Island—a wildlife preserve—and a stone jetty from the mainland.

Moxie downed his second shot of Duggan's Dew O' Kirkintilloch as Ben took small sips from a huge stein of ale. "Well, what do you think of Vickers?"

"First rate yard. If we get anywhere with *Neptune*, I'll recommend that the British version be built here."

"Don't count us out yet, Ben. I'll take a little heat anytime over your radioactivity. Soon we'll have better insulation and an extra cooling intake for anything over twenty knots. You can 'ave your uranium and plutonium. I 'ere that stuff makes you bald and sterile . . ."

"In that case, I'll have to make babies fast."

"Naw! You'll be marrying Betsy?"

Mount nodded sheepishly.

"MacDoon," Mulford jumped up from his stool, "did ye hear that? My friend is going to take the big step. Give us a round for everyone—" he eyed the crowded tables—"at the bar."

"Aye, Commander—and you're fortunate that we're not as full as yesterday." The bartender drew three beers for a group near the taps.

"So, laddie; when's the day?"

"Around the end of May."

"I'll be there—if I'm invited!"

"3000 miles to kiss the bride?" Ben hiccuped over his beer.

"I have gone further . . ."

"For a kiss?"

"Mon, I shall not incriminate myself. Now . . . we have got to arrange a bachelor party. I'll get a few o' th' blokes together, and we'll put you on an aircraft in the morning. It's about time you got drunk like a man. Things like this do not happen often."

"Do you mean a *first* marriage?"

"I suppose, mon. Say, how about a round of golf this afternoon with the yard superintendent?"

"I only play stickball; we didn't have much grass where I grew up." Ben's beer stein wavered. Only two fingers to go.

"Stickball? You mean a stick, and a ball? Is it anything like your baseball?" Moxie ordered a third Scotch.

"It is, except that the game stops everytime a car drives over the playing field."

"Can't the traffic be re-routed?" Mulford spun round once on his stool as a tight-skirted hostess wafted by.

"Can't be. Stickball has to be played in the street."

"Why is that?"

"Because of the sewersh . . . sewers."

"I give up. You'll be all right till the party, then?"

"I'm going up to see the ruins of Furness Abbey, in the 'Vale of the deadly nightshade.' "

"Eh?"

"Have you seen the ruins?" Ben opened a travel folder and held a picture of the Abbey in front of Moxie's mustache.

"Can't say I'm much for ruined churches—or new ones for that matter."

Leaving his bicycle in a rack, Ben paid a shilling admittance to historic Furness Abbey. He was happy to have come when he did because the exhibits were to close in a week until October. In addition, there weren't many tourists—and no children. One of Ben's practices was to try to be alone in a Museum, alone with the particular painting or sculpture that he was interested in. It made him nervous to view a work of art at the same time as a stranger, so he would wait patiently until the room or area was vacant, or nearly so, then swoop in and study the piece for as long as he was alone.

Peeking and darting into one room after another, he admired the fine red sandstone transept and Jacobean windows . . . the convoluted arches on the cloister wall, and the vaulted ceilings.

Methodically, Ben penciled off all the points of interest until but one remained—the Infirmary. According to the guidebook, the two praying stone effigies of Norman warriors in full armor were among the best, if not the best of their kind in the world. It promised to be the highlight of Furness Abbey.

After a short wait at the entrance to the 14th century room, Ben went in; gloriously alone with history. High ceilings, empty halls on either side. Elbow room and such a change from the nemesis of interior claustrophobia. Small apartment rooms, small submarines, small toilets. Oh, for the grand scale of Piranesi!

He approached the closer of the stone figures. Prone on his back, with bullet-like helmet, chain mail and armadillo armor, the knight's broadsword lay on his torso—hilt partially covered by praying gauntlets. Ben ran his hand over the striated chisel marks of the figure's powerfully hewn stone shoulder and along the arm.

There was something amiss. The effigy was twisted, askew. Larger than life, the heroic, heavy stone lid was at an angle to the supporting rectangular pedestal. It was hollow and Ben peered into the triangular opening at the corner under the shoulder.

The sarcophagus was empty!

Had there been a mummy within?

Had it been stolen?

Something was afoot—or was it the big stein of ale he'd

had earlier that afternoon? Sense of symmetry disturbed and appalled at such wanton desecration, Ben hurried from the room in search of the custodian. Hardly had he left, when an elderly gentleman, wearing a Burberry raincoat similar to his, sallied in and leaned over to read a descriptive plaque. Crouching behind the sarcophagus, Danny Towers, in mufti, and a beefy accomplice were unaware that their quarry had left.

In one lunge they were upon the hapless tourist, a deadly wire garroting him by the neck as a sack was pulled over his bulging eyeballs.

When Ben came back with a guard, he was bewildered and meekly apologised. The heavy effigy lid was in perfect position on its base. Dismayed, he ascribed his plight to an hallucination brought on by the influence of W.E. Mulford, and continued his tour of the Abbey.

Chapter 16

"Ben," the gaunt admiral tried to lift his head, but fell back on his pillow weakly, "I'm serious—and you know, a Kirkland is as ornery as they come—but this," he tapped his chest, "those fag doctors say everything's gonna be all right. Bullshit. I figure I've got a fifty-fifty chance."

"Dad," Betsy puffed up his pillow and tried to calm him down. "Don't be so . . ." She looked away.

"Look Bets; at fifty-fifty I can't lose. One way I'm with you, the other I'm with your mother."

Betsy nodded into her handkerchief and one hand felt blindly for Ben's. The admiral smiled. "That's what I like, Ben—someone to care for my Bets. Promise me, Ben. If . . . you'll take care of my Bets. And that's an order."

"Aye, aye, sir. In fact I've been thinking that it's about time I settled down a little, and, well . . ."

"Say it, man." Gar Kirkland struggled up on his elbows.

"If I may, I'd like to ask your permission to—"

"Permission granted. It's about time you put in for my

daughter, but better late, as the schoolteacher said. Hey, how long have I got; I mean till visiting hours are over? This is the night I go on a countdown.'' Gar winked at the nurse.

"How 'bout that, sweetie?"

"You've got ten minutes, and then I take over." The buxom nurse struck a provocative pose.

"I'm looking forward to it; say Bets, I've got to talk a few minutes with my future son-in-law. Man talk."

Ben pressed Betsy's hand, then reached for the umbrella they'd brought because of the forecast. She dried her eyes and smiled. Ben had insisted on smuggling an airlines jigger bottle of Red Label into the hospital, inside the folded umbrella. She followed the nurse out into the corridor.

Ben snapped the umbrella open and extracted the tiny bottle of Scotch, peeled off the cap and was about to pour it into a bedside glass when Gar snatched it out of his hand.

"Son, do you realize there's water in that there glass?" Gar tipped it back and guzzled it down, then ceremoniously dropped the empty bottle into the waiting umbrella. "First mission accomplished, Captain Mount," he sighed and slumped back. "Let's get on to the next operation. Are you with me?" Kirkland spoke as if he was on a ship's bridge.

"Right, sir," Ben played the game.

"Betsy told me you were ready to bury the tomahawk."

"It takes two, sir—"

"Gar!"

"Gar."

"That's good, son, a right smart answer. It takes two to do anything in this—" he looked right and left—"fuckin' world."

"You're fuckin' A right, Gar."

"Don't make me start laughing, Ben—now the major operation, damn that word, is *Operation Neptune*. Right?"

"Right, sir . . . I mean Gar."

"Just in case," Gar tapped his chest again, "I want to lay it on the line. I've seen my share of men buy the farm in my time, and who am I to expect different? Where was I?"

"*Neptune.*"

"Neptune, right; funny how Neptune, the Roman god of *fresh* water beat out Poseidon, huh?"

"Must have been some fight."

"Or Neptune had a better press agent." Gar smothered a cough and reached for his water glass. "Let's make it quick, I don't want to spoil my chances with sweetie nurse." He turned grim and pale. "I know you'll be all right with my Betsy, but there's something else." Gar sipped water through a bent plastic straw, then fell back, exhausted and panting. "I'm OK, don't worry. Now I want you to know that I've put in a few words to Bureau of Ships, and the Secretary of the Navy about *Neptune*. Somebody had to. If this country only knew what a head start those Russkies have on submarines—well, I want to tell you Ben, that the U.S. Navy, and the U.S. people, and most probably, the whole goddamned free world needs *Neptune*. We've got to take the helm again—regardless of what my politics are, what yours are . . . what separates us. Now don't get us flag admirals wrong. We're sons o' bitches, but deep down we're on your side. It takes time, like in all hierarchies. You might find it tough to make rank, but hang in there. Do you understand, Ben?"

"I know I've stepped on too many toes . . ."

"Ben, we're losing the foot race, so maybe what you've been doing ain't all wrong. But officially we can't admit it; there are too many guys out there who won't understand, and they're right. Get what I'm tryin' to say?"

"Got it, Gar."

"Enough said then—and one more thing. I know what you're going through. This is no easy establishment to buck, if you know what I'm getting at. And they don't take easy to people who are—"

"I know I'm different, Gar, but so are the Russians."

"Guess you got somethin' there, boy. Let's shake on that."

It rained that night, and a small, empty Scotch bottle fell from Ben's umbrella. Ben and Betsy picked up the pieces and walked a block to the nearest trash can. It was warm for January.

Gar Kirkland died the next morning.

Betsy and Ben were married in late May—a small ceremony at the admiral's home on Kent Island, across from the Academy. As threatened, Moxie Mulford flew in from England and Ben's Naval Propulsion group mixed with Betsy's newspaper chums in the heated pool built earlier that year. Viewed from the widow's walk atop the main house, the pool was in the shape of twin dolphins.

"He wanted so much to commission the pool," Betsy recalled. "He planned to order all submariners to swim a lap underwater before they could qualify for a drink."

"I'd a swum it blindfolded *and* submerged for a drop o' Duggan's Dew o' Kirkintilloch," Commodore W.E. 'Moxie' Mulford lit into the soft-shell crabs with ouzo after they were flambéed.

Jack McCrary sent apologies for being unable to attend, and Senator Southerland was reported as having a recurrence of a nervous ailment—the result of a traumatic experience a few months earlier.

Ben amused the party by demonstrating a makeshift periscope that he'd designed to use with the snorkeling tube in the pool. By nightfall, Moxie had managed to find some firecrackers and had had to be restrained from throwing them at Ben before he was completely submerged.

There wasn't much time for a honeymoon. But for Betsy, it would have been "put off" till after the Idaho trip. But she insisted that Ben get away from his work. They drove to the Shenandoah and stopped at mountain inns and motels until they found one that was secluded, quiet and provocative.

At Hawksbill Gap, 4000 feet up in the Blue Ridge chain they registered at a precariously perched stone "castle", complete with cylindrical tower and "magic fingers" beds.

Sunset enhanced the river, a meandering silver ribbon to the bright west. When Betsy saw Ben take a briefcase out of the car, she made him hand it over and locked it in the trunk, detaching one key from Ben's key chain.

"You can have your briefcase only once a day," she bargained, "and that is after we—" she looked coyly at the big bed.

"I may need the specs more than once a day," Ben counted sternly on his fingers.

"Now I know why you were picked for the *Neptune* project," Betsy kicked her shoes off as the blinding golden sun broke through a stand of pine, casting fanciful patterns that seemed to change the very room itself into a throbbing forest.

The Argonne Laboratory in Chicago . . . Bettis' Lab in Pittsburg . . . The Hanford Works on the mighty Columbia . . . Berkeley . . . Los Alamos . . . the lava fields of Idaho. Ben's unlined raincoat and spare toothbrush were permanent residents of his blue Air Force bag.

In the midst of all this came the promotion review board. Ben didn't make admiral. Some said that he'd stepped on too many toes—was too pushy; others, that he didn't have enough sea duty. The Secretary of The Navy, in self defense, pointed out that there was no slot for that rank for an engineering officer. There were even a few whispers about anti-Semitism.

The early fifties was a time for "loyalty" in these United States. The idea of Communism became a dayglow red flag with the entry of China into Korea and the people cheered as a gruff Senator from Wisconsin entered the arena.

Klaus Fuchs had been found out and the ripples of Soviet espionage reaching out, a vast, spidery network, were caught in glaring klieg lights. The inquisition called for blood—as no doubt the enemy would do, had their atomic secrets been divulged. The Rosenbergs were condemned and scores of suspects charged or deported. In Michigan a beauty contest winner was dubbed Miss Loyalty instead of Miss Detroit.

Even former General of The Army, George C. Marshall was denounced as the center of an international conspiracy against the nation. J. Robert Oppenheimer, the brains behind the bomb, was cashiered because of two reasons— his refusal to work on the hydrogen bomb, and his friendships with scientists of the leftish persuasion. There had been talk of his wife's "parties" with Klaus Fuchs at Los Alamos, and David Greenglass . . .

It was also a time for the underdog and the press was quick to capitalize. *Life* magazine found a story in Captain Benjamin Mount and the mighty machine put pressure on the Pentagon after receiving a "hell, no," and a slammed-down phone as an answer to a request for an interview. It took a direct order from the Secretary of the Navy to get Ben to agree to be photographed.

The lead article declared: ". . . there had been much more progress on the A-Sub than the tight-lipped AEC would have the public believe," and it described "beady-eyed and frugal" Ben Mount as going down in history as the Robert Fulton of the Atom. That the atomic submarine was not a challenge to the captain. It was an "obsession born of necessity."

By the summer of 1951, the gaunt captain was a national figure, along with Willie Mays, Ed Murrow and Patti Page. At Oak Ridge it was, however, respected that the captain, when visiting the plant, expected Mozart to get equal time on the jukebox with *Tennessee Waltz*.

Early one morning in September, an unusual craft submerged off Kent Island in the Chesapeake. Shortly after, the mallard population of South Point was scattered by the sound of explosions. Not hunter's shotguns, but depth bombs.

On the beach a lone turtle-necked figure at a portable easel washed in some cerulean blue for sky on his watercolor block pad, then scrambled behind a boulder that faced south toward Poplar Island. He unwrapped a sixty-power spotting scope, tightened its swivel nut and set the blunt tripod on a gull-whitened rock. His hawknose level with the eyepiece, the artist focused. At a distance of a mile, he watched the naval buoy tender. It was tied up to a channel marker. "Normal maintenance" to anyone who didn't know. But Colonel Rudolph Ivanovich Abel knew. The powerful scope sucked 6000 feet into 100, hardly more than the distance from home plate to the pitcher's rubber, a distance that kept few secrets. The Colonel's analytical mind was clicking and recording: the temperature, the wind, the water surface and tide—as only a man with many facets could. Abel was adept with classic guitar, spoke five languages, painted admirably and was a superb craftsman in the normal spy arts of photography, ham radio and mechanical deceit. His long fingers gripped the instrument tightly as an object popped to the surface next to the tender. The sleek form filled half the 100 foot field of view of the spotting scope, a fifty-foot long model of the experimental nuclear submarine! He watched patiently as a shock of white hair bobbed among the larger boat's crew on the fantail. Grown men playing at war. Instinctively, Abel ducked as the white-haired man seemed to look directly at him.

The painted black model indicated a miniaturization scale of about seven to one, since the first photos sent by Järvi from Arco projected the prototype to be 350 feet overall. With a diameter of thirty feet, *Neptune*'s model research components would have a vertical measurement of not more than thirty divided by seven, or 4.3 feet—an important consideration in "diverting" such components in transit.

The agent trembled with excitement as the model submerged again and scaled-down depth charges erupted under the direction of the energetic captain whose photo had appeared in *Life*.

As the tender, towing its charge, chugged across the Chesapeake, the artist brushed a covering sepia tint over the foreground of his painting, obliterating a code which recorded the test. The code would remain invisible until the water-color paper was backlighted with a cobalt blue. Abel finished his painting of the beach and, while packing up, concerned himself with a more pressing task, the transmission of data from an agent in Dr. Teller's group at Los Alamos. The first hydrogen bomb had been successfully detonated in the Pacific. And Stoyanov was the impatient type. In addition to all this, the Colonel was instructed to set up a new agent who would soon be arriving from Stockholm, under cover as a picture agency photographer. The KGB was anxious to install an expert on submarines in the states, someone who could weed out the nonessential data and reduce the danger inherent in multiple drops. A former German U-boat officer, he had acquired the necessary "legend" and was known as Peter Pryda, a specialist in nature photography.

"That's very nice," the woman's voice startled Abel. He turned about slowly, calculating his next move, were it a trap. Relieved at the sight of an attractive woman, seemingly alone and oblivious to his calling, Abel relaxed, thankful that he'd already wrapped up the scope.

"I hope I'm not trespassing," the Colonel had decided that a French accent was most appropriate in disguising whatever Russian was noticeable.

"Beauty belongs to everyone," Betsy Mount twirled her summer-blue skirt and came closer to the easel.

"Besides," she added, "you're standing below the high-tide line."

"Then I will be most grateful if you don't see me walking back to my automobile."

"Done. You know, I really like your painting. Is it for sale? We have just the spot for it. You see, we've only been married a few months and we're still decorating. Our house is just up the beach. I know my husband would be delighted."

"I tell you, madame. I cannot sell it this moment because my gallery, she expect to see it first. Perhaps I find out and I write you. No?" Abel hadn't counted on this.

"May I?" Betsy reached for a charcoal pencil on the easel.

"Allow me," Abel took a fountain pen and a small spiraled pad from his paint box. "My name is Emil . . ."

"Glad to meet you; I'm Betsy Mount, Mrs. B. Mount will do, Kent Island, Maryland."

"Mount, like mountain?"

"Oui, Monsieur. Like *montagne*."

"I see," Abel forced a smile and hurriedly dismantled his easel. "I will get in touch with you."

"Say, Emil; my husband will be getting home soon. He's been over at the Academy. Perhaps you could come over and show him the painting while you're here . . ."

"Good idea, Madame Mount—but not proper, and besides it would be more fun to surprise him. No?"

"Then you'll sell it?" Betsy squealed with delight.

"I won't sell it to anyone else."

"Then I won't watch you going back to your car."

"Madame," Abel bowed graciously, "it's a deal."

The miniature reactor, engine connections and equipment placements were examined for simulated damage by the toy depth bombs. Components were shifted and strengthened, then the model was towed out and bombed again and again until the most efficient formulas were decided upon.

The next step was a full-scale test. Ben requested the use of two of SS *Ulea*'s seven compartments to lash in prototypes of *Neptune*'s instrumentation components and propulsion units, short of an actual reactor. The obsolete submarine, used for testing "Guppy" equipment was rigged with remote controlled steering and diving as well as a battery of motion picture cameras and shock-testing sensors. The crewless boat was depth-charged with the latest weapons in simulated war conditions.

Many were the contractors who received a package containing a print of the test film, some chunks of their broken components and a sign lettered "SHOCKPROOF!" courtesy of Ben, the showman.

An odd sight at Groton was the *Gato* Class boat *Haddock*. She lay alongside a dock for six weeks. For all purposes she looked like a mothball boat without the cocoons. But the boat gurgled and huffed, blew garbage from its tubes and watched the shoreside goings-on with both periscopes.

Inside were 54 men, a complete crew, including cooks and captain. It was a test of the life-support systems that were designed for *Neptune*: oxygen regeneration equipment, carbon monoxide detoxification units, refrigeration and air-conditioning and sanitary systems. It was also the first test of man crammed into the extended psychological time warp of nuclear existence.

The bearded crew emerged and were adjudged healthy enough considering the ordeal, then interviewed and debriefed by mental, physical and mechanical specialists, and the findings incorporated into the final plans of *Neptune*.

The keel was laid in June of 1952. President Harry S. Truman led the list of notables attending at Groton while Ben Mount watched from an obscure seat deep in the grandstand.

Some weeks later, Ben was called to the Pentagon at the behest of the Secretary of the Navy. Finding himself surrounded by reporters and cameramen in the lobby, he asked what was going on and was told that he was going to receive a medal.

During the ceremony an aide read:

". . . he has held tenaciously to a single, important goal through discouraging frustration and opposition, and has consistently advanced the submarine thermal reactor well beyond all expectations; his efforts have led to the laying of the keel of the first nuclear powered ship well in advance of its original schedule. His careful and accurate planning, his technical knowledge and ability to clarify and resolve the many problems arising between the AEC, The Bureau of Ships, and the contractors have proven a contribution of inestimable value to the country's security and reflect great credit upon Captain Mount and the Naval Service . . ."

The Secretary of the Navy pinned the legion of Merit on Ben's gray civilian suit lapel and shook his hand so vigorously that the slight captain recoiled in pain.

Flashbulbs popped as a diagrammatic scale model of *Neptune* was unveiled. The Secretary was embarrassed; not one top-level admiral had shown up, despite invitations. The highest rank attending was another captain, a friend of Mount's.

After a short speech protesting that the medal should be cut into pieces and distributed among half a dozen associates, Ben decided to celebrate by taking a weekend off with Betsy and his month-old daughter, Deborah.

"We've just got to have more zirconium." It was Lieutenant-Commander Cal Crowe, calling from Idaho where he was liaison with the Westinghouse engineering group.

"Well, buy some, goddamn it," Ben cradled the phone on his bony shoulder as he sorted out mail.

"At a thousand bucks a gram?"

Ben gulped and did some mental calculations. "Okay, Cal, so it's about a half million a pound. So how many pounds do you need? Who's the supplier?"

"But Ben, that's just it. All the suppliers together can't put together more than a breadbox full—and we need enough for a bakery window. It's all produced in labs by hand."

"Damn," Mount slammed a sheaf of letters down on his desk. "If we could build the bomb in two years, we should be able to build our own zirconium in less time. The formula's no secret; right?"

"Sure, but the machinery doesn't exist—"

"So we'll build the machinery first. Don't worry about it, Cal. We need super bearings to stand super heat, and we can't stop right in the fucking middle of this job. From now on," Ben boomed, "you can call me Captain Zirconium."

Mount cornered some private industry acquaintances and informed them that the Navy was looking to change a few contracts on the carrier program. Within a month, certain machinery had been modified and by the end of January, 1953 zirconium was being produced quickly and cheaply.

A Congressional committee later queried Westinghouse as to how they managed to come up with the rare metal, to which they answered: "Captain Mount ordered it."

An engineering officer working at the Argonne Laboratory in Chicago phoned Ben with the news that he'd been promoted and had the commission in hand but the Navy had not told him where to go and get sworn in.

Mount perused the problem, then replied "Go find a Bible; buy one if you can't find or steal one, then call me back."

When the officer called back, Mount told him to put his left hand on the Bible and to raise the other. Next, he read the oath from his Naval Handbook and congratulated the officer:

"You are now a full commander in the U.S. Navy."

As a result of his success, Ben was given a free hand in hiring his own help from the ranks and civilian sources. Normal navel channels were incapable of finding reliable and talented specialists with standard interview procedure, so the Bureau sat back and let Captain Mount use his bizarre but effective methods of interrogation and evaluation.

One young officer decried the paperwork in his current job and the fact that nobody ever read his reports. Mount told the nuclear aspirant to stop submitting those reports. The lieutenant replied that he couldn't because his commanding officer maintained a "tickle" file, a card on each subordinate, who if remiss, would have his card pulled automatically for reprimand.

Mount puzzled the enigma, then shot back: "Why don't you take your card out of the tickler file?"

Several days later, Mount received a call that included the pre-arranged code phrase, "tickler complete."

"You're hired," Ben answered, "I'm putting your transfer through." The condition, of course, was absolute secrecy or Ben would have been court-martialed, but such was his uncanny sense about people that he was not compromised.

On a higher level, one of the senior admirals recommended a friend for Mount's program saying: "Jim, here, has had over twenty years of sea duty which should come in handy . . ."

An interminably dull interview ensued with Jim. When it was over, Ben phoned the admiral . . . "I've seen your man with twenty years' sea duty. Could you send me a good, used deck winch instead? Some of those have had *thirty* years' sea duty.''

Ben's attitude toward standard procedure did not help his popularity among the Pentagon brass. One admiral's cigar dropped out of his mouth when he read a bulletin Mount had posted outside of his headquarters.

IN THIS OFFICE AND JURISDICTION, RANK DOES NOT DETERMINE PRIORITY. IF A CIVIL-IAN IS MORE COMPETENT THAN A NAVAL OFFICER IN DOING THE SAME TASK, THEN THE OFFICER WILL REPORT TO THE CIVILIAN. THE SAME HOLDS FOR GS RANKS.

It was determined by project engineers that per given power unit, ships could move faster underwater than on the surface, giving rise to proposals that transports and destroyers be designed for underwater propulsion, where the effect of waves would not have to be overcome. Reports stated that the nuclear alternative would soon revolutionize the old Navy, sending shudders through the establishment admirals and adding black X marks to Ben's personal promotion sheet.

Parallel to building the reactor, a second group of engineers were developing the perfect underwater profile for *Neptune*. It was based on the result of pulling an air-inflated balloon underwater at great speed. The concept, though valid and yielding several extra knots submerged, was held for incorporation into the second generation and a conventional hull was modified to simplify the program and get it afloat. Even so, the hull was much larger than the standard fleet sub design and recalled a period during the 1920's when the world's navies built a series of clumsy dual-purpose submersibles armed with battleship guns and carrying seaplanes in deck hangers. Giantism, a development from German World War One transport subs proved obsolete under diesel propulsion. Now it was being revived— scaled to a new "torpedo", one that fired vertically, through the sea of air and sub-stratosphere; one that was designed to destroy entire cities.

Initially, Westinghouse had proposed a prototype reactor system that spread like a plan, over an area the size of a city block. Components in separate buildings connected by tunnels and covered corridors would be safe as well as easy to maintain and conducive to experimentation and modification.

Captain Mount showed the plan to his naval group and all turned thumbs down. "You see," he told the chief Westinghouse engineer, "I'm not the only one who thinks it can be built better to the size it is intended for. You've got a week to do new drawings, and you've got thirty feet diameter by fifty to fit it into."

Not only did Westinghouse come through, but they revamped the Argonne Laboratory concept of an encapsulated total power package in favor of a "strung out" power take-off. As Mount had known from experience in fleet subs, a way had to be found to allow routine maintenance of moving parts. The problem was solved by allowing for quick radioactivity run-off in secondary components, such as the pumps and heat exchangers.

A frantic call came in from the General Electric site where the back-up liquid sodium reactor was being built: "Captain, we can't get enough quarter-inch steel plate for the Mark A containment sphere. All the big mills are contracted for three months for the *USS Forrestal* and BuShips won't budge . . ."

Ben did some quick thinking. The Hortonsphere at Schenectady was essential. The 225-foot diameter steel sphere was designed to contain an accidental explosion and protect the populated dairyland from radioactive contamination.

During a stint in the Pacific during the war, Ben had been impressed by the way a SeaBee Petty Officer had managed to find emough metal on an atoll in the Marianas to construct a first rate dock for servicing damaged submarines. Bulldozer Boyle went into the construction business after the war, but Ben had cajoled him to lend a "30-day" hand at the onset of the *Neptune* project. Now, almost two years later, "Bulldozer", his job done, had gone back to private industry. No pay or promise could get Boyle back for this one "last job." Finally, in desperation, Ben offered to buy him a drink. Boyle caught the next plane out of Pittsburgh after explaining to his associates that he would never forgive himself if he missed the miracle of Ben Mount buying a drink.

Boyle inveigled a friend in the War Production Board to issue him a directive permitting the acquisition of steel "without affecting the construction of ships under contract." Over the screams of BuShips, he pointed out that the 70,000 ton aircraft carrier, *Forrestal* could wait several months because of working-up delays in the ship's turbines, and that the steel, delivered per contract, would rust in the Newport News shipyard.

Fireworks followed as the steel was routed to Schenectady. Ben, true to his word, ordered drinks and downed his before Boyle. "Bulldozer," he slurred, "I'll buy you another drink if you can find more steel to replace the stuff we stole, and what's more I'll buy it right here and now." Ben's eyes were almost crossed.

"Begorrah, they won't believe it in Pittsburgh," Boyle was stunned, "two miracles in one day."

the steel whale. The submarine section inside the tank was exactly as it would be on *Neptune*, double hulled and completely functional. It contained the reactor and its protective shielding. Extending aft, through the water tank, was the interior hull, ribs showing, of the 64-foot engine room. Missing was the tapered aft section containing the crew's quarters, drive shaft and propellor. The power take-off was attached to a paddle wheel in the tank.

High above, like a spider in a steel web, a bootsole edged cautiously off a girder. It was worn smooth and had a small hole in the center—hardly noticeable because the bootsole was two inches thick. Joseph Elk's right leg was shorter than his left and needed an orthopedic boot. The Nez Perce Indian had not let his deformity keep him from being employed. He was admired by all for overcoming his handicap when he could just as easily have languished on the reservation with the indolents. Joseph was proud of his job as cage elevator operator. He felt like one of the boys, even to his white plastic hard hat, which he decorated with an eagle feather. He flexed his right toes and the thick sole emitted a faint click and whirr. It was more that Joseph felt it rather than heard it. Had an eye been looking through a magnifying glass into the hole in Joseph's boot, it might have seen the tenth of a second reflection of the reactor assembly in the tiny lens—providing the eye and glass were not obstructing the field of view.

The Indian liked his job, but he also liked the extra money he was getting for taking these pictures; one a day since his agreement with the Finn six months earlier. Already his mattress was bulging green in his attic room at Arni Järvi's house. He was impatient for Arni to do as promised: to put the money into a proper bank under another's name. The plan was he would make enough money taking pictures in one year to enable him to buy back the land bordering the Clearwater's south fork that had been stolen from his great-grandfather, Speaking Owl, by ruthless gold-seekers during the gold rush of 1879. In addition, he was reaping revenge on the nation that had allowed its "long-knives" to murder Speaking Owl, who had been described by Idaho historians as "eloquent, sagacious, and noted as an Apollo among the belles of the tribe . . ." He was beginning to gain prominence as a leading spokesman of the anti-white faction of the Nez Perces when he was cut down during the Sheepeater War.

"Joe, let's go," the crane handlers' shouts shocked him out of his reverie.

"Sorry, I didn't hear the whistle," Joe guided his caged platform down to the concrete floor. It was lunchtime. Joe sat and ate his sandwich along with the boys while watching and searching for instruments and machinery that would benefit his assignment. Noting a complex component waiting to be installed, Joseph would casually stretch his afflicted right leg out on a box and flex his toes. The lens was such that everything two yards away or more was in focus. Closing his battered lunch box he noted his "calendar", a series of vertical scratches in the box's blue paint. The last group was due this day for a diagonal scratch, finishing the fourth week. Joseph flicked open his folding knife and scratched in his "Saturday" mark. Tonight he would meet Arni Järvi at the "drop."

The town of Salmon, Idaho, was a good three-hour drive from the north gate of the AEC Testing Center. Far enough away to be spurned by the payday drinkers from the Center, even if the Naked Truth Saloon had the best pinball machines in the state. It was a cozy, safe-feeling town on the Salmon River where it branched out into the Lemhi, nestling amongst three mountain ranges south of the Continental Divide. Nearby was born Sacajawea, the Indian woman who guided Lewis and Clark from Lemhi Pass, across the savage and uncharted wilderness.

The original Naked Truth Saloon had flourished in Boise during the Gold Rush, and closed as the city became respectable at the turn of the century. Shortly after the war, an entrepeneurial army veteran had sunk his mustering-out pay into the establishment after finding an old sign at a Boise auction. Below the saloon's name was a message which read in part:

> "Friends and Neighbors: Having just opened a commodious shop for the sale of liquid fire, I embrace this opportunity of informing you that I have commenced the business of making: Drunkards, paupers and beggars for the sober, industrious and respectable portion of the community to support . . . I will undertake on short notice, for a small sum . . . to prepare victims for the asylum, poor farm, prison and gallows . . . and cause fathers to become fiends, wives widows, and children orphans . . ."

Local people, mostly sheep farmers, sat below the sign which dominated the antique bar, jabbering about the snows that were sure to come before Pearl Harbor Day, and the radiation danger to their sheep, having brought them down from the Bitterroot heights. Surely one mistake in that contraption they were building—or was it already the reason for the sheep's coats being shorter? One good southern breeze out of Arco into the spring grass . . .

Arni was already practicing at a pinball machine when Joseph, wearing his new salt-and-pepper English tweed under a sheepskin clomped in. He picked up a bottle of Shasta beer at the bar and joined the Finn in the dark-wooded rear of the saloon, walls bristling with moose antlers interspaced with framed photographs of proud hunters and fishermen displaying their catches of grizzly bear and cutthroat trout, of cougar and the Chinook salmon.

The Finn, not noted for his abstinence, was experimenting with American-style boilermakers. He dumped his double shot of Canadian Club into a glass of beer as Joseph fed the machine and propelled his first steel ball with a snap of his wrist; an expertise that irritated Arni because he couldn't do it and usually lost as a result. Losers bought the next round of drinks.

True to form, Joseph's first shot caroomed off a barrier pin with such spin that it hit the highest-scoring cushion counter, then proceeded, accompanied with bell clanging and toteboard lights flashing, to roll up additional scores.

29030 . . . 29030 . . . 29030. The steel ball had hit the elusive jackpot, Mount Everest. The bar's patrons gathered round to watch the rare play which opened the way for a 100,000 single roll, numbers corresponding to the height of the world's most famous mountains, in feet. CLANG, the ball ricocheted off Mount McKinley . . . then Chimborazo . . . and Rainier . . .

84340 . . . 84340 . . . 84340! Only 16000 more buys drinks on the house for a year. The Grand Prize! The glistening stainless ball had almost lost its momentum; on its last course before the machine bottom groove, it swerved toward Popocatepetl—over 17000 feet high! And then away toward Pike's Peak, which at a mere 14110 wasn't enough. Suddenly, another swerve, and the lights flashed as the score went up and over the top. Shouts and screams tore out into the street—and then subsided. The score that had flashed for an instant, running digitally over 100,000 had been wiped out by four large, pulsing letters:

TILT

As the only person touching the pinball machine was Arni Järvi, it followed that he had caused the TILT; had also caused the steel ball to defy the laws of gravity by jostling the machine. Nothing short of an earthquake or explosion in the street could jar the foundations of The Naked Truth Saloon. The proprietor let go a deep sigh and went back behind the bar.

"Shee-it," Arni used local vernacular and guzzled the rest of his boilermaker.

"Have one?" Joseph took a paper bag out of his jacket pocket and slid several bright red pistachio nuts on the pinball glass top; red UFOs hovering over snow-capped Kilimanjaro, 19340. He flicked one of the shell-dyed nuts toward Järvi, who picked it up, looked it over, then popped it into his mouth. Järvi despised pistachio nuts, especially nuts that had been glued together by Indians. Järvi rolled the nut into his cheek and put another quarter into the sliding slot. It was now his job to get the minox film that was inside the nut to Walla Walla.

Complicated system, but a certain amount of personal contact was necessary between the impersonal "drops" such as under mailboxes and behind roadsigns. There was always the danger of the CIA intercepting a planted message and staking out its route—catching the whole string of operatives. No, Stoyonov wouldn't like that. Järvi watched his shot bump weakly off a low-scoring cushion and drop into the bottom groove. He thought of the real Arni Järvi and his family: three frozen bodies, thawing and freezing every year, buried somewhere in the woods outside of Oulo in Finland. He wondered whether the bodies, buried since 1933, looked like Peruvian mummies, since they'd not been embalmed.

Bidding a drunken goodbye, the Finn staggered out, bemoaning his depleted funds and teetered toward his old Chevy, leaving Joseph a twenty to square up the bar bill. Huffing frosty clouds, he leaned on the battered old car parked next to his and buttoned up his mackinaw, while simultaneously slipping a tiny, sealed envelope into a pried-up corner of the car's locked trunk lid. The Colonel had worked it all out, making Järvi sign a voucher for each of the little envelopes. Two hundred dollars. Four fifties folded tightly in each of the original twelve envelopes. Enough to buy one acre on the Clearwater south fork.

Norman Benedict squinted through his coke-bottle eye glasses, askew, and pressed on the floor. Boots walked back and forth in the half-inch space between the heavy

door and the saw-dusted plank floor. Norman squelched a
sneeze and slid his polished steel explorer scout mirror
under the door. The poolroom was empty and his broad
behind was eclipsed by one of the three green-felted tables.
Besides, a bell on the front entrance double door would
give him ample warning of a customer. Norman recognized only one pair of boots in the ante-room, his father's.
One of the two strangers wore city shoes, black shoes with
perforated decoration. He slid the mirror as far in as he
dared, just enough to see above the competition table, as it
was called. He waited, scarcely breathing as the balls
clicked and one of the players went round the table for a
cross-side bank shot. He could see a baldish man leaning
over—only his eyes and his nose were visible above the
antique Brunswick. Eyes, piercing like an eagle, but from
his clipped accent not the American Bald Eagle. And he
had a beak that cast a triangular shadow over his tanned
cheek.

"Emil," it was his father's voice, "leave some for
me." But Emil racked off, moving round the table. Deftly
using a bridge for difficult shots, he sank the fourteenth
ball of his straight run to a congratulatory fusillade of cue
stick butts on the floor.

"Ain't nobody run a rack off like that here, except the
bettin' boys," Norman's father boomed out from his high-
chair referee's perch next to the locked door. "And with
good position—pretty good fer a foreigner."

The hawk-nose rumbled two more scores along the canted
oak rails, then missed. "But I'm not a foreigner, I'm from
Brooklyn, born in Manhattan."

"Brooklyn's foreign enough," Big Al Benedict plucked
his Menjou mustache and straightened out the 8-bore buffalo rifle on its wall hooks. Al was proud of the W. W.
Greener gun which once belonged to Czar Alexander II,
and was used on a buffalo hunt in which the Russian was
accompanied by General Custer. Benedict, a man wary of
his enemies, also kept the gun loaded to blow a hole

through the door should he be cornered. His business contacts in Fairbanks were unsavory and ruthless in their dealings with him on real estate, so much so that he feared for his life after accepting "payments." Big Al knew they were working with the Soviets and had a respect for their methods. Emil Goldfus and his associate were different, though the very difference suggested an equally lethal danger—one that a cagey plainsman was at a loss to counter.

The blond man called Peter fussed with his camera as Al ran off five balls and scratched. Emil noted Al's nervousness but said nothing. It would be in his report to Stoyonov; perhaps it was time to replace the Northwestern cover agent.

Norman's glasses slipped off one ear and he uttered his one expletive, "Gawd damn." Nobody in the back room heard, but one of the many cats scurried away, frightened of the outwardly docile youngest son of Big Al. The cats were aware that Norman was the same breed as his brother Leo, the cat killer, who had been committed to the Yakima County Asylum because of a strange ritual he practiced— that of dispatching stray and neighbor's cats with bow and arrow while wearing the warpath regalia of a Yakima Indian medicine man.

Norman pressed his plump right cheek to the floor and listened. Who were these strangers? Business had not been good; Norman, a math major at State University and home for the summer, had seen the books. Garage, so, so. Worse than the year before. Billiard Hall, a loss for 1952. Real Estate, also dwindling in transactions. Where was the money coming from? Had his father sold out and juggled the books? Had he— Norman growled at the thought. His father's gold—his stake to get out of Walla Walla and study art instead of becoming a drab math teacher. With Leo gone he was the heir to a knapsack of twenty-dollar gold pieces. His mother had told him about the gold that had been buried in a cavern in The Craters of The Moon

National Park near Arco, Idaho the year he was born. 1934, when Big Al, rather than convert to paper money in accordance with the Gold Reserve Act, buried the proceeds he'd received from a real estate deal with his Alaskan contacts and moved his business to Walla Walla. His mother had told him about the gold during one of her "bourbonic trances," and then had forgotten. A spasm of total recall brought on by Wild Turkey brand bourbon had described the cavern and its location well enough for Norman to ascertain the lode's existence. He'd counted almost eleven hundred coins before repacking them and replacing the heavy lava slab over the natural safe deposit box. Enough for a fancy new Jaguar convertible and a studio in New York. And a set of new body-building weights. Double-breasted white linen suits. He would show them all, those people who laughed at him because he couldn't grow a beard, because he was 4-F and blind without glasses. Norman's glasses fogged up when he recalled the note he found in his High School yearbook, marking the page on which his picture appeared:

> Indians can grow no beards,
> Neither can Norman.
> Yakimas kill cats,
> And so can Norman.

Click, swish, the scoring beads slid along the overhead wire signalling the game's end. About to slide the mirror back, Norman saw a hand—his father's, by the sleeve— slip a small card into the center table pocket.

Later that night Norman, as usual, swept the floor of saw dust and cigarette butts and hosed out the spitoons while his father was tending to the gas station receipts up the road.

Door locked, he eagerly brushed the felt of the competition table and reached into the center pocket. Finding the card tucked up inside the leather cushion, he quickly read it:

Chapter 18

Emil Goldfus stopped by at the Walla Walla Post Office and picked up a package addressed to him, care of General Delivery. The wrapping bore the stamp of a mail-order house in Boise, Idaho.

That evening, the Colonel prepared a sea food dinner for two, with clams on the half-shell as appetizer.

"I prefer a knife," Abel pressed down on the chromed handle of the clam opener and split the last of a dozen cherrystones. He set them on plates of crushed ice and handed them to Peter Neilson to put into the refrigerator. Next, he dried his hands and selected a screwdriver from his toolkit. As a precaution, he went to the front window of his rented skylighted studio and peered past the windowshade into the street below. Good. A deserted vista. He returned to the pullman kitchen and sat at the table, turning the clam opener around as Peter poured two beers.

"This one," a sensitive fingertip prodded one of the four steel screws that anchored the metal blade stand to the

base wood block. He carefully inserted the screwdriver
into the Phillips slot and backed the screw out several
turns. Pressing down on the block with one hand, he
gripped the screw head with a pair of pliers and pulled
firmly upward. The screw head came off its tiny vertical
spline tracks. Abel smiled as he deftly extracted the tightly
rolled, quarter-inch film cylinder. He was proud of his
handiwork, having machined the screw himself on his
miniature lathe. One more reason that he was the top agent
of KGB's North American sector.

Twenty minutes later, after finishing the clams and turning down the gas flame under the sizzling panned trout,
Abel went into his darkroom, made a few prints and put
them through the hypo and wash.

They studied the blow-ups over coffee. Handing a postcard sized print to Nielson, the Colonel tapped his surgeon's
fingers decisively on the table. "Looks like they've done
it—hooked up the reactor to the power plant."

"Which means," Peter studied the print, "that they'll
have it revved up to full power in about a month."

"Which means, my dear Peter Pryda, that our expedient
plan is now in effect. I wish you luck," Abel raised his
coffee cup in a mock toast. "You know I would go there
myself, but you're such an athlete—one of the prerequi-
sites of a saboteur. And what do you make of this one?"

"It's a chart of the Atlantic Ocean."

"Joseph Elk deserves a bonus for this shot. I do believe
that the Jew captain intends to simulate an Atlantic crossing as a test for the *Neptune* program. Very clever." Abel
tore the prints into small shreds, dropped them into the
sink and set them afire. Then he set a wrapped-up *Double
Bubble* gum on the table.

"Peter, your teeth are younger than mine." He rolled
up the negative film and pressed it back into the hollow
screw, pressed the screw head back on and extracted the
entire unit. He then laid the screw next to the bubble gum
and grinned.

* * *

At dawn the next morning, Nielson set up his tripod and Rolleiflex in the Walla Walla railroad freight yards. The summer sun played on the tops of the Wallowa range to the south, then dipped into the lush plains as the photographer snapped his cable release, capturing Americana for the thirsty readers of Europe. Colorful cabooses, coal and refrigerator cars, with their distinctive stenciled signs: *Northern Pacific, Canadian Pacific* . . . *White Pass & Yukon.* . . . After running off half a roll of film on the Alaskan freight cars, Nielson unwrapped the pack of *Double Bubble* and stuffed it into his mouth. Finishing the roll, he took the pink wad of gum out of his cheeks, pressed the hollow Phillips screw into it and nonchalantly stuck it under the sliding door frame of the blue box car forward of the red caboose emblazoned with the *White Pass & Yukon* seal.

Two days later, the pink wad would be plucked off at the Fairbanks freight yard, the screw removed, and driven into the wooden stemhead of a fishing trawler that wended down the Yukon River once a week after delivering its cargo of salmon.

For Nielson-Pryda, it was east to Arco, Idaho, under cover of a picture story about one of America's great National Parks, The Craters of The Moon facility—just 15 miles from the new atomic reactor testing station.

Emerging into Norton Sound, below Nome, the trawler *Kwikpak* steamed west for its routine rendezvous with a Russian counterpart off St. Lawrence Island near the International dateline.

Vodka flowed, and so did used American greenbacks into the coffers of the surly Captain of *Kwikpak* after a screw was removed from the stem of his boat with a borrowed Phillips tool by the Soviet agent from Kamchatka Oblast.

Emil Goldfus had done his job out west, had laid out the information drops and spot-checked the operatives from

Chicago to Alaska. As the inventor of a photographic color print system, his western trip was completely documented though unsuccessful. He compiled a list of corporations in California, Washington, New Mexico and Alaska that he had made presentations to. The trip was entirely deductible for tax purposes.

By late June, 1953, Rudolf Abel, alias Emil Goldfus was back in the Upper West Side of Manhattan, managing the drop sites, one of which was a sign at the entrance drive to The Tavern on The Green Restaurant. He had decided on a new cover, that of a fine arts painter and set about finding larger quarters. He'd paid his rent for almost four years at addresses in the ninetys and seventys. There were those who began to wonder at his strange hours and disappearances for months at a time. He would find a studio in Brooklyn rather than in Greenwich Village, where he had occasionally visited Julius and Ethel Rosenberg before their arrest. Now they were dead by the electric chair. Greenglass had put the finger on them in return for a shorter sentence and the chief KGB man, Yakovlev had fled from his cover job as Vice Consul in New York. Things were still a bit hot. The Colonel looked forward to having an extra back room for the Hallicrafter transmitter kit he was assembling.

The turbine whined as superheated steam blasted back from the reactor inside *Neptune*'s truncated prototype. Whorls of seawater sloshed along the steel hull and against the side of the giant, round tank as power was taken off by the submerged paddlewheel, simulating ocean conditions and stresses. Lieutenant Commander Calvert Crowe, at the throttle console in the remote control room, eased a lever slowly forward. Inside the lead-shielded reactor, seven long rods of hafnium, a neutron-absorbing metal, rose out of the uranium core container, starting the fission reaction by allowing neutrons to be absorbed into U-235. The higher the rods, the more fission, the more heat was transferred from the primary loop to the steam loop. All the signals were "go" as maximum power was reached, scientists and technicians congratulating each other with hand gestures and smiles, while the military men remained stoically indifferent. All but Ben Mount who was as exuberant as a little boy with a new toy.

Outside the stark building, snarling Doberman Pinschers strained at their leashes, now and then howling in counterpoint to the turbines, as if their primitive instincts had been stirred by something frightening, akin to the forces that, had erupted eons earlier, forming the pocked lava landscape and tortured stone sculptures. The perimeter of guards and their dogs at twilight appeared as an ancient ritual, ringing the white monolith.

In a hidden gully behind a power shack, a Doberman's teeth gleamed through its turned-back red jowls in a last, frothy spasm of death. Next to the dog lay its dead handler, eyes bulging and several fingers cut off in a futile attempt to stay the razor wire that descended about his head when momentarily lax in attending his convulsing dog.

A stealthy figure, wearing the dead corporal's identification badge on his fatigue jacket, slipped into the dark service tunnel, feeling its way along the conduits and switch boxes toward the sound of turbines. At the end of the corridor, Peter Nielson, hearing commotion and voices beyond a locked door, sat down, exhausted, and drew another wire garrot from his pocket.

"Twenty-four hours, Captain, that's it." Commander Nash Watson jutted his chin out. "We can't expect any more than that at full power."

"But Nash, baby; we're only off Nova Scotia. That's no trip for *Neptune*. Hell, let's at least make the Grand Banks," shouted Ben Mount with bravado.

"Captain Mount," there was a tone of finality in the

Commander's delivery, "as Officer-in-Charge of this facility, I must point out that in the concensus of our engineers, it is advisable to shut down the reactor before something goes wrong. Since I am responsible for thirty million dollars of government investment in this prototype, I must—"

"Look, Nashy—I didn't put that chart up for nothing. This is the culmination of years of effort and I'm not going to come in with a whimper when we can really sock it to 'em. Where's your sense of adventure? Would Stephen Decatur stop *now*? Would Farragut go into reverse?"

"I have orders from Admiral Woodburn—"

"FUCK ADMIRAL WOODBURN." Ben walked away.

The great circle plot line crept red across the ocean chart as the mock-up crew went on standard four-hour sea watches. The imaginary *Neptune* sped submerged toward England: thirty hours, forty . . . fifty. Over two day's constant running as Ben Mount caught catnaps on a folding cot with orders to wake him every four hours to personally inspect the test data.

At 4 A.M. an electrician, going off duty, made the fatal mistake of taking a shortcut through the power shack. Nielson slipped into the blue-lit reactor room and crouched between the sea tank and a building wall abutment. The metal tank, set into concrete, loomed ten feet over Peter's head and was ringed with a six-foot-wide circular catwalk. Looking at his watch, he timed the guard's circuit by noting the footfalls. The average, taken from three circuits was forty-seven seconds. That meant the armed guard would be furthest away, at the opposite side in about twenty-three seconds, thus facing away from Nielson's position between eleven and twenty seconds after passing over him. An extra advantage was that, since the tank was bisected by the test hull, the segment of water closest to him was hidden by that part of the hull that was above the surface.

Nielson took a clear plastic bag containing a gray powder from his fatigues pocket and counted down with his sweep-second luminous watch, rehearsing the action twice:

Zero . . . stand by. *Five seconds*: press the little plastic vial inside the sealed bag. *Ten seconds*: cock arm to throw. *Fifteen seconds*: flip the bag over the catwalk, into the seawater tank . . .

The cigarette pack-sized missile landed in the water and with a sizzling sound, disintegrated, releasing a cloud of gray particles that sank toward the bottom, forty feet down.

Drawn by a powerful suction, the gray particles were sucked into a scoop inlet on the steel whale's belly along with tons of cooling water, running through two cylindrical steam condensers. Twenty feet aft, the heated water emerged through an outlet, but the gray particles, having expanded from the condenser heat had become lodged, growing into clumps and depositing a sticky sludge in the condenser tubes. This reduced the amount of cooling water and raised the reactor temperature. Red lights flashed; alarms went off.

Jolted out of a dream which concerned Jack McCrary's kid sister, Arabella, Ben alerted the engineers and soon the test hangar was swarming with Lilliputians. Control lights flickered erratically as power fell off. An eerie wail was emitted from the very heart of the fission reactor itself as one of the hafnium rods strained at the heat before the remote throttle could be eased, dropping the rods and decreasing the neutron bombardment. Shortly after, a main condenser tube failed and the pressure plummeted, driving most of the technicians to safety.

Upon the insistence of a Westinghouse representative, Ben put a Mayday call through to the Pentagon and turned the power down by fifty percent. The senior technical staff of the Naval Reactor's Branch was called into a pre-breakfast session and voted for an immediate abort. Mount, so advised, agreed but decided to give the machine a little extra time in case it was flooded—like a testy one-cycle gasoline lawn mower.

Under confusion's cover, Nielson escaped the same way he'd come in, elated at the apparent success of his effort. Mount, undaunted, ordered that only volunteers need remain in the building. Soon he was alone, except for Calvert Crowe.

"Cal, you're crazy," Ben throttled up to seventy-five percent power.

"Look who's talking," the thin officer scurried from one control to another, checking and adjusting while blurting out short strains of a current hit tune:

'I'm walkin' behind you . . .'

The red chart line leapt ahead . . . two thirds across, under Iceland . . . closing in on Europe. *Neptune* surged at a simulated 28 miles per hour. As fast as the crack surface passenger liners—underwater all the way!

The technicians and engineers trickled back to their posts. They returned uneasily, but they returned, eager to be part of history, to share in a great American triumph. The throttle backed down again—then regained speed. The world's first nuclear machine was being slapped on the behind. It was being born, and "borning" for the first time just had to be more difficult.

Five hundred miles to go. Twenty hours . . . ten. Down a third . . . full power again. Anxious eyes and hesitant smiles as the red line approached Ireland. Just a few more hours. Just one.

A resounding cheer reverberated through the cavernous structure as the last chart gap was closed and the power suddenly cut off; only flesh and blood vibrated until the realization set in.

"Might as well put into a peaceful place like the

Shannon,'' Ben Mount adhered a silhouette of *Neptune* to the Irish river estuary as Commander Watson swabbed his forehead in relief.

"Now, now Nashy," Ben joshed, "I told you we weren't going all the way across. Much too dangerous."

Chapter 19

"It's about time you took a day off," Betsy gathered the picnic utensils and packed them neatly into a wicker basket. "I'll bet if I hadn't come out here you'd still be in that horrid bunker."

"It's a test building, love."

"It's concrete and damp, and not good for you. You must be the only senior officer in the entire country who doesn't have a nice healthy sun tan. I'll be glad to loll on a beach in Hawaii and get you away from all this radioactivity."

"The reactor shielding is designed to give a man less radiation than one gets in normal life . . ."

"Designed is one thing, but nobody really knows. Why I just read that—"

"Nice of your aunt to take Debbie," Ben interrupted as he locked the back door of his AEC station wagon. "C'mon, let's take a walk; I've been working here on and off for two years and I've never explored the place."

"I don't see how anyone could get excited about this—

nothing but strange rocks. It gives me the creeps," Betsy
hung on to Ben as they sidestepped along the edge of a
crevice marked by a sign:

GREAT RIFT, Depth 450 Ft.
Craters of The Moon National Park

"Just imagine," Ben read into his guidebook, "that this
lava field covers 200,000 square miles. A sea of red hot
lava!"

"All those poor animals," Betsy moaned as Ben inspected the glass-like blue formations, some resembling
the bodies of deflated reptiles.

"Incredible." Ben marveled at a field of solidified froth
cones and picked up a teardrop-shaped stone. "Look at the
form, this thing was a large drop of molten lava that
spurted up out of a volcanic opening and solidified as it
cooled in mid air. I'll have to bring this back for the hull
design boys."

"I didn't know *Neptune* could fly too."

"You never can tell where an idea will lead," Ben
parried Betsy's observation. They were well matched; he
the blue-skying dreamer and she the practical wise-guy.
Ben needed the balance and counted on her intuitions to
help him over his excesses.

Ben and Betsy were, in their playful joy, oblivious to a
man who had slipped into a cavern ahead of them after
removing a danger sign, warning of a "bottomless pit"
that was off limits. The man was tipsy and acting on his
own initiative, hoping for a cash bonus from his superiors
for the annihilation of one Captain Benjamin Mount by
way of an unfortunate accident. Arni Järvi was an agent in
a hurry.

The Finn's fervor overshadowed his caution as he wandered
deep into the dim-lit cave, once a haunt of renegade
Shoshone. As a resident of the area, Järvi was well ac-
quainted with the pitfalls of Crater National Park, and had

more than once, considered its "advantages" to the business of espionage. Järvi, out of breath, picked up a stone and slammed at the restraining chain that marked the off-limits tourist area. He broke the wall shackle and flung the chain and stanchions into a crevice, then ducked behind a stalagmite wall to await Ben mount, and, if necessary, help him into the dark, yawning bottomless pit in the shadows.

But it was not to be. There was something already in command of the position: the deadly muzzle of a double-barreled, 8-bore buffalo rifle. The Finn opened his mouth but words never came as a flash told him that all was over and a millisecond later, with no time to assess the consequences of such a weapon's destructive capability, he was lifted off his feet and into the beckoning bottomless pit—in two limp, dead pieces.

Amidst the multiple reverberations of the powerful powder charge and the screeching of frantic bats, Ben stopped short at the sight of the myopic, sweating figure in a white linen plantation suit. The formidable short-barreled rifle was leveled and Ben flung Betsy behind him.

Norman's eyes blazed madly. Another enemy stood before him; another schemer after his family fortune. He blinked the salt sweat from under his fogged-up glasses. "I'm sorry," Norman backed up, foot by foot. He hadn't expected a woman; women drove him crazy, especially women who were not Indians. Norman had a secret: he was part Indian—just like everyone suspected back at High School. His father was a full-blooded Yakima. That's what had driven his mother to drink.

"Sorry," Norman was about to lower the buffalo rifle when a furry creature rubbed on his booted ankle. Taken aback, he stumbled and accidentally stomped on the animal. It was a cat. His cat—a mixed breed with one brown eye and one green eye. "Gawd Damn," he screamed to the cavern's heights. "Gawd Damn," the echo answered.

Ben, protecting Betsy with his body, clung to the damp

cave wall, daring not to move lest this madman pull the trigger. Norman knelt down gently over the shivering kitten and examined it; ran his pudgy fingers over its soft skull. "Gawd damn," he snarled and stood up, a full 200 pounds of nervous indignation and animal rage. Rifle still pointed at the two motionless figures, Norman raised a heavy booted foot and stomped down on the kitten's head.

"It was your fault that this happened—my best kitten," tears welled up in Norman's eyes. He tore off his planter's hat and took aim. "You see, I have to do this—there is no other way." His finger squeezed the second trigger and Ben embraced Betsy, sparing her the sight and knowledge of the end.

BOR-OOOM

Ben felt the blast against his back; but no pain. Was he in heaven . . . in hell? No blood? He gripped his wife by her trembling arms. Their eyes met in one great realization.

They were alive.

Ben whirled and stopped, aghast. The madman was gone. A rifle, its barrel shattered like a metal banana peel lay over the dead cat. Beyond was only a black void, recipient of the couple's long shadows from a distant, bare electric light bulb.

After reporting the bizarre episode to the Park Ranger, they drove back to Arco. Ben was ready for one of his rare drinks. Feeling more of this world after two "New York Style" martinis and a plate of spaghetti and meatballs to Betsy's Rob Roy and chef's salad, they danced through the Arco Inn's lobby. A poster by the door caught their eyes. It showed a handsome Air Force pilot and a mascara-eyed beauty looking soulfully at each other. A monumental title proclaimed: *ABOVE AND BEYOND* . . .

> "The Love Story Behind
> The Billion Dollar Secret!"
> CRATERS OF THE MOON DRIVE-IN
> US 93 (4 Mi. S. of Arco)
> 8:30 & 11:00 P.M.

The incandescent fireball glowed green, then smoldered into a sequence of pulsing hues as the now-familiar mushroom cloud burgeoned and bubbled up. Awe-struck faces reflected the blinding flash through quickly cleaned patches in dusty windshields; cars parked like lemmings, stalled on their march to the Great Silver Drive-In Screen. Gangling tow-heads rose from their jalopys' bowels from the dark havens by eight-ball and stainless steel spherical gearshift knobs, leaving squirming sixteen-year-old bobby soxers in panting disarray. Microphones dangling like snakes through open windows crackled under the increased volume of the Hiroshima explosion taped in by a hungry Hollywood.

Cut to a grim-faced Robert Taylor at the controls of *Enola Gay* as shock waves rock the bomber. Close-up of somber, resolute glances between soft-capped Colonel Taylor and his co-pilot as *Enola* banks away from the conflagration.

Dark against the star-specked sky behind the Drive-In's flickering screen loomed the Lost River range, capped by Mount Borah, Idaho's highest peak: mute testament to the horrific forces of nature with its snowy summit of marine limestone—forces that have now been matched by man.

Peter Nielson was conspicuous in that he was alone in his open Jeep as he pulled up to Sound Station 267 in the last, sparsely parked row of the Drive-In lot. He couldn't help but notice the shadowy young people doing things inside their automobiles. Post-war love—American style. Ripe young girls squealing in back seats. He was getting an erection just thinking about ravishing one for himself. But he was on assignment and this time it wasn't photography. The main feature ended with a flight of glittering B-29s into the sunset. Peter watched as a slide came on, advertising the food and refreshment stand, then he got out of his Jeep and tested the speaker as he plucked a magnetized screw from under the pedestal unit. Joseph Elk's alternate drop—microfilm of the final reactor tests. Data and meter readings of the remote systems.

Putting the screw under his metal dashboard, Peter walked down toward the refreshment stand behind two giggling, but curvaceous minors. A *Bugs Bunny* cartoon came on—with the buck-toothed rabbit full-screen like a stuttering dinosaur against the backdrop of dark mountains.

Ben Mount, in studded western boots and Levis was paying for cherry cokes as Peter walked up to the counter. He'd passed Betsy who was waiting patiently by the entrance, looking up at the big sky for shooting stars to wish upon. She hoped that the stirring within her would be a boy this time. A companion for her husband; something to tear him away from his work.

"Would you like a soda? I'm buying," the stranger flashed a roll of green at the two unescorted cuties. Betsy did notice that the man was much older than the girls, and attractive, but she continued her reverie, noting also that the girls were provocatively dressed. "Would you like a soda?" The phrase had a strange ring—as if she'd heard it before . . . long ago. Then she realized it was not what he said. It was the accent.

Where? When? In England, during the Blitz? No—before. On a boat. A Navy trawler . . . On the same day she'd first met Ben. He was directing the rescue of *Sebago*'s crew by the diving bell. The accent—she'd first heard it then. A Swedish officer who had been among those brought to the surface as she covered the story for her first newspaper assignment.

A cold chill shot through her body and she started to tremble. It couldn't be—not here in the middle of the desert. Must be mountain fever, or the Rob Roy she'd drunk earlier at the Arco Inn. Betsy recalled Helen McCrary's revolting account of what he'd done to her and Moxie Mulford at the Admiral's cottage in Dorset during the invasion scare. Betsy found herself drawn to this blond stranger; she had to know that he wasn't Peter Nielson.

"Peter," Betsy called out softly. There was nothing wrong with that, so she thought. If it was not Peter he would not respond.

His shoulders seemed to hunch a bit, but he ignored the challenge and continued his pursuit of the giggling girls.

Betsy stepped lightly around him as if to select some candy from the counter stand. "Excuse me," she smiled and took a good look at his face.

Then Betsy saw it: the Egyptian silver symbol that Moxie had worn at the cottage. The charm that Helen said had been ripped off Moxie's neck by Nielson. More than a coincidence.

Peter blinked, then saw the white-haired man with the big nose coming toward him. It came to him all at once: Movie about the bomb . . . Atomic sub reactor . . . Ben Mount.

He turned but Betsy held him by the sleeve and shouted, "You are Peter Nielson . . ." Peter pushed her away and ran out just as an Idaho State Trooper swaggered in.

"What on earth—" Ben held his wife close.

"It was Peter Nielson, I swear it," Betsy sobbed. "He just went out," she pointed weakly as the other customers looked about in confusion. "I'm all right, Ben—he's getting away. What is he doing? Is he after you?"

Ben ran outside and spotted the stranger walking toward the parked cars. He sprinted and caught up with him, their giant shadows cast upon the screen from the sunken projection booth. Two figures in combat against the colorful cartoon of Bugs Bunny being chased by a clever cat.

"Down in front," they yelled from the blackness. "Outa the way," the chorus of irate shouts drowned out the sound. The shouts turned to screams as the dark silhouettes grappled and one, the larger, grabbed the smaller by the neck. The smaller shadow slumped to the ground and the other ran off as Bugs Bunny chomped on a carrot, disappeared into concentric circles, and popped out once more with his "Tha—tha-that's all F-Folks."

.* * *

Ben sat on the edge of a bed in the small Reactor Center Hospital. He'd been treated for shock and abrasions about the head and neck. The local police, after being given a description of the assailant had left. Ben had cautioned Betsy not to tell the whole story about Nielson. This was a matter for the CIA, not the local police, and agents were already flying out from Seattle.

As they turned out the lights that night in their quarters, Betsy snuggled up to Ben. "You recognized him too, then?"

"No, I didn't. It was too dark and the projection light blinded me—but I knew it when he called me 'a dirty Jew.' "

"Hey, I've got something on our intrepid Navy," the bespectacled young lawyer tossed a report on the congressman's desk.

"It's about time, Roy," the junior Senator from Wisconsin rubbed his five o'clock shadow and scanned the missive. "Shee-it, wouldn't ya know," Joseph McCarthy relished what he read:

"Benjamin S. Mount, Captain, US Navy . . . Born 1915 . . . Litovsk, Russia." He rolled his tongue over his lips. "This is crazy," he continued. "Parents Lev and Ida Berg, to New York City in 1919 . . . It's something, but not enough."

"Read on," the lawyer replied smugly.

"Signed Stockholm Peace Petition, November, 1950 . . ." McCarthy slammed the report down. "Why the sonofabitch signed that pinko sheet while he was an officer in the American Armed Forces—while the Commies were stickin' it to our boys on the Yalu. Why that bastard might just be the guy to play both ends for the Navy. What is it with these people? Don't they like this country?" Tailgunner

Joe counted on his fingers: "The Rosenbergs, Gold, Brothman, Moskowitz, Sobell, Greenglass, Coplon . . ."

"And let's not forget Bentley, Chambers, Hiss and Remington—and it took a Shapiro to catch a Coplon."

"Big deal, give him an FBI medal for fuckin' her."

"Maybe we're all catalysts."

"What's 'at?"

"I mean Jews. We make things happen."

"*That's* no shit," he handed the Mount report back to Cohn. "Make me a copy, I'm gonna see some Navy brass."

In his unique capacity as hiring boss for the nuclear navy, Ben was developing novel testing ideas. He cut one inch off the front legs of his applicant interview chair, so that the aspiring candidate would have "that sinking feeling" and be at a disadvantage which would further test his ability to adjust. The practice soon became expected but wily Mount confused them all by having two more identical chairs in the act—one normal, and the other, one inch shorter on its *back* legs.

One of the first young Lieutenants to be tested was a buck-toothed cracker from Plains, Georgia—on the prototype chair.

"Lieutenant Carson," Ben paraded around the green chair with the child-faced officer sitting perpendicular despite the incline. "If the citizens of Washington, D.C. decided that they had to eliminate a naval officer or a street cleaner, for whatever reason, who would you side with?"

The Lieutenant, with all the fervor of a ventriloquist's dummy, answered quickly, as if programmed: "Sir, though I realize that streetcleaners are important, I would imagine that the officer could do his job, whereas the street cleaner could never command a United States Naval vessel."

"Then you would eliminate the street cleaner?"

"Not quite, sir; as an officer, I would—er, *the* officer would use his position to save the street cleaner."

"Well said, Lieutenant—there seems to be something wrong? Are you comfortable?" Ben scribbled some notes on his pad.

"Yes, sir; ah jus' caint tell ya how much it means to get into somethin' real solid like th' nukular program. Ah feel jes like an entraypenoor in a vast new frontier."

"Then you went to Annapolis looking for a challenge?"

"Well, my Daddy and kid brother are handlin' the business pretty well—besides, I kinda like the water, and the friggen plantation is so dry . . ."

"Plantation? What does your family grow?"

"Peanuts, sir."

Chapter 20

NEPTUNE UNDER WAY NUCLEAR

The communications officer of the world's first atomic powered submarine read the short message, saluted, and went below to the radio room. Ben and Betsy had stayed up late the night before. Ben was happy that his wife had dissuaded him from using one of his earlier phrases which sounded too much like advertising slogans: NEPTUNE NUCLEAR NOW . . . and GO NUCLEAR, GO NEPTUNE.

It was Betsy who first insisted that the boat's trial run be observed with a proper and memorable epigram, a motto to go down in history with "Fire when ready, Gridley," and "Damn the torpedoes, full speed ahead."

Ben was proud, standing in the conning sail of the dream that, in less than eight years, he had pushed to reality. Many skeptics had said it would take ten or fifteen years to accomplish. Even Robert Oppenheimer had expressed doubt. Now the glistening bows were gliding down the Thames, only a year after Mamie Eisenhower had first wet her down with champagne.

And Ben had been lucky. The McCarthy thing had fizzled, with the Senator's Congressional censure the previous month. The witch-hunt balloon had burst and with it, the last obstacle had been removed between Ben and the big brass as to who would be the first commander of *Neptune*. After successfully circumventing the old hassle about a Captain being too high a rank for a sub, enter McCarthy, to the delight of certain Admirals. The Secretary of the Navy had already advised Ben to recommend another commander, one who was less "visible." And this partially because Ben was born in Russia. But now he was at the helm of his baby, and no force in the world—or under the waves was going to deprive him of whelping this steel whale. Even Admiral Woodburn's eyebrows rose when Ben resolved to wear a uniform during all duty hours as commander of *Neptune*. Pentagon scuttlebutt had it that Ben was so eager for the command that he'd purposely irritated his superiors in order to be turned down for promotion to Admiral, which would have scotched the assignment and nailed him to a chair.

Instead, Ben took the boat to Puerto Rico in May, 1955. The shakedown cruise took only ninety hours to travel almost 1400 miles—the entire trip submerged. From an average of sixteen knots, Ben coaxed *Neptune* to over twenty on a second run to Key West.

The prototype reactor at Arco was refueled after two years of continuous operation, with a new grapefuit-sized core that accomplished a revolutionary feat: sixty-six days continuous running at full power. This was roughly equivalent to going round the world twice without stopping. In April, 1957, *Neptune* got her second core after logging over 60,000 miles. The same distance on conventional diesel oil would have required enough oil to fill 217 railroad tank cars—a train two miles long.

*   *   *

It was a pivotal year for Ben and the Navy. Promoted to Rear Admiral, he undertook the entire fleet nuclear program and ushered in the *Skate* class boats, a hybrid of *Neptune* and *Albacore*, the first hydrodynamic teardrop-shaped hull. This test boat, powered by radial diesels and trebled underwater batteries hit a top submerged speed of thirty-three knots, sending Soviet designers back to their drawing boards. Already, the first production line nuclear boats based on *Neptune* were obsolete.

Ben went through his papers and was amused at a directive dated about the time of the Berlin airlift. It was an extract from Operation *Dropshot,* a plan for war with the Soviet Union in 1957. It stated in part: "... a prototype combat submarine should be available by 1956, having a top submerged speed of twenty-five knots with an endurance of twelve hours, and a total submerged endurance of two days." He tore the memo into long, thin shreds and dropped them ritually into his waste basket. *Neptune* had taken part in the NATO exercise called *Strikeback*, a residual ripple of *Dropshot*, but Ben had other plans, among them, drawings for an inverted fathometer which he slipped into his briefcase along with a copy of an explorer's memoirs. Sir Hubert Wilkins, in 1931, had borrowed a US Navy sub, O-12 and fitted it with overhead "skis" to run under the arctic ice and attempt to reach the North Pole. He closed a folder marked "Brickbat 0-1" and locked it in a steel wall safe. In it were plans for yet a new type of submarine; one capable of launching sixteen programmed missiles from below the ocean surface. The system was to be called "Polaris" and was destined to change the definition of war for all time.

When Ben arrived home late that night, he was surprised to find Betsy still up. "I told you not to wait up," Ben stopped in the middle of his sentence when Betsy lifted the lid of a pot of steaming Chinese-style vegetables in the kitchen. His favorite dish. "What happened?" Chinese vegetables only happened when something else happened. "Good—or bad?" Ben hung up his uniform jacket on a doorknob and loosened his necktie.

"Can I make you a vodka and tonic?"

"Why?" Ben sat on the kitchen stool.

"Moxie Mulford died," Betsy got out the vodka.

"Two jiggers," Ben saw the letter and picked it up slowly.

"I thought it would be better not to call you at the office. The weather is so bad—and that bridge . . . in the rain," Betsy set a drink near Ben and took his jacket to the hall closet.

"With everything he's been through . . . a heart attack . . ." Ben read on, mumbling a word now and then. He set the letter down solemnly and lifted his glass.

"To Moxie."

Betsy joined in the toast. "Do you think it would make sense? That is—is it legal?"

"The boy is a minor, and I'm his Godfather. Adoption is adoption, especially since it seems to be in Moxie's will. There's nobody to contest it. But what about you, my love—suddenly a sixteen-year-old young man in the house."

"Darling, we have so much room, and the poor boy has never had a real family." Betsy set the dining nook. "I even bought some chop sticks for you . . . and extra shrimp in case . . ." Betsy took a foiled container out of the oven. "I tried a new sauce recipe."

"Betsy, you're great."

"If the Chinese can see joy in sorrow . . ."

"True . . . true," Ben reflected, "they see death as a rebirth, more than we do. But Rudi Mulford . . ."

"What is it, darling?"

"Tell me about our children. Were they good today?

Chapter 21

The pendulum had swung.

Admiral Ben Mount demonstrated the proper way to whirl a hula-hoop on the foredeck of the first Fleet Ballistic Missile Submarine, SSBN *George Washington*. The audience was his daughter, seven-year-old Deborah, and the launch crew, the politicians, brass and commissioning crowd having filtered out to their watering holes in Connecticut and New York in preparation for Auld Lang Syne, 1959.

It was a gala day, and compensated for the commissioning of SSRN 586 only six weeks earlier. *Triton*, the largest, most powerful and expensive submarine ever built, was already obsolete. Designed as a radar picket on the basis of World War II needs, with twin nuclear reactors and a surface cruising intent, had been leap-frogged by electronics technology and cancelled as a class. It was one of Ben's mistakes. Her huge bow got in the way of a railroad at Groton and had to be sliced off. *Triton*'s stern hung too far out over the Thames River, so it had to be built at another shipyard. Its seven-story high tail fin had to be cut shorter to fit under the hoist cranes at launching. Twelve feet was blow-torched off and later replaced. Heavier than a medium cruiser, *Triton* needed special launching gear lest her weight carry her across the river into a mud bank. Even so, the river had to be dredged around the slipway.

It was the only major launching of a nuclear sub that Admiral Mount did not attend. In a message to the President of Electric Boat, Ben said: "I regret that I am not able to be present at the launching of *Triton*, for I consider this to be a significant event in naval history . . . It symbolizes the submersible capital ship of the future . . ."

Costing 100 million dollars of taxpayer's money, *Triton* was a potential thorn in the side of the new Polaris program. Something had to be done with this white elephant. Mount, with a burst of energy after receiving his Admiral's stripe, came up with one of his expedient solutions.

Triton was going to "sell" the nuclear product.

Triton was going to retrace the world's first circumnavigation. It would follow Ferdinand Magellan's route of 1521; three years and 31,000 miles around the globe. But *Triton* would do it in about two months—SUBMERGED ALL THE WAY!

In September, 1959, Rudi Mulford, with some help from his Godfather, was accepted at Annapolis. It was Moxie's request, but Ben had his own reasons. The "little Aryan," had astounded his foster father. In his two years at Kent Island, the orphan had developed into the child that Ben would have liked as his own progeny. Rudi had a natural affinity for the sea, storm and calm . . . dinghy and ocean-racing sloop. It was so uncanny that Ben, in anticipation of such questions that were imminent, hired a missing persons bureau in Hamburg to find out what the Red Cross hadn't, according to Commodore Mulford's solicitors.

Ben locked the Hamburg Bureau's findings away with

his top-secret "Brickbat file." It all fit. Rudi was found under the prefab sections at Blohm and Voss' electro boat assembly yard in Hamburg. With the incentive of American dollars, a private investigator scoured the back streets of Hamburg, offering a reward to anyone who could identify the "adopted" boy from a snapshot taken by Commodore Mulford in 1945. The search ended in a bar on the infamous "wicked mile" of the Reeperbahn, shore leave haunt of the German Navy during the war.

A retired bartender recalled a romance between one of the "good" girls and a U-boat officer who had vowed to marry her as a result of the birth of a son, who was given the name "Rudi" after the father, Kapitänleutnant Rudi Müller. A wedding was planned for June, 1942. Operating with the "Trutz" wolfpack group, Müller's boat, U-227 was detected and attacked by the American Escort Carrier, *Bogue* off the Azores. One of the escort's Wildcats was shot down by U-641, but U-217 was depth bombed and sunk. Müller's boat was damaged but submerged and was not claimed as a kill by *USS Bogue*.

Hope gave way to despair as days, then weeks passed with no word from U-227. The boat was officially declared "missing" and its commander's photographic portrait posted with the many others at the Kriegsmarine Officers' club—with a black border.

Every afternoon, for some months thereafter, a young woman was observed, carrying an infant and waiting by the docks till dusk. Even during the final year of the war, she walked with her child once or twice a week along the waterfront, as if expecting her fiancé to miraculously appear.

The old bartender thought her name might have been Lisa, and that she was from Cologne. Both Lisa and her son were never seen again after the firestorm that resulted from an air raid just prior to German's surrender.

Ben wondered just how hard Moxie had tried to find little Rudi's parents after the war, and suspected that Moxie's impetus had been hindered by a need to replace his younger brother, Nicky, who had died along with 800 other tars after the torpedoing of HMS *Royal Oak* in Scapa Flow, early in the war. A chill went through his lean frame when he recalled the Crater Drive-In incident. Peter Nielson's cover as a Swedish photographer had been disclosed during the trials of the year before that had led to the conviction of the masterspy, elusive Colonel Abel. Nielson had made good his escape—back to the Soviet Union before Abel's arrest. Nielson, by his own admittance, partially responsible for the *Royal Oak* disaster, was also the warrant for little Rudi.

Sputnik was the culprit. America, having been accused of a "missile gap" had to come up with an answer to the Soviet's lead in rocketry. Across the country, over 30,000 private companies, universities, government agencies and shipyards were set into motion—the largest single effort since Manhattan District.

The initial contributor to Polaris was the SINS Ship's Inertial Navigation System, developed at MIT and used on *Neptune* during its historic submerged trip across the North Pole. Where traditional magnetic systems went beserk near the Pole, SINS, sensing the shorter rotation period of a point on the Arctic Circle as compared with a point on the Equator, knew how far that point was from the Pole. Combining this, with time, speed and direction, it was a simple matter to pinpoint position. The next step was to design a miniature system to fit into the Polaris missile. This was accomplished and tested in a submarine simulator at Sperry Gyroscope's plant in Syosset, Long Island in conjunction with MIT.

Simultaneously, the missile itself was tested in a miniature ocean simulator tank called LUMF, for Lockheed Underwater Missile Facility. The tank could generate any type wave or tide found in the ocean to determine the effect on various shaped projectiles as they were fired from a fixed underwater launcher. Over 3000 launches were logged in determining the initial Polaris configuration—that of a near bowling pin.

Another test series was known as Operation Pop-up, in which redwood logs were fired and photographed. In leap-frogging the Soviet submarine missile program, the Americans went to solid fuel enabling underwater launchings. Aerojet of California responded and soon an operational missile was perfected. All this to the credit of a Naval flier turned missile developer, Vice Admiral William Raborn.

The Polaris missile was ready; atomic warheads were ready. But the delivery platform was three years behind.

"Can you do with a boat that makes two knots less at operating speed than the specs call for in "George Washington?"

The Navy, the Federal government and the Think Tank people answered Ben in the affirmative. Gain three years, lose two knots.

"We've got *Scorpion* almost ready on the ways," Ben told the combined committees in closed session, "and we can cut the fucking thing in half and stick in an extra section for the missiles, just like the Germans did with their cargo and minelaying U-boats during the war." So *Scorpion* became *George Washington*, and the SUPERSUB was born by Caesarean section.

Chapter 22

Vice Admiral Konstantin Kulov's decorations covered his broad chest, glinting gold in contrast to the dark-suited party functionaries sitting before as many unlabeled bottles of mineral water.

"Our adversaries are but five short years ahead of the People's Soviet in nuclear submarine production. But for the unrelenting efforts of Comrade Kulov, the gap might well be much more. It was Comrade Kulov who—without the fanfare of his imitators in the aggressors' camp—brought the Soviet Navy to a position where it is now ready to challenge and surpass all existing underwater weapons systems.

"It was Comrade Kulov who, realizing the limitations of the last war's ship propulsion systems and obsolete missile systems design, set out and succeeded in replacing certain reactionary sectors of our invincible Navy with his new technology. The Soviet Navy, superior in forces, stands now at the threshold of domination of all the world's oceans, should we so deem it necessary."

"It is with great pride that we award Comrade Kulov with . . . the Chairman exhibited the decoration, then waiting for the committee to rise, set the ribbon over the Admiral's bowed head, ". . . with the Order of Lenin . . ."

"Comrades," the Chairman waited for a round of applause to subside. "the Committee is pleased to announce that Admiral Kulov, in addition to his other duties, will be in charge of a Soviet Naval mission that shall eclipse all previous underwater records. The world has seen our pre-eminence in space programs, starting with Sputnik, almost 10 years ago. The world knows the power of the Soviet Army; now the world shall know of the superiority of our Navy. In 1960, the American nuclear submarine, *Triton*, followed the route of Magellan around the world, submerged—30,000 miles in 60 days. In the same year, the first American ballistic missiles were fired from a nuclear submarine. In a short time, the Soviet Navy will surpass both of these. Our new *Sturgeon-Class* boat, more powerful than the current American *Lafayette* class will, in commemoration of the 100th anniversary of the publication of Jules Verne's great classic, *Twenty Thousand Leagues Under the Sea*, double the *Triton's* record. In addition, the boat will carry 16 SS-N-6 missiles equipped with improved atomic warheads . . ." Chairman Mikhailin of the Naval Committe raised his arms to stay the applause which echoed through the venerable marble halls of the Admiralty, turning the heads of boatmen on the Neva and strollers on Nevsky Prospekt.

"Kostya" Kulov acknowledged the congratulations of associate officers and official dignitaries as he left the hall with his aides, Captain, First Rank, Zinoviev and Captain, Third, Nielson.

"You two will have to get to know each other better," Kulov walked between them with his arms over their shoulders, "60,000 miles under the sea is a quarter of the distance to the moon."

Zinoviev, smooth and catlike, had, in his teens, studied ballet at the Kirov under Aleksandr Pushkin, the teacher, 8 years later of a Tartar-cheeked youth from the Urals, Rudolph Nureyev. Andrei acknowledged his superior's little joke. He was used to being ribbed because of his life style. All work, never married, and a tendency toward the finer trappings, both military and civilian. As a child he'd been torn between extremes. His father's side of the family were scientists, including his grandfather, a famous rocket designer and biographer of the space theory pioneer and patriot, K. Tsiolkovsky. Maxim Zinoviev was a renegade and a purist; during the twenties he patented a rocket engine that developed 350 *Goosepower*, in honor of Fyodor Geshvend, another space pioneer and practicing architect, who died ironically, in 1890 after being committed to an asylum built from his own blueprints. So enthralled with his work was Maxim that he named his children after the heavens, Andrei's father answering to "Mercury."

By contrast, his mother's family excelled in music, and his aunt Sophia, with whom he stayed in Astrakhan during the war, introduced him to theater and the ballet.

Back from the rocket weapons factory after Germany's fall, "Mercury" and Alexis Zinoviev pulled their only child back into the laboratory and thence to the Nakhimov Naval School in Sevastopol.

Called "The Dancer" by his adversaries, Andrei was both respected and feared. Never had a Soviet Naval Officer attained the rank of Captain, First Class in peacetime before the age of forty. And Alexei was thirty-seven. Never had a man so different fit in so well. There was no question that he was the best, and most ruthless younger tactician in the submarine service.

Little notice was taken at the selection of the "foreigner", Petrus Nielson as weapons officer. His record of over 20 years service, first with KGB Naval Division during the early nuclear development period and his subsequent commission as a propulsion engineer under Admiral Kulov was sufficient to warrant a slot. Petrus, at 53, was more an observer than a combatant, and his ability with several languages was considered an asset for the 60,000 mile cruise. A few years' short of retirement, he had asked for sea duty in order to obtain information to complete a study he was doing on the Soviet Nuclear Navy.

Nielson, who had met Kulov while turning over an experimental German U-boat to the Soviet Navy, had again contacted him in 1954 with duplicate plans for the American reactor intended for Captain Mount's *Neptune*. From there on they helped each other, as well as the Soviet Navy. Just as Ben Mount was synonymous with the U.S. Nuclear Navy, so became "Kostya" Kulov—at least to his superiors, public fame being anathema under the Red flag.

The Russians were still behind. Even the *Sturgeon* Class— its sixteen missiles had a range half that of the American "Poseidon" thermonuclear-tipped projectile. And Soviet missiles were not "Multiple re-entry"—the Poseidon carrying 14 independently programmed warheads to only one on each Soviet counterpart. But Kulov knew it was only a matter of three or four years and all would be even—all except the surveillance and tracking war, in which the Soviet technology was hopelessly inept as far as multiple array underwater sonar systems were concerned.

What good will the *Delta* boats be? Larger and more powerful than the comparable American vessels, when they can be detected better. And the *Typhoon* series, more potent than the adversary's much vaunted *Tridents*? Will the *Alpha* design, with its 50 mile-per-hour speed and its titanium hull, enabling 2000 foot dives be able to elude capitalist Bell Telephone's CAESAR-COLOSSUS sound surveillance network, its anchored arrays, its towed arrays, its suspended arrays . . . and the CAPTOR homing torpedo?

Konstantin Ossipovitch Kulov, great nephew of Admiral Makarov, the hero of Batum, had a plan. It was worthy of the twin bearded Admiral himself, whose daring torpedo tactics earned him the title of "Father of The Imperial

Russian Navy." So, it had been first proposed by Captain Zinoviev, then presented in a top secret session with the Naval Committee that included General Secretary Leonid Brezhnev—it was he, Kulov, who had badgered the plan through.

The boat chosen for the cover mission was *Vyatka Sturgeon*, third in the class called *Yankee* by NATO. Named for one of the sturgeon-teeming rivers of the Caspian Sea, she was 426 feet long, displacing 9000 tons, and powered with a 24,000shp reactor. Top dived speed was listed by Jane's as 25 knots and her complement was 120. The first two boats, *Volga Sturgeon* and *Ural Sturgeon* were already deployed.

The Soviet Armed Forces newspaper *Red Star* announced the mission, under the name "Operation Nemo," as a tribute to the great "people's writer," Jules Verne, and a gesture of defense against encroaching capitalistic agression. Officially, the four-month trip would start, as did the fictional voyage of M. Pierre Aronnax, a shipwrecked professor of natural history, aboard Captain Nemo's *Nautilus*, at a point 200 miles off the coast of Japan, and finish in a maëlstrom off arctic Norway. In all, 37 geographical "stops" were plotted; the first was an island north of Oahu in the Hawaiian chain, called variously, Crespo or Rocca de la Plata—"Silver Rock." Unofficially, the itinerary was surprisingly parallel to U.S. Naval facilities round the world, and dismissed as "coincidental" by Soviet authorities—another example of agressive paranoia on the part of *ComASWForPAC*, or Commander, Anti Submarine Forces, Pacific Fleet. A terse note from the Commander of the U.S. First Fleet at Pearl Harbor "recommended" that Operation Nemo's first stop be short of the Island of Crespo, whose coordinates, 32°40' north lat. and 157°50' west long. were within the Hawaiian defense perimeter and off limits to Soviet missile-carrying submarines.

The First Fleet Commander, a fan of Jules Verne, offered to allow safe passage to Crespo only on condition that the Soviet crew be taken off and replaced by an American crew within the defense perimeter. The offer was refused.

SOSUS was the acronym for "Sound Surveillance System," the progenitor of which was known as CAESAR and deployed in the early 1960s. The original Atlantic system detected the Russian subs that precipitated the missile crisis in 1962 off Cuba. CAESAR stood for "Passive Undersea Surveillance System, Submarines." The next generation, COLOSSUS, was deployed in the Pacific and around Hawaii. The Hawaii installation, known as SEA SPIDER, incorporated with standard arrays, ten-foot diameter hydrophones anchored in three mile depths and powered by nuclear batteries. On the American drawing board was SAS, a single mammoth tripod tower with "legs" sixteen miles apart, bearing transducers and hydrophones of such great power on long cables that "one tower per ocean would suffice for complete 'insonification'."

NATO allies used a variation of SOSUS called BARRIER and BRONCO in the Atlantic and the Mediterranean, while the U.S. installed fixed arrays and sonobouys on French-built towers surrounding the Azores; called AFAR for Azores Fixed Accoustic Range.

Behind the American warning note was a big stick. The SEA SPIDER array perimeter had a radius of 1300 miles from Oahu—approximately 80 miles longer than the Golem II, operational missile of the standard Soviet submarine. In the late 60s, anticipating a breakthrough in range for the Yankee Class boats, SEA SPIDER extended its western-facing arc by some 300 miles and equipped this arc with CAPTOR prototypes, mine casings containing the Mark 46 torpedo, an accoustic homing submarine killer with a reputed atomic warhead. KGB was wary, and so was Kulov. Nemo's course was to be altered accordingly; the details were left to Captain Andrei Zinoviev.

"The Dancer" was also a chess player who enjoyed using pawns for gambit. He assigned a *Golf* Class ballistic

missile sub to scout the first leg to Crespo. It was not a
coincidence that the boat selected was commanded by
Sergei Grodnov, an insensate bear of an officer with a
reputation for following orders to the small print. The
noisy, obsolete diesel boat was a pet peeve of the
Captain's—an unsophisticated weapon that should be retired before it brought shame to the service. Yet no one
was aware of his real motive.

He craved insanely that which was not to be had; one
promised to another. Natalya, the elegant daughter of the
Admiral, now grown from the child he had once held on
his knee. Was it lust? Was it duty, or ambition that drove
him? Andrei had not thought of her in this way—until
Senior Lieutenant Artemon Kalinin once beat him in chess,
to the delightful giggling of Natalya. It was the last game
. . . the only game. He lost gracefully, but burned with
jealousy and confusion within. Tactician that he was, no
one ever suspected, nor had they reason to. Natalya was
for him alone. It was ordained, regardless of her immature
promise to the studious young engineer. It was only too
obvious, even to her father, that an officer who was more
excited about building dams and bridges than about blowing them up, promised meager glory to the name of Makarov
or "Kostya" Kulov.

Oiled black hair glistening, The Dancer did a quick
pirouette in the metallic privacy of his small stateroom on
the upper level of *Viatka Sturgeon*, rolling gently in the
ice-flecked Kola under the Aurora Borealis over Murmansk.
It was the day before St. Nicholas Eve, January 4th and
only hours before his flight left for icebound Leningrad,
500 miles to the south. Andrei looked forward to a ten day
leave while his able First Officer took *Vyatka* under the
Arctic ice and across the polar sea to Vladivostock, no
small feat in itself. He would fly out and take command
later.

He picked up his brass dividers and set one point on the
island of Oahu on his chart of the central Pacific Ocean.

Chapter 23

The barrel-shaped officer from Baku cheeked his plug of Turkish tobacco and bared his yellowed teeth. "Down to snorchel, Lieutenant." He took a last, long look from the conning tower of Number 780. A flock of Red-tailed Tropic-birds shrilly announced their presence and circled the chugging diesel boat once before flying off. From his previous service in the Pacific, Lieutenant Commander Sergei Grodnov knew that the "bos'n birds" with their long forked red marlinspike tails, ranged up to two hundred miles from their island roosts, and they were headed, as was 780, to Midway Island. Waiting for the deck officer to disappear through the hatch, he spat to leeward and followed the watch down.

"Bear" Grodnov clumped off the tower ladder and over to his first officer who was plotting a course on the chart table.

"How much further?" He leaned heavily on the table.

"We're over the Emperor Ridge right now, Sir." Lieutenant Artemon Kalinin gestured at the fathometer.

"Good God," Grodnov recoiled, "1500 feet—and the last time I looked it was 15,000."

"Seems to be holding at that, sir . . . a sort of plateau. Must be an uncharted sea mount. It checks out with the inertial data; we're about 250 miles northwest of Kure."

"How far outside of SEA SPIDER?"

"250 miles, sir, another 30 hours run."

"Plot a tangent to Crespo that keeps us 100 miles from the SPIDER circle—that is, to the closest point we can get to Crespo, north of Oahu."

"Aye, sir, that'll put us about 550 miles north of the position in Comrade Verne's book," Artemon set his parallel rule tangent to the SPIDER perimeter and swung one end toward 780's position. Next, he drew a course line and checked it against the compass rose declination and the tide and current data.

"Come to zero five eight," he ordered the helmsman as Grodnov nodded and went forward, anxious to finish a crossword puzzle he had started in *Krokodil*. Two seven-hundred mile legs around SEA SPIDER would take about a week under snorkel. Eighty-six men, apprised of this interval, went into various stages of nautical hibernation. Three diesels hammered out 6000bhp in counterpoint to a lively balalaika in the forward torpedo room crew's quarters.

Kalinin was glad he had transferred out of Zinoviev's nuclear boats, for had he not he might well have been on *Vyatka*. Four months away from Natalya. He longed for the finish of this mission . . . a month more and he would be back in Leningrad—before the ice melted on the Neva.

Back in Leningrad . . . walking along the riverside, and planning the future with his Natalya.

Chapter 24

A cascade of white-hot sparks and metal chips showered down into the cavernous hull. Two men, caught as they were crawling through a confined corridor below decks shouted up to the workmen, but the racket drowned them out.

"Let's get the hell outta here," Ben swung down to the next deck, his London Fog raincoat sleeve smoldering from a hot flake of metal.

"I'm sorry, Ben—this all happened because of me." First Lieutenant Rudi Mulford brushed cinders from his uniform jacket.

"Let's say, this was your baptism under fire. If it's anyone's fault, Rudi, it's mine; I should have told the foreman we were going inside. Anyway," Ben rubbed his cold hands and blew warmth into them, "that entire 'sail' area gets flooded when she dives. The ports are just for surface looking. Right here," he slapped one of the steel ribs, "is where the reactor goes. This is called a 'hoop'. All the steel in this baby is the toughest made, HY-80. It can take 80,000 pounds per square inch, and it ain't cheap. The next step up is titanium; starts at 120,000 and goes right on up to 200,000. Titanium alloys have another thing going for 'em—they're not magnetic. Won't register on MAD systems, besides being the best corrosion resistant alloy there is, especially in sea water.''

"Then why are we still building steel hulls?" Rudi inspected one of the through-hull fittings.

"There ain't enough ore in this country. Funny thing," Ben mused, "a German discovers the metal, an American invents a way to extract and produce it in quantity—and now it turns out the purest deposits are in Russia, India and China.''

"We're expecting a Soviet titanium sub?"

"It's one way they can beat our magnetic ASW system."

"How deep could a titanium hull go?" Rudi winced.

"We'll plant CAPTORS on the bottom.''

A crew of hard-hatted workmen snaked past, flattening Rudi and Ben against a bulkhead, giving them a less than cordial glance. One of them made a muffled remark which amused the others.

"They don't like Navy brass, . . . I think they recognized me. I oughta dye my hair next time," Ben led the way aft. "I guess they think I'm checking up on their work.''

"Aren't you?"

"This is a tour, not an inspection," Ben replied stoically.

"Sure got a lot of people working on one boat," Rudi changed the subject, noting he'd touched a sore spot.

"Takes about 18,000 men and women to put one together— and that's twenty-four hours a day, 365 days a year.''

"Lots of overtime, I'll bet."

"There's lots of gold at Fort Knox, so let's use it," Ben quipped as a pneumatic hammer turned the hull into the inside of a trap drum. They passed two large, roaring fan ducts which were sucking out the combined fumes generated by the welder's torches, cleaning solvents and packing grease. "There have been people gassed and electrocuted in this program, just like in any other building program . . . the pyramids . . . Empire State Building—

"The Pentagon?" Rudi interrupted.

"That's classified," Ben smirked, "but don't touch any loose wires. We don't need any more publicity."

"I'll hold my breath, too," Rudi entered a long compartment sudded with vertical columns. "Sherwood Forest?"

Ben grinned. "You've done your homework. "Yep, this is where it's all at. We're putting C-3s into all of 'em now. No fuckin' around. There won't be a city we can't hit." Ben stuck his unruly head into a tube access opening. "Sonovabitch," he voice echoed hollow inside the launch tube, "now there's some sloppy welding." Ben retracted his head, took a pad from his coat pocket, and noted the tube number. "Shoulda been ground down and buffed." Ben looked inside all sixteen tubes. "Just like buying a car . . . don't take the saleman's word that everything's in shape just because you can't see it. There ain't much difference between Detroit and Groton: Profit, Profit, Profit—regardless of shoddy workmanship." Ben peeked into the next compartment aft.

"Maneuvering Room," the slim Admiral ducked in. He screwed up his face at one of the deck mountings, then looked at his watch. "Let's see the rest of the boat."

"Next time you come by, we'll drive down to Norfolk and look at the boat you'll be assigned to. She's almost ready and you should get a preview—see 'er stripped to essentials before the trimmings hide everything. I want to check 'er out myself anyway," Ben hit the brakes and his six-year-old Nova skidded to a stop beside one of the Delaware Bridge's toll booths. "Sorry," he handed the astonished attendant a handful of nickels and dimes.

"Zebulon Pike is a strange name for an SSBN," Rudi

turned on the radio as they sped across the southbound span of the tandem bridge. ". . . where have you gone Joe DiMaggio . . ."

"Not as strange as," Ben mimicked a southern accent, "*George Washington Carver*, dere. I wanted to call your boat *Jean LaFitte*—get a little action back in the fleet. But the brass was afraid of the pirate image."

"I can see the jolly roger waving now . . ."

Simon and Garfunkel gave way to the matter-of-fact newscaster's beat:

"Noted author and pediatrician Benjamin Spock was indicted yesterday on charges of conspiring to counsel young men to violate the US draft regulations . . ."

Ben turned the newscast low. "Somebody ought to cut off his nuts. What the hell is happening in this country? Traitors shooting their mouths off and making money at the same time. There's another Yale prick born with a silver spoon. All they want is more publicity; that's all everyone wants."

Rudi's eyes caught Ben's in the rear-view mirror. They were both glad when the pop music picked up again.

Chapter 25

Andrei moved closer to Natalya. He picked up the striped purple silk bolster she had set between them and tossed it to the opposite end of the mauve Victorian divan.

"I've waited a long time for this," the fastidious Captain reached over with his gold rimmed blue sleeve and toyed with a pendent under Natalya's auburn hair.

"You're going to miss your flight," she shrugged away from his grasping fingers.

"I've decided to spend my leave in Leningrad. I like cozy fires in the dead of winter—like yours."

"But you told father you were leaving tonight—"

"That's why he accepted my tickets to the Kirov. He knew I wanted to talk to you. Besides, Tanya hasn't been to the ballet in years. So everyone benefits." Andrei filled Natalya's brandy glass as she stared into the marble-cased fire. Admiral Makarov looked down from his frame over the mantel. Natalya closed her eyes to escape his stare. Suddenly she felt a cold hand on her back. A button was undone and the coldness crept around her, almost within her. "Andrei," she squirmed defiantly as the hand slid inside her blouse and tugged at the clasp of her brassiere. Momentarily shocked as the brassiere slipped down, she tore from his grip, only to be caught by his other arm and pulled down onto his lap on her side. With his left hand restraining her about the neck and shoulder, he forced his right hand around her and caressed her uncovered breast. She started to scream and kick but his hand closed over her mouth. Then she bit his left hand and he flung her onto the thick Heriz tree-of-life rug where she lay dazed among the palmettes and peacocks. Andrei licked his wound.

"You little devil, look what you've done," he let some blood rise on his skin.

"I'm sorry Andrei, but you . . . I . . . , can we forget what happened. I won't say a word. Please?"

"*Please*, she says." Andrei took off his uniform jacket and draped it over the divan. Then he leaned over her. "Drink this," he handed Natalya her filled glass. She tried to get up from the floor but each time he pushed her down again.

"Drink."

She drank, afraid of what was in his eyes.

He unbuttoned his silk shirt, feeling a power over her, sitting at his boots in front of the flickering flames.

"Andrei, what are you . . ."

He kicked off his boots and rolled off the divan. He wrestled her to her back and clawed at her blouse. She felt her skirt being pulled up—fire's heat upon her thighs and a quick hand caught her off guard.

Natalya screamed, but his hand closed over her mouth.

"Now, now, my treasure—screaming will be bad for everybody . . . your father . . . and . . . you must think about Artemon. Natalya's body went limp at the name. She stopped struggling and he removed his hand from her mouth. "That's much better," he pulled her sheer claret blouse up over her winter white breasts. Natalya closed her eyes as she felt his hands, his hot breath and his impassioned, hungry lips. High above, the antique grandfather's clock joined the Admiral and looked down on her. Chimes struck quarter of ten; her parents would not be home until past eleven.

"You said 'Artemon'?"

"Yes, the studious Lieutenant I just—the young man who went to Vladivostok. I believe I met him here a few months ago. There aren't many Artemons in the submarine service.

"What have you done to him?"

"His boat is on an important mission."

"Why did you say 'I must think about Artemon?' " Natalya tried to shake off the effects of the brandy.

"Just that we wouldn't want to get him into trouble, would we; and only a few months more service."

Natalya was quiet. How did Andrei find out. Not even her father knew that Artemon wanted to resign. She shuddered at the idea of Artemon being refused his option. She felt Andrei's hand, now warm on her knee; he was sitting like a child with a new toy. She tried to turn away, but he knelt between her legs and pinned her down with one arm. Then he forced her legs apart, whispering "Artemon . . . Artemon." The ceiling spun round her head; chandelier . . . portraits . . . curtains. All upside down. Again, the fireplace warmth between her thighs . . . an animal grunting . . . snapping of garter belt and he was upon her, clawing at her bare hips. Natalya struggled up on her elbows and she saw him. A bald spot behind slicked black thinning hair—pressed into her. "Don't . . . please," she whimpered ashamedly. The blue and gold moon's phase face glittered between the clock's hands. Then it stopped; Andrei had stopped and she fell back, relieved. Another sound. She ran her hands down her side, over her stomach. Thank God he'd stopped; she felt defiled enough with what he'd already done. At least she would be, would appear chaste for Artemon when they were married.

Slowly she raised her head, expecting to find him gone.

It was so quiet and she dared open her eyes once more. When she did, shock set in, such was the apparition as he closed in on her, a hairy animal, out-of-focus and cutting off the very light and air about her. Thrust up against the divan, fingers pried at her mouth as the animal forced its way in, pulsing and wet; choking her. Then, a faraway dull, intruding pain darted within her but she dared not move, had not the strength to resist—nor the will. She tried to think of Paris and the Ecole des Beaux-Arts, of the museums and the paintings she loved. Cezanne . . . Renoir . . .

Then an image of Edvard Munch's *The Scream*—a blank-faced young girl on a bridge, screaming in silence. And now a vortex of tortured shapes and colors . . . jagged brush strokes . . . streaming, dripping paints—blood-red betrayals of white linen canvases.

Chapter 26

The magnetic tape spun, then stopped—then spun once more as signals were fed into the computer bank at the ASW Force center on Oahu. Intelligence Center Electrician's Mate Ann Tucker pressed a print-out button. The computer clicked and buzzed, disgorging a strip of paper. She tore it off, inserted it in a blue envelelope and put in on a message belt. Seconds later it was fed into a decoding machine; the myriad zeros and ones on the strip were deciphered into words and figures, then routed through a tube into a locked access vault in the duty officer's room.

Chief Warrant Officer Sid Newman put down his air-mail edition of *The New York Times* and read the latest from SEA SPIDER:

USSR GOLF 780 DEP VLAD 6 JAN 0800- 2800T
320 X 25 X 22- 17.6/17- 6000BHP- R22700- 3 SSN5
700R- TSUGARU V- 10J- 4H

Newman read the last three entries once more. A Soviet diesel missile sub was headed for the defense perimeter. If it didn't change course in under 4 hours it would trip the system.

Information had been leaked that SEA SPIDER was larger than the original radius as a deterrent for new Soviet missiles. KGB Naval Section couldn't miss the tip. But it was still coming in. Were they calling our bluff? Was it a feint—preceding another Pearl Harbor, this time on the U.S. Pacific coast? Newman put the transcript into a red envelope, sealed it and hand-carried it to CINCPAC Section, down the long corridor of the air-conditioned data fortress. Red envelopes were rare, this being the first time Newman had occasion to use one. They were so rare that Newman discarded the first envelope because it had been discolored on top of the stack.

He handed it directly to the Admiral's aide and waited till he saw a flurry in the old man's office.

Lieutenant Artemon Kalinin was in command of 780. He knew, everyone knew that the "bear" would stay in his cabin . . . come out of hibernation only under duress or danger. One more hour and he could also dream. Dream of Natalya. The balalaika had been joined by men's voices, transforming the boat into a resonant metal instrument, dampened by the sea's passage along the hull and the diesel's constant beat. Artemon tapped his boot lightly in rhythm with an ancient Russian folksong and imagined he was dancing with Natalya under the summer lanterns of Lenin Park by the Planetarium. He wore his resplendent white uniform and she, a daring Parisian miniskirt.

It was the last wordly image that Artemon saw. The 2800 ton craft shuddered violently, catapulting crew and equipment into blackness. An automatic alarm blared and trailed off. Artemon's image was eclipsed by green and white fireballs. His hands felt cold metal under rushing sea water. Warm liquid coughing out of his mouth. Natalya reappearing smaller and smaller, spinning into a distant point of light. Jackhammer throbbing in the midbrain. Then *nothing* as the sepulchal steel tomb hurtled ever deeper, seams crunching, toward the eternal primordial ooze of the sunless ocean floor—three miles down. 1000 pounds seawater pressure per square inch on flesh and fixture . . . 2000 . . . 5000 . . . 7000.

Skulls and bowels bursting and imploding, People's Submarine Number 780, falling at over 100 miles per hour, impacted and buried it's crumpled bows deep in the black mud, stirring up vast legions of luminescent microorganisms.

February arrived and there was still no word of Grodnov's boat. Complex code queries gave way to world-wide commercial radio broadcasts appealing to individual crew members under various misleading contexts by the Soviet-controlled media. Unlike the United States press coverage of the 1963 *Thresher* disaster, and *Scorpion's* loss, there was no mention of 780's disappearance.

But *Vyatka Sturgeon* left Vladivostock on schedule with Andrei Zinoviev commanding—confident of his eventual conquest of Natalya as well as the Soviet Fleet. The Captain had gambled on the Admiral's daughter and won. 780 would be listed as missing and the search trawlers recalled—in due time, during which Natalya would accept her father's counseling. That she was already "compromised", Andrei considered an advantage and a prerogative of the classic masculine warrior.

By mid-March *Vyatka* had logged almost 8000 French leagues—over 22,000 nautical miles—marking in the passage, calls at eighteen of *Nautilus'* 37 anchorages, including the Marquesas, New Hebrides, Vanikoro and

Chapter 27

/

First Lieutenant Rudi Mulford stood in the lead-lined reactor tunnel of SSBN *Zebulon Pike*. It was just past midnight as the *Lafayette* Class boat cruised at 21 knots, 800 feet below the surface of a moonlit Indian Ocean. After threading the Laccadive islands and passing through "8 degree channel", the black whale turned east for a ten hour run to the "come about" point off the southern tip of the Indian peninsula.

Ben Mount's adopted son looked down through the lead-treated thick glass window in the tunnel's deck. His boyish face gleamed green from the glare of the reactor's fission chamber as he knelt down for his periodic inspection as engineering officer. Reaching for a handle on the wall of the 25-foot corridor, he turned it slowly, activating a polished titanium mirror below the window and rotating it to observe a series of sight guages in the chamber. Bunched snake-like conduits and eccentrically-shaped tanks in the tunnel picked up the green glow, imparting a science-fiction aura to hard reality: full circle, from Verne to verity and back.

Deep inside, the viewing of nuclear incandescence frightened Rudi. He fingered his polarized goggles to make sure they were set to maximum opacity. There were too many things about nuclear fission and fusion that were still unknown. The effects of cumulative exposure to radiation would take years to determine . . . With new particles like quarks and anti-quarks being isolated, who is to say that there is not yet another particle being emitted that pierces lead or changes the composition of the very air we breathe? It occurred to Rudi that even Ben had not been exposed to the eerie green light as much as he had been during his seven years in the nuclear navy. He watched as the control rod cam lowered slightly, pushing its multiple boron shafts deeper into the tubes of U-238, damping the neutron exchange and lowering the heat in response to a change in power demand.

The square window to energy heretofore claimed only by the sun and the universe was a warning—a kaleidoscope of the future, a view into peace—or war. Infinite energy in a world of confusion and enmity, and this was only the beginning. He was two years older than the splitting of the atom . . . five years older than Hiroshima. What will happen when the energy has lived a lifetime's span. Two lifetimes? Did anyone expect that the war twin of the green window be leashed anymore than those other doomsday weapons, the cross-bow . . . the machine gun . . . the V-2 missile.

Rudi had almost spoken his mind at a party given by Ben and Betsy before his assignment to the Blue Crew on *Zeb.* *Almost* because of Debbie Mount, and what happened. His 15-year-old "sister", complete with provocatively torn jeans and "ooh-wow" vocabulary ambushed him with grass as he was taking a beach breather from Jack Daniels. Rudi stared into the greenfire window as Debbie's taunts mingled with the engine's beat aft:

"Rudi—I didn't think you'd do it: stay in the service after all the Viet-Nam shit. Nobody under 30 does it—at

least, people I get along with. The bomb sucks, and you
want to be a bomb jock—drivin' sixteen *mirvs* around.
Don't you feel wrong?

"Debbie, I didn't come here to be—"

"Then why did you come at all?"

"For your father . . . My stepfather."

"Bullshit."

"Debbie," he declined her offer of the roach.

"They can't hear us. They didn't last year—when we
. . . you . . . Isn't beach property nice—I mean the sound
of waves an' all."

"What do you mean by *me*? It was that stuff you gave
me to sniff. I didn't know what it would do. I went crazy."

"You sure did," Debbie's tongue moved over her lower
lip.

"It was wrong, I shouldn't have . . ."

"Man, there's nothing wrong with a nice hard-on. In
fact they're getting very rare nowadays."

"That's because women have changed." Rudi took the
grass roach and dragged deeply on it.

"So have men," Debbie pressed into him.

"But you tricked me—it was almost like—"

"Incest?"

"You said it, I didn't." Rudi picked up a flat stone and
skipped it on the night-flickering water.

"But you're so different from an incest-type brother. I
don't like to mess with dull people like David and all their
hang-ups. Your body is so great—not flabby like David's.
I always used to watch you when you came home on
leave."

"What do you mean, "watch me?""

"In the cabana when you changed. You know the locker
that was hard to open? I could fit in it. You used to stand
so close to me that I almost went crazy." Debbie embraced him and pressed herself into him. Rudi's hand
found a rip on the seat of her jeans and Debbie encouraged
an exploration.

"You *are* crazy, Debbie. This doesn't make sense at all."

"It could, Rudi. Give it up. I got these friends in Frisco. We can crash for a few months." She lit up a fresh joint.

"Sorry. No go. I like you, kid. But this is far enough."

"Want me to scream?" She took a deep breath, breasts thrust forward in the moonlight.

"You wouldn't," Rudi started to walk back.

"I've got nothing to lose. I've already dropped out of school, so who cares."

"Ben and Betsy care; so do I."

"Then let's go to the cabana."

"Why," the grass was getting to him.

" 'Cause I wanta be screwed by the U.S. Navy," she whispered and nuzzled him under the ear.

"Your mother's perfume?" Rudi was responding. He slipped his hand between their bodies.

"If you screw me, we'll be even and I promise not to tell anyone about your taking advantage of a minor last summer."

"You strike a hard bargain," he ducked under some bushes behind the cabana as voices were heard from the house.

"It runs in the family," Debbie led the way calmly.

Framed at one end of the wardroom, a reproduction of a painting of Brigadier General Zebulon Montgomery Pike, in high military collar and tassled gold epaulettes gazed benignly toward the flowered drapes behind Commander Bradford "Red" Sweet. Seven officers sat, caps before them around the long, formica wood-grained table. They waited until the mess steward had closed the door behind him. Coffee steaming and several cigarettes alight, the men in short-sleeved summer tans waited tensely for the Captain to look up from his daybook. Rudi was impressed by the fact that the mess steward was no longer a separate ethnic type, but managed to look like an amalgam of Oriental, Black and Spanish-American—a tribute to the new Navy's central casting section.

"Men," the Captain pointed toward a chart hanging over part of the wardroom plotting window on the access corridor side. "If you haven't heard yet—the reason we've cut speed is that we received an order during last night's star fix. The *Nemo* Yankee that's due through these parts didn't pass inspection. One of our PC-3s picked him up on magnetic detection south of the Cocos yesterday. Routine data processing at First Fleet came up with a bogey. Magnetic had him at 8200 tons, but the bank came up with 9700 for the first two of her class, from operational magnetic fixes." Sweet sucked on his cigarette placebo, made a face and set it down next to his mechanical pencil. "Aerial surveillance photos of *Nemo's* launching at Severodvinsk show a standard *Yankee* configuration—sixteen tube humpback deck and a low sail. He's on a vector to Manaar Gulf and the updated plot puts him off Sumatra."

There was a red adhesive disk on the chart, just south of the Equator near 80 degrees east longitude.

"So there you've got it. Our job is to shadow him and make sure he stays out of the Persian Gulf. There's something fishy about that displacement disparity." Sweet's plastic cigarette rolled briskly off the table and Ensign Adams bumped his head while retrieving it as Zebulon Pike swung gently on his well-lighted wall.

"Fifteen hundred tons is like a whole World War Two fleet boat lighter," Lieutenant Commander Jack Woolhiser was doodling female forms on his notepad.

In eager schoolboy style, Rudi raised his hand. "Maybe *Nemo* doesn't have any missiles aboard, which could account for the weight difference."

Commander "Red" Sweet's black coffee went down the wrong way. "What's the point," he sputtered, "of sending out an empty SSBN instead of an attack boat? Gorshkov needs all the firepower he can get *in* the water."

"One thing though, Red," Woolhiser closed his pad. "The Russians don't do anything without an ulterior motive. Suppose there are no missiles aboard. They could have delivered them somewhere. Maybe Rudi's got something."

"It's not like the Soviet Navy. They would have used it in propaganda. An unarmed boat going around the world. You know—the 'peaceful' bit." Sweet drained his coffee and got up.

"What's his next port of call," drawled the navigation officer, Lieutenant Begole. "That is if he sticks to the 20,000 leagues schedule as Verne wrote it?"

Sweet peeked into his daybook. "Gulf of Oman. Then Gulf of Aden and The Red Sea."

"It *would* be the Red Sea," quipped Woolhiser.

"*Nemo* might try to slip through the Straits of Hormuz and get a look at MIDEASTFOR," Begole traced his finger on the window chart from Ceylon to the Gulf of Oman. The Russkies got pretty pissed when one of our guys got under an *Echo* boat in Vladivostok harbor and photographed his bottom."

"*And* got out again," Captain Sweet added laughingly. "Admiral Gorschkov must have shit when we mailed him the prints a year later. But there's no way they're getting into the Persian Gulf, and they know it."

"That's what the British said about Scapa Flow and the U-boats in 1939," added Woolhiser. "With all the Commie arms being shipped in for the Dhofars, I wouldn't be surprised to see a few Russian ETs playing around with our channel arrays at Musandam. Another possible way in is to dredge one of the peninsula channels—*on* Oman territory and haul the *Yankee* through."

"There'll be a surprise when they come out the other side," Captain Sweet went forward to his stateroom, followed by his exec.

"Does that mean CAPTOR is operational," whispered Woolhiser.

"No comment at this time," replied Commander Sweet with an affirmative air.

0400. Ensign Adams had replaced Rudi in the Maneuvering Room and a new watch crew was manning the panels and the steam wheel. Across the central corridor, the "still" gurgled in its unremitting task of transmuting the ocean into fresh water for the cooks, the crew and the washing machines. Climbing a ladder out of the engine room, Rudi passed the Auxiliary Machine Room and stopped in the Reactor Tunnel for his last check of the green window. Then another Machine Room crammed with thrumming generators. He walked under the armored ceiling cables of Sherwood Forest, counting steps to himself. Forty-seven steps for the Missile Room. It varied, more or less by one step—or a half step—depending how tired he was. The red interior lighting, corresponding to night in the real world, tired him, slowed his responses and steps, while the white "daylight" had the reverse effect. He patted the last missile tube for luck—"Luck" that the Captain would never have to use that infamous key of his and loose the "sharks of war."

Entering the Navigation Center, Mulford always felt as if he was an intruder inside a giant electronic brain. Though he had taken basic courses and could tell a "flip-flop" from a "Schmidt trigger," he was in awe of the ETs as electronics technicians were classified. A different breed, they appeared as programmed as the profusion of knobs and dials they manned. Rudi walked carefully through the maze of electronic stations, noting the overhead Inertial Navigation binnacles, the NAVDAC computer and the Multi-Speed Repeaters and the wall consoles with their large "selector wheels."

Suddenly, the tone of *Zebulon Pike* dropped an octave.

Power had been cut back and the digital knotmeter flicked slowly downward, settling between four and five knots—just enough headway for steering. *Zeb* had come up for a star fix.

Pristis Clavata lay basking in the starlit waters off Kelai Atoll, over the Maldives shallows. Clavata bore one pup within her womb—a strapping 60 pound male. Clavata slapped her nine-foot sawbill on the surface playfully as she rolled over under the milky white ring of the heavens, sparkling with constellations: Lupus . . . Cëntaurus . . . Carina—and proud Crucis, the Southern Cross.

She was lithe and long—as long as the much-vaunted white shark, without counting her saw: sixteen inches across at the base, it was studded with 32 six-inch bone daggers on each side.

Her domain stretched from the Maldive Archipelago to Manaar Gulf and was uncontested by her cousins, the killer sharks. For *Pristis* was named by men who knew of her power and exploits—her position in the evolution of the shark. She was the progenitor, as in the terms "prime, prior," and "private." It was not her lack of strength that doomed her specie to smaller and smaller domains, but the ascendence of a new kind of survival in the sea:

Multiple offspring.

Clavata, a rare, evolutionary throwback, could have but one.

But the Great White, *Cacharodon,* and the Hammerhead, *Diplana* bear up to thirty pups—survival of the most. Clavata rose up from the bottom-groveling ways of the rays to become the scourge of the seas. Her combination of slashing blade and shark's body held sway over eons, when continents were still part of the ocean floor.

Now, her kind had dwindled, but where they lived, they reigned supreme. Throwbacks to the Devonian epoch. Sharks, those dreaded fish held little fear for the pearl divers who chased them off with noise, but Clavata knew no such fear. For it was the sawfish that panicked the Tamils—the raking razor bill that had cut many a diver in two.

Clavata lay, comfortably spouting from its topside spiracles and expelling water from its underside gill-slits . . . resting for the ordeal ahead.

A plume of white slid along the water's surface, startling the basking sawfish into a sudden erratic dive. A force of 9000 tons—the leading edge of *Zebulon Pike's* superhard steel sail struck Clavata in the soft underbelly. Staggered, she slashed at the gigantic dark whale with her bill, but it passed by—leaving her trembling in the pangs of premature labor. Screaming inside, she tortuously expelled her pup. She had carried it for the best part of a year. Clavata nudged it lovingly.

But it did not respond. The pup's white belly was up as it drifted away from its mother. It was dead.

And it was the whale that killed Clavata's pup.

"No damage that I can see, sir." Master Diver Anthony L. Karas climbed up the sail ladder rungs and handed his flashlight to the OD. "There were some scratches in the paint, like we mighta hit a chain or somethin'." He unzipped his wet suit top and slipped down through the conning hatch. The decks were already awash when the chief dogged the hatch.

Zeb went down to periscope depth again for the fix. One piece of floating debris in several month's patrol wasn't bad. It could have been worse—a local fishing trawler . . . or an eighty-foot whale. Captain Sweet ordered an immediate check of the sonar ranging system and went back to his bunk.

Lieutenant Commander Woolhiser, who'd drawn the lobster shift, called out star fix orders from his saddle seat on the Type Eleven periscope. Designated "Optical Star Tracker", it was located in a raised cubicular compartment at the forward end of the Navigation Center. Once again, the SINS reset procedure started, as Mulford stood by, intent on becoming more proficient himself.

The SINS or Ship's Inertial Navigation System was the heart of the boat, indeed of the entire global function of Polaris. But it was not perfect, having a tendency to introduce tiny errors in position and attitude because of "Gyro Drift." After 3 or 4 days, the cumulative error could be enough to shift the data that was continually processed by the NAVDAC computer to a degree that the missiles, if fired, might miss their targets 2500 miles distant.

Buttons and switches were activated in sequence. NAVDAC reached into its memory and found two facts: The brilliant star, Canopus would be spotted at -53 degrees 49.6 minutes south declination and 102 degrees 15.3' azimuth. This data was based on the other fact that SINS calculated the *boat's* position a millisecond earlier for processing by NAVDAC. The exec pressed another button; the Star Tracker scope wormed around, turning the stealth-coated head—plumed white wake following on the sea's surface—toward Canopus. Another electronic signal from NAVDAC, and the elevating prism behind the electrically-clearing entrance window pivoted upward, stopping at the NAVDAC solution.

Lieutenant Commander "Jack" Woolhiser, bloodshot eye pressed into rubber, focused on a wavering pinpoint of light. NAVDAC had pointed good, but not good enough. The star image swung crazily in and out of the field of view, leaving a subliminal "W" shape in Jack's fertile mind. The "W" reminded him of woman—viewed by a man from a vantage somewhere between the lady's ankles, assuming the lady's kneecaps were higher than his eyeballs.

The gangling officer, draped around his Type Eleven scope, switched to maximum enlargement. Canopus was sucked into his eyebrain six times as big as at first. Still it roamed in and out of the target rectangle in the circular viewing field.

Time for manual correction. It felt good that a man had a final say over automation. Woolhiser twirled a ribbed knob, moving the star image to the right. Centered horizontally, it now remained to be fixed in declination or altitude. Another slow turn and Canopus rose, But it still swayed within the target rectangle. Apparently the wind had picked up or there were swells on the surface that caused the scope to rise and fall, to pitch and yaw.

Jack pressed the attitude compensation button.

NAVDAC computed the boat's pitch and yaw, then transmitted a negative command: The periscope mirror obeyed: it moved in equal but contrary attitudes to *Zebulon Pike*'s centerline. Canopus was now still—centered within the periscope's target rectangle.

"Mark," the exec called out.

"Mark," replied the NAVDAC ET as Woolhiser's hand correction data was assimilated by the computer and relayed into the SINS system, correcting its cumulative error.

Firing a 2500-mile range Poseidon missile is comparable to a rider trying to hit a bull's eye at a quarter of a mile with a handgun, firing from a bucking horse. In addition, the problem involved stage separation at the proper instant— the piggyback bullet.

NAVDAC gobbled up the updated data. Should Red Sweet be ordered to use his doomsday key, it was ready to mix its solutions with the port and starboard optical trolleys as they determined each missile's alignment attitude by means of a mirror laser system, assuring update guidance in sixteen programmed packages. With a maximum range of 2500 miles *Zeb* was programmed to hit sixteen cities and military centers from Moscow south to Iran. At its apogee or farthest point south in the Indian Ocean, the sixteen Poseidons, carrying more devastation than all the bombs used by all sides during the five years of World War Two were automatically programmed to obliterate the three southern Soviet "Oblasts" bordering Iran and Afghanistan.

Hiding a yawn, Rudi passed by the steering cockpit, noting the *Conalog* "television screen" steering station. Manned by two ratings, the starboard station screen showed the Indian Ocean surface as a perspective plane while the digital repeater hovered around forty feet. The ocean surface plane was delineated with a grid that extended to infinity. Below a horizontal centerline there was another plane—much like a long highway, which indicated the boat's keel plane.

A correct "on course—on depth" heading showed a perfect balance of planes. Change of direction or depth signals altered the graphics to appear as a right-turn highway or a rising grade. In all cases the boat's attitude was represented by a center-screen star. It was reminiscent of an amusement park automobile driving machine.

In practice, *Zebulon Pike* was controlled with aircraft-style equipment, enabling it to climb, bank and dive. The major difference was that the air was liquid. Rudi felt a drop in temperature as he walked past the Chilled Stores compartment and wondered what the cook had in mind for the next day's dinner. He patted his stomach and hoped he'd not gained as much weight as some, considering the average sixty-day mission consumed 4000 pounds of beef, 3000 of sugar, 1400 pounds of pork loin, 1000 ham, 800 pounds of butter, 3400 of flour—and 12,000 eggs. Pushing these images away, he hurried past the crew's mess, adorned with plastic flowers and into "officer's country." Closing the door of his empty two-man compartment, Rudi stripped off his uniform and sighed into the lower bunk. Yes, rank had its privileges. An officer could burp and not be clobbered with wisecracks. So he did.

Flicking on his reading lamp, he opened a book, marked by a playing card joker.

Chapter II

A NOVEL PROPOSAL OF
CAPTAIN NEMO'S

ON THE 28th of February, when at noon the *Nautilus* came to the surface of the sea, in 9°4' north latitude, there was land in sight about eight miles to westward . . . On taking the bearings, I knew that we were nearing the Island of Ceylon, the pearl which hangs from the lobe of the Indian Peninsula.

Captain Nemo and his second appeared at this moment. The Captain glanced at the map. Then, turning to me, said—"The island of Ceylon, noted for its pearl-fisheries. Would you like to visit one of them, M. Aronnax?"

"Certainly, Captain."

Well, the thing is easy. Though if we see the fisheries, we shall not see the fishermen. The annual exportation has not yet begun. Never mind, I will give orders to make for the Gulf of Manaar, where we shall arrive in the night." . . .

"Agreed, Captain."

"By the by, M. Aronnax, you are not afraid of sharks?"

"Sharks!" exclaimed I . . .

Rudi read on for several more pages. M. Aronnax described the dangers inherent in hunting the shark in its natural element and gave scientific details about the pearl to Ned Land and Conseil:

"The pearl is nothing but a nacreous formation, deposited in a globular form, either adhering to the oyster-shell, or buried in the creature's folds. On the shell it is fast; in the flesh it is loose; but always has for a kernel a small hard substance, maybe a barren egg, maybe a grain of sand, around which the pearly matter deposits itself year after year successively, and by thin concentric layers.''

"Are many pearls found in the oyster?'' asked Conseil.

"Yes, my boy. There are some that are jewel caskets. One oyster has been mentioned, though I allow myself to doubt it, as having contained no less than a hundred and fifty sharks.''

"A hundred and fifty *sharks*!'' exclaimed Ned Land.

"Did I say sharks?'' said I, hurriedly. "I meant to say a hundred and fifty *pearls*. Sharks would not be sense.''

Mulford put the book down on the deck beside his bunk, and flipped off his reading light. In twilight sleep he envisioned Manaar Gulf, with its seabed glittering—covered with opening and closing oysters displaying millions of lustrous pearls. Sea mounts of pearls, rivers and strands under the sea—with man-eating sharks swooping and hovering . . . diving and gorging themselves with oysters and pearls so the jewels were flung from their gills.

Verne's words from the mouth of M. Aronnax flashed across the strange feast:

". . . one oyster . . . having contained no less than a hundred and fifty sharks.'' Rudi stirred and awakened. Pearls . . . sharks . . . the curious misplacement of terms by M. Aronnax . . . Why not a hundred and fifty oysters in a shark? Or pearls in sharks; strings and caskets of pearls inside sharks . . .

Rudi sat up and bumped his head on the top bunk.

Pearls inside submarines.

A STRING OF HYDROPHONES INSIDE *NEMO*!

He would see the Captain at reveille.

reefs of the far distant islands of the Hawaiian chain before
the introduction of cultured pearls by the clever Japanese
at the century's turn. For they had been taught by Lunalilo,
the last of the divers who knew the secrets of fabled Pearl
and Hermes Reef . . . who had faced the shark, the devil-
ray and the great tsunami.

It was a toss-up among the family whether Tony had
learned to swim or to walk first. At the age of five he was
bringing up spiny lobsters from the flats and river bed. At
seven he was into scuba with an aqualung purchased from
the income of his personal fishing ventures. The summer
before entering high school he was allowed to go with his
uncles aboard *Mahimahi* to learn "big fishing" in the
Leeward Islands and for the first time go out of sight of the
island mountains he knew so well—of the dormant volcano,
Waialeale that lifted Kauia from the ocean floor to become
the "Garden Island" of Hawaii and the wettest place on
earth.

Before the summer was over, his uncles, daunted by
Tony's speargun captures of grouper and jack, had bought
their own flippers and tanks. *Mahimahi* went scuba.

Large families breed businesses, so a combination dive
shop and fishing boutique was added to the business of
fishing. Keala and one of her three brothers manned it.
The booming tourism of the sixties encouraged the store
and soon eclipsed *Mahimahi's* original calling. Equipped
as a dive boat, it took babbling rich Americans to the pearl
reefs while Tony ran the dive school between high school
classes and on weekends. There was something missing.
The wildness had left the ocean; beercans and plastic
bottles lined the tidal beaches. Tony went into the rain
forest more and more—for solitude and and a sense of
undefiled nature. He studied the flowering vines and bushes
along the Waimea Canyon rim, the *akuli-kuli* and golden
hala. In the verdant mountain forests he found the pearl-
like *pikake* and on the lava slopes of Waialeale, the flame-
red *ohia lehua*, tree blossoms sacred to the fire goddess

Pele. And Tony hunted the exotic forest orchids: purple and vermillion beacons against the wet umbers and deep emeralds of primeval jungle.

After graduation from high school he had to make a decision. Go into full-time work at the store and develop the dive shop—or attend The University of Hawaii at Honolulu.

He did neither; he surprised everyone by joining the Navy. It was time to leave the island, and the prospect of being drafted into the foot-slogging Army and going to Vietnam was depressing.

Recruit Tony Karas advanced through the enlisted ranks, excelling in Underseas Weapons School and was assigned to a demolitions unit. In August 1965, his Frogman unit swam ashore from a task force off the Chu-lai Peninsula in Vietnam. They mapped the reefs and blew up new landing entrances for the 1st and 3rd Marine Divisions which were assigned to "neutralize" a hard core contingent of Vietcong that had dug in at the port city of Hue. On the night preceding the assault, young Karas led a stealthy recon detail through the coral studded, shark-infested tidal flats and located major enemy gun emplacements to be knocked out by a rocket barrage prior to the landings. At 0600, when the first wave hit the beach, the Marines were amazed to be greeted by a bullet-riddled wooden sign propped in the sand:

WELCOME MARINES
COURTESY UDT-5

With the blue and gold Distinguished Service Navy ribbon on his whites he came home to Kauia, a local hero. His record more than qualified him for a choice of service in continuing his enlistment. Within weeks after applying, Tony was assigned to the submarine school at New London for eight weeks, and then to the Class C school in Dam Neck, Virginia. Learning the Polaris system in simulators along with electronic and missile technicians—ETs and MTs, he was part of a test group the nuclear brains under Admiral Mount had deemed essential to a submarine now that it had attained the size and grandeur of a capital ship. What the nuclear sub lacked was a small force of combat-trained men who were capable of instant deployment in support of their ship and related missions. The force was to be called "SEAL" which was an acronym of "sea, air and land." Aside from tactical units assigned to fleets and airdrop squadrons, SEAL was to provide a small but competent detail to each SSBN and SSN—a kind of "underseas Marine detachment."

Petty Officer, 2nd Class Karas was picked to head the first test squad aboard *Zebulon Pike*. Known by the crew variously as *Rubbernecks* and *Bangstick Boys* because of their aluminum rods capped with 12 gauge shotgun shells— sure death for sharks if detonated against the predators' brain. Unlike the storied peacock Marines in Naval history, Karas and his squad were not exempt from humdrum duty—as much as there was aboard an automated vessel.

One thing there was a lot of on board *Zeb*—was time. Commander Sweet spent his, reading books on becoming a four-striped Captain. Lieutenant Commander Woolhiser, in the privacy of his upper level stateroom, alternately ogled his copies of *Playboy* and stripped his personal competition Colt 45 automatic blindfolded. Lieutenant Mulford, before his revelation from Verne's classic, had tried to absorb Joyce's *Ulysses*, but settled instead for *Mein Kampf* in a paper wrapper.

Some of the crew took Harvard-prepared college courses with co-ordinated film and text sessions. Others slept or practiced with whalebone scrimshaw carving sets.

But not Tony Karas!

The delicate vermillion orchid had not done well during *Zeb's* first week on "Blue Crew" patrol out of Bahrain in the Persian Gulf. This was his third two-month cruise, and his third attempt to grow an Epidendrum orchid. The others had succumbed; weak stems from a lack of nutrients in *Zeb's* distilled water. Bothered by the limp plastic petunia and pansy arrangements in all four corners of the messroom, Tony had teamed up with Sylvan Rossiter, an up-and-coming doctor by way of Navy Pharmacist's Mate to nurture the first real plant ever grown on a submarine without nature's help. If successful, the process was to be submitted to Admiral Ben Mount who had encouraged similar ventures—with due rewards—to the Polaris crews. In this case, Rossiter had an uncle, a lawyer, who he would first consult before turning over the nutrient formula to the US Navy. A matter of procedure. Twenty-four hours earlier, Tony had doused the plant and its sandalwood-enriched pot of soil with Sylvan's latest liquid solution. The stem had been propped and tied lightly; strong when brought aboard, it had drooped after three days out—despite the grow-lamp and the dampness of the compartment below the reactor, which was called "The Mushroom Cave."

Tony stopped halfway down the ladder. The orchid seemed to glow like never before. *Zeb's* cellar housed the blast-off gas generators—one under each launch tube; their function was to provide pressurized gas to push the missile out of its tube to the ocean surface, after which the rocket engine ignited and continued propulsion. *Epidendrum,* small and frail as it was, stood erect among the gray metal trappings of destruction—a living thing.

Carefully, Tony untied the supporting string and drew the stick out of the potted soil. Removing his hand from behind the stem, he drew a deep breath. The orchid didn't move. Success.

"Hey, muff diver," one of the crew joked as he put a nickel in the juke box slot and pushed three selection buttons, "find any nice mermaids out there?"

"I'll save you seconds," Karas cringed as the raspy lyrics of Tiny Tim and 'Tip Toe Through The Tulips' invaded the messroom. He drew a cup of coffee from the urn and sat down at a corner table, away from the perennial poker and backgammon games.

"How's the patient?" A dark, curly head, protruding ears and freckled hose emerged from a pre-med textbook.

Tony just smiled.

"You mean—" Rossiter's jaw dropped.

"It's lookin' good. Whatever you put in the water yesterday musta done it." Karas put the string and support stick on the formica table and stirred his coffee.

"Tony, if it's true, we'll be famous—and maybe rich. This will go down in Naval annals like the appendectomy done with knives and forks during the war . . ." Rossiter closed his textbook and jumped up excitedly. "I gotta take a look-see."

"What did you do different this time with the solution?"

"What did I do this time?" The Pharmacist's Mate pulled at an earlobe, collecting his thoughts. "H_2O . . . natural rainwater, which is best for all plants . . . contains dissolved gases from our atmosphere . . . as well as traces of CO_2, chlorides, sufates . . . nitrates and ammonia . . ." He covered his eyes. "I can't remember—but I know I wrote it down . . . somewhere."

"*Somewhere?*" Tony moaned, "this is our big chance. Just think: the end of plastic flowers on submarines . . . maybe the beginning of herb gardens in all the Mushroom Caves . . ."

"Or fresh mushrooms— What the hell did I do with that note?" Rossiter flipped through a loose-leaf binder. "I know I wrote down the ingredients and amounts, but I draw a blank. I got everything down here for the last three experiments," he held up the binder for Tony to see, "except for yesterday."

"Oh, Jesus," Karas slumped back against the booth rest, under a corner arrangement of plastic flowers.

*　　*　　*

Captain, 3rd Rank Petrus Nielson was satisfied with his inspection of the hangar-like void, aft of *Vyatka's* navigation room. 120 feet long and 30 feet in diameter, the cavernous compartment was unobstructed except for catwalks, port and starboard, that connected the aft propulsion section with the control and crew's compartments under the sail and forward. This Soviet atom-powered submarine had been designed to capture a section of the newly-completed American sonar detection array, COLOSSUS.

A series of steel beams crossed the hold athwartships, under the sixteen false muzzle hatches. Attached to the bottom of each beam was a drum of wire cable powered by a central lift motor The cable ends were fitted with remote-control grapples. Below, 2 long watertight "bomb bay" doors were ready to be opened hydraulically after pressurization of the hold. Designed for relatively shallow underwater depths, the system resembled the standard open bottom caisson, long used in marine salvage and seafloor construction.

Lieutenant Kalinin's plan as originally described in a letter to Captain Zinoviev was to maneuver the salvage craft lengthwise over a stretch of the Colossus system with one of the twenty-seven foot high cylindrical nuclear-powered transformers in the center of the pick-up bay, then cut the cable fore and aft, and winch the entire assembly up into the hold. Equipped with umbilically powered cutting tools, a team of six divers could cut and separate the array in ten minutes. Another five and the bottom bays would be closed as the array, winched up, was secured. The operation would be too fast for US Naval sea or air retaliation. Once underway, the sub would be beyond reproach or inspection without international incident. With Kalinin lost and presumed dead, Zinoviev stood to gain as he presented the brilliant idea to Kulov as his own, first swearing the originator to secrecy pending its success.

KGB, Naval Section, seething after intelligence reversals brought about by the ambitious American operation "Holystone", went all out to pinpoint Colossus to save face and avoid a shake-up. A combination of infiltration of the American contractor, Western Electric with help from a wealthy Kuwait sheik and equipping a Ceylonese fishing boat with transistorized sonar, hidden in its trawling nets, established the location of Colossus. Just installed, it reached from the Indian continental shelf, all the way across the ocean to Cape Leeuwin, Australia, over 3000 miles. Two giant tripod supporting towers had been erected—one atop the 'Ninety East Ridge', parallel to the Cocos, and another, on a flat-topped sea mount north of the Ob Trench, a 22,500 foot abyssal canyon bordering the Diamantina Fracture. Like pylons of a suspension bridge, the towers, each four times as high as the Empire State Building, with three legs, spaced ten miles apart at their bases, supported the string of hydrophones and transformers, the latter having some degree of built-in floatation.

It was now up to *Vyatka* to bring glory to the fleet. Captain Andrei Zinoviev, chess player and devotee of French scientific élan and associated literature had prevailed well. Nielson could not take issue with Andrei's performance. It was the execution that counted.

Execution. Nielson pondered the term. It was only in English that the word meant death. French and German variations had no such connotations. He wondered why he was thinking in English and then realized it was his built-in strategic habit, a phenomenon that occurred before engaging the enemy. His ability in languages was another weapon in combat. *Execution* . . . Artemon Kalinin. Nielson folded the idea into his memory.

Though it was barely dawn above, *Vyatka* was swarming with life and sparkling with light. Helium tanks were readied and compressed air generated. Forward and side-scanning sonar reached into the dark waters, feeling for Colossus' huge transformer—looking for a reflected impulse. Sounds that would be data computed and appear on the conversion screen as a large, suspended buoy. KGB had fixed the northern terminal of Colossus at coordinates corresponding to a point 52 miles south of the tip of India.

Vyatka, true to *Nautilus'* journey, one hundred years earlier, was in the Gulf of Manaar, but not for visiting pearl fisheries—or donning diving suits and searching for Captain Nemo's coconut-sized pearl. *Vyatka* was about to win a battle of "The Wet Cold War."

"ZHEHMchyoog!"

A husky cry rang out in the navigation room.

"A pearl indeed," Zinoviev smiled at Nielson as the signals increased and the ghostly greenish-white image glimmered on the sonar screen.

After resting in the Kelai kelp beds for some hours, Clavata was in need of sustenance. Her underside pained and she'd chipped a few sawteeth but swimming was not impaired, in fact the pain abated when she exerted herself. Fighting the ocean current was good medicine for bad memories. Lonely nevertheless, after the loss of her pup, Clavata sought companionship . . . remembered the haunts of her youth, the spawning waters of Trincomalee on the sunrise side of Ceylon. With strength born of hope, the distraught sawfish veered toward the Manaar Straits, her thousands of sensory pores reacting to minute variations of light, taste and current . . . transmitting natural 'data' through nerve channels and into a bank of jelly-filled brain sacks called ampullae. The fresh stimuli, compared with previous sensations, retrograde passages and phases of the heavens, advanced navigational directions to the giant sawfish's cartilaginous rudders in response to her desires.

Halfway across the Maldive Straits, after finning along for three hours she spotted a school of glittering mackerel near the rippling surface and gave chase. Spiralling up toward the light she caught some stragglers before the silver hoarde became alarmed. The pulsating cloud of slow-moving fish suddenly elongated, following the experienced leaders in flight from the dreaded scourge of Ceylon.

The joy of chase in her, Clavata forgot her wounds and became determined to catch the fleet mackerel, wherever they led her. Maintaining a speed that man has only attained in the nuclear navies, the twenty-six-foot shark gained on her weaker prey, first slashing at small orbital schools, then powering into the core and exploding the school into shreds of bloody guts—flailing the massed mackeral out of the swells against the red twilight.

As the remnants dispersed, Clavata glided down in circles, snapping up the scaled chunks and yawing striped heads with her smallish mouth—grinding with her crustacean molars until she felt sated once again. On the bottom, at the edge of the continental shelf she rubbed her bill in the sand and seaweed, cleaning the sawteeth of clinging flesh and bone fragments before continuing on her way east. And then it came.

Distant, but unmistakable.

The faint water-borne vibrations of a whale.

A whale she had encountered only once before.

Zebulon Pike lay quiet. All but the most vital organs were shut down. No laundry now, no deep-sea Bobbie Gentry, no Sean Connery capers. Even the great Green Sea Turtle, ponderously hauling his 500 pounds accepted the high, looming submarine sail as another rock, nestled in the eel grass he was accustomed to feed on. Brightly striped yellow and black Skipjack Tuna swam round the black sail while tiny, glowing anenome fish passed between the periscope standards. *Zeb*'s round bow nuzzled into a sandy oyster bed while, over 400 feet aft, her stern lay over a cavernous rift, covered with swaying kelp.

The only sound aboard was the humming of a rotating fish-eye sonar unit, one of a group of instruments projecting from the sail. Originally designed for and used on

Neptune during its crossing of the North Pole ten years earlier, it determined the distance between surface ice and the sail. Operation "Holystone" had used an improved version to record the bottom of a Soviet sub in Vladisvostok harbor.

Now it was focused on another form of submersible—the vertically oriented Colossus transformer. The vertical component was set at six diameters magnification, and stationary, while the revolving sensors within the fiberglass dome were set for normal maximum-field scanning . . . expecting a visitor. *Zeb*'s conversion screen showed a white disk at the far left, and a small blip near the right edge, which corresponded to aft.

A Mark 48 wire-guided torpedo had been programmed, and was ready to be ejected from *Zeb*'s bow if needed. Two more were standing by. Far aft, in a ready room under the escape hatch, Tony Karas checked out his SEAL team. Armed with anti-shark "bang-sticks", grenades and an underwater compressed gas carbine, the five *aquamarines* were "qualified" for 350-foot dives from the surface and considerably deeper when working out of a submarine. There was no "track record" however, of rising to an objective and then diving back to the "mother ship" so Captain Sweet, in concurrence with his officers, decided that *Zeb*—should the occasion occur—would be the aggressor. This was still not a shooting war and the SEAL detachment was not to be put into danger. *Zeb* was prepared to blow and rise to within striking distance.

"What happened to your wing, sailor?" Captain Sweet broke the tension in the Sonar compartment. There was a plaster cast on the operator's right forearm.

"Doesn't bother my duty, sir," the slim black Sonarman flexed his cocoa-colored fingers at the officer standing behind him.

"How did it happen?"

"I'm embarrassed to say, sir—I was goin' to the head last night, and when we hit that debris I lost my balance . . ."

"Don't worry about it. Line of duty . . ." Sweet leaned over the operator's shoulder and read his nameplate, then added ". . . Nowis."

"Simon, sir, you read it upside down."

"Er, yes. *Simon*, of course. I see many of the crew have signed your cast."

"Could you sign it too, sir?"

Red Sweet had no choice. He upcapped his gold-plated ball-point Schaeffer and looked for a blank space. After signing, he decided he should get to know the names of his enlisted men better. He was surprised that he'd no recollection of the EM whose name he had signed under: "Pot Nitra." He had to pull himself together before it got around that he occasionally had a memory problem. Sonarman Simon he could remember by association with Simon Legree, the brutal slave driver, but be careful about calling the negro Legree. He would start with Seaman Nitra—which was about in the middle of the alphabet, and work alternately toward A and Z. It just might make the difference in facing the promotion board.

Leander Simon pressed his left earphone tight. The ambient background sounds included a click, like a scratched record. He tirned up the screen "gain" and there it was. A pinprick flash every fifteen seconds; it was bearing Red zero three two—coming in off the port bow from the southeast, just as Lieutenant Begole had thought it might.

"He's coming in fast," Captain Sweet watched the blip grow—and thought of Simon Legree. "How long?"

"About nine minutes, Cap'n Sweet. He must be doin' almost thirty knots 'cording to NAVPAC."

"What do *you* think, Jack?" Sweet sucked on his plastic cigarette and paced right and left.

"Could be Mulford was right. We wouldn't get a signal like that from a whale; it's too solid. If I were *Nemo*, I'd come in flat out . . . do a hit and run."

Chapter 29

"All systems on standby, sir," Nielson threw a short salute.

"Excellent, Commander—you know what this means?"

"With an intact transformer-to-hydrophone module, we'll be on a par with—"

"Par, my foot. We'll be *ahead* of them. Already our boats are bigger . . . like our space rockets . . ."

"Of course, sir." Peter agreed with his volatile Captain, an eye on the course control panels at the steering station. "It's been almost two months since Kalinin—I wonder whether he's been heard from . . . or found."

"Why do you bring him up *now*?"

"Didn't he have an idea . . ."

"Yes—what idea?" Zinoviev glared fanatically.

"Nothing, nothing at all. I'd better go aft."

Vyatka throttled down as orders rang out. "All stop" . . . "Half astern," The boat moaned as its six-bladed propeller clawed at the ocean.

"Current is stronger than calculated, sir," the helmsman called out as the chief engineer increased reverse power.

"Bring her about," ordered Zinoviev, "we'll hold forward way against it. All stop . . . half ahead . . ."

"Rudders . . . hard right . . . Planes up thirty."

The 425-foot craft swung around, bow toward the bobbing transformer, and blew some main ballast. Lighter and more buoyant, she rose and crabbed sideways till she lay directly over, and in line with the Colossus cable. The down-angled sonar was shunted to the viewing screen.

"Slow ahead."

Vyatka crept forward, as if pulled by a string.

The transformer's round disk glowed on the sonar screen.

"Lined up."

"Mark. Hold position . . ."

"Keel to objective, 40 feet . . . 30 . . . 20 . . ." Tons of water rushed into the diving tanks.

"Mark . . . Hold Depth . . ." The Captain picked up his intercom, "Commander Nielson, commence salvage."

One red light persisted.

All the rest were green on *Zebulon Pike's* ready board.

"Port stern plane jammed, sir."

"Goddammit," Captain Sweet almost lost his cool as he glanced at the sonar screen. A long silhouette had occulted the transformer pattern.

"May I suggest . . ." Mulford offered.

"Okay, okay, Mulford."

"Send out two divers. We might be fouled on giant kelp.

"What can we lose? Go ahead, do it Mulford—but hurry!" Sweet bit his plastic cigarette in half. "Of all times. Redmond," he barked at the Chief, "Let's try full power, ahead and astern. Maybe we can rock 'er loose."

"Aye, sir," Redmond called the maneuvering room and relayed the orders. Another red light blazed on the panel.

"What now," glowered the balding officer.

"Shaft, sir. Can't get our revs up for the vibration. Shall I call Lieutenant Mulford—as long as he's takin' a look . . ."

"Very well, Redmond—but I don't think it will matter."

"Aye, sir. So close and yet so far."

Chief Diver Tony Karas and one of his SEAL team, a Tampa man, Ed "Stonefish" Mason, stood in the escape hatch pressure chamber as water rose around them and was pressurized equal to that of the outside depth of 540 feet. The frogmens' tanks were charged with a helium and oxygen mixture which allowed them to work in deeper than normal depths with minimum narcosis, or bends.

"Stonefish," an amateur weightlifter, who came by his name because of a facial skin condition, carried the anti-fouling tools: cable cutter, demolition grenades and an underwater pneumatic chain saw. Both divers were equipped with bangsticks and powerful headlamps as well as shin-knives and intercom.

When the chamber pressure gauge needle lined up with the outside sensor repeater, the hatch sprang open at a touch. Following Karas up the ladder and onto the missile deck, Stonefish attached his pneumatic cable fixture to a deck outlet and pulled his saw trigger. A cloud of bubbles rose from it and he stomped twice on the deck. The two walked cautiously aft, while 300 feet above their heads, a beam of light filtered down.

The Soviet submarine had opened its bay doors.

Karas slid down onto the port diving plane and examined a mass of tangled seaweed that trailed back into the marine jungle below the boat's control surfaces. Training his head-lamp, he could not see any part of the twelve-foot propeller beyond the rudder because of a mass of kelp that enveloped it. He drew out his diving knife and slashed at the seaweed, tearing off the heavy tendrils as Mason waited for a signal to help and kept shark watch from the sloping fantail deck.

Suddenly, Tony shrank back as his lamp revealed a pinkish slime-covered texture under the kelp. Milky white suction cups yawned at his arm. Alive!

A quivering tentacle as thick as his own thigh was jammed between the hull and diving plane. There was no telling whether it belonged to a giant squid or an octopus. He crawled to the trailing edge of the rudder and played his light below at the continuation of the sucker-studded, kelp-swathed apparition.

Clouds of sand and seaweed swirled up out of the dark, almost blinding Tony's goggle vision. Upon dispersion his light beheld two red-tinged eyes—as large as dinner plates, with luminous yellow and black slit-like pupils. Unblinking, the wide-set orbs hypnotized him momentarily—and a realization set in: from the spacing of the eyes, the creature's head was as wide as a Volkswagon. The eyes rose under an enormous balloon-shaped sinuous pale head, and stopped at Tony's level. The pate of this head was as high as *Zebulon Pike's* 12-foot dorsal rudder! It moved closer and Karas, from experience with small octopuses knew that the bristling skin of the creature was a sign of anger. First reporting his confrontation to the control room by intercom, he motioned Stonefish to come down on the plane and use his chain saw. Tony slashed and sawed with his knife, then relinquished the task to Mason's bubbling saw. The monster, which Tony now recognized as a giant octopus, recoiled at the slashing of its arm, wedging it yet tighter as bluish green blood seeped from the wound and spread in the light beam. The octopus, enraged, unstuck one of its anchor tentacles from its rock lair and curled it slowly upward.

Stonefish's pneumatic saw shredded through the nine-inch thick mass, flinging flesh and gaping suckers in all directions. Severing the tough, mangled arm at the trailing edge of the aileron, he inserted the bubbling teeth between the hull and inboard edge, chewing out the wedged remains.

The muscular diver turned triumphantly only to be shocked at what he saw.

Karas was locked into a double turn of tenacle, close up to the creature's blazing eyes. Struggling, with his rubber suit torn and six-inch suckers adhered to his chest and back, he was lifted off the plane by the foot-thick tentacle.

Diving off the plane, Stonefish caught Tony's flailing arm and he brought his chain saw up to bear on the massive coil. A cloud of bubbles and green blood enveloped the clashing knot of man and monster. As the murky mixture dispersed with a rush of seafloor turbidity current, a pack of hammerhead sharks, drawn by the green blood and tentacle shreds, spiraled down and circled hungrily. Just as the saw was slicing in spurts and stops, single-handed by Mason—his other arm wrapped around the coil at his buddy's chest—the octopus reeled backward, snapping the pneumatic cable and catapulting the chain saw into darkness.

"Mayday, mayday," Stonefish screamed into his scuba microphone. No answer, only the silence that precedes death. The octopus reared up, exposing its parrot beak, snapping and spitting out empty lobster carapaces and claws as large and bleached as cleaved human skulls. The natural pale pearl of its bulbuous dome turned color, erupting into mottled brown, then rust, and glowing red as it snapped closer, barely a yard from Stonefish's borrified head. The diver reached down instinctively to his belt and unclipped a grenade. Almost unconscious from exertion, he pulled the pin with his teeth as the scuba mouthpiece, pushed aside, flailed free, emitting a stream of bubbles.

A blinding flash of light was the last thing Mason remembered as he was flung back by the concussion. Two more divers, sent out after the intercom failed, hit the deck, then lowered themselves to the bottom and dragged their stunned comrades from under the tangled horde of writhing tentacles and torn, ink-engulfed mantle and head of *Octopus Gigantis*.

A dark blur, the other denizen streaked toward the luminous black whale. Approaching from below, with intent to rake the stationary enemy with her deadly sawtooth lance, she saw little live things—wiggling down from the whale's body.

The whale was giving birth!

The whale that killed Clavata's pup!

With aggravated frenzy, three tons of cartilage and bone speared into the group of descending frogmen, slashing the helmeted head from one and impaling another through the gut. Flipping quickly, she swerved upwards after the others, and with a flick of her powerful tail, shot through the bright rectangle, rising clear of the surface, into *Vyatka's* gaping hold and catapulting the impaled, bloody Soviet sailor against the ribbed metal ceiling. The beserk fish thrashed frantically in search of escape, smashing an electrical transformer and a catwalk manned by technicians, before diving amidst a shower of high-voltage sparks. Nielson, straddling the injured on the collapsed catwalk, called for the ship's surgeon while Clavata, getting her bearings in the body-strewn depths below the Colossus array, sucked in a strange-tasting fish head before turning north toward the Manaar Straits.

Klaxon sirens rang out to frantic shouts echoing in the blood-spattered hold: "*GAH-yoo, GAH-yish*" . . . Help! "Tuh-ruh PL'OOS" . . . Hurry!

The grappling hook whirred up to its drum and the ponderous bay doors groaned closed. Pumps chugged and sucked out the trapped water as the engine pulsed and rumbled to life, pushing the big craft, her bow falling off to the west.

SSBN *Zebulon Pike*
27 - 28 Feb. 1968
7 48'06'' N Lat., 77 21'32'' E Long.
2115:SECURED AT BOTTOM, 459FT. UNDER TRI COLOSSUS

0412:   SONAR CONTACT 102MAGN.
0416:   IFF NEGATIVE, STANDBY ALL STATIONS
0423:   ID YANKEE BANDIT, CLOSING 24KN
0431:   POSITION YB PROX TRI, COMMENCE
        INTERCEPT
        SCRUBBED, JAMMED AILERON & SCREW
0435:   DEPLOYED SEAL AFT
0439:   REPORT GIANT CEPHALOPOD & STAND-
        BY
0444:   INTERCOM DEAD, DEPLOYED 2ND SEAL
        AILERONS RESPOND, SCREW SLUGGISH
0447:   SONAR CONTACT UNID VIC YB, TRI
0451:   EM MASON, KARAS RESCUED, MASON
        ARM SEVERED,
        KARAS SHOCK & LACERATIONS. EMERG
        LTCOM WALLIS
0453:   DAMAGE REPORT SHAFT OUT-OF-LINE
0455:   COMMENCED INTERCEPT, SONAR YB
NEGATIVE
0501:   DEPLOYED SEAL TRI, REPORT NO
        DAMAGE
0522:   RADIO REQ EMERG MEDICAL
0703:   SURFACED & TRANSF 2 EM VIA AIRMED

Commander Bradford Sweet II set the Xeroxed log copy
down next to his rough draft of the report titled "Encounter,
SSBN 668/YBX." Three days had lapsed since putting Karas
and Mason on the SH-3 copter from *Enterprise*. He picked up
his Schaeffer gold-plater, thankful that, unlike Mason, he
still had a right arm—and shuddered at the image of the
raw, red circular patches of flesh left on Karas' body after
the tentacles had been cut away.

Zebulon Pike, also wounded and running at reduced
speed because of her out-of-line shaft, was 350 miles off
Bombay on her way back to Bahrein for repairs. The
Captain had one week to put his report into shape for the
Sixth Fleet Review Board. Had he failed? Should he have

checked out the bottom under Colossus first—or hovered at depth. He could have dropped the hook. Sweet saw himself sitting at the focus of the board; imagined huge magnifying glasses over him—broiling rays pinpointing him.

He looked at it another way. Why not recommend the frogmen for medals. That would look good, after all, they may have saved the boat. Saved 140 officers and men . . . Averted another tragedy: *Sebago* . . . *Thresher* . . . *Scorpion*. He could not bear the thought of not making Captain. February 27th was a blot on his career record. SSBN 841 might just as well have stayed on SLBM course, for all the good it accomplished. Bradford Sweet would hereafter be whispered about: 'Brief encounter Brad' . . . 'Did he, or didn't he—'' Sweet put his ballpoint cap between his teeth and tried again.

'Deducing that the potential adversary—'

"Yes, come in," he replied to the Ensign's name and covered the report with his khaki service cap.

"Excuse me, sir," Ensign Adams popped his sunburned face in. "The enlisted man you assigned me to check on—"

"Seaman Pot Nitra."

Adams nodded. "I couldn't find any such name on the roster, so I signed ET Simon's plaster cast."

"And?" The captain put a hand over his eyes.

"I found the signature. There were numbers written after it—same handwriting. Same color ink—a funny purple."

"Go on."

"So I asked Simon and he said it was the Pharmacist's Mate who signed in purple. It was right after the cast had set. Gave him the idea to get more signatures in the first place. So I copied it all down and went to see Rossiter. He's the surgeon's assistant when he's not running the drug store."

"I was afraid of that," mumbled the captain. "Continue."

"Well, Rossiter said it was a formula used in making plaster casts more resilient to shock and cracking. Pot Nitra was just shorthand for Potassium Nitrate."

"At least that's something."

"What is, sir?"

"Nothing, Adams—that will be all."

"Yes, sir." The willowy ensign closed the door quietly.

It *was* something to Brad Sweet. It had worried him for three days—on top of the Colossus screw-up. There was scarcely a corner of *Zeb* that at one time or other hadn't reeked of marijuana, but the excellent air purifying system had been put on overtime, so he preferred to ignore the problem rather than make an issue that would ultimately draw adverse publicity.

Pot Nitra, he'd feared, was code for an organized conspiracy—if not the name of a pusher—that meant to do him in.

Chapter 30

Vyatka proceeded on its prearranged course, in the words of M. Aronnax as set down by Verne:

"... the island of Ceylon disappeared under the horizon and the Nautilus, *at a speed of twenty miles per hour, slid into a labrinth of canals which separate the Maldives from the Laccadives. It coasted to the Island of Kiltan, a land originally madreporic, discovered by Vasco da Gama in 1499, and one of the nineteen principal islands of the Laccadive Archipelago, situated between 10° and 14° 30' north latitude, and 69° 50' 12" east longitude.*

We had made 16,220 miles, or 7500 (French) leagues from our starting-point in the Japanese Seas.

The next day (30th January), when the Nautilus went to the ocean's surface, there was no land in sight. Its course was N.N.E., in the direction of the Sea of Oman ... an outlet to the Persian Gulf ..."

"*For four days, till the 3d of February, the Nauti-*

lus *scoured the Sea of Oman, at various speeds and
depths. It seemed to go at random, as if hesitating as
to which road it should follow, but we never crossed
the tropic of Cancer.*

"*The 8th of February, . . . Mocha came in sight,
now a ruined town . . . once an important city, containing six public markets, and twenty-six mosques,
and whose walls, defended by fourteen forts, formed
a girdle of two miles in circumference.*

*The Nautilus then approached the African shore,
where the depth of the sea was greater . . . through
the open panels we were allowed to contemplate the
beautiful bushes of brilliant coral, and large . . .
rocks clothed with a splendid fur of green algae . . .*

*. . . What new specimens of submarine flora and
fauna did I admire under the brightness of our electric lantern!*

*There grew sponges of all shapes, . . . foliated,
globular, and digital. They certainly justified the names
of baskets, cups, distaffs, elks'-horns, lions'-feet,
peacocks'-tails, and Neptunes'-gloves, which have been
given to them by the fishermen, greater poets than the
savants.*

"*As to the fish . . . The following are those which
the nets . . . brought more frequently on board:—*

*Rays of a red-brick colour, with bodies marked
with blue spots, . . . some superb caranxes, marked
with seven traverse bands of jet-black, blue and yellow fins, and gold and silver scales . . .*"

" '. . . Ah! It is an intelligent boat!' "

'Yes, sir, . . . It fears neither the terrible tempests
of the Reed Sea, nor its currents, nor its sandbanks.'

'Certainly,' said I, 'this sea is quoted as one of the
worst . . .'

'Detestable, M. Aronnax . . . It is . . . a sea subject
to fearful hurricanes . . . which offers nothing good

either on its surface or in its depths. Such too, is the opinion of Arrian . . . and Artemidoris.'

'One may see,' I replied, 'that these historians never sailed aboard the Nautilus.*'*

'Just so,' replied the Captain, smiling . . . 'It required many ages to find out the mechanical power of steam. Who knows if, in another hundred years, we may not see another Nautilus? *Progress is slow, M. Aronnax.'*

On March 3d, 1968, U.A.R President Gamal Abd-al-Nasser vowed in a radio speech that the Arabs would liberate all areas occupied by Israel as a result of the six-day war the previous June. The Suez Canal had been closed since that war—blockaded by Arab boats sunk below and above the Great Bitter Lake, in the south of the canal zone. It was more than a coincidence that several of the steamers trapped in the lake by the action were American and British oil tankers. Israeli monitors intercepted a phone call between Nasser and Jordan's King Hussein in which the two conspired the assertion that British and American aircraft were supporting the Israeli drive. Shortly after, a Baghdad Arab convention instituted the first oil embargo against Britain and the U.S. The Arab fabrication of air support paled a few days later when Israeli planes attacked the American intelligence ship, USS *Liberty*, killing 34 and wounded 164, despite its prominent display of flag and signals. The incident, to this day, has not been explained by Israel

President Nasser received another message, one that neither the Israelis or Americans picked up. It was from the Kremlin and it ''suggested'' that the Suez Canal blockships be turned sideways at sundown on March 5th for a period of 12 hours. In addition, the Egyptian Navy was ''asked'' to provide a powered dredging barge and await further orders at the southern terminus of Port Tewfik.

* * *

At four the next morning, a rusty scow anchored in Lake Timseh, under the night lights of war-scarred Ismailia, ancient city built at the junction of a Pharoah's waterway to Alexandria. Lying parallel to the canal, the naval dredge *Saratân el-Báhr* let go lines fore and aft on the port side and the top of a conning sail dipped beneath the surface. At 6 knots, the barge, with *Vyatka Sturgeon* secured alongside, ten feet of her sail above water and hidden from Israeli infra-red scopes on the east bank, had navigated about one half the canal's length.

The Soviet Navy had prudently decided to take no chances with an Israeli homing torpedo attack on what they would have claimed to have been mistaken for one of Egypt's dozen World War II diesel submarines. *Vyatka* was to spend the day quietly on the bottom of the lagoon-ringed lake, invisible to undercover Israeli agents on Ismailia's waterfront. Unfortunately, the Suez Canal's depth was only 49 feet, which was 10 feet short of the Sturgeon Class' minimum submerged requirement.

The Russian edition of *Twenty Thousand Leagues Under The Sea* lay on the wardroom table before Andrei Zinoviev, who read with a theatrical flare:

'Well, unless the Nautilus sails on dry land, and passes above the Isthmus—'
'Or beneath it, M. Aronnax.'
'Beneath it?'
'Certainly,' replied Captain Nemo, quietly. 'A long time ago Nature made under this tongue of land what man has this day made on its surface.'
'What! such a passage exists?'
'Yes; a subterranean passage, which I have named the Arabian tunnel. It takes us beneath Suez, and opens into the Gulf of Pelusium.'

"That's odd," Nielson ventured, as he moved his knight's pawn into into hostile territory. "If the Suez Canal was going to be opened in 1869, only a year after his book was to be published, why didn't Verne set the period one or two years later and have the Nautilus go through on its own power. That would seem logical, considering the author's dedication to detail."

"Because the French are so impetuous. Like the rest of the decadent countries who have seen their best years, and fear the decline, they have little patience left—a quality that we—the Soviets have in abundance . . ."

"Might that attribute be an Eastern trait?"

"I think that can be said to a degree, M. Nielson."

"In that case, The People's Republic of China might become a major adversary."

"Ah, but they lack the technology, and will for years."

"That's what the Soviet Navy thought about Japan, in 1904, only fifty years after coming out of their feudal state."

"Don't remind me, M. Nielson," Captain Zinoviev turned a few pages and read aloud:

'At a quarter past ten, the Captain himself took the helm. A large gallery, black and deep opened before us. The Nautilus went boldly into it. A strange roaring was heard round its sides. It was the waters of the Red Sea, which the incline of the tunnel precipitated violently towards the Mediterranean. The Nautilus *went with the torrent, rapid as an arrow . . .'*

"Now here's the clincher," Andrei smirked and skipped a few paragraphs:

" *'At thirty-five minutes past ten, Captain Nemo quitted the helm: and turning to me, said—'*
'The Mediterranean!'

In less than twenty minutes, the Nautilus, carried along by the torrent, had passed through the Isthmus of Suez.''

"One hundred and ten miles in twenty minutes?'' Nielson whistled and mentally calculated. "Why that's 330 miles per hour; even Verne should have known such speed was impossible.''

"Ah, but it isn't, M. Nielson; a boat cannot go that fast—but a wave can. Tsunamis have been measured to exceed 350 miles per hour. A little sensationalism from M. Verne!'' The Captain moved his bishop, trapping Nielson's pawn.

Chapter 31

"Where is the fucker now?"

"Ben!" Betsy cautioned her husband, "it's Easter."

"Well, that's what they are, eh Rudi?" Ben turned the big globe on its axis.

Mulford, in civilian sport jacket and slacks, pretended he hadn't heard Mount's expletive. "You'll have to look *under* the globe. Air recon picked them up with infra-red, right on course . . . making for the Falklands. Radio Moscow said they'd been at the South Pole."

"Go on," Ben snorted, "The Pole's on a *solid* continent."

"Part of Operation Nemo's crew were *flown* over the Pole; They were picked up at Bellingshausen, one of the Soviet Antarctic stations by an IL-38."

"That's not fair," Ben was on hands and knees, searching the underside of his library globe.

"Latitude's about seven-oh . . . at the tip of the polar peninsular below Cape Horn," added Mulford. "It's on St. George Island."

"I got St. George—, what are they trying to prove?"

"Oh, you know the Russians, dad, historically, they don't know when to give up," fourteen-year-old David Mount leaned his tennis racquet against the empty fireplace and picked up the sports section of the *Washington Post*.

"For a meshugga kid, you seem to know an awful lot . . ."

"*Ben*," Betsy looked up from the newspaper.

"So, it's Passover, too."

David, perched on the top step of a mahogany footladder, peered over a front-page photo of the Cardinal's Bob Gibson, warming up for opening day. "At school, we talk about world political situations and then present solutions."

"Next time we have an impasse with Brezhnev, I'll tell the President to put you on the hot line."

"We can't do much worse, dad—" David gathered up his newspaper and left the room.

"Have you heard from Debbie?" Mulford thought it right to ask. He was also concerned.

Ben spun the globe once more. "She's back. Frisco got too crazy for her. She got a job with the Post Office easy enough, but moved in with a fast crowd. Marijuana was a picnic compared to what she got into. I had to fly out and bring her back. She's living in New York. The east village. I think she's running around with a schwartze."

Betsy got up and went toward the kitchen.

"I like what the folksinger said—the guy with a group called 'The Limelighters.' Ben rolled the globe closer to his brown leather chair and sat down. pensively running his finger over the Atlantic Ocean, while Rudi remained standing, occasionally pulling a book from the shelves and flipping through it. Ben went on, legs stretched out on an ottoman. "He said 'Hippies are the first wave of an encroaching ocean of technologically unemployable people created by snowballing cybernation in American industry.' "

"Cybernetics, as a word, is used a lot, but it doesn't

have to be all bad," Rudi took out a tobacco pouch and pipe.

"Moxie's old brand," Ben noticed.

Rudi nodded and lighted up. "Some of those kids know how to be part of complex electronic systems. Take the Polaris ETs. You don't hear much about the kids who *can do*. It's the liberal loudmouths who get all the press."

"I'd like to kick Abbie Hoffman in the teeth . . . and that bitch actress who went to Hanoi," Ben growled. "Hypocrites, that's all the lot of 'em are. All just as pushy as medicine salesmen. They'll cheat each other blind, soon enough."

"David seems to be doing well," Mulford was becoming uneasy about Debbie. Drugs have been known to make people talk. How much had she told her father about the 'affair'? And why did it bother him that she was 'running around with a schwartze?' Somehow, he felt more than just sorry for her.

"David's a genius, but he'll never make a sailor—not even the Jewish navy—our Coast Guard, that is, so . . . I guess my dynasty is not going anywhere." Ben reflected: "It's my fault, about Debbie. I was away too much; no time to be a father."

"But look at your son."

"He's the baby. They always get more attention—besides, it works crossover: father and daughter . . . mother and son. And David has the analytical mind. Debbie's the dreamer."

"She doesn't like being replaced by transistors."

"That's some of it, Rudi, but I wonder what I would have been like as the child of an Admiral."

"Don't blame yourself, Ben," Mulford sat down on the flowered sofa. "It's not just us . . . this country. It's happening all over," he held up a news photo of a left-wing youth demonstration in West Berlin.

"Nothing I can do about it now, except keep the door open," the white-haired engineer changed subjects: "Now how about my other son. I'll bet you're looking forward to getting back on old *Zeb Pike*—especially now that she's gonna work out of Norfolk.''

"Once we're under, it doesn't make any difference where we are. You know that. It's not like your war was . . . coming into port every week or two.''

"Sure, kid. A little joke there, but I'd much rather stick my periscope up off Jupiter Beach than Ceylon—eh boy?'' Mount winked devilishly and looked around the book-lined room.

"Now that we're alone—just where is that fucker going, and why? Gorshkov wouldn't send a new boat around the world for nothing. Scuttlebutt around town has it that if that *Nemo* boat did screw up with the Colossus system, it'll try something else. NI's got some dope that their CO is no ordinary officer. He was cleared through a top-level session.'' Ben put on his half-frame glasses and examined the coastline of South America. "So the Bandit comes up and around Brazil's hump, according to Jules Verne. Hmmm.''

"See something?'' Rudi sprang up.

"Can you get me the book; its one of those near the window—with the gold filigree on the back.''

"Ask me, I've read it.''

"Okay, smartass. Is he due to stop anywhere around Florida?''

"*Nautilus* ran into an octopus off the Bahamas.''

"It's in the ball park,'' Ben slumped back. "Gorskov is itching to take a look at our underwater test center, but the Bogey will have a problem getting inside. Even if he tried, he'd probably trip our Atlantic Colossus; it's much better than old Caesar—the one that picked up the Cuba Bandits back in the '62 crisis.''

"AUTEC will take precautions anyway?''

"With Brad Sweet out there, who needs precautions?'' Ben had disappeared behind the funnies.

                            *   *   *

A smoky red moon hung over Skull Valley, on the edge
of Utah's Great Salt Lake Desert—just enough light to
mark the utter desolation of the land. A dense mist clung
to the valley and the summits of surrounding mountain
ranges; of the Onaqui, the Cedars and Granite Dugways,
floated ethereally alone. The valley, had, in the words of
an early traveler, "no voice of animal, no hum of insect to
disturb the tomb-like solemnity . . . All was silence and
death."

Chad Magill had Utah in his long bones and the chill
dawn invaded his dream. Fourteen years of herding sheep
in the valley where indian skeletons were found in great
numbers by Fremont and Carson had taught him to listen.
The valley was silence, but not with seven thousand head
of fine-fleeced Targhees wakin' up over on the south
slope, hardly a quarter-mile away. And with a warm breeze
a herder could 'spect some lowin' and bleating.

This was going to be a good year for the Magills, not
only with a bumper shearing of number 60 fleece, but with
a fine lamb crop from the breeding ewes. For the first time
since he bought the spread with his accumulated back pay
after fourteen months in a Yalu POW camp, he was certain
it had all been worth it. Helen . , . the kids . . . the sweat,
and the loans. He buttoned his trousers and shirt going
down the stairway and stopped in the kitchen for a pre-
breakfast slug of milk out of his personal paper container
in the fridge door. Then he grabbed his shearskin jacket,
pulled on his boots and went out to the stable, sheltie dog
at his spurred heels.

Taking a short cut off the road, he spurred his old roan
across a salt flat as lofty Mount Deseret caught the first
rays of morning sun—standing guard over the Goshute
Reservation. Chad reigned up short at the ridgetop as his
dog sniffed and whined, running in fits and starts.

The grizzled herder squared his hat against blinding sun

and squinted in disbelief. The snow-patched field was littered with dead sheep. His sheep; stiff limbs stretched skyward—a forest of black hooves and white wooly mutton legs. And death-twisted muzzles. Almost seven thousand prize Targhees, dead—as if struck by lightning. But there had been no storm . . . no thunder. Only the blood-red moon. Twelve hours earlier, a herd of healthy animals. Now none.

Chad dismounted, leaving the reign loose and took off his hat . . . walked slowly toward the grazing field. What had gone wrong—and why to *him*?

He knelt near a newborn lamb. Born dead! Then he looked up at the mountain above the morning mist, and shrieked an unintelligible curse across the valley.

Chapter 32

When, during the Korean War, human waves of Chinese Communist troops were overwhelming the American forces, the Pentagon brass had to come up with an answer. World War II was "more equal", a given number of ground troops against a similar enemy force, or at least a comprehendable force. Fighting the Germans or the Japs was a question of logistics: the greater number of enemy troops deployed, the greater number of bombs, guns and rockets deployed against them, and America had a limitless supply.

But the Chinese Communists! Hundreds of Thousands, like locusts. The Joint Chiefs and President Eisenhower decided that a new weapon was needed. Super-automatic weapons, flame-throwers, clustered needle-bombs and napalm simply did not work.

Digging into captured Nazi chemical warfare documents, the Pentagon came up with "Sarin", a nerve gas so lethal that a few pounds, dispersed effectively, could kill many thousands of attacking troops. In fact, Sarin was so lethal that one *ten-thousanth* of an ounce in the human lung was fatal.

By 1955, the army was producing—in Indiana—thousands of gallons of this gas in liquid form, under the code designation, "GB". Developed by German chemists in the late 30s, it was almost used—on two separate occasions. Hitler called a conference to discuss the use of nerve gas against England in 1943. Present were Field Marshal Wilhelm Keitel and War Production Minister Albert Speer. The key speaker was Otto Ambros, Germany's foremost authority on toxic gases. He briefed the conference on gas production, but then argued against its use, since he did not know what retaliatory gases the English possessed. Hitler canceled the plan.

Two years later, recalling the briefing, Speer ordered a cannister of Sarin to be dropped into the air-conditioning system of Hitler's bunker, thus avoiding a last-ditch battle and total devastation by the immensely superior and enraged Russians who were descending on Berlin. I.G. Farben, the manufacturer, refused to supply the gas on the grounds that it would disperse and kill thousands of Berliners.

After the war, American companies vied for Ambros' services in this country but he was tried and imprisoned as a war criminal.

GB found its application in the warheads of more than 100,000 M-55 rockets. The six-foot long projectiles, looking like slender stovepipes with fins, were stockpiled largely in Okinawa, on orders from President Kennedy.

In the early sixties, a more potent nerve gas was developed by Great Britain. Called "VX" it soon supplanted GB in rocket warheads and land mines. VX was five times as lethal as GB; one ounce could kill 50,000 troops . . . people . . . or sheep.

The original GB warheads contained 11 pounds of liquified gas, plus a two-pound "burster" charge to insure a deadly spread upon landing in the target area. The rocket itself, was powered by propellant enough for a four-mile trajectory.

There was no evidence of combat usage of nerve gas during the Vietnam War, despite the proliferation of the weapon. However, the rocket cases, corroding from long periods of storage during which unstable chemicals were released, posed a delicate problem for supply commands all over the world.

An international incident developed when an M-55 rocket broke open at a depot in Okinawa, injuring 24 people. Following this, the Japanese government demanded that the stockpiles be removed from their islands. As a result of this pressure, vast shipments of rockets were routed to Ordnance depots in the States for "neutralization". In 1967, "Operation Chase" was instituted. "Chase" was an Army acronym for "Cut Holes And Sink 'Em. The first shipments were scuttled in the Atlantic, 140 miles off New Jersey. By the end of the year, an all-seasons mass production dumping terminal had been set up in North Carolina, using de-mothballed Liberty Ships, and sinking them, loaded, in a deep canyon off the Bahamas. All of this was going on without "certain" members of Congress knowing about it.

When VX was confirmed by Army experts as the gas that killed the sheep in Skull Valley, the Pentagon hot lines all but melted. And this in an election year.

Shortly, a smooth-talking colonel drove out to Chad Magill's house with a government check for double the market value of the dead sheep. He offered it to Magill on condition that all press interviews be turned down should the Dugway Weapons Proving Center, twelve miles south, be implicated in the skeepkill.

The herder asked that the government also buy his lands and house for a fair market price—or there would be no deal. Within a week, Chad Magill and his family were on their way to California. It had been a good year.

Meanwhile, in Washington, scientists and military experts were hurriedly called into special "Tank" sessions. With hundreds of thousands of unstable nerve bombs threatening to erupt, President Lyndon Johnson gave the Joint Chiefs of Staff a month to solve the problem. They settled on "coffins". An enterprising Engineer General had proposed that all the rockets be cast inside concrete blocks eight feet long by four feet square, and these blocks be further encased in quarter-inch steel vaults. Each coffin when completed, would weigh over seven tons and contain thirty rockets.

The records of the Anniston, Alabama Army Depot, one of several that prepared the coffins, would eventually show that over 1600 of them had been dumped at sea in the year ending June, 1968—before Congress passed a bill requiring that the Army give advance notification of such dumpings.

In April, 1968, a special shipment of rockets were airlifted from the Rocky Mountain Arsenal in Denver to the Blue Grass Depot near Lexington, Kentucky. Many of these rockets contained the super-lethal VX, but were not properly labeled. All were entombed in concrete blocks and loaded into gondola freight cars marked for delivery to the dumping terminal at Sunny Point, near Wilmington, North Carolina.

Elaborate safety and security measures were taken; more so with this shipment, because of the labeling foul-up. It was not known which of the 287 coffins contained the VX rockets. The 43-car train rumbled out of Lexington's freight yards, following a pilot train that scouted the curving tracks ahead. This train carried a platoon of armed troops, decontamination units, and piggyback ambulances and fire trucks. Hospitals along the route received surprise stocks of atropine, a nerve gas antidote. To detect possible leakages, each of the loaded freight cars were equipped with caged rabbits, fore and aft.

The Liberty Ship, *David Low Dodge*, sailed on schedule with its deadly cargo, and was towed by a Navy tug, escorted by a destroyer and a Coast Guard cutter to the dumping site, 283 miles due east of Cape Canaveral. An eight-man team of Naval ordnance experts boarded the *Dodge* and checked the holds of the 7000-ton veteran, in which six white rabbits had ridden—the only passengers on the ship during its 350 mile trip. The rabbits were examined and declared healthy. After rigging hydrophones and depth charges to record the sinking rate and direction, the Navy team removed salvageable equipment, including the rabbits and opened the seven main flooding valves. The destroyer escort, *Hartley* stood by to record the position as *Dodge* went down, stern first.

As Colonel S.M. Burney, commander of the Anniston Depot would testify before Congress in June, "the operation came off without even a nosebleed."

Eastern Star had seen her best times. In the five years following World War II, 7000 blue whales per year had been caught, and she'd taken more than her share. Sperm oil for the steel-rolling mills of Russia; for tanks, tractors and submarines. By 1962, the world's catch was down to 1000 per year, with Russia and Japan accounting for 80% of the kills.

In 1964, 110 were slaughtered.

Two years later only 20 blue whales were caught.

The rusting factory ship was given a new job. Taken over by the Soviet Navy, it was equipped with the latest electronic surveillance devices and manned by technicians as well as whalers. Again she plied the oceans, from polar to polar regions, acting visibly as a factory ship for Soviet trawlers to transfer their catch into for processing into fertilizer and oil. The 640-foot steamer still maintained its stern slipway and reveled in catching a stray whale to haul up the steel incline—regardless of international agreements to restrict the taking of endangered species.

It was no secret to NATO that the main function of this

gray hulk was tracking American missiles fired downrange from the Kennedy Space Center at Cape Canaveral. There was nothing that could be done so long as the boat observed the 12-mile limit in cruising and the 200-mile limit for fishing or dredging.

What American Intelligence did not know was that, along with *Vyatka Sturgeon*, the whale factory had been modified as part of *Operation Nemo*. Her hull had been bisected and a false hold installed to camouflage the change. Bow and stern remained as before. The box-within-a-box game, long a strategem of the East, had been applied to Navel steel and the wet cold war. *Eastern Star's* capacity was one 8000-ton nuclear submarine.

By skirting the coast of Brazil, *Vyatka* had evaded airborne detection and slipped by Trinidad into the Caribbean. Staying outside the maximum detection area of Colossus, it made for the safety of Cuba's southern coast where it rendezvoused with *Eastern Star* off Santiago. As a submarine, *Vyatka* could not cross the hydrophone perimeter that guarded the Bahamas, but as part of a surface vessel and invisible to sight, infra-red, magnetic and acoustical detection, it cruised merrily past the big American Naval Base at Guantanamo and turned north toward the Bahama Banks.

Drawing only 22 feet, about the same as the submarine secured between her twin hulls, Eastern Star maneuvered carefully over the shallow sand banks south of Andros Island—a 75 mile stretch studded with purple-brown coral heads until it reached "Tongue of The Ocean", a dropoff of over 2000 feet.

Lieutenant Commander Russel Gill, USN had been quoted in the February issue of *National Geographic* and translated into Russian for *Operation Nemo:*

"Tongue of The Ocean is a perfect site—a big bathtub with no steamer traffic to interfere with our listening devices. We've planted hydrophones beyond the barrier reef and built optical towers above, all tied together by cables and computers. Thus, for example, we can track a rocket missile fired from our sub until it breaks the surface, then follow it through the air and back into the water, all the way to a submerged target."

"I couldn't have stood the stench much longer," Captain Zinoviev sighed as *Vyatka* dropped from the whaleship's bosom into the cobalt blue depths, one hundred miles south of the Navy's Underwater Test and Evaluation Center off Fresh Creek.

Peter pinched his nose in agreement. He'd kept his affliction secret from the Soviet Navy. He suffered from migrant *Paranosmia*, the result of an electrical shock injury received during a test at Flensburg Naval Academy to determine his stamina, a prerequisite to commanding a U-boat. Paranosia was the medical term for a condition in which one odor or taste was confused with another—often quite opposite. An afflicted person, upon sniffing a rose, could receive the sensation of onions instead.

Petrus Nielson did not tell Zinoviev that to him, the whaleship smelled like lavender.

"Two hundred," sang out the control room mate.

"Down to a thousand, and rig for sonar scan." ordered Zinoviev. Aft, the twin screws of *Eastern Star* were picked up accoustically as they receded, back toward the shallows.

"What do you make of it?" Lieutenant Burger snapped up his sunglasses and banked the twin-motored jet for a second look.

"Damn, Max baby, guess the mudderfucka's runnin' scared. Bringin' her ass in 'cross th' bank. Ah do think *our* presence is a prime factah in this here day-tant scene," Lieutenant JG "Jewel" Newell blew on his pinky ring diamond and rubbed it against his sleeve. "Besides, they ain't no whales in heah . . ."

"You know, *nigaro*—I think you is right," Burger continued the dialogue stoically and headed the dumpy Lockheed Viking Tracker back toward Andros Island.

Twenty-one hours later, *Vyatka*, running silent, rode the ebb current through Northeast Providence Channel out of Tongue of The Ocean. Twelve miles—from Andros, as well as from New Providence with its glittering white cruise ships clustered in Nassau's harbor, was still the international accepted limit—for surface ships. Zinoviev was exhilarated . . . the second phase of *Nemo* had been a total success. AUTEC had been scanned and the findings taped for processing by KGB Naval Section. A veritable "cat's cradle", the new testing center scanned out to be almost ninety miles long by fifteen wide, and more than one mile deep. *Vyatka's* sensors, picked up a test firing of the new "Harpoon" missile from a submerged *Lafayette* Class boat. The surprise, however, was a series of impulses that dove from the bay's surface at speeds of over sixty miles per hour, to depths *lower* than the 2200 foot level that *Vyatka* was hovering at. Her maximum.

The control room crews were quietly jubilant as the boat coasted out of dangerous island waters into the deep Atlantic. "Fleet Headquarters will be very pleased with our research," Andrei smiled. "This will erase the stigma of the Ceylon fiasco. Even at the onset of *Nemo*, I only had hopes of *one* objective being successful . . ." The Captain flexed his wrists, a carryover from ballet practicing.

Nielson sat behind the tandem helmsmen, hawk-like watching the contact analog screen and the forward navigation sonar. The operators sat, poised before the aircraft-type steering wheels—ready to take over should the automatic pilot be cut off.

"Perhaps we could use the same tactics to get inside *Sea*

Spider and take a look at their Pacific testing center off
Kauai in the Hawaiians," added Nielson.

"I do plan to make such a recommendation when we get
back to Murmansk. Admiral Kulov should be most
interested." Andrei envisioned Natalya Kulov—softened
after several months . . . resigned to his demands because
of Kalinin's "disappearance", and her father's depen-
dence on *Operation Nemo*. Should she reject his proposal
of marriage, he could always go directly to Admiral of The
Fleet Sergei Gorshkov. Andrei motioned to his duty officer.
"Lieutenant Zuyenko, prepare for a little celebration at
dinner tonight. Break out caviar and beer for the off-duty
watch . . . and . . ." his eyes rolled zealously.

Zuyenko saluted. He read those wild eyes: a sign among
certain kindred men. There would be vodka in the wardroom.

"I've never seen anything like that before," Nielson
gaped at the peculiar, long blurry shape on the sonar
screen. Diagonal, it appeared to be falling. The electronics
operator corrected the vertical field.

"It's big—five or six hundred feet long," observed the
former German officer.

"Too big for a submarine, unless the Americans are
even further ahead than we thought." Andrei was perplexed.

"I think it's out of control," snapped Nielson, "the
trim is uneven and it's yawing. Don't lose it, Chernavin—"
Nielson caught a blighting glance from Zinoviev.

"Close in, helmsman," ordered the Captain. An electronics rating checked the digital read-out of the recording
tape system as the odd image grew. With a turn of the gain
knob, spindly appendages appeared . . . and superstructure
amidships.

"A surface ship . . . sinking," exclaimed Zinoviev.

"We're at maximum depth, sir," warned Cheravin, and
I'm losing contact . . . picking up interference . . ." The
screen became covered with wavering shapes, almost oblit-

erating the falling image. Suddenly, a white mass loomed up from the screen's bottom.

"Seamount," shouted the helmsman as he switched to manual and both pulled sharply back on their tandem steering wheels, throwing several of the crew off balance. Profanity echoed fore and aft as *Vyatka's* bow rose sharply.

"Very well, trim and let's get away from here while we can. Any ship that sinks around here is good news."

Nielson waited until the Captain had gone to his quarters, then walked over to the navigation center. The seamount image was vivid in his mind and he recalled something odd about it. Conical, with a flattened top, he'd noticed a smaller, rounded peak to starboard as *Vyatka* swerved. And, just at the screen's edge, there was a double notch that separated the undersea masses. The silhouette had been etched into his visual memory: white against the black of ocean. And the notches—immense gunsights, marked the spot where the ship had disappeared: *beyond* the notches, and *before* the rounded seamount. Nielson penciled a note inside a match-book cover. The inertial navigation read-out was 29°15'45" N Lat., 77°51'32" W. Long. After finding the general area on the strip map and noting down the time and course heading, he studied the depth soundings. There was an extraordinary fall-off: from 500 fathoms to 2700 within a distance of 40 miles. About a hundred miles to the southwest there appeared a dotted circle. It was over a 500 fathom depth and had an inscription within:

REPORTED US ARMY EXPLOSIVES DUMPING AREA

It couldn't have been a munitions ship—missing the site by a hundred miles. Nielson filed the enigma in his congested memory bank as *Vyatka* headed for its second rendezvous with *Eastern Star* at coastal navigation buoy 41002, a six-hour run NNE.

* * *

Chapter 33

August saw the boiling over of unrest in Chicago. 15,000 protesters gathered at Grant Park to demonstrate peacefully at the Democratic National Convention. Everyone showed up: Allan Ginsberg, Jean Genet, William Burroughs, and Norman Mailer, who was too chicken to march with his subjects. There was Dick Gregory, Rennie Davis, Rubin, Hoffman. They shouted "PIG,PIG,PIG" at the plexiglassed policemen, and chanted "OM . . . OM . . . OM" before they pelted the "Pigs" with stones and bricks, bringing down the billy clubs and tear gas.

Never were so many photographs of police brutality ever taken in so short a scuffle.

Weatherperson Kathy Boudin was there with Cathlyn Wilkerson—so was Deborah Mount. They were all arrested for planting a stink bomb in the Hilton's lobby and for spray-painting obscene statements about the CIA on a Federal building.

Ms. Boudin, fractious daughter of a leftist-aiding, liberal lawyer, moved into a town house in Greenwich Village, owned by Wilkerson's millionare father and played with homemade bombs. Rumor had it that the older girls recruited younger girls for more than idealistic purposes. Debbie Mount naively fell into the latter group—but not before she'd met her hero.

Ted Gold was 23 to her 16. Along with Mark Rudd, he'd fanned the Columbia University student riots, and gone to Cuba with Boudin, paying homage to slain Che Guevara. He went to Mississippi to help the black man and survived. He wrote lyrics for a Weatherman songbook, such as "I'm dreaming of a white riot" and told former classmates that "communes cure us of such bourgeois hang-ups as privacy and monogamy." When one graduate student aquaintance asked him how he made a living, Gold answered "we steal."

Kathy Boudin used Ted Gold and the town house; she was the queen who would be king, and demanded her favors from the realm. But Ted Gold had stolen the Admiral's daughter from the leftist princess.

On March 6th, 1970, a dynamite explosion destroyed the Wilkerson crash-pad. Kathy and Cathlyn staggered from the ruins and disappeared, leaving three bodies in the smoking rubble. Two were unidentified; one was baby-bearded Theodore Gold. Debbie Mount was in Maryland at the time, visiting her parents and trying to borrow money.

Robert M. Dixon had, among other misfortunes, the stigma of being the first president to be in office during a nerve gas squabble. In August, the first publicized nerve gas trains left the Blue Grass Depot for Sunny Point. Carrying 418 concrete "coffins" of GB and VX, again unlabeled. There had been evidence that the unstable VX was eating into the propellent tanks.

Dixon had approved the move at Secretary of Defense, Baird's behest. But Governor Kirk of Florida didn't like the idea and sued the government. Ralph Nader martialled his forces and Britain flew over a delegation to contest the dump site.

After running a gauntlet of demonstrators along the route, the two trains, one almost a mile long, were unloaded and the 2675 tons of lethal cargo put into the holds of the Liberty Ship, *Le Baron Russel Briggs*. A Federal judge restrained the freighter from sailing pending further study of the hydrolization of toxic gases in sea water. Confronted by civilian experts, the Army embarrassedly admitted that it had been ill-advised to encase the rockets in concrete in the first place. Secretary Laird promised that this was the last such shipment. Future neutralization would be by chemical means, not dumping. Queries by the UN Seabed Commission were met with terse assurances that human and marine life would not be endangered.

The judge finally agreed with the powers that appointed her on condition that the Army seek a shallower site than 16,000 feet. She had been advised by experts that the great pressure at three miles' depth would rupture the concrete, causing quick gas dispersion, whereas a shallow site would enhance hydrolization by gradual gas seepage from the vaults.

So *LeBaron Russel Briggs* was towed out and scuttled, with full press coverage and a Naval escort. Despite a Court of Appeals motion and an emergency session of the Bahamiam Cabinet.

Ironically, the scuttled ship had been named for "one of the gentlest souls that ever lived,"—a professor of literature and Dean of Harvard, and a writer of operatic lyrics.

But, to America, it was Dixon's boat.

Two unusual events transpired in 1974. One was the demise of President Dixon, and the other, the incredible feat of raising a sunken Soviet submarine from a 17,000 foot depth in the Pacific Ocean by Howard Hughes' salvage rig, *Glomar Challenger*.

Among the remains of the 86 officers and men that were disinterred from the Golf-class Soviet submarine after six years under a seabed pressure of 7000 pounds per square inch, were recovered clothing and personal effects which were quite indicative of the crew's deployment and everyday life aboard the sub.

An important discovery was the crushed body of a nuclear weapons specialist. A junior officer, he was identified from his metal dog tag as Lieutenant Artemon Kalinin. Found next to him, in a narrow bunk was his personal diary, which covered every phase of student training and nuclear missiles duties. Like the other printed manuals and code books salvaged, it was put through a high-vacuum drying process to restore legibility. In addition, six "Serb" nuclear-tipped missiles were salvaged.

A funeral service, in Russian and English, following the Soviet Naval Manual procedure was conducted aboard *Glomar Challenger* before the bodies were once more consigned to the deep.

In the officer's diary was an unfinished letter addressed to Admiral Konstantin Kulov, the Soviet Navy's Benjamin Mount. It accused one Captain Andrei Zinoviev of ordering Kalinin's boat to sea without adequate and up-to-date intelligence of the American ASW systems in the Hawaii area.

After collating the information, the CIA followed up with a disruptive ruse based on the letter and planted it for the Soviet Navy to find. Zinoviev, already enraged by Natalya's rejection of him, blamed Nielson because of his friendship with Kalinin and had the Swede court-martialed on trumped-up charges of being a double agent.

Incommunicado for six years in a labor camp, his health waning, Nielson smuggled a letter out with an escapee who mailed it from West Berlin. It was addressed to Admiral Benjamin Mount, c/o The Pentagon, Washington, D.C., USA.

* * *

"Yesterday was a very sad day for our country," Secretary of The Navy Robert Murray said sadly as he faced over 5000 invited guests at the launching ceremony of SS Michigan, second of the giant Triton boats. An overcast afternoon in April, the day after the disastrous attempt to rescue the hostages in Iran. Murray continued: "But today is a great day for the Country, the Navy, and the state of Michigan. This is not a ship designed for war, but to preserve peace."

Outside the security fence milled a thousand anti-nuclear demonstrators who had tried to block the gates. 211 had been arrested in the scuffle that followed by the state police. One of them—as Ben found out that night, was his daughter, Debbie.

Standing with the Admiral of Second Fleet in the sail observation position, high above masses officers on both diving planes and the broad, rounded deck below, Ben felt like a God. Outwardly adverse to publicity and adulation, he really craved it. All those small, servile people out there. All those yea-sayers; how he detested them. Now they were all here, paying homage, as well they should . . .

The 19,000-ton black behemoth, bow covered with a circular flag, large white star, surrounded by smaller ones on a blue field, slid backwards down the ways into New London harbor, with a hundred white-capped officers saluting port and starboard. All that was needed was the music from "HMS Pinafore".

In the library of his Maryland home, Ben opened a wrinkled letter. Stamped MIT LUFTPOST, it had been forwarded from Washington by official pouch with other material while he was away. The letter had been written in pencil, and dated over a month earlier.

Admiral B. Mount:
Please accept my apologies for what happened at the drive-in movie so long ago in Idaho.

This letter, should it reach you, offers your government a great opportunity to obtain classified information about the Soviet submarine branch.

I am, at present, a patient in the Hospital at the Correctional Labor camp GULAG at Kotlas, 300 miles SE of Archangel, from which—with appropriate help—it is possible to escape, as did the bearer of this letter. My motives in divulging information are simple. I am sick, though ambulatory and have little time left. In return for information resulting from over twenty years service with the Soviet Fleet, I ask two things. One—a meeting with my son in West Germany, and two—arrangements to allow me to live out my remaining days in safety—perhaps in your western forests which so remind me of my birthplace in Sweden.

If such an "exchange" is possible, please hurry.

It was signed, as Ben saw before reading it, "Peter Nielson."

Ben recalled the week's events . . . the protesters . . . Debbie in jail . . . the disheveled young woman who screamed at him when he crossed the demonstrator's lines at the gate in Groton:

"The Trident is nothing to celebrate . . . nobody wins in a nuclear war. Everybody gets radiated."

NOBODY WINS. What do these indolent children know about war. Surely they don't expect us to surrender and become slaves. They'll be the first ones to complain if we did. If the bomb is ever used again, it will be by a crazy Iranian, or an Israeli. The "wet cold war" is a global chess contest played with MIRVED missiles, and won by predicting the enemy's moves—using any means available.

Ben picked up his phone and dialed the coded number of the man considered by many as being America's master spy, electronics wizard, Vice Admiral Billy Ray Gwinne, director of Naval Intelligence from 1974 to 1976, and currently Director of the National Security Agency, with a budget larger than the CIA's.

". . . now all you good people in the Daytona Beach listnin' area; hold on before you take a walk on the beach. We've got eight more people admitted to the emergency room at Memorial Hospital with those same symptoms— irritation of the eyes and throat, and nausea. That makes twenny-nine good people in the last two days . . ."

"And here's th' kicker, folks. We've got Mr. Saul Ratzkin up here from Smyrna Beach, and he's really got somethin' to tell you. Remember, you heard it on WDAY, your station for news and newsmakers. Go ahead, Mr. Ratzkin."

"Thank you, Jerry. Well, I've been living at the beach since I retired eleven years ago. It was during "tricky Dixon's" administration—1970. The Army comes in and fills up an old Liberty Ship in North Carolina, and they haul the boat out in the ocean a couple hundred miles off Cape Canaveral and they sink it. Guess what was on that old boat? . . .

"Nerve gas, that's what. Thousands of tons of nerve gas! It was in all the papers. Governor Kirk tried to stop them, but Dixon went right ahead anyway. Even the Army admitted that the gas had been leaking out of the rocket's warheads. I have a clipping I kept, right here. It says the Federal Judge on the case at the time was afraid that the gas would escape when the containers were crushed too fast in deep water, and some scientists recommended that the Army find a shallower place to dump. But no, Dixon didn't care any more about what people said than he did later, at Watergate. Nobody's gonna get me out on that beach anymore."

*　　*　　*

"Hello, Bob," the President-elect spoke to the ex-President through a scrambler telephone. Sorry to spoil Monday night football, but something's come up."

"No problem, Don, I'll switch on the Betamax." Dixon examined the scrambler attachment that had been installed a few hours earlier in his Manhattan town house by a Federal agent. "Does this gilhooley on the phone really work?"

"It sure does, Bob. And we can change the scramble code by a remote signal. Don't be afraid to lay it on the line."

"I should have had one of these years ago," Dixon laughed. "What's up?"

"There's been a small epidemic in Florida. People getting irritated eyes and throats. We're getting reports from all along the coast—St. Augustine down to Canaveral. Some people think it's caused by nerve gas that the Army scuttled in 1970."

"Oh, oh," Dixon blanched.

"What do you know about it, Bob?"

"There was a lot dumped. The gas was supposed to disperse in sea water—but who knows, some batches may have been different."

"I've done a little homework, Bob. The Navy tells me they have fixes on all the boats that were scuttled, except one that went down in '68 . . ."

"Before my time," Dixon sighed.

"Maybe so," the voice drawled across the continent, "but nobody out there knows that. It was all classified before your time. If it *is* nerve gas, we're going to be blamed. Not Carter, not Ford, but US. For the country's good we can't let on that we were dumping already in '67. It sure ain't a good way to start off in January . . ."

"What can I do?"

"Okay. Seeing as you're going off on that "trading trip" this week, we've arranged another meeting for you. Admiral Mount is onto something about the missing Liberty ship, but his source won't divulge the location unless there's a U.S. Government representative present. He's been sprung from a Soviet prison where he'd spent the last six years. The only name he reacted positively to was yours. He's never heard of any of Ford's or Carter's people—and probably hasn't seen any of my movies. He's a former U-boat officer who defected to the Soviet Navy after the war.

So here's the plan . . . ''

On Friday night, at 6 PM, the reactor core rods of an attack submarine were raised, activating nuclear fuel and generating heat. Next, the steam valves were cracked and the primary water system warmed up. At 7:45 the steam turbines and generators cut in. Aboard, with Ben Mount, was Robert M. Dixon and two aides, one a Chinese-American. There had been no advance notice of the ex-President's arrival; even the Groton town police were not informed. Besieged by ravenous reporters at the pier gate, a Navy spokesman called the trip ''an all-night familiarization and orientation cruise,'' but declined to give the destination.

The ''688 Class'' *Cincinnati* powered darkly down the Thames, past its night-building cousins, Ohio and Michigan, and sluiced across Long Island Sound to the Race. Then it turned southeast and submerged off Cerberus Shoal to follow the deep-water canyon course around Montauk Point into the Atlantic Ocean.

On the way out, Nielson was called to the wardroom where charts were spread out on a long table. Recognizing the former President, Nielson agreed, over a signed affidavit, to pinpoint the location of the boat he had observed sinking, on *Vyatka's* sonar screen. With *Cincinnati's* communications officer operating a video camera over the charts, Nielson compared the submarine topographical contours of Blake's Basin with a navigation chart. He set a transparent yellow disk over a sharp depression that ran between two sea mounts—one, flat-topped, and the other, smaller and rounded.

With Nielson escorted to his cabin under guard, Mount and Dixon discussed the lagging *Trident* program in private. Ben blamed it on the current administration's soft union policy and named names at Electric Boat, in the government, and in the Navy.

Dixon shook his head and accepted a sealed report from the Admiral. "No wonder *Ohio* is thirty months late," he moaned.

"It's all in the report, Bob. Those Soviets wouldn't stand for it with their boats," Ben held his hand edge-on to his scrawny neck and made a slicing motion.

"Then, with a few 'changes' *Ohio* could be ready by June instead of December, as certain people claim?"

Ben just cocked his head.

Chapter 34

Breakfast over, Dixon was given a tour of the boat, meeting some of the key officers and men.

"Too bad you can't hang around another night," said the ship's cook. "Every Saturday night we have international cuisine. Tonight is Italian night—lasagna . . . checkered table cloths . . . garlic bread, and soft Italian music . . ." He hummed a bar of "Torna a Sorrento."

"Maybe next time. I like lasagna," Dixon replied.

"Maybe you could bring some Chianti, sir?"

At 0900, the motors cut back and the navigation center came alive. Aft, a detail of SEAL scuba divers were already clambering out of the pressurized escape hatch unto the bright morning water where *Cincinnati* hovered, a hundred feet below the surface. Just deep enough to be safe from an accidental collision with a surface ship's keel—a standard procedure in case of navigation systems failure.

One SEAL team ranged along the port side, checking out the long rubber fenders that had been attached the night before. With a whirring sound, steel bollards rose fore and aft as a second team of divers stood by, lines in hand.

A mirror-image moved slowly alongside. The boat's sail, however, was squatter and more streamlined than *Cincinnati's*. As the craft came closer, it proved to be somewhat shorter than the American submarine. Divers were also stationed on the approaching deck, with mooring lines ready. The other boat's prop spun in reverse, casting a sparkling spray of bubbles as it nestled parallel, several yards away. As one, both teams of line-handlers rose off their respective decks and flippered across the void. Rafting lines lines were secured to the bollards—bowlines, sternlines, and crisscross spring lines. An underwater ballet.

Meanwhile, the second SEAL team had broken out a collapsible accordion tunnel, six feet high by three wide, and was attaching the ends to the escape hatches of both boats. Tunnel secured, the diving teams all swam forward and awaited their turns to re-enter through the forward escape air-locks.

A powerful surge of compressed air blew out the tunnel water as Dixon waited below, with his interpreter. They climbed up and ducked through the tunnel, to descend into the other boat where Dixon was greeted with the Chinese equivalent of ''Good to see you again.'' They were led forward to a large cabin where an oriental gentleman sat, alone at a table furnished with a delicate tea service. While Dixon was in closed conference, the two boats exchanged crews; enough American crewmen were put aboard to navigate the boat to a secret Naval facility on the Sound.

The plan was to study and evaluate the Chinese-produced attack submarine for a week, then re-instate its original crew for the return voyage to Shang-hai by way of the Panama Canal.

Among the subjects Dixon discussed with his old friend and Politburo member, Yao Wen Yuan, was an exchange of goods.

"I cannot speak for the present administration, as you may well understand . . ." He waited for his interpreter to finish, "but in January, we intend to resume the cooperation between our countries that we enjoyed during my time in office . . ."

"You will speak to the new President about the F-16 jet fighters?" Wen Yuan sipped his tea under penetrating eyes. "Chairman Deng Xiaping is most anxious to acquire them."

"You have my word. Early in the next year we will send the new Secretary of State to Peking to work out the details."

"And who will that be?"

"I'm not at liberty to divulge that, yet," replied Dixon.

"Understandable, sir. I have also been asked by the Chairman to request of your country that another joint electronic tracking facility be constructed. We feel it necessary to monitor our northeast border."

"I'll include that in my recommendations."

"The People's Republic of China sincerely hopes that your Navy will like our craftsmanship. Most of the material used in this replica of a Soviet *Victor* Class submarine is from China. This boat represents the class that preceded the *Alpha* series, one prototype of which is the famous titanium-built boat."

"Our Navy is certainly interested in your titanium mines."

"We expected it to be so. Perhaps we will be allowed to build one of your *Trident* boats in my country. It will not cost as much in Shanghai as in New London . . ."

Cincinnati sped back to Connecticut, arriving in mid-afternoon. A waiting government limousine drove Dixon and Mount to Groton Airport where they boarded a Navy jet.

Landing in Washington, they transferred to a helicopter that carried them over the crowded throughways to a pad behind the National Security Agency building near Fort Meade. Met by Admiral Gwinne, the two were ushered into a well-guarded conference room where Dixon unsnapped the briefcase tether from his wrist and extracted its contents. Among them was a packet of specifications for the Soviet submarine . . . and a video cassette of the meeting with Peter Nielson.

Chapter 35

It was midsummer Sunday as Ben watched *Ohio* coming up the Thames, surrounded by pleasure boats: sailboats, with striated light-wind foretriangles . . . powerboats pulling water-skiers . . . a tanned girl in a bikini, swerving on a sailboard.

Ohio had been delivered in June, as Ben said it would. The new administration had acted. He felt alone, nevertheless, without a Navy man in office. Dixon had been Navy, and so had the next, elected President—one of his own nuclear officers. At least Dixon was back, if only in the wings.

A small group of Electric Boat people and Naval Officers were on the Navy pier, waiting for the black whale to be nudged in by a chugging tug. Ben watched the docking intensely—how *Ohio* took the wind, on turning. Was the sail too high in a crosswind? Did she ride level on her waterline . . . was there too much turbulence on her squarish foredeck while surface running? He was oblivious of his family, standing beside him. It was good that they were all together again, but this was a really special occasion. Five hundred and sixty feet long, 18,700 tons. This was no mere whale.

IT WAS A DINOSAUR!

And Ben didn't want to face the fact.

A recent theory on the extinction of the dinosaur, held that Plutonium and Iridium radiation from star collisions or supernovae may have zapped our planet during the dinosaur's reign, seventy million years ago, resulting in mutations that could not survive. Another theory projected that mammals, a minor group in the dinosaur's era, could better hide and burrow—away from the deadly radiation and climactic changes of the period.

Now there was talk of man-made radiation that, unlike previous energy: light . . . sound, and electricity—could pierce the deepest depths of ocean, uncovering Trident's lair. One, electronics firm, GTE, had already demonstrated a laser beam that could communicate with deep-diving craft.

With such a beam possible—how much longer till a death ray? A communication beam was enough for a submerged missile to lock onto. Even Senator Jack McCrary was drum-beating in Congress for a re-evaluation of the Trident program. Instead of fourteen more large boats, he was advocating forty small ones.

Full Circle! David had told him last January.

"Dad," his son's voice startled him. "We have to leave now." Debbie came over and kissed Ben on his cheek.

"Bye, Dad . . . Mom, see you after Labor Day."

"Go along now, and have fun—but please call us when you arrive; you know how I worry about you both." Betsy waved.

"Labor Day? Ben tried to talk and watch *Ohio's* crew at the same time as they popped out of the hatches and lined up.

"Don't you remember, Ben? Betsy chided in fun, "They told us last week."

"Told us what?"

"They're driving out to Cape Cod. Debbie's got a summer job aboard a whale-watching boat . . . and David is doing a report for his Defense Analyses people. Something to do with endangered marine species at Woods Hole. It's a sort of sabbatical; he said the Institute encourages an occasional look through the other end of the telescope—"

"Sweetie pie, are you trying to tell 'ol Ben Mount something?" He turned and smiled at his wife. "You're a much better gardener, but if it makes you happy . . ."

"Oh, the garden's fine . . ."

"Especially without my two left feet."

"There *is* one thing that would make me very happy."

"Flowers?"

Betsy batted her eyelashes quickly.

"Shoot."

"That letter that you 'found' a few years ago."

"I did answer him—you mean the kid with the orchids."

"I know, darling. We wrote a very nice letter—my God, it was so long ago . . . but wouldn't it be nice if—after all, the *Ohio* is *so* big and I have so many plants that need homes . . ."

"Yes, dear . . ."

THE WAR-TORN

A remarkable five-book mini-series depicting the World War II experience as lived by five families in five nations around the world: America, Germany, France, Japan, and England.

THE AUTHOR

Robert Vaughan has served or traveled in over thirty countries, and was a helicopter recovery officer in Vietnam, where he served two tours of duty, and received many decorations for bravery in action, including the Distinguished Flying Cross. He has over 9,000,000 copies of his books in print, under his own name and various pseudonyms.